I0549812

Wings to Redemption

An Alex Boudreau Adventure

Paul H. Landes

K. Rogers

Hunter and Gatherer Publishing Company

Davis, California

Hunter and Gatherer Publishing Company

This book is a work of fiction. Names, characters, places and incidents either are products of the authors' imaginations or are used fictitiously. Any resemblance to actual events or locales or persons, living or dead, is entirely coincidental.

Copyright © 2012 by Paul H. Landes and K. Rogers

All rights reserved, including the right to reproduce this book or portions thereof in any form whatsoever. No part of this book may be reproduced in any manner whatsoever without prior written permission except in the case of brief quotations embodied in critical articles and reviews.

Cover Design by Robin Walton Design

Book Formatting by Maria Liza Chu-Plaza
http://www.thefastfingers.com

Cover photo of Golden Gate Bridge from
©Deposit photos/Radoslaw Lecyk

Cover photo of Eagle wing from
©Deposit photos/Maxim Petrichuk.

ISBN: 978-0-578-11206-0

For more information about this book and other works by the authors, visit: www.paulhlandes.com

To Hunter and Reema
who gave us so much more than any human ever could. This is dedicated to
your memory as you were always the wind beneath our wings.

and

To all those who dream of writing their first novel.

Make your dreams your reality

"True redemption is when guilt leads to good again. . ."

Rahkim Khan, *The Kite Runner*

"The eyesight for an eagle is what thought is to a man.

Dejan Stoyanovic, *The Creator*

Sydney, Australia
February 26, 1999

PROLOGUE

THE LARGE COURTROOM WAS UNUSUALLY QUIET. Somehow, it seemed odd that such a beautiful and stately room, paneled in rich walnut, was about to become the chamber in which Denis Wilkinson's fate now rested. Denis' lawyer, Joshua Bolden, sat awaiting the verdict, his muscles chained across his spine, squeezing his lungs. Half breaths were all he could manage. With his unblinking stare fixed on his white knuckled, laced hands, Joshua mumbled, "In all my years. . . never seen such a travesty. . . injustice. . . so sorry Denis. . . so sorry. That one piece of evidence. . . that *one* connection. . . just gotten our hands on it. . . convince the judge. . . so sorry, Denis. . . so sorry."

What really happened? Denis would drift back and forth, from the reality Joshua represented and the now-obscure past. How could a man such as he be subjected to a court of law which now held ultimate power and authority over his life—a life that had been molded from unwavering principles, hard work and a deep humanitarian spirit.

Denis Wilkinson was a model citizen and his altruistic achievements and business acumen were admired not only in Sydney, but throughout Australia. His company, Wilkinson Mining, Ltd., was the largest mining company in Australia with operations spread throughout the world. Australia has the largest known reserves of uranium in the world and Wilkinson Mining had been its leading producer. Uranium ore is used for medicine, power plants and military weapons and it is highly regulated around the world. Denis had always maintained a strict policy that uranium sales would be for peaceful, non-explosive purposes.

In the early days of uranium mining, the ore was stored in steel drums and protected by no more than a wax seal and string. Denis was at the forefront of the international movement that established strict storage, accounting and safety procedures for this prized ore. The use of double low-carbon stainless steel containers was used by Wilkinson Mining long before the International Atomic Energy Agency adopted policies mandating their use.

So, that day when the Commonwealth's Attorney General and the Commissioner of the Australian Federal Police appeared unannounced in his office with an arrest warrant, Denis was stunned. He was charged with the exportation and sale of 200 pounds of uranium 235, a weapon grade isotope known as enriched uranium. The Australian Safeguards and Non-proliferation Office was notified months earlier by the International Atomic Energy Agency that canisters with this uranium were discovered in a foreign country that was not a signatory to international non-proliferation and safeguard agreements. The Safeguards Office undertook its own investigation that led to the charges against Denis and Wilkinson Mining.

Denis and Joshua spent countless hours undertaking their own investigation into what Denis knew was a theft. Bill of

Ladings had been altered by an outside intrusion indicating that the canisters were shipped to a country that was a party to bilateral safeguards agreements. In spite of the vast investigative resources at Denis' disposal he was unable to find any hard evidence that could be used to support what he knew was a third party sabotaging of the accounting records and ultimately the theft of the weapons-grade uranium.

Denis sat with his head bowed and his thumbs pressed tightly together under his chin. His energy was drained and his mind remained stuck on what must have happened. What did happen?

"Mr. Wilkinson, will you please rise." Judge Ramsey instructed Denis, without so much as a glance in his direction.

Denis, along with Joshua, slowly rose and looked directly at Judge Ramsey. Outwardly, Denis appeared stoic and impenetrable. Inside, his guts wrenched and his mind twisted, anticipating the Judge's pronouncement.

"Upon careful review of the evidence before this Court and the existing laws covering the issues raised here at this trial, this Court finds it is bound by precedent to strictly construe the Customs Act of 1901 as it relates to the manufacture and export of uranium. That Act, and the regulations promulgated by the Minister for National Development, each require that all contracts for the exportation of uranium be subject to the approval of the Minister for National Development. The purpose of this is two-fold: first, to ensure the price stability of uranium; and second, and more importantly, to ensure that the materials exported are for peaceful purposes only. It is this second issue which has been central to this trial."

The Judge had been looking down at his notes up until this point. Now he focused his attention on Denis as he drew closer to the awaited verdict.

"Mr. Wilkinson, the evidence presented at this trial shows that beyond any reasonable doubt, Wilkinson Mining supplied uranium to a foreign government and that government intended to use that supply of uranium for the production of nuclear weapons. Throughout this trial, you have personally denied any involvement or knowledge in this scheme by either Wilkinson Mining, Ltd., or yourself. There has been, however, no direct or even circumstantial evidence presented by you to support your contention that Wilkinson Mining and you were in fact victims of a much larger conspiracy—a conspiracy, as you allege, that was masterminded by an unnamed foreign government or corporation. This Court cannot accept such a baseless and unsubstantiated defense in light of the severity of the crime."

Denis dropped his head. He could no longer look into the eyes of the man who was about to raze his longstanding and honorable reputation, brick-by-brick. Joshua continued to stare at the Judge, in an angry manner now, as he clamped down even tighter on Denis' arm.

"Mr. Wilkinson," the Judge continued, "this Court is acutely aware of your stature within this country and you have, in the past, demonstrated a firm commitment to advancing many charitable and social causes. While that is certainly commendable, it is not, in and of itself, sufficient to mitigate the obvious violations of the Customs Act of 1901 or the applicable provisions of the New South Wales Crimes Act. Accordingly, this Court finds you guilty on each of the charges brought against you, and sentences you to fifteen years of incarceration to be served in the New South Wales prison. I'm sorry. I have no choice."

The silence in the courtroom broke in unison. The hushed crowd began to stir and their rumblings quickly whirled over the sound of the Judge's gavel as he repeatedly demanded order in his Courtroom. Photographers' flashbulbs clicked in rapid uninterrupted succession and reporters, with their notepads and recorders waving, clamored for position to get that first quote.

With his head still slightly bowed and his arms dangling motionless at his sides, Denis closed his eyes and stood frozen in time. Although his outward appearance did not reflect his inner turmoil, he knew his future hopes and dreams were at this moment unsalvageable. In his last moments of freedom, the words ricocheted across the weary pathways of his mind,"... incarceration in the New South Wales Prison. . . no choice!"

Joshua, now clutched Denis' arm even tighter, turned toward his friend and whispered, "What do we do now, Denis? What the hell do we do now?!"

As the bailiff approached Denis to escort him from the courtroom, Joshua raised his hand in the air and motioned to give them another moment together.

With a tear in his eye, Denis pivoted slowly toward Joshua, placed his hands firmly on each shoulder and said, "My father always told me that nothing and no one could ever destroy a Wilkinson. It's over now. I'm sorry Joshua. I'm sorry father."

PART ONE

Paris
August 30, 2010

CHAPTER 1

H IS SECRETARY'S VOICE FOLLOWED THE BUZZER, "Mr. Broussard, your two o'clock appointment has arrived."

A razor-sharp, crisp voice rapidly replied, "I shall be right out—hold all my calls."

From out behind the solid mahogany double doors stretching to the ceiling marched Andre Broussard. With his right hand he reached toward the person he knew as Alex—they locked grips. In that instant, Andre remembered that old competitive spirit he had always admired in his longtime friend.

"It is great to see you again, Andre. You have not changed a bit," Alex said, while noticing the deepened lines in his forehead and the darkness under his eyes.

"Nor have you, I might add," Andre replied with a slight bow at the waist. Andre escorted Alex into his office, turned to his secretary, cupped his manicured hand around the side of his mouth and calmly whispered, "Under no circumstances am I to be interrupted."

Alex entered the office and remembered how Andre always did have the taste of the bourgeoisie. The corner office of the 32nd floor in the Tour Monteparnasse, the tallest office building in Paris, framed an eye-catching view of the Eiffel Tower. The furniture was Louis XIV era, a style exhibiting showy elegance rather than comfort. At the far end of the office rested his large mahogany desk with ornate brass mounts. Two high-back black leather armchairs with cabriolet legs and an intricately upholstered sofa with carved and gilded wood were arranged in a seating area in front of the desk. The floor was covered with parquetry in geometrical designs, and the artwork looked as if it belonged in the Versailles Palace.

Alex couldn't help but notice the odd incongruity of this man's slight build and the overpowering opulence of his office. Andre gave the impression that he was born to wear hand-tailored silk suits, drink from Waterford crystal, and walk on hand-stitched Persian rugs. But to Alex, Andre always seemed to over-compensate with his material surroundings for what he surely felt nature failed to give him. The irony was that Andre was one of the most powerful men in the world who directed one of its largest multinational corporations, yet needed continuous reinforcement through his surroundings in order to fill the giant shoes he so awkwardly wore.

Andre peered out at Alex from behind his desk. He remembered those mysterious eyes that could pierce right through him, almost as if they become the gauge, the check by which no lie or piece of false information could pass undetected. He remembered that mystique which enabled Alex to dissect the faculties of even the most perceptive and shrewdest of adversaries.

Andre sat with his back rigid and his chest pushed forward. With his neck slightly crooked, he tried to appear at ease. He began, "Thank you for coming such a long way on such short notice."

One would never know that Andre was raised in a working class family and was educated in the French public school system. He had mastered the nuances of several languages and spoke in the formal manner used by the French nobility. His eyes were fixed on Alex as he continued, "I know you are one to move directly to the point so I will not insult you with any small talk. You have not had enough time to think about what we discussed the other day, and I certainly understand your initial concerns. I do, however, want you to hear me through before you make any final decisions." Andre paused, his eyes remained firmly fixed on his long-time ally sitting stock-still across the desk.

"I will not lie to you," Alex said. "Your offer sounds very intriguing. It does. Remember though, Andre, I am no longer in the business. I know you understand that livelihood is short and I have already surpassed the time limit. It is good to see you though, and I am flattered that you have asked me here."

Andre remained outwardly calm. He edged forward in his seat, his arms resting heavily on the desk. The art of give and take was foreign to Andre. He was a master at intimidation and had taught himself to stare endlessly without blinking. His eyes were quick and set deep in his sockets, his lush lashes hiding the whites.

Staring directly into Alex's piercing eyes, he continued, "Alex, you are by far the best. The very best, Alex. You have no equal and I trust you with my life. If I do not somehow acquire this information, it will most certainly have serious repercussions on my company—and quite possibly on me as well."

"If it were five years ago, or even two, you know I would jump at this chance," Alex responded. "But, the way things are now, I just cannot, Andre. My whole life has changed since I saw you last. I have to go back and forth to Morocco to care of my mother, who has been very sick since my father died. I have no extra time, nor do I have the enthusiasm needed for this line of work anymore. Believe me, I would love to help you. I do know a couple of other people you could contact who would do an excellent job for you. I am sorry, Andre. It is just that I made the decision to get out and I cannot turn back."

Andre was out of his chair and standing in front of the picturesque fixed-glass tinted window. Pivoting to his left, he began to pace back and forth in front of its twenty-four foot span. The silence was broken only by the measured clicking of his spit and polished black leather shoes against the wood flooring. He turned toward Alex and began his deliberate seduction. "Alex, you and I have known each other for many, many years. I gave you your first job here at CS Generale when you were in college. You began your training here. Maybe I was selfish, or perhaps a bit naive, but I had always thought you would be my protégé and in due time take over the helm of this company. I now know, of course, that will never come to pass because of the exciting turn your life took when you left here. I admire you a great deal, Alex. There are few, if any, people in the world that can do what you do to such perfection.

"I will never forget the masterful way you handled the Singapore assignment. You were splendid. I can only imagine the thrill that must go with that kind of work, and you cannot sit there and tell me you do not miss the adventure of it all. It is in your blood, Alex. Once you have tasted heroin, it is hard to walk away. I can feel the strength of your intensity in this room and I know you have not lost the hunger or you would not have come here today. This is not simply something you can turn your back on and leave as you would a lover. I know you too well, Alex. Your spirit is too strong, too determined to let go."

Alex remained silent, but inside began to feel the inner frustration as the struggle ensued. It was always the struggle from within that was so torturous. Andre had retained Alex's services five years ago to pirate certain research information that was being developed by a small Singapore company—Hetero Singapore Pte Ltd. The company was working on the development of several drug therapies based on p53, the tumor suppressor gene that protects the cell in response to damage and stress. p53 brings everything to a halt, and then decides whether to fix the cell or, if the cell is beyond repair, to destroy the cell. This protective function of p53 is disabled in most cancer cells, allowing them to multiply without check. Restoration of p53 activity in tumors could potentially inhibit tumor growth and even shrink the tumor. Hetero had not yet perfected this treatment, but it was close and Andre wanted to get his clutches on the research so that CS Generale could introduce the treatment and reap the millions, if not billions, of dollars that this treatment would bring.

"There was little risk in the Singapore assignment. Their government is not nearly as sophisticated as the United States. You are asking me to do a job in an arena that could potentially expose you and your company to enormous legal risk, not to mention long prison terms, and could possibly impact the French government as well. Then there is the little problem of endangering my own life. I am past the adrenalin rush, Andre. I am trying to create a calm and peaceful life for myself now, and I think I deserve it. I have earned it. You, more than anyone, should know that. I no longer want to assume the risks associated with these high stakes."

Alex loved and hated this work. The thought of jumping back into it posed the unsolvable dilemma. On the one hand, Alex longed for stability and normalcy. Yet, on the other, Alex was like a recovering addict, desperately trying not to give in to the thrill, the rush that comes with the drug. That chapter of Alex's life was supposed to be closed forever. Yet, here was the pusher offering another needle. . . another high.

Andre had been slowly pacing back and forth, like a leopard closing in on its prey. Suddenly, he stopped, turned and stared straight at Alex. With short, deliberate steps, he walked to the front of his desk. He sat on the corner and his narrow fingers stroked his finely tapered chin. Leaning over he stared directly down at Alex and looking unwaveringly into those eyes, he delivered his final blow, "As I see it, you have no choice. Have you forgotten your father's accident? Who flew him to the best hospital in France so he was able to receive the finest medical care that ended up saving his life? Who paid for all the surgeries to repair his broken body after that horrible accident? You were still in school back then and your family had very little money. Remember how frightened you were? Of course you do. It meant a great deal to me to be able to offer my assistance to you and your family. Your father was an honorable man. You and I both know he would most certainly have died if you had left him in that wretched hospital in Morocco. I did it all for you, Alex. Now you must do this one thing for me."

Andre paused just long enough to see Alex blink. "You know why I am bringing all this up now, do you not? You promised me that night I sent my private jet to pick up your father that if I ever needed you for anything—no matter what—you would be there for me. Well, Alex, I need you to be here for me now. This is that moment. I am calling in my marker. You owe me, Alex. I need this to be done and you must do it. No is not an acceptable answer."

Andre's unblinking stare threw a net of silence over the room. Alex knew only too well that his silences could be as searing as his rants. Frozen in the chair, Alex continued to return Andre's stare knowing that their rapiers had crossed. Soon one would lunge, the other would counter-attack; a coule, a moulinet, a remise— the duel was on. Facing the unwinnable dilemma, Alex's hands clenched even tighter. Finally, Alex parried, "I appreciate what you did for my father. No one in this world would have done what you did. But that was a long time ago, Andre, and I have paid you back dearly since then. What about Singapore? You knew then that was my final assignment and you were okay with it then. No, Andre, that was your marker. You have been paid in full."

Still leaning over from atop his desk, Andre concealed his impatience, but wasn't about to cede the field. He remained fixated. His stern and forceful tone rose, a tone which Alex had heard countless times before. His saber-tipped tongue lunged, "No, Alex. That was an assignment for which you came to me. I gave that to you simply because you convinced me to do so. You were paid handsomely for your services, I might add. This time you are not coming to me—I am coming to you. Again, Alex, *you owe me*. I have always known you to be someone whose word I could trust. Will you prove me wrong today?"

As Alex sat listening to those sharp words out of the mouth of this pompous man who was too forceful to deny, a bitter coldness swept through the room and the reality became only too clear. There was no choice. No turning back. Alex owed this man and the job had to be done. The drug would be taken one last time.

Alex stood upright and walked behind the chair hoping the touch of its cold leather would soothe the inner turmoil. Alex stared into the eyes of the man who had won yet another battle.

Knowing that his last thrust had landed and there would be no riposte, Andre rose from the corner of his desk and stepped toward Alex. With the chair between them, symbolizing a bottomless chasm, their outstretched hands clasped once again and Alex conceded, "You have a deal. You have won. But this is the last time. I will do this for you under one condition—after this is over, my debt has been repaid in full. We will be even, Andre."

Andre's ferret eyes widened; he blinked several times and heaved a sigh of relief. With a grin he tried to hide from Alex, he said, "I knew you would come to your senses. Yes, Alex, we will be even. I am looking forward to working with you once again. We need to start immediately. Unfortunately, there is so little time, but I can promise you this will be over rather quickly as long as it is done correctly. I know you can produce rapid results. You always have."

Motioning toward the conference table at the far end of his office, Andre continued, "Please, let us sit down at that table and go over the details together. I trust you bear no hard feelings." Andre appeared rather smug and confident.

Alex was more than mildly annoyed for having to accept the albatross this man brandished without any remorse. However, Andre was right—a sacred debt needed to be repaid.

They walked over to the conference table and Andre placed a large stack of dossiers in front of Alex. They each pulled up a chair and began the task of familiarizing one another with the mission, as well as the plot. It was as if no time had passed since the two of them had worked together. They were very much alike in certain ways. Both loved to dream-up elaborate schemes aimed at countering each anticipated move of their corporate target. They would spend endless hours until each attack and counterattack was known and checkmate was the only conceivable result.

They worked for several hours, until Alex finally rose from the table and said, "That is it Andre. With any luck I will not need to speak with you again until I return to France."

Andre escorted Alex to the double doors and said, "Luck is always on your side. I do hope you are not angry with me and you realize that you really are the only person I can turn to for this task. Thank you, Alex, for doing this. I know this has not been easy for you."

"Good bye, Andre." Alex opened the doors and walked down the hall to the elevator. Andre stood erect and motionless, unable to take his eyes off of the figure moving away from him. The elevator doors closed. Andre took a deep breath, in part to regain his composure after the struggle and in part due to that distinctive presence he had forgotten could linger hours after departure.

Andre stepped forward and told his secretary to book a flight the next morning to San Francisco.

"Who is it for, Mr. Broussard?"

Andre, with his arms folded and looking as though he had just won a boardroom battle, replied, "It is for Alex Boudreau."

"No! Wait!" Andre remembered the operative name. "Make that Ms. Alexandria Pancini."

CHAPTER 2

B ACK IN HER FLAT LATER THAT SAME AFTERNOON, Alex began to pack for her trip to San Francisco. She pulled out her largest travel case, threw it on the bed and opened the top. Stuffed inside a zipped pocket, she found some old pictures from Hong Kong. Her first thought was why on earth were those still around? She was usually more careful about disposing of any links to her previous assignments. Then it all came rushing back—Hong Kong, the intense danger, and the catalyst it had become for her to finally walk away from it all.

A little over a year ago, Alex had an assignment to access and gain critical information from HSCB Holdings, based in Hong Kong. HSCB manufactured various chemotherapy drugs used only in rare forms of cancer, such as Burkett's Tumor, a brain tumor that afflicts a small percentage of children. The economic benefits to a company manufacturing a new drug, which successfully eradicated any disease, were immense. Companies would initially experiment with these drugs in countries which had little or no regulatory control in the hopes of producing documented results which would eventually lead to the drugs' approval in the most lucrative market—the United States.

Her long path to the Hong Kong assignment was littered with scores of companies that had lost valuable trade secrets, innocent people who had been charged with her criminal activities and clients who profited handsomely from diplomatic, yet indiscriminate acts. Alex had worked with Andre on half a dozen assignments over the years. Yet it was that very first assignment that sent her down that crooked path.

She had first met Andre when she was an intern in Paris during the summer before her final year of graduate school. During her internship, Andre had offered her a full-time career position with CS Generale. She was to be fast-tracked through the management training program, and she saw her opportunities there as endless. She embarked on her new career with the same hard-hitting gumption she used to tackle any challenge that faced her. Within her first two years she had exceeded Andre's expectations. She quickly ascended the corporate ladder and was in-line to take over the lead position overseeing internal controls within the company.

She had worked closely with Andre on several high priority projects, so when he asked her to help out on a special assignment she jumped at the opportunity. As Andre explained it, there was a company, Prymirian Pharmaceuticals, which manufactured a drug called Reflamkin which was used as a first line of defense in Tuberculosis cases. Very few drugs were available for this disease, since it occurred primarily in economically poor regions of the world and drug manufacturers tended to focus their research and manufacturing capacity on the world's higher socio-economic regions. In the sub-Saharan region of Africa alone, 1,300,000 new Tuberculosis cases occurred that year. The figure was exactly twice that for Southeast Asia.

Prymirian had cornered the market with its Reflamkin drug and Andre, with his convoluted logic, was convinced that they were participating in a price-gouging scheme where they were selling vials of the drug for three times the price in less-developed areas of the world. Andre wanted to expose this unethical practice for what it was and restore balance to the pricing system.

Alex had flown to Tangiers and met with a person that Andre had hired to gather enough information to expose Prymirian. The man was having difficulty accessing Prymirian's internal computer network, and Alex was to take the lead and finish off what he had been unable to complete. A critical part of the assignment was to obtain the research background and manufacturing specs on Reflamkin. As Andre schemed, when Prymirian was exposed they would surely run into serious financial problems and once CS Generale began to manufacture the drug itself, it would continue to flow to the needy patients at a reasonable and fair cost.

Alex, born in Morocco, spoke fluent Arabic, knew the customs of the region intimately, and had the skills necessary to perform this mission. The fact that no one other than Andre was to know what she was up to and that she was to have a completely separate identity while in Algeria seemed a natural byproduct of the operation. Secrecy, speed and resourcefulness were the keys to its success.

Industrial espionage was nothing new, even back then, but Alex succeeded in raising it to a new technological level. She spent her days using her shrewdness and wiles to befriend several employees of Prymirian. Through them she learned all about the internal computer systems used by the company. She spent her nights developing a sophisticated Trojan horse that she was able to install in the Prymirian computer system. This program, which she named

DownTuber, would retrieve and send out specified information each time a particular program within the system was used. In this case, DownTuber was hidden within the financial reporting files. Each time this system was employed, the Trojan horse would randomly search the data banks for files connected to the Reflamkin drug, bundle copies of those files and send them back to Alex.

Two days after Alex launched DownTuber, she was on a plane headed back to Paris. She was unaware of Andre's true intentions, but she had injected the intoxicating drug for the first time, and she was hooked. Her life was set to take on new, yet unchartered, dimensions.

As Alex reminisced, she carefully built a fire—a ceremonial fire of sorts. It was a warm August evening and this fire was not to provide heat, but to become a burial ground for old memories. She took the remainder of the pictures and threw them, one by one, into the flickering yellowish flames in an attempt to lay to rest that period of her life. She sat on the brown and white marble hearth with her arms clutching her legs to her chest. She leaned slightly forward and watched the flames turn gray-blue and swirl upward, carrying the burnt remnants of her past with them.

Hong Kong was the first and only time she had been detained by the authorities as attempts were made to connect her to the theft of HSCB's clinical research. The hours spent in the interrogation room were enough to convince her that she had too often beaten the odds, and that if she were to get out of there unscathed, it would be time to find a new line of work.

Alex slowly pushed herself away from the open flames that made her face flush from the heat. She watched the sputtering flames smolder and fade away. She rose and walked to the sofa at the far end of the room. She reached over to the table next to the sofa and picked up a photograph of her family, a family whom she missed terribly.

Alex had grown up in a remote village in the eastern part of Morocco. Desperately poor, her parents struggled to do everything they could to provide her with the bare necessities. Her parents, tenant farmers on a small wheat farm, lived at the base of the easterly slopes of the Middle Atlas Mountains near the small village of Sidi Lahcen.

Sidi Lahcen was a festive village steeped in humble, yet rich, traditions and cultures. Twice a year, once in the spring just before the harvest and again in the fall just after the harvest, a large celebration would occur. The *mawsim* was a special time when all the villagers and farmers made sacred contracts with their Saints in the hopes of producing a lucrative and bountiful harvest and to protect them throughout the year. Alex always loved the fall celebration, especially after a fertile harvest. The *mawsim* was like a Thanksgiving celebration and Alex remembered her father's laughter, and the pride that always radiated from her mother's face as she joyfully watched her husband perform the traditional ride into town on his horse with the other men, each dressed in traditional and colorful clothing and firing their guns randomly into the air.

She attended school each day in a small, one room school house that was built from limestone rocks quarried from the nearby mountains. It was there that she first learned that she had a real hunger for learning. In no time, she was able to sit along side the older children in the small schoolhouse and learn about the wonders outside of her small world.

Alex had one younger sister, Christina, whom she cared for while both her parents worked. Christina was sick most of the time and eventually died from what appeared to be a lack of good nutrition. The family never really knew exactly what caused her death and Alex never recovered from the loss of her sibling. She felt, somehow, that it was her fault since she was responsible for her sister while her parents were away working. Alex tried, as best she could, to attend to her sister's health. She would only eat half of what she was given at school so she could bring the rest home to share with Christina.

Alex's fingers softly stroked the image of Christina in the photograph. Young, beautiful Christina. She closed her eyes and could hear her soft child-like voice.

"Not now, Alexandra."

"Christina, please. You need to eat this rice. I have brought it home especially for you."

Christina looked at Alex with her pale skin and dark eyes, and quietly murmured, "Not now, Alexandra. I just do not feel like eating right now."

Alex waved the small spoon back and forth, coaxing her little sister, pleading with Christina over and over. "Please Christina. Please. I cannot stand to see you this way. Do it for me. Please."

Alex would have done anything back then to save her little sister. Try as she might, nothing worked, and Alex felt she had failed. No matter what her parents said to her—that it was not her fault and that they were responsible, not her—none of it made sense to her. The loss of her sister was etched in her being. Alex knew that she should have done something to save her sister's life. She had failed.

Unable to let the death of her sister pass, Alex turned her pain into a driving and consuming obsession. Somehow, she decided, she would make it out of this life of poverty. She would work harder, be smarter and never let anyone beat her again. She knew that only she could save herself from the loneliness and the pain of losing her sister.

Alex already had a real hunger for learning, but now that hunger became a competitive spirit to win at all costs. She set the highest goals for herself that she could possibly imagine and she isolated herself into a distant and obscure world she could barely imagine, but *would* occupy one day, no matter how high the price.

Alex withdrew from her normal sociable and effervescent self and threw herself headlong into her books. By the age of 12, she had progressed to an educational level well beyond her years. In fact, her teacher had Alex assisting children four and five years older than herself. Unable to provide this gifted child with the educational challenges she needed, her discerning teacher went to the local priest in hopes that he may have an idea of what to do with Alex. He did. He suggested that she be sent to Paris for the remainder of her education where she could attend a good high school and prepare for college. Of course there was no money for such a venture.

Alex's mother, Thérèse, was a French citizen who met Youcef, a Moroccan soldier, while he was in France for training. Thérèse fell in love with Alex's father, and they moved to Morocco shortly after he completed his training. Thérèse had never renounced her French citizenship, and that became the entry for Alex into the French schooling system.

Alex reached into the drawer of the table next to her and pulled out a copy of the letter the priest had sent to a friend in Paris—the letter that had opened the doors to the cage of poverty and loss in which she had lived for so long.

Dear Roland

I am writing to you to ask a very special favor. There is a young 12 year old girl, Alexandra Boudreau, who is a member of this Parish and who is gifted with extraordinary talents. Her teacher has advised me that she has already progressed well beyond the schooling available here in Sidi Lahcen, and from what I know about this young girl I quite agree. I believe she has all the talents to rise to great things if only she could be given the chance to continue with her education.

I am hoping that you may be able to call upon several of your most favored acquaintenances to see if there may be a way for her to continue her education in France. Her mother is a French citizen and that may be of some help.

This child's fervor for learning and her determination is what makes me certain that she would live up to my highest expectations.

I am enclosing a record of her school performance, but that is only a slight indication of this child's true brilliance.

Thank you, Roland, and any assistance you could provide would be most welcome by all of our Parish members as she is highly thought of by each.

Henri Groues

Alex was soon admitted into a prestigious French boarding school. Afraid to lose the last of their children, Thérèse and Youcef knew that the only chance Alex would ever have to free herself from the same dire poverty they had grown accustomed to, was to let her go to France. Alex never thought twice about this opportunity. Even as a young child, she knew what this meant. She had read enough books about France and the rest of the world to know that this was her opportunity to escape—to take herself far away from the origin of her pain.

Before she went back to her bedroom to continue packing, she rose and walked toward the phone in the corner of the room. She sat down in the upholstered Bergere chair next to the phone, dangling her legs crosswise over the armrest. Taking a deep breath, she prepared to dial her mother in Morocco. She dreaded having to make that call. When she left her mother yesterday to meet with Andre she assured her that she would return in a day or two. She knew her mother needed her now in the same way Alex had needed her mother as a child.

In the past year, Thérèse had grown frail and more depressed. Alex thought it was because the only man she had ever loved, the man with whom she had spent her entire adult life, the man for whom she gave up her future, was now gone. An emptiness grew inside her mother not unlike the unacknowledged loneliness Alex had felt ever since Christina died. Alex swore she would never sacrifice her life for any one person the way her mother had. In a way, she resented her mother for leaving France to begin a life of poverty. Her mother always told her it was for love. That never made any sense to Alex. She often wondered about that tangled, convoluted emotion. Love shouldn't make you give up your dreams, your home, and your life. That kind of love would never happen to her—at least not in that way.

Once Alex had completed her studies and began working, her parents no longer had to work long, endless days to support their impoverished existence. She regularly sent them money to ease their financial burdens. Then one day, over a year ago, after working in the wheat fields, Youcef and Thérèse went home, cooked dinner and laughed together in the same treasured and joyfully routine way they did every night. This time, however, their happiness ended suddenly when Youcef fell to the floor, breathless.

Alex flew home from Paris immediately when her mother called. The funeral was extravagant for a small village, though Alex knew her father would have been proud to witness what she had done for him. As with Christina, the loss of her father devastated her. But, as always, she rose to the occasion by becoming the strength her mother needed to lean upon. After all, her childhood training prepared her well for another day of suffering.

After Youcef's death, Thérèse began to visibly deteriorate. Alex watched her mother's struggle to get out of bed in the mornings and could see that she showed little interest in working the farm. She paid a few laborers to tend to the field, and never returned again to inspect the crops. The only time she ever left her home was when she took flowers to Youcef's grave. The neighbors brought her food, so she didn't have to go to the market. Alex was afraid that her mother would not survive long without her husband, so she made a special effort to spend as much time as she could with her mother over the past year. She urged her mother to move to Paris with her, but Thérèse insisted that she couldn't leave Youcef's side—even in death.

Again, Alex wondered about this love her parents shared and the sacrifices her mother made in its name. Yes, it seemed beautiful and romantic, but at what price?

Alex heard the ring in her ear, and then the frail voice in the native accent du midi Southern French dialect on the other end, "Hello?"

"Hello, mother. How are you feeling?" Alex waited for the usual reply.

"Oh, I am alright dear. Surviving. Tired. I miss you." Thérèse's voice always dropped off at the end of her nondescript, patent answers.

"Mother," Alex continued, "are you eating and sleeping alright?"

There was an obvious pause before Thérèse answered, "Yes, dear. Please do not worry about me so. I am fine."

"Are you thinking about father again?" Alex asked.

Another long pause. "I am, but I know he is with Christina and they are taking care of each other in heaven."

That stung Alex. She felt the guilt well-up at the thought of telling her mother she would be gone for a while and would be unable to return immediately to care for her. And now her mother's words brought a fresh flood of guilt at the mention of Christina. Why was that memory still so fresh, so painful after all those years? Alex thought. Why did her mother have to mention her sister's name now, and not just talk about father? There was pain in the loss of father, but not this burden of guilt, this burning question from which she could never escape, 'why her and not me?'

Alex remembered the day she had overheard her parents talking soon after Christina's death. Her mother's words still ached in her heart and reminded her of her failure, "Alexandra is so lucky that she is so strong and healthy. I know she tried hard to save Christina, but what could she do? I guess we will never know what happened to our little girl, why God chose to take her and leave us Alexandra."

Alex clutched her temples, closed her eyes, and delivered what she knew would be a blow. "Well, mother, I have a bit of bad news." Somehow, it was easier now to say this because the mention of Christina had turned pain into anger. She continued, "I have to travel to the United States for a few days on business. I will not be long and I will call you as often as I can."

She heard her mother begin to softly cry. "Mother!" Alex said little sharply, "Please do not make such a big deal out of this. I will be back soon and we will spend time together."

"I know, dear. It is just that I am so alone here and I miss you and your father so much."

Alex thought about the years she spent at the boarding schools in Paris and how she would not hear from either of her parents for months at a time. She understood now how hard it was on them to send her away and how difficult it was for them to keep in touch with her. But, as a child, she couldn't reason that way. When she wouldn't hear from them for months, she felt that they no longer wanted her as part of their family and that rejection was probably due to her failure to keep Christina alive. The logic of a child only knew that when you are left alone, it must be that you are not wanted, that it is somehow your fault.

That childhood logic made no sense to Alex now, but the gap between the mind and the heart is wide. That emotional and physical abandonment were now, she thought, safely locked away, only a faint memory, deliberately buried deep within the chambers of her mind. And it was those deep unacknowledged feelings that only fueled her burning need to achieve.

Alex always had a hard time when her mother talked about missing her. It never made any sense, yet she pretended to understand and said what her mother needed to hear, "I miss you too, mother. I promise I will not be gone long. I will call you from California."

"Okay, Alexandra. Please be careful. Bye, dear," her mother ended the call in the same cheerless tone.

"Good Bye, mother."

Alex sat by the phone staring at the receiver. Be careful? She has no idea what I do or what I have done. She could never even begin to understand my world. She has no idea what I have done for her. . . for father. . . for Christina.

CHAPTER 3

"Now boarding United Airlines Flight 1052, nonstop to San Francisco at gate number ten. Please have your boarding pass ready." The overhead speaker startled Alex as she sat, trance-like, in the black plastic seat, her arms propped on the shiny silver metal armrests, concentrating on the documents Andre had given her to prepare for this assignment.

She folded up her burgundy leather attaché, closed and locked the outer clasp and headed down to the gate. This briefcase had seen its last days, Alex hoped, as she rubbed the well-worn leather with its faded scuff marks. She was dressed in frayed blue jeans, a blue Italia sweatshirt and her jet black hair was neatly braided, hanging down past her mid-back. She looked like the typical traveler who was off to the States for a mix of business and hopefully some relaxation.

As she entered the boarding ramp to the plane, the old feelings of excitement began to sift through the cracks in the blockades and walls she had so successfully built up over the past year. Never again, she thought, would she be boarding another plane on a mission to destroy an entire corporation. Never again would she prostitute herself for the greed and ruthless desire of others too spineless to do so themselves. Never again would she place her own life in peril. Never again would she do what she was about to do.

But now, as she stood watching the flight attendants greet the passengers entering the plane, as the pilot turned and offered a smile as she entered the cabin, and as she carried the future of CS Generale in her attaché, the thrill was too powerful to ignore. She knew there was no turning back. Making peace with herself would have to wait until some other tomorrow.

Alex always flew First Class. There was no alternative. Her competitive nature never allowed her to be less than or even equal to others. She always wanted more. She felt a special sense of entitlement, the same that was accorded to the old establishment. The best of everything was what she deserved. She could now afford to surround herself with every material pleasure that, for all practical purposes, made her appear confident and content. However, her persistent struggle to reach the unattainable, that utopian level, left an unfillable emptiness she had learned to push into the same solitary dimension where her lifeless, hidden pain resided.

She sat in the body-hugging leather seat, closed her eyes, leaned her head back and felt the surge of the jet engines lift the plane from the ground, calming the tingling nerves nipping at her conscience. This was her favorite part of flying. The take-off. This was the beginning. And this was the end.

As the plane began its so-familiar ascent, Alex, with her eyes still closed, spread her fingers evenly and clutched the armrests of her seat as the thought of this assignment—another assignment— started to become real. She began to feel the frustration of giving in to Andre. Why did I not stand my ground? she wondered. Why did I ever get involved with Andre in the first place?

The *Direction Générale de la Sécurité Extérieure*, known simply as the DGSE, is a secret intelligence and counterintelligence agency that operates under the defense ministry of the French Government. Formed to protect French national interests, the DGSE had worked closely with intelligence agencies from allied countries to monitor arms proliferation and counterintelligence. It expanded its turf over the years and had freely stated that it aggressively collected economic and technological intelligence from other countries and multinational corporations in order to assist French companies to become more competitive in the international marketplace. French companies were offered incentives to participate in these operations and they could share in the 'take' which might not otherwise be accessible to them.

The DGSE employed sophisticated recruiting methods to enlist qualified recruits into its covert operations. Still, the trusted old-boy network was a favored option, and typically the most successful.

Alex knew that Andre's connections cut deep within the Agency, but she had no idea how deep they ran. During Alex's internship with CS Generale, Andre had spoken with her in great detail about doing "something stimulating" in the Foreign Service. Patriotism was an honorable calling, he told her. She was intrigued, and countered with probing questions, but ultimately, she remained focused on completing her schooling, obtaining her degrees, and forging her own life of independence and self-importance. But, when Alex returned from her Tangiers assignment, it took no persuasion from Andre before she passed the entry level examination and was accepted into the Intelligence Service training course.

Alex was initially assigned to the Division des Operations based in Quelend, France. She underwent nine months of rigorous physical and mental training that pushed her body and mind to its utmost limits before she became a specialist in nautical activities. Similar to the U.S. Navy Seals, this division was deployed on clandestine missions knowing that their cover was unprotected by their homeland. Failure meant sure torture, isolation or the loss of one's life.

Alex's rapid success and tenacity had caught the attention of several top-ranking DGSE officials who re-assigned her to a highly classified technological spy network—code named Service 7. There, she underwent a twelve month training program and was trained in small arms, computers, ciphers and communications. In each step of her training, Alex received the highest scores and bested all her male colleagues. Her career course was set and she entered the secretive world of espionage.

Until a few days ago Alex thought she had buried this secretive world behind her and started a new life. There were to be no more of these escapades. This *had* to be the last one. When this is over with, she attempted to convince herself, I can begin the search for what has been missing in my life. . . what has been missing? She had everything any person could ever want. . . yet she had nothing. There must be more. . . something deeper. . . not material possessions. . . but what? She had often wondered since her father died, why was he so happy with so little? What did he have that I do not? He was a humble man with little more than a broken roof over his head, a job that barely supported a meager existence, and a woman who loved him desperately. Desperately.

"Ms. Pancini," the flight attendant was standing over Alex. "Excuse me, Ms. Pancini?" Alex looked up, noticed the attendant looking at her and suddenly remembered her new name. It was always a strange transition on these flights when the first person to call you by your name was the flight attendant. She always thought it was good practice before arriving at her new assignment. This time she was taken a bit by surprise, however. After all, she had retired from this racket over a year ago and had begun to get used to her real name once again.

It used to be amusing for Alex to assume different identities. The clients she worked for always gave her a new name, passport, and residence in foreign lands. She had no problem mastering a new identity. It was all a game to her. She was fluent in seven languages and could easily adapt to any accent throughout the world. She studied long and hard in the schools and universities of France, Switzerland and Germany. She had obtained the equivalent of a baccalaureate in World Languages at the age of 18, a dual master's in International Business and Law in Switzerland at 20, and another master's in Computer Sciences from the University of Paris at 21.

The work she had done for various clients was just an extension of the game she had mastered in the educational systems of Europe. There was nothing more electrifying to Alex than to have a challenge thrown at her; like the tiger in the forest, you stalk your prey, learn its habits and its movements, slowly close in on it, then, when its back is turned, you devour it. Devour she did. There was no challenge too great or too dangerous. That was her drug—her sustenance.

And now she was back. Back into what could potentially be the most demanding and intriguing challenge she had ever undertaken.

"Oh, yes. Sorry, I was drifting off," Alex said, recovering her focus.

"Can I get you anything? Some champagne? An espresso?" the flight attendant asked.

Alex always liked to over-indulge on these First Class trips. Normally, prior to an assignment, she had plenty of time to prepare for what was to come. This time she only had the ten hour flight to learn everything there was to know about the next new world that she must conquer. As much as she craved the caviar and champagne, with a slight pout she said, "I will just have an espresso. No, make that a double please," she added.

"Do you have a lot of work to do, Ms. Pancini?" the attendant queried.

"Yes. I am afraid so," Alex smiled. "This will be a working flight."

The flight attendant returned to the galley and Alex unlocked her briefcase and carefully pulled out two white, over-stuffed plastic binders, and placed them on her lap. She always sat in the aisle seat and made specific arrangements so the window seat next to her was vacant. This wasn't always easy to accomplish, but it was always done. She used the other seat to spread out her material, and the highly classified documents could be seen by no one but her. Over the years, she had learned to put blank sheets of paper over any sensitive materials that might be visible. One could never be too cautious and no one was beyond suspicion.

The documents were neatly organized so that Alex could progress at a swift pace and learn what was needed. The task of learning about new territories, a new country, a new corporation, a new victim—it was all easy and exciting for her. She loved the intellectual challenge of it all. She began by opening up the thick folder entitled: GENETIC ENGINEERING NEXUS

She scanned the overview, and then began to methodically peruse the contents.

This initial overview will provide you with general background on the above-named company and the products it produces. Appendices are attached which detail the specific scientific data, research and methods which are crucial to your understanding of the targeted information.

Genetic Engineering Nexus, commonly known as GEN, was formed in 1987 by a group of former employees of Amdel Biosystems, Inc. They were initially funded by government and private grants to decipher DNA sequences based upon known human genes. At the formation of GEN, less than 5% of all human genes were identified, yet, the ability to create protein from human genes represented potentially huge profits for the biotech industry. GEN was on the cutting edge of a potentially multi-billion dollar industry. By 2004, GEN's sources of grants were dissipating and it was forced to file a Chapter 11 Bankruptcy in an attempt to continue its operations.

Benjamin Hunter, whose dossier is attached, purchased the majority interest of GEN through a court ordered reorganization plan. Mr. Hunter's interest in GEN was linked primarily to his interest in Cystic Fibrosis research. GEN was a company fully equipped from a research point of view; they owned DNA synthesizers, sequencers and Fume Hoods which, if purchased on the open market, are very expensive. In total, Mr. Hunter purchased his controlling interest in the company for less than 40 cents on the dollar. Mr. Hunter has capitalized the company and devoted considerable resources to GEN's further research in the area of Cystic Fibrosis.

GEN's 2011 total revenues amounted to $6.2 million, most of which was earned from selling access to its gene sequencing data base. This data base is the most complete one of its kind.

GEN has applied for patents before the U.S. Patent & Trademark Office seeking protection for a new protein producing gene it has identified. Through a process known as "Gene Therapy," GEN's newly discovered gene could be placed into lung and pancreas cells to cure Cystic Fibrosis. In addition, they have developed a "Smart Drug." Smart Drugs have the ability to bind the receptors on human cells which carry the dysfunctional genes that cause disease. In GEN's case, its drug is intended to provide therapy for Cystic Fibrosis. GEN is also awaiting approval from the U.S. Food and Drug Administration permitting the commercial application of both discoveries. Approval is expected to be granted within the next thirty days.

The economic benefit to GEN from both of these applications is enormous. We conservatively estimate this market to have a current value of $675 million, with the potential to balloon into a multi-billion dollar market within five years. By way of comparison, Amgen Inc.'s top selling biotech drug, Neupogen, generates over $1.2 billion per year.

A lex sat back and leaned her head against the seat. She smiled faintly as she pondered what she intuitively felt was Andre's motive. As usual, she had been retained to appropriate proprietary information and deliver it to a company which either lacked the sophisticated technology or financial resources to compete, or simply operated on the strict principles of greed. In either case, they were always morally bankrupt. Morals, she thought, who am I to even care if someone is morally equipped or not?

Now it was time for Alex to pick her prey. Andre provided her with bio-sketches of the seven board members at GEN. Knowing this was what she demanded, Andre left it up to her to choose the one person she felt could best lead her to the information she needed. Even though this was routine for her, and she had become very skillful in choosing the perfect victim, she always felt nervous about making a critical error in judgment. She knew she had one opportunity to choose the *right* person. She had great confidence in her decisions, but there was always that slight margin of error: did she choose the right one? This was the only time in an operation that Alex ever hesitated.

She pulled seven folders from her attaché. Each folder held a brief description of the individual and an attached detailed biography. Each attachment contained carefully gathered information about past and present business dealings, professional career and personal facts.

Alex was not normally superstitious. This time, however, she closed her eyes and randomly chose the first folder. Another game.

She read the folder on Gary Kimball. Not interesting enough.

She read the folder on Jessica Wasserman. Nothing there.

Then she opened the folder on Benjamin Hunter.

BOARD MEMBER

BENJAMIN HUNTER

NAME:
Benjamin Hunter

AGE:
41

ADDRESS:
1150 Skyview Lane
Mill Valley, CA 94923

PHONE:

415-555-5562

ADDRESS:

Double Bar Ranch

Ennis, Montana 99999

PHONE:

406-555-1423

OCCUPATION:

Cattle Rancher, Investor, Philanthropist

PROPERTY:

1. 22,000 acres—Montana
2. **5 acres—Mill Valley, CA**

BUSINESS INTERESTS:

1. GEN: 1,250,000 shares
2. Hunter II Trust: Co-trustee with Northern Trust. Income derived from government-grade securities. Estimate trust value: $242 million.
3. Farallon Pacific Trust: Sole trustee. Trust assets consist of investment in corporate-grade stocks and bonds, real estate holdings in Oregon, Nevada, Wyoming, Indonesia, Australia, New Zealand. Estimate trust value: $600 million.

PERSONAL INCOME:

Estimated at $4.4 million/year

PHILANTHROPIC ACTIVITIES:

1. Founder: William Hunter Foundation. Devoted to research in Cystic Fibrosis.

2. Donor: Democratic National Party

3. Numerous nonprofit groups with emphasis on humanitarian needs

HOBBIES &`INTERESTS:

1. Open-water swimming

2. Abalone diving

3. Scuba diving

4. Sailing

5. Travel

IMMEDIATE FAMILY:

Married to US Senator Constance Hunter in 2006.

No children.

OTHER FAMILY:

Parents:Ian Hunter, Jayne Hunter

Both parents died in single engine plane crash in the Philippines, December 2, 1992

Siblings:William Hunter: Died of Cystic Fibrosis: July 28, 1980.

Without hesitation, Alex flipped to the attachments. She began reading the descriptive bio. Intensely, she read and re-read every word of the forty-two page sketch. Time stood still as she read, plotted and planned. On each page of his bio-sketch she made extensive notes. She became fixated on the details of this man's life and the quest of winning the game. In her usual methodical and organized manner, Alex had, within a few hours, masterminded an entire plan to capture the one she wanted—Benjamin Hunter.

"Ladies and gentlemen, please make sure your seat belt is securely fastened. We will be landing at San Francisco International Airport in approximately thirty minutes. We hope you have enjoyed your flight. Have a wonderful time in the City by the Bay." The pilot's predictable comments brought Alex out of her deep concentration.

She closed Benjamin's folder, put everything back in her briefcase, locked the outside clasp, and placed it on the floor near her feet. She smiled as she looked out the window at the sprawling Pacific Ocean stretched beneath her. Her plan was workable, she knew it, but it would have its challenges. Such a beautiful city. Such an interesting man.

The plane began its descent. Alex felt the pressure change in her ears. She leaned her head back once again against the cushy leather. Enjoying the familiar feelings of satisfaction and accomplishment, she knew she had now found the hook that Benjamin Hunter would swallow and her plan would not fail. The prey had been identified and the hunt had begun.

CHAPTER 4

"I REALLY CAN'T WAIT TO GET OUT OF THIS SHIT HOLE. I'm going stir crazy down here." Henry Block stood on the roof-top deck of the research facility overlooking the vast emptiness beyond.

Evan had the exact same thoughts. "Well, your wish may come true sooner than you think. I was on the phone with the higher-ups this morning, and they've given us the go-ahead to test our product as soon as we think it's ready."

"Well let's get on with it, then. If it doesn't work as planned no one will ever know the difference. I don't really think anyone knows what's going on down here anyway," said Henry.

Evan turned away from the railing and walked toward the door. "Come on Henry, let's head back in. I think we should get the others together and see exactly where we are on this project."

Evan Rogers had been the lead scientist in charge of the SyNAPSE project since its inception. The original work for the SyNAPSE project started at the National Emerging Infectious

Diseases Laboratory in Boston, later moved to the Galveston National Laboratory at the University of Texas, and six months ago the operation was transferred to the Health Containment Laboratory in Brazil. HCL, as it was known, was built by the United States government in 1962 as part of its bio-weapons offensive program. It was officially closed in 1973, after the United States signed the Biological Weapons Convention Treaty of 1972 however; it remained open and "officially" operated as a facility conducting genetic engineering research for the development of vaccines for infectious diseases. Unofficially, HCL was a biolevel 4 facility with a small army of highly specialized scientists and technicians. Anthrax, Ebola, Marburg virus, Junin virus, and a host of others were stored there, and while there were only two official repositories in the world storing vials of smallpox, this was believed to be one of the three "unofficial" storage facilities housing that deadly virus.

HCL was a totally self-contained facility located in a remote region of the Amazon rainforest some 300 miles south of Manaus. Situated near the confluence of the Rio Roosevelt and the Aripuana River, it was only accessible by boat or helicopter, and one would be hard-pressed to find human inhabitants for over fifty miles in any direction. The region was first explored by Teddy Roosevelt and his party during his noted expedition down the River of Doubt in the early 1900s.

Such an isolated location would seem to require less security measures however, HCL was equipped with the latest and greatest in modern cameras, multi-zone intrusion and escape detection systems, microwave and infrared technology, biometric radars and biohazard containment systems. Starling Defense Applications Corporation was one of the largest defense contractors supplying countries throughout the world with everything from weapons to radar technology to security services. They had a staff of over sixty personnel stationed at HCL to monitor the security equipment and patrol the compound.

In 1998, President Clinton read a newly released novel entitled, *The Cobra Event*. The novel's underlying theme involved a genetically engineered super-virus, and it heightened President Clinton's concern that a bio-terrorist attack was a real potential threat. HCL became the beneficiary of President Clinton's directive to address national security deficiencies related to biological and chemical terrorism warfare.

Seated around a small conference table, Evan brought Henry and the two other scientists up to date on his phone call earlier in the day.

"Isabelle, where exactly do we stand on the circuit board? Is it fully operational at this point? Can we run some tests with the virus inserted in the mosquitoes?" Evan asked.

"Well, both the size and weight are manageable and we've been successful in over 150 test cases where we've controlled the flight sequence well within our margin of error. I think we're definitely ready on this end." A single nod of his head showed Evan's complete confidence in this scientist. If Isabelle said things were a *go* on her end, there was no need for any further questions. They were a *go*.

Isabelle Roberts was a credentialed scientist with a reputation for innovative testing techniques and boundless energy. She received her Ph.D in Nanotechnology from Columbia University, and was a Fellow at the Nanoscale Science and Engineering Center at Columbia for three years. Her research there led to the conceptual design of the nano circuit boards that were being used on this project. Microscopic in size, the boards were inserted in the mosquitoes' peritoneal cavity, and the insects' flight could be directed for distances up to 40 miles. Isabelle was confident that within a short time the flight control would be effective for distances of up to 100 miles, maybe more.

"Henry, you and I have already talked extensively about your progress, but why don't you bring the others up to date?" Evan pointed to Henry and handed off the discussion to him.

"We're a bit behind Isabelle on this end, but I think we'll catch up when we conclude our testing in the next few days. We've gone through countless mutations on each of the synthetic genes, and in all but two cases these mutations have stabilized. In those two cases, the mutations produced different results than the others, so we need to isolate the factors behind the breakdown to see whether it was just an anomaly, or if it will require further work. My hunch is that this won't present any problems. In two or three days we should be good to go."

"Great. This is all very encouraging," Evan said. "If we can run the operational tests in a matter of a few days then we may just be able to finish up and get out of here a couple months ahead of time. Unless any of you are enjoying your stay so much that you would like to hang around a little longer?" Evan received the reaction he knew this good-natured dig would bring.

The group stayed together and discussed the specific procedures they would each be following in the coming days. If this project was successful, the results would not only be groundbreaking, but the potential uses would be immeasurable. The ability to inject a mosquito with a microscopic circuit probe and control its flight would have unlimited uses for the U.S. military. The new synthetic genes that were being created for insertion into the synthetic virus would give the military the means of thwarting virtually any human offensive before it was even launched. All of this was being undertaken as a way to protect lives in the event of potential attacks by a terrorist group or rogue nation. That was the official company line, anyway.

Finally, Evan placed both hands on the table and pushed himself back. He stood and said, "Okay, that should do it. Let's get back to work. I'll see you all at dinner tonight. Matt, can you hang around a bit? I have some other things I'd like to go over with you."

Henry and Isabelle walked out of the room together and the smiles on their faces reflected the "we're going home" mood of the discussion.

Matt Triplett remained seated. He had a casualness about him that always seemed to deflect criticism or concern. He had worked with Evan for a number of years, and the two shared a parallel outlook on the role science should play in the future of mankind. There was a divide within the bioethics community as to whether genetic engineering of human germ cells would alter the trajectory of human evolution. Many of the arguments against this type of technology were couched in not only moral and religious terms, but over the concern that the advancement of this technology could not be adequately regulated. Evan and Matt had always rejected these arguments in favor of pure evidence-based scientific research.

Five years ago, Matt Triplett led a project that combined two of the most exciting current fields of research, biotechnology and computers, to produce the DNA-processing nanocomputer. It was an actual computer, but was so small that a trillion of them could fit in a test tube. The tiny computer consisted of DNA oligonucleotides and DNA-processing enzymes, both dissolved in liquid, thus its input, output, and software were all in the form of DNA molecules. The purpose of the nanocomputer was to detect abnormal variations in the human genome. Scientists could use this information to create remedies for these abnormalities.

"Matt, I need to see if you can keep a distant eye on Henry. I don't think he has any inkling what it is we're really trying to do here, but when we get into the final testing methods, it's going to be difficult to keep his mind in SyNAPSE mode and not find out what you've been up to. Have any ideas?"

"I was thinking the same thing." Matt's fingers were interlocked and he twirled his thumbs. His boyish grin covered the bottom half of his face. "I don't think he's suspicious of anything at this point. In fact, I think he's genuinely excited about this whole SyNAPSE project and what it could mean."

"I agree, but I don't want to run the risk of him getting overly suspicious now that we're so close to wrapping things up," Evan mused.

Matt lifted his right foot and placed it on the edge of the table. He leaned forward and retied a loose shoelace. "I'll spend some time with him this afternoon and probe around a bit, just to make sure. He's pretty anxious to get home. Maybe we could find a reason for him to go home early if we need to?"

Evan stood up and walked over to the window and gazed out at the deep green forest. "You know," he said, "sometimes when I go for a walk out there I wish I'd become a biologist or maybe a botanist. That's an unexplored laboratory that's waiting for someone to come along and discover some truly incredible species. There may already be lethal toxins out there far more deadly than anything we're trying to create in here."

Evan turned around, leaned back against the window and faced Matt. "Anyway, I thought of that too, but Henry has been with us since Galveston, and I know he wants to see this through to its conclusion."

"A well-placed phone call could result in a reason for him to head back to the States," suggested Matt. "I think he'd jump at the right opportunity. We could always arrange for some teleconferencing sessions and include him in the mix."

"Yeah. Good idea." Evan pushed his square chin upward and rubbed the side of his neck. The tone of his voice reflected the slight smirk that passed as a smile. "You should have been a salesman, Matt. I think I'll go ahead and make that call today, just in case."

CHAPTER 5

Benjamin Hunter sat at his desk at home and gazed out the window that framed Mt. Tamalpais to his left and San Francisco Bay to his right. His bare feet were propped on the desk top, his left foot crossed over his right, and his hands were loosely gripped behind his head. This bulky, wooden desk once belonged to his grandfather and was one of the few possessions he had to remind him of that man.

Oftentimes, when he prepared his lecture notes, he would sit at this desk and immerse himself in the view to spark his creativity. Today was one of those perfectly clear, crisp Bay Area mornings—the kind that turned photographs into works of art.

Benjamin had purchased his home four years ago. He was instantly captivated by its panoramic view and the privacy it afforded him. He treasured his privacy and was always careful to preserve it. He loved his ranch in Montana for that same reason. This location was also ideal because he was in San Francisco often, due to his board position on GEN and his Foundation based in the City.

He was outlining the speech he would deliver tomorrow afternoon to the Alumni Association at Stanford University about establishing nonprofit medical research foundations, when he instinctively reached for an old fishing lure placed neatly in a dish on the side of his desk. He twirled the lure's brass swivel in his fingers and his thoughts drifted back to his brother Will.

Benjamin grew up in an outlying area of Auckland, New Zealand, where he and his twin brother spent most of their free time riding horses and fishing on their family's 2000 acre ranch. Almost daily, they would go down to the lake after breakfast. When Benjamin and Will started school, they switched their morning fishing routine to the evenings. They had hoped that this might prompt their father to fish with them, but he was rarely at home, and had little time to spend with his two sons.

Benjamin's parents had met in 1965 in New Zealand while his mother was there on holiday. His mother, Jayne, was from extreme wealth—the same wealth Benjamin was accustomed to today. His father, Ian, was from a family of moderate means. Ian was a large, physically fit man. Handsome and dashing, he always had women vying for his attention. A partier in every sense of the word, he loved to close down the local pubs, get in a fight or two, and take home whoever was left at the end of the night. It never mattered to him. He just wanted the fun and thrill of being out of control and chasing women.

Then he met Jayne. It was she who would change his life. She, who would briefly save him from his daily routine of drunken emptiness. They met one night before Ian had crossed the drunken threshold. Some say they fell in love at first sight. Others say he fell in love with her money. The truth was that Jayne saw the wild spirit of a bronco that could take her away from the boring, monotonous life she had led as a pampered rich child.

Here was a man full of life and excitement. The thrill and risk of it all overwhelmed her. They were married a month after they met.

Settled in New Zealand and, estranged from her parents, Jayne's life soon became a sad and lonely existence. She loved her two children, and hated the man she lived with. There was no recourse for her. She was forever stuck in a loveless marriage with only the joy of Benjamin and Will. When she married Ian, her father told her never to come home again until he was out of her life. Somehow, the old man knew that this renegade was only interested in one thing.

Jayne's father had known that Ian would never be able to provide for her, so he gave her enough land and money to survive in a moderately comfortable lifestyle. He had also set up a sizeable trust fund for each of his two grandchildren, even though he had never known them when they were growing up. He had been careful to place into the trust enough protective clauses that neither parent could ever lay a hand on the money. If one of the children died, the other would inherit the deceased brother's trust fund. If they both died before reaching the age of majority, the money would revert back to the grandfather.

Jayne had done all she could to give her children a loving home—a fatherless home most of the time—but a secure and warm home nonetheless.

When the twins were just nine years old, Will began to slowly develop breathing difficulties. Jayne thought it was allergy problems due to all the agricultural activities in the area until one night Will awoke gasping for breath. Scared, Benjamin quickly helped his brother get dressed and they went with their mother to the local emergency room. Will was admitted for several days and numerous blood chemistry and x-ray tests were administered. It took several weeks for the results to come in. The words "Cystic

Fibrosis" soon became the central topic of discussion. What did this mean? Would Will die?

Watching his brother become sick and unable to play or do the things he had always done had been very hard on Benjamin. Twins have a special bond unlike most siblings. Some say it's because they've shared a womb together. It has also been theorized that twins had a peculiar "one" sense of each other, as if they were one soul. Truly, Benjamin and Will were examples of this special bond.

It was Benjamin who had begun to investigate this disease. His mother had been paralyzed from the fear of potentially losing a child. She had no where to turn. Her husband had been gone most of the time, and when he was around he was drunk, drinking even more after Will's diagnosis. Jayne had been too afraid to tell her father about the diagnosis, she thought he would blame her for not taking proper care of her son. With only Benjamin to lean on, Jayne had watched her healthy young son's strength evolve. He became the family protector, and the provider of vital information about this dreaded disease.

Over the next year, little Benjamin Hunter had written away to medical universities in the United States. He had known the right questions to ask. After all, he was the one spending hours at the libraries learning everything there was to know about Cystic Fibrosis and he was the one who was determined to save his sick brother.

Benjamin would gather his mother and brother together and organize trips to the Kelleher Medical Center in Wellington where further tests and treatments were administered. He had become the supervisor of his brother's treatments. The medical staff had been amazed at the knowledge young Benjamin had accumulated in such a short time. They had even tended to consult with and advise him rather than his mother.

Information poured in from abroad about Cystic Fibrosis. Everything indicated that it was a fatal disease and that most children never lived to see their 16th birthday. On rare occasions, a person with Cystic Fibrosis could live into their 20's. Benjamin was certain that his brother would be one of those lucky few. He had plenty of time to continue gathering information and planning trips for his brother to visit other doctors and medical facilities.

In spite of Benjamin's confidence, Will had gone downhill fast. The fluid suffocating him was thickening at a very rapid pace. No amount of research or experimentation had been able to halt the inevitable.

On the morning of July 28, 1980, Benjamin had awakened early and run into his brother's room, as he always did, to get him up for his breathing treatment and breakfast. Will hadn't moved when Benjamin called to him. Benjamin saw the tiny lifeless body under the covers. Crouching over his brother, he had touched the cold face, then turned and ran. He ran faster and harder than he had ever run before—out toward the edges of the property, past the herd of sheep and the grazing horses and into the lake, where he swam and swam, never wanting to stop. All he had known at that moment was that he had to get away—as far away as possible from the pain under the covers, from the face that no longer smiled, from the memories in his mind.

Benjamin had climbed out of the lake, still in his night clothes, and had fallen to the ground. Pounding the earth he had screamed, "Take me, not him! Why can't you take me? I hate you. I hate you, Will. Don't leave me. Come back. . . come back." The tears had poured from his eyes and mixed with the cold lake water streaming down his shivering body. The pain of losing his brother was as devastating to Benjamin as the fact that he should have saved him. He did not do enough. He had failed.

Benjamin had no way of knowing then that his brother's death would give him a purpose and conviction which, in time, would change the course of his life forever.

Now, wiping tears from his eyes, the ones that always came when he thought of his brother, Benjamin continued to review his speech. He was very proud of his nonprofit foundation devoted to Cystic Fibrosis research, and his involvement in GEN, which was responsible for identifying the gene that caused this dreaded disease. He had become one of the most revered members of society because of his philanthropic devotion. It was never for him, however. Always, it was for Will.

The ringing of the phone stirred Benjamin from his altered state.

"Hello?"

"Hi, Ben. How's it going?"

"Hey what's up, Phil?

"Not much here. Just checkin' in to see if you're ready for your speech?"

"Well, I'm almost done. Just putting some final touches on it," Benjamin replied.

Phil Morgan was one of Benjamin's closest friends. They were two connected spirits, and loved to spend hours together pursuing their outdoor hobbies. They both competed in the local open-water swims and were avid abalone divers along the northern coast of California. Other than Murray Paulson, the CEO of GEN, who had been Benjamin's mentor over the years, Phil was the only person Benjamin truly trusted.

"How's Baldy doing?" Phil asked.

"Ah, he's great. Seems to be healing well. Should be back on his feet in no time. Wish I had half his strength."

"Well say hi to the old bird for me. Are we still set for a swim tomorrow afternoon?"

"You bet. I'll see you at the Club around 4:00."

Okay. Great. I'll talk to you soon and good luck tomorrow."

"Yeah, thanks Phil. Later."

"Down the road." It was Phil's personal rendition of goodbye.

Benjamin hung up the phone. He noticed his inbox was flashing with new email. Seeing the email was from Murray Paulson, GEN's CEO, he clicked it open.

Ben–

I am calling a special Board meeting for this Thursday at 2:00pm. We have received some new information that will require the Board's immediate attention. Please call to confirm your availability.

Thanks

Murray

CHAPTER 6

THE APPLAUSE WAS ALWAYS BENJAMIN'S FAVORITE PART. He felt his speech was well received, but he was glad it was over. He still couldn't clear the conversation he had with Murray earlier in the day from his mind. He walked out from behind the hand crafted cherry wood lectern, down the side steps of the podium to the floor of Stanford University's Memorial Auditorium. He began to greet people, some familiar, others he had never seen before.

"Thank you, Mr. Hunter. I really enjoyed your presentation. I've been on the Board of the Packard Foundation for several years and am excited about the prospect of new and innovative foundations emerging here in California. You have some wonderful ideas and I would love to discuss them further with you," said a deep, throaty voice from the audience.

"Thank you very much." Benjamin appreciated these kinds of endorsements, especially from other foundation board members. "Yes, please contact me." He reached into the inner pocket of his tweed blazer and pulled out several business cards. Handing one over to his new acquaintance, he said, "Here's my card."

Another voice from the auditorium, "Oh, Mr. Hunter, thank you so much for your inspiring presentation. We need more people like you to promote private medical research."

"Mr. Hunter," he shook another hand, "my child died of Cystic Fibrosis several years ago. I can't tell you how much your work means to me and my husband. You're a Godsend."

Over and over, Benjamin shook hands or received hugs from people and listened to their praises. He never hesitated to reference Will any chance he got. After all, this was all for him.

The crowd of several hundred people began to disperse. Benjamin chatted with some of his old friends from the University, and then walked back toward the lectern to gather his materials. Suddenly, he heard a voice that stopped him in his tracks. A very strong accent, soft, yet forceful said, "Mr. Hunter. Please, if I may have just a few words with you."

He pivoted abruptly. What he saw when he turned was a vision too intriguing for any man to ignore. He felt his heart pound in his throat. What is this? He had met hundreds, no, thousands of women in his travels and career who had asked the same question: "Excuse me Mr. Hunter, may I have a word with you?" He was never at a loss for words—until now.

"Of course," was all he could manage. Studying her as she moved closer, mesmerized by her grace and stature, wondering how could any woman have eyes like the sea and hair as black as the night? Who was this powerful presence?

With an outstretched hand, Alex introduced herself, "My name is Alexandria Pancini. I am a journalist from Rome. My country is very interested in assisting and promoting private foundations devoted to medical research such as yours. We are, ourselves, exploring various ways to expand our own research capabilities and believe that someone, such as yourself, could be of great assistance to us."

He was paralyzed. This hand he was holding and trying to formally shake was so fragile, so soft, yet so strong and gripped him so tightly. He tried to let go of her and stop staring while he searched for words to engage her in some form of conversation. What was happening? Almost as if he was afraid she knew what he was thinking, he pulled his hand away from hers before she could feel it tremble. He took a step backwards, put his left arm on the lectern for balance, and attempted a response.

"It's nice to meet you, Ms. Pancini."

"Please, call me Alexandria. And I enjoyed your lecture. You must be so proud of your accomplishments. There is so much I could learn from you that would be helpful."

He felt a rush of pride and nodded, "Well thank you. Thank you very much. What can I help you with, Alexandria?"

Alex stared invitingly into his brown, intelligent, deep-set eyes. His face was chiseled with sharp features, prominent cheek bones and a deep set dimple in the center of his chin. In her distinctly confident Italian accent, she replied, "I think what I need to learn will take much more time than what you can give me here, or what I have time for today. Could I be so presumptuous as to ask you for some time later this week to learn more about the private foundational system here in America, as well as your own research endeavors?"

His arm was still propped against the lectern and he took another deep breath hoping she would not notice the awkward tension he was somehow unable to control. He reached into his pocket with his free hand and pulled out a business card. Handing it to the person he now knew as Alexandria, Benjamin said, "I do have some free time this week. Please call me when your schedule permits and we can make an appointment. I would love to hear about your interest in this area. As you've probably gathered, this subject is very dear to me, and I'm always interested in others who feel the same way." That was his patent answer. All he could think was, thank goodness he had one.

Alex took his card and moved closer. She shook his hand and said, "I will be in touch very soon. Thank you, Mr. Hunter. I look forward to seeing you again."

His arm was still frozen to the lectern. He needed to feel grounded, balanced. She had pushed him to an edge he had not felt in years. "Goodbye, Ms. Pancini." He then corrected, "I mean, Alexandria."

He turned and walked to the back of the lectern and now faced the auditorium once again. He tried, unsuccessfully, not to look out toward the auditorium entrance. He hoped no one was watching.

Again, hypnotized by this woman, he watched as the striking beauty glided up the flight of stairs to the open doorway at the top. Suddenly, she stopped and turned to look at him one last time. The sun shined brightly through the windows just behind her and the shadows placed a veil over the refined and delicate features of her face. The silhouette that stood above him had sinuous and supple curves that stirred his senses and aroused his passion. He could not take his eyes off her. He knew he should. He felt completely fixed in time. Just as suddenly, she turned and disappeared through the light. A slight tremor rippled through his body and warmth enveloped his core. He looked down at his notes, unable to see them, trying to regain what little composure he had left.

Professor Hill approached Benjamin and said, "Thank you, Benjamin. As usual, a stunning presentation."

"Thank you, John. I enjoyed being here."

And he truly had.

Alex drove back to her hotel in San Francisco and reflected upon her brief interlude with this intriguing man. Could she get the information she had been paid to uncover? Was the strength she felt from him too unyielding to pierce? Of course she could break this man, she reminded herself. She had broken some of the most powerful men in the world. She had him. There was no doubt. She would win.

She pulled into the Fairmont Hotel at the top of Nob Hill. Leaving her rental car with the valet, she walked into the lobby and asked for her messages. There were none. She moved toward the elevator and pressed the Penthouse button. On the 31st floor, she slid her electronic key in the door and entered her suite overlooking the Golden Gate Bridge.

Upon her earlier arrival at her room, she claimed a work space on the large desk set next to the window overlooking the Bay. The desk was fashioned from walnut with inlayed burl and polished brass drawer handles. The aniline covered mid-back chair was the same moss green color as the leather fixed to the desk top.

Alex's educational background in computer sciences and her years of experience in computer information systems gave her the expertise to operate any computer system. She had owned this particular laptop for fewer than two years. The Powermaster was custom built by the British company Premiergent Hi-Tech. With a one terabyte hard drive and i5/i7 Turbo boost performance, she had all the power she needed for complex analysis and the capacity to store endless data. It was probably more than she would ever need, but in her line of business one never really knew what was needed until one was immersed in the work, so she added every upgrade she could without losing speed and versatility. She had set the system up to give her access to every phone call, E-mail and facsimile either sent to or received by Benjamin.

Entering her room, she saw a blinking red light on the upper right corner of her display screen. Instead of reading the message, she walked over to the window and brushed the curtains aside. The entire Golden Gate and beyond was at her disposal. She thought once again about the man that lived on the other side of that bridge—a bridge she knew she should never cross.

With her impressive practiced ability to block her senses, she turned around and walked back toward the computer and checked on the message she had apparently received. An email from Benjamin's computer lay before her and she began to read:

Ben—

I am calling a special Board meeting for this Thursday at 2:00pm. We have received some new information that will require the Board's immediate attention. Please call to confirm your availability.

Thanks

Murray

CHAPTER 7

MURRAY PAULSON STOOD AT THE DOOR, COFFEE mug in hand and was chatting with another board member, Ed Schickman, when Benjamin arrived.

"Afternoon, Ben," Murray said while briskly shaking Benjamin's large calloused hand. Benjamin was known for his handshakes. His hands were large and rough, yet there was a gentleness about him whenever he shook someone's hand—almost as if he wanted people to know his God-given strength was not in his physique, but in his heart.

"Glad you could make it on such short notice." Murray continued. "Let's go ahead and get started. We have a lot to cover and you don't want to hang around here all day, I'm sure."

Ed Schickman greeted Benjamin and asked, "Hey, did you catch the Giants game last night?" Ed was a successful venture capitalist who was instrumental in arranging needed funding for GEN. He was a tall and wiry-slender guy who usually made a point of pulling Benjamin aside to catch up on the latest football, baseball or basketball scores, depending on the season.

"Nah, I missed it, but I read about it this morning," Benjamin replied.

"It was beautiful, just beautiful. Twelve strikeouts for Lincecum. This could be the year."

Benjamin shook his head and smiled, "Yeah, maybe, but I think I'll wait a few more weeks before I run off and buy my playoff tickets. Hopefully, they won't let me down like the past few years."

"This is the year. They have winner plastered all over them. Buy your tickets!" Ed put his arm around Benjamin, "Come on, let's head into the conference room."

Benjamin and Ed walked into the modest-sized conference room, and Benjamin sat down in one of the small, beige, padded swivel chairs directly across from Murray. Murray had been the CEO for the past six years, since Benjamin first purchased a controlling interest in the company. His educational background was in the sciences, with a Ph.D. in Genetics from UCLA. However, it was his keen business acumen that landed him the CEO position of such a potentially powerful and progressive company. Prior to this position, he was CEO of Neurogenics, Inc., a leading pharmaceutical manufacturer.

Benjamin admired this brilliant man who had been a great support to him when he began the William Hunter Foundation. Murray spent untold hours advising Benjamin on how to best invest the foundation's resources in various research projects. Benjamin trusted Murray like a father, and gave him full rein to run GEN as he saw fit. Murray was 64 years old, and his tall stature hid the fact that he was slightly on the heavy side. His eyebrows were bushy and thick and spaced wide apart, making them appear half-sized. Their jet black color was a sharp contrast to his peppered gray hair, slightly thinning but always lying neatly in place. Smartly dressed in a tailored suit and his trademark

Hermes tie, Murray looked every bit the success that he truly was. Benjamin sat fixed on his mentor, curiously awaiting his unveiling of the details contained in the urgent message he had received two days ago.

Even though Murray was a board member at GEN, he never forgot that his position as the Chief Executive Officer was subject to the Board's scrutiny at all times. He shuffled some papers, stacked them neatly in front of him and peered across the table at his colleagues.

"Let's get this meeting started," he began. "First though, let me again thank each of you for coming here today and taking time out of your busy schedules to meet on such short notice. I know you all received my email two days ago. We have a few issues to discuss that are highly sensitive. I am sure I don't need to remind any of you that the information we gather and discuss in these meetings must remain confidential." Murray paused and picked up a stack of papers and continued, "That leads me into the reason I have called this meeting today.

"As outlined in the materials you received, the FDA has given us a formal letter apprising us that it will be at least another six months before it is able to issue a ruling on our Cystic Fibrosis drug and gene therapy process. Our research is now complete so this poses some obvious security problems to your company. You know that the economic value of this drug is immense, and there are at least a dozen companies throughout the world who would use any means necessary to obtain our background information on this drug.

"We already have adequate security measures in place to protect our research, but I believe this additional timeframe imposed by the FDA necessitates that we increase our security procedures immediately. Remember Cynor Corporation? Three other rival companies were able to infiltrate their research data banks while they were held up by the FDA for a number of months, and they lost millions of dollars.

"I'm giving you sealed packets to take home and study." Murray rose from his chair, circled the conference table and passed out a packet to each board member. Standing behind his chair with his hands firmly grasping its top, he stood erect, reached up and gave his left ear a slight tug and continued, "This information will provide you with a detailed plan of the security measures I am proposing. These security measures have been developed by G4G Security Solutions, and they represent state-of-the-art procedures. It covers setting up checks and balances to prevent the specific types of problems encountered by Cynor, as well as assuring that there are no leaks within our existing corporate structure. This includes, I may add, specific safeguards designed to protect and monitor all communication among the Board Members.

"I'd like to have someone from G4G Security come to your homes and offices to install these security devices. We're going to change the current password authentication process for each of you to enter our network here. Under the new system, you'll be given a wide range of password options that you'll use and you'll be given an authenticator—a device that will give you a second password you'll need to enter the network. The authenticator changes the password every 60 seconds."

Maryanne Taylor leaned toward Murray with a puzzled look on her face and queried, "Now, Murray, do you really think this could happen to us? Aren't you overreacting a bit?" Her hands waved in sync with her sing-song voice and she continued her questioning, "Doesn't the security system we already have here afford us adequate protection?" Maryanne was not only strikingly beautiful, but extremely animated when she spoke.

"Murray, I thought we had the best security money could buy," interjected Ed.

Murray allowed the members to pose their questions—questions he was more than prepared to answer. He always knew ahead of time what potential questions could arise. This was one of his greatest strengths, always ready for every angle, every possible twist and turn.

"Well, I think each of your concerns is well-founded. I've no actual way of knowing whether we're in fact at risk of having our research pirated. I am, however, paid by you to not only promote the corporate assets of GEN, but to protect them. I know very well, as do each of you, that the proprietary value of our research is undoubtedly our greatest asset. When it comes to protecting this asset, I would much rather be accused of over-reacting than under-reacting.

"Our current cipher suites are using Blowfish to encrypt our stored electronic data. It's still an excellent product, but there are better ways to protect our stored data. Let me just add that Cynor was using Blowfish at the time their data was stolen. G4G intends to change our system over to Advanced Encryption Standard. This is used by the U.S. government, and is the most secure system worldwide. The cost to implement these additional security measures is minimal in comparison to the substantial risk if we do under-react to this potential threat."

Jessica Wasserman was tapping her fingers on the table and shifting nervously in her seat. A small round woman with flame red hair, she was an Adjunct Professor at Stanford University. Recognized for her work in Pediatric AIDS, Jessica always kept the meeting agenda focused.

Murray pointed to Jessica. "Jessica, it looks like you have something to say."

With her chin leaning on her right fist, Jessica began the questioning she already knew the answers to, "Murray, I'll certainly read this packet you've provided to us and it will most assuredly answer my questions. But to understand you correctly though, you're saying that each of our personal and business phones, fax machines, computers and other communication devices will be monitored, not only with respect to communication among those of us here, but also with respect to our other business and personal activities?"

"Yes, Jessica. That is precisely the circumstance," Murray replied.

Jessica continued, "Well, this requirement presents serious concerns to me. As a physician I'm bound to protect my patients' confidentiality." She picked up her packet, held it up and looked over at Duncan. Duncan Smith was a senior partner in a major San Francisco law firm. He was a husky man who obviously shunned exercise, and he tended to be quite eccentric. He looked at Jessica and gave her a sharp nod.

Jessica focused back on Murray and continued, "Duncan has the same confidentiality requirements as well. Any interception of my professional discussions with my patients or about my patients would be an obvious breach of that confidentiality."

Another anticipated question. Murray responded, "Jessica, I understand your concern. I do. However, we can't make any exceptions to this security plan. As a physician, you'll have to find your own way to monitor your communication with your patients so you don't violate your code of ethics. If you feel unable to do this, you may need to consider temporarily removing yourself from the Board until this issue has been resolved. This seems harsh, I know, Jessica. But, I believe it's necessary for the security and future of this company."

The meeting continued for another hour with the Board members asking their questions and voicing their opinions. Murray explained the security measures in greater detail and the Board finally approved Murray's plan. Jessica and Duncan abstained from the vote, each saying only that they needed more time to contemplate their personal quandaries.

Crossing the Golden Gate Bridge in rush hour traffic was usually something Benjamin was able to avoid. After his Board meeting, he was anxious to get home so he called Phil and cancelled their Bay swim. Driving more slowly than normal, trying to avoid the monotony of stop and go traffic, he thought about Murray's proposal. He really liked the idea of extra security measures. After all, he had nothing to hide, nothing of any great interest was occurring in his life. Nothing ever did. They could tap his computer and his phone. His phone. But, what if Alexandria called for an appointment? Ah, that's no problem. It was just a meeting to gather information about U.S. foundations. But, those eyes, that voice, the sun beaming through that silhouette.

He looked at his right hand that steered the slow-moving car and he could still feel her soft, small touch. He glanced at his left hand on the other side of the wheel and saw the gleam on his fourth finger. Of course it doesn't matter if she called, he thought. He would just make an appointment and that would be that. That would be that.

He pulled up under the shaded oak tree canopy in front of his house. He rarely pulled into the garage—too much hassle. He jogged up the inlayed cobalt brick stairs to the main entryway and opened the front door. He never locked the front door—too trusting, Phil always said. He kicked off his shoes and walked to the kitchen to grab a cold beer from the refrigerator. Out of the corner of his eye he saw the flashing red light on the answering machine. He punched the message button and continued toward the refrigerator. He pulled out a cold one, popped off the cap, slowly savored that first sip and then he froze. Once again he heard the piercing accent.

"Hello, Mr. Hunter. This is Alexandria Pancini. I hope you remember me."

Benjamin, immobilized, spinning, thought—remember you? The silhouette, those eyes, the voice, the sun.

He was hypnotized by the sultry accented voice. "I was at your lecture at Stanford and asked if I might contact you for an appointment. I am sorry I missed you. I will call back soon. It was a great pleasure meeting you. Ciao."

Where are you? Why didn't you leave your phone number? Will you call back? When? The security system. . . GEN Corporation. . . will they find out about Alexandria. . . who cares. . . Senator Hunter.

CHAPTER 8

B ENJAMIN PARKED HIS CAR AT THE FOOT OF JEFFERSON Street in front of the Dolphin Club as he routinely did nearly every morning around 9:00 am. Parking was a challenge at this end of the street, but he always seemed to have great luck when it came to getting what he wanted.

The Dolphin Club was founded in 1877, and was the oldest swimming and rowing club in the City. Benjamin joined the Club five years ago because of his love for swimming. He learned to swim as a child in the lake on his parents' property. He remembered swimming with Will and how much fun they used to have racing to the other side of the lake and then back again. So, swimming for him was not only physically satisfying, but it served as an important link to his childhood memories.

He walked upstairs to the locker room, slipped into his suit and headed toward the Club's beach bordering Aquatic Park. As he walked, he put on his bright orange neoprene swim cap. Stuffing his wavy chocolate-brown hair into the cap, he looked out at the six or seven other swimmers, each stroking through the currents in various parts of the cove. The cove was bordered on the left side by a long city-owned pier and on the right side by the Hyde Street Pier. The two piers ended at the farthest point off-shore, leaving a small opening for boats to enter the open waters of San Francisco Bay. The cove was perfectly sheltered from the choppier waters of the Bay and was an ideal place to swim.

It was another beautifully clear day. The sun reflected off the water, and the two old historic schooners moored alongside the Hyde Street Pier bobbed slowly to the rhythmic up and down beat of the waves. Benjamin, knowing how to assess the tide by the direction the smaller moored boats were facing, knew that an ebb tide was just beginning. It doesn't get much better than this, he thought.

Benjamin walked over to the edge of the water, put his feet in and felt that familiar shock of the icy Bay. He stood in the gritty sand for a few moments planning his course and trying to get used to the temperature around his feet. This time of year, the water temperature hovered around 54 degrees—about the same temperature as the morning air.

While he stood in the shallow water, one of his old swimming buddies, Brian, came swimming toward him. He stood up, waded out toward Benjamin and chided, "Hey old man. Get in the goddamn water. What's the matter? Too cold for ya?" Brian always had a few choice, spirited words for Benjamin to get his blood circulating. He figured he probably needed it today, since his mind had been so preoccupied lately.

He looked out again at the sheltered cove and saw a woman moving through the choppy water with a grace only a seasoned open-water swimmer could pull off. Who is that? he thought. Never seen her out here before. Maybe a new member.

His feet were firmly planted in the wet sand and he took a few more minutes to stretch. He was about to begin the plunge into the ice-cold water when he heard splashing coming toward him. He looked up and saw the woman he noticed earlier. She exited from the water, her head was down and she was pulling off her purple swim cap when Benjamin said, "Where'd you learn to swim like that? Very impressive!"

She pulled her cap off. Down fell that coal black mane. It tumbled around her neck, down to her waist. Then the accent, "Oh, I have been swimming in the Mediterranean since I was a child." Now she was completely out of the water and stood several feet from him.

Benjamin was stunned. There was no lectern to lean on, no balance in the sand. She was more beautiful than he could have possibly remembered. Her body was like that of a young athlete. She obviously had spent many years sculpting that creation. Her legs were like a gazelle, long and powerful. Her slender hips and taut stomach set off the fullness of her breasts. Her shoulders were broad from the years of swimming and her arms were long and graceful. Then there was that face. Her skin was smooth and dark. Her features molded to perfection—a small well-defined nose and high set cheek bones. She had an exotic look found only in dream-like exotic places. As if from mixed race, she was dark, yet had piercing aquamarine eyes. How could anyone have such beauty, such radiance, such mystery?

It was all Benjamin could do to just say, "Hello, Alexandria. Uh, I didn't know you were a swimmer?"

The hook, she thought, "Yes, Mr. Hunter. I love swimming. And you? You swim as well?" She knew the answer.

Benjamin shuffled his feet in the sand and fidgeted with his swim cap as if trying to adjust it, then replied, "Please, please call me Ben."

"Oh, you were introduced at your lecture the other day as Benjamin Hunter so I presumed you would go by Benjamin."

"Benjamin is my formal name but my friends call me Ben." He danced from one foot to the other as he spoke.

They stood knee deep in the chilly water and Alex noticed this man—her prey—as he confidently stood in the water in nothing more than a small nylon swimsuit. How could she not be aware of those broad shoulders and strong sturdy arms that looked like they could envelope any woman they wanted, that muscular chest and perfectly defined abdomen, those forceful legs—that suit—back up to those eyes. His eyes showed a familiar pain in his soul and a fire in his heart. His six foot two inch frame was that of perfection; that of an athlete; that of endurance; someone no woman could deny. Except Alex, of course.

"It would be nice if someday I, too, could be considered a friend, but until then, if you do not mind, I would prefer the more formal given name."

Alex coiled her hair in her hands and gave a tight squeeze. Water trickled out, she looked back at Benjamin, and her long lashes fluttered, "I am surprised that you are a swimmer". She was always good at the game of pretending not to know as much as she really did. "We should swim together sometime. I will only be here a short while, but I would love to learn about some of the different types of open-water competitions you have in this area." The hook was set.

"Yeah, I love to swim, especially here in the open waters of the Bay. I haven't met too many women who do this sport, so forgive me if I am taken a little aback by your interest." He thought that was a good way to excuse his fumbling for words.

Benjamin, desperate to make conversation and to try to keep her here, to learn more about her, then heard the words he knew would eventually come, but was unprepared to handle.

"Oh, I see you are married." Alex decided to bring this point out into the open, almost as if she wanted to see if she could make him feel uncomfortable or out of control.

No, not really, he thought. This is a marriage of convenience, a loveless, empty existence. She trapped me when I was vulnerable. We married and have never really lived together. She is in Washington, D.C. and I am here—alone.

"Yes, I am," Benjamin said, looking down at the sand. Back up to her eyes, he continued, "She is a very busy woman and spends most of her time in Washington D.C. What about you? Are you married?"

This was an easy one to answer, Alex thought. But, why did she have such a hard time forming the words. So she wasn't married. She had no time for such foolishness. No time to be distracted. But, still, there was a hesitation in her response that made no sense to her. "Uh, no. I am not. I suppose I, too, am a busy woman."

She pulled her hair over her shoulders and gently wrung the last drop of water and continued, "I need to get going now. I have an appointment. Nice to see you again. Goodbye, Benjamin." Why, she thought, was this so uncomfortable? I was supposed to make *him* feel awkward, not myself. Maybe, she thought, I am just cold.

As she walked past Benjamin, he tried to say good bye, but he was trying to figure out a way to see her again — soon. Oh. . .wait.

"Wait, Alexandria. I got your message yesterday. Would you still like to get together?"

Why on earth had she forgotten about that? Was it the swim, the cold, the tension? What was happening to her? Of course she needed to see him.

"Oh, yes. I would love to." Back to the hunt. "Does this afternoon work for you?"

"How about 3:00? We could meet at the Olympic Club on Post Street. Do you know where that is?"

"No," Alex replied. "But, I will find it. I will meet you there and, thank you very much."

"Goodbye, Alexandria."

"Ciao."

Benjamin tried not to watch her walk away. He turned for a moment back toward the Bay. He shuffled his now frozen feet in the water. With no thought, he turned around. There she went. Up the steps toward the locker room. What grace, what elegance. From behind, she was just as beautiful as she was standing next to him in the sand. Is there any angle that is not perfect? Her wet hair bounced and tumbled with every step. He was again mesmerized. She was gone. And so was he.

In the locker room, after his swim, he took an extra long hot shower. Standing under the warm water, he continued to think about Alexandria. His hour-long swim did little to ease his growing tension. He leaned against the tiled squares and let the warm water flow over his head and cascade down his back, slowly soothing the cold tingles wedged in his skin. He visualized her next to him, gliding stroke for stroke, in synchronized rhythm, through the winding currents.

Benjamin's mind gradually cleared and he cursed at himself. Damn, he thought, I should have told her about how bad it was with Constance and how miserable she has made my life. I need to think of a way to tell her about this nonexistent marriage—this lie I have lived for too long.

Benjamin had met Constance when they were both 34 years old. He had been scuba diving in Monterey, California. Politicians and their staffs had gathered there for a seminar on Social Media fund-raising. Constance worked for a State Assemblyman and was in Monterey the same time as Benjamin. Constance loved politics.

Her father had been involved in government her entire life, which helped introduce her into that world at a very young age. She had the dream that many young political aides had—to become an elected official someday. Her career plans were well-calculated and she made sure she always put herself in the right place and circulated with the right people. The only thing she lacked was money. If only she could get the money she needed, she knew she could make it to Washington, D.C.

Then she had met Benjamin, an extremely handsome, unassuming man. He had been captivated by her energy and beauty. He was much more reserved and contemplative than she, and, for a while, it had appeared they brought each other to a state of equilibrium. At least, Constance had been careful to have Benjamin think so. It hadn't taken too long for them to fall in love. They married and her career had taken off.

She had convinced Benjamin to back her in the Senate race in Montana where they lived. After two years of marriage, she was off to Washington, D.C. Her life had been set and his had become lonely. He had really loved this woman. He wanted nothing more than to live a peaceful life with her and their children. She had always said she wanted children before they married and then had every excuse imaginable why "now" was not the right time. Benjamin's hopes and dreams had withered. He had begun to grow very bitter toward this woman he rarely saw. He had thought many times about divorce but knew that it was not the right thing to do. You marry for life, his mother had taught him. After all, she had stayed with his father all those years, even though he was never around. Benjamin often wondered if his life pattern had somehow modeled hers.

Now, Constance was on one coast and he on the other. Over time, Benjamin had grown into this lifestyle. He had the freedom to do whatever he desired and he decided to spend most of his time doing philanthropic work and enjoying outdoor sports. In all those years, married to a woman he had only made love to a hand full of times, he had never had an affair. Again, he was raised to respect women and the institution of marriage. Only now were his more basic desires beginning to stir. Only now were the morals of his upbringing being challenged by an instinctual need. Only now was he thinking about risking it all.

For Benjamin, marriage was more than a piece of paper signed years ago by two people who had completely grown apart. His marriage offered nothing more than a lonely life. Meeting Alexandria made him remember the feelings he first had with Constance. That was the way it should have stayed—exciting, alive, sharing, and sexual. Yeah, sexual. What happened to all of that? Was he to live out the rest of his life alone? Never to feel the touch of those soft slender hands? Never to gaze into those aquamarine eyes or touch that brown smooth skin?

Who was hunting whom?

CHAPTER 9

S ITTING BENEATH A LIGHT TAN CANVAS CANOPY ON THE third story roof of the HCL complex, Matt and Henry were protected from the harsh sunlight, but still endured the stifling heat and muck. A typical mid-afternoon in this far-away humidifier.

Macaws, hidden amid the ancient Brazilian nut trees and the canopied Kapok trees, cackled and screamed in unison. Blue-eyed Kingfishers, with their long black beaks, darted about in furious pursuit of the unlimited insects that infested this region. The rooftop deck was equipped with hi-tech insect shields to ward off the swarms of gnats, berne flies, wasps and other stinging pests that would cover one's body in welts within seconds if given the opportunity. Far in the distance, eerie sandstone cliffs rose 3,000 feet above the blanket of green that covered the unknown multitudes of creatures that wandered below.

Henry sat in one of the several makeshift chair hammocks dangling from the overhead beams that held the canvas canopy in place. His right arm drooped down and his left hand stroked his bushy salt and pepper beard as he swung gently back and forth. With his eyes closed, he reminisced out loud, "You know, I think I may actually miss this place. I don't think there's anywhere else in the world where you can sit outside and be entertained by more sounds than you ever thought imaginable. It's damn amazing here. I should try and record this sometime. It's probably the only way I will ever convince Barbara that I really did spend months in the jungle. This is a far cry from our condo in Alameda."

Matt chuckled. Henry's quirks, and sometimes sarcastic wit, were not appreciated by some, but Matt had really taken a liking to Henry. The two men had known each other only casually before they began working on this project together in Galveston almost a year ago. In Galveston, they were two scientists among scores of other professionals working on a wide array of projects, not just the SyNAPSE project. They did spend some time together socializing there, but while here at HCL, they spent much of their off-duty time together. Henry rarely missed a chance to accompany Matt on his twice-weekly forays into the jungle, where Matt would point out fauna, invertebrates, insects and other living things indigenous to this species-rich biome. He explained that the bark of the Chinchona tree was used to make Quinine, and he would point out a camouflaged Anaconda coiled tightly around one of the 300 different species of trees found in just one acre. Their regular nightly chess games were standing room only occasions, and Henry would often entertain everyone with his sharp Henryisms. "I'm nothing but a recovering assaholic," was a favorite, or his use of the baseball phrase "can a corn," whenever he described something easy or simple.

Yes, Matt had grown quite fond of Henry, and if it weren't for the fact that they were down here working on completely divergent goals, Matt felt he could carry on a long and close friendship with his colleague.

"If you need to prove to Barbara that you really spent time in the jungle and weren't just barricaded in your lab, I'll forward her some of my pics. Like the one of you where you're pantomiming a monkey and there's a python slithering down the tree behind you. Or, remember the one where you out-ran a Tapir trailing behind you?"

"Won't work, Matt. She'll for sure think those were Photoshopped."

The two men shared a good laugh together, but were abruptly interrupted by the loud whirling sound of the approaching helicopter. Henry spoke first, "Those guys are right on schedule, as usual. I hope they managed to get us some decent veggies this trip. It's been a while since we've had something that resembles anything fresh, let alone edible."

They both stood and walked over to the railing at the end of the deck and watched the chopper plunk down on the pad below. Four times a week this same Jet Ranger made the two-hour flight down from Manaus, shuttling food, supplies and the occasional visitor. They stood and watched as crates of supplies were unloaded and the ground crew readied the chopper for its return fight.

"I've seen that guy here a couple times before. Do you know who he is?" Henry asked, as he eyed the man who had just exited the chopper and was searching through a stack of boxes on the ground.

"Yeah, I've seen him too. His name's Alan Price. He's some head muckety-muck with Starling Defense Applications. I don't know much about him except he meets with Evan while he's here and other than that he just wonders around, as far as I know."

"You really miss being home, huh Henry?" Matt asked as they walked back to their hammocks.

"Yeah, yeah I do." Henry had resumed his sprawled out position. "I miss Barbara, my dog, my condo, traffic jams—everything. This is the longest I've been away from home probably since college."

"Well, we're close, my friend. We'll be back in the good old U-S –of-A before we know it," said Evan.

"I hope you're right." Henry swatted at an errant mosquito that had somehow penetrated the "impenetrable" insect barricade. "Hey, remember my lab partner, Rick, I told you about? Well, I spoke to him a few days ago, and he said they expect to hear from the FDA any day now about the new gene therapy we've been working on these past umpteen years. I definitely want to be around for the party when *that's* announced."

CHAPTER 10

BENJAMIN ARRIVED EARLY AT THE OLYMPIC CLUB, the oldest private athletic and social club in the country. The membership consisted of many prominent San Franciscans—sort of a "who's who" in the local societal world that he so painstakingly avoided. He enjoyed this place for the simple reason that some of the best athletes in the area belonged here, and it gave him the opportunity to participate in some highly competitive sporting events.

He walked into the front entrance of the Club and greeted Walt, the Club's assistant manager, who oftentimes sat at the front desk, making sure no one entered without proper credentials. "Hi, Walt. Good to see you today. I'm expecting someone to meet me here shortly. Could you escort her to the second floor dining room where I'll be waiting?"

"Sure thing, Mr. Hunter. What's her name?"

"Alexandria Pancini," he felt a touch of pride as he said her name.

Benjamin bee-lined to the elevator and it ferried him to the second floor. Few members frequented the Club at this hour which was one of the reasons he thought this would be a good place to meet—not to mention it was an impressive venue.

The dining area was an old, stately-looking room with high ceilings and rich dark cherry wood paneling that invoked memories of old San Francisco. A crystal chandelier was perfectly centered overhead and shot shimmering rainbows in all directions. Each table was set with crisp white linen tablecloths and lead crystal glasses.

A few tables were occupied on the right side of the room, so he asked the Maître d' if he could be seated by the window on the left side.

"Of course, Mr. Hunter. And how are you today?"

"Great, thanks Jim." Benjamin gave a fleeting nod. Today he was too preoccupied and too nervous to have any sort of conversation with anyone.

They walked to his table and Jim asked, "Are you expecting anyone, or will you be dining alone this afternoon?"

"Yes, there will be one more person arriving shortly," he responded, thinking, don't ask me any more questions.

Benjamin sat near the window overlooking Post Street. Watching the cars race by, he thought about Alexandria. Yes, he was captivated by her beauty, but there was much more to her than that—much more. Her confidence and intelligence revealed a past that was laden with hard work and a deep drive to succeed. He could feel a true sense of commitment in her voice when she spoke. He wanted to know everything about her. Where did she come from? How long will she be here? Why did she become a journalist? Where is she going? What is it. . .

"Hello, Benjamin."

Oh God—that accent.

"Am I late?" Alex asked.

Startled out of his wandering thoughts, Benjamin awkwardly stood to greet the beauty before his eyes. Her hand was already at his side before he could lift his. He shook the now-familiar hand, looked directly into those entrancing eyes and said, "Hi, Alexandria. You look great after that long swim. Please, please have a seat." He moved around behind her, pulled out her chair, and as she sat down, he leaned just slightly into her, enough to catch her fragrance, and enough to send a warm shiver down his spine. He moved back to his chair and said, "I'm so glad you could make it here. Did you have any trouble finding it?"

She looked down trying to get situated in her seat and with her right hand she brushed the cascading black mane from her face. "No problem at all. I took a taxi so I would not have to even think about it."

Alex wore a loose-fitting ivory colored cashmere sweater with a draped cowl neck. The corners of Benjamin's eyes were glued to her revealing neckline. His stare was broken seconds before Alex lifted her head, but his awkward embarrassment was revealed when he stammered, "Um. . .Well. . .Are you hungry?" He reached over and grabbed his napkin, gave it a quick snap and placed it in his lap. "The food here is more than edible. It's. . .um. . .actually pretty good."

"I am really not hungry. But, thank you anyway. I would like to find out more about the foundation you have started here in America. Your lecture was so fascinating and I am very curious about how it all began."

"Well, thank you. How about a glass of wine though, before we get started?" Benjamin asked, hoping that they could first spend time getting to know each other better.

Alex replied in a professional, matter-of-fact tone, "That would be nice, thank you."

She pulled out a pad of paper and a pen and placed them on the table as if she was actually interested in his foundation. Now she had to go through a litany of questions on a subject she had to pretend to care about. This had to be done. The key to her search might lie in one of his answers.

But first, "Maybe you could tell me some things about yourself? It would help me greatly if I got to know a little bit about your personal background, maybe some of the other things you are interested in." She smiled and gently pressed a finger to her lips.

Benjamin tilted his head to one side and met Alex's gaze. "I've never really thought about how to explain something like that before. Let's see. I guess that between the foundation and my involvement with another company that does research in the area of Cystic Fibrosis, I don't really have the free time that I used to."

He held both hands out, palms facing upward and continued, "I do make a regular habit though of spending as much time as I can outdoors. You'd be surprised at all the things there are to do here. But, what about you? Tell me what makes you tick? What are some of your interests? As a journalist I would imagine that you do a lot of traveling?"

"I am afraid I am mostly all work and no play. But, I too, enjoy spending as much time as possible in the outdoors. It seems there. . ."

The waiter approached them and, posed in a tin soldier stance, asked, "Would you like a menu or perhaps you would like to start with something from the bar?"

"Well, what would you say to a bottle of Pinot Noir? Maybe a DuNah, 2008?" His head turned, he looked at Alex and continued, "This is a little-known specialty winery in the Russian River Valley appellation just north of here that produces some excellent wines." Benjamin thought how stupid it was to not even ask if she liked red wine.

"I am not familiar with DuNah. But, Pinot Noir sounds perfect."

No, Benjamin thought. You are the only thing here that is perfect. "Then Pinot it is." He turned, looked up at the waiter and said, "Please bring us a bottle. Thank you."

Benjamin felt relieved that a bottle of wine was on its way. Maybe that would help calm his nerves. He fiddled with the lapel on his navy-blue herringbone blazer and held his breath as he looked back at Alex.

"May I begin now, Benjamin?" Alex asked. It was time to start probing for her clues.

He exhaled, "Certainly. Fire away."

"Well, let's see. How long ago did you start your foundation?" she began.

"The William Hunter Foundation started in October, 2006. However, I spent several years before that doing the necessary preparatory work to get it off the ground."

Alex was intently taking notes.

He noticed everything about her. How she held her pen in that distinct crooked style only left-handed people do. How she looked down at the paper and back up at him after a few strokes of her pen. How her hair was slowly drifting back around toward her face. He began to even anticipate the right hand flinging it back behind her again.

Alex continued her probing, "Perhaps you could go into some. . ."

"Excuse me." The waiter appeared out of nowhere.

"Ah, here we go," Benjamin said and slid his wine glass toward the waiter.

The waiter pulled the cork from the bottle and poured the customary amount into Benjamin's glass. His thumb and two fingers delicately cradled the stem, and he slid the glass toward Alex and asked, "Would you like to do the honors?"

She smiled, camouflaging her thoughts, and said, "Oh no. I am sure you are a much better judge than I. Thank you anyway." She always was good at pretending she knew nothing about the finer things in life. Of course she knew how to examine the cork, swirl the glass, test for its nose and bouquet, and hold a slight sip in her mouth. She also knew how to appear less refined and cultured than all her years of schooling and travel had taught her.

Benjamin performed the ritual and told the waiter it was just right. Please, just leave us alone, Benjamin thought. Don't come back for a few hours. Time to gaze back into those eyes.

Benjamin lifted his glass from the table, tipped it forward slightly and proposed a toast, "Here is to your trip to our beautiful city and," he raised his glass higher and smiled, "to the day when you feel comfortable calling me Ben."

Alex laughed. "I, too, hope that day will come."

Their glasses touched.

She took another sip and said, "Now where was I? Oh. . . could you provide me with some details about how you determine what particular research projects you eventually fund?"

As much as Benjamin enjoyed discussing the foundation and all its achievements, he was burning with questions of his own. Are you in love with anyone? If not, why not? Then. . . how does your skin feel. . . how would it feel to be under you with that silk-like mane covering me. . . could I be enough for you. . . do you feel what I feel. . .

With his fingers rubbing the stem of his wine glass he began, "As you may remember from the lecture, the foundation focuses almost exclusively on Cystic Fibrosis research. This makes it easier to narrow the pool of grant applicants. When we decide on a few, and there are not many organizations in this country, or anywhere in the world for that matter, that do this type of research, we do our own investigation into each applicant's qualifications. We look for the capability of the organization to not only formulate sound research, but whether or not they can complete what they have projected. This is done by checking their past performances, staff credentials and their technical expertise. I suppose when you review these applications enough, you begin to develop your own sense of what is needed to perform this critical research. It really becomes second nature. Basically, when all is said and done, you often decide at an instinctual level." Benjamin sipped his wine thinking, that sounded impressive, didn't it? He sat back in his high-backed upholstered chair, pulled his shoulders back and pushed his chest out slightly. He had regained his control and composure.

The right hand, the toss of the mane behind her back

Alex was still taking notes. She placed her hands on her shoulders and unconsciously gave her sweater a slight upward tug.

"Just a moment, please. I am trying to get this down." She had it down. Her thoughts were interrupted by the overwhelming presence across the table. This was not her usual prey. He had composure, a confidence and a sincerity too many men lacked. She made a note of the application process and thought about how his eyes gleamed with pride as he spoke, how articulate he was, how obviously brilliant. It was this mix of humility and strength that confused Alex. Here was one of the richest men in all of America, yet she felt as though she was sitting across from the "salt-of-the-earth," a man similar to her father.

Focus Alex, she thought. The hunt. . . the hunt.

Alex fidgeted in her seat. Her hand brushed through the side of her hair and she continued, "Benjamin, could I ask about the name of your foundation? I remember from your lecture that the foundation was named in honor of your brother. Do you mind telling me more about that?"

The inevitable question. This was always asked. Benjamin had a solid, business-like answer, "My twin brother died of Cystic Fibrosis when he was only ten. I always wanted to do something for him, in his name. This was the perfect choice."

"Your brother was only ten when he died of Cystic Fibrosis? I am so sorry. That must have been terrible for you?" She blocked.

"Yeah, it was." He gazed out the window. "I can still see him running and playing in the open meadow. Full of so much life." He always mentioned Will's name in his lectures and oftentimes gave a quick synopsis of his short, but meaningful life. But, it had been a long time since he had spoken to anyone on a personal level about his brother. Most people were uncomfortable discussing death. He looked over at her. Not in a wanting way, but in an emotionally connecting way. He looked into her eyes and he felt a connection to her. He wasn't certain what it was, but somehow he knew she would understand. He had begun—he would continue.

"I haven't talked to too many people about the impact my brother had on my life. It's a long story and an emotional one for me, but if you'd like I could give you the Readers Digest version? It may help you in understanding why this foundation is so important to me."

Benjamin had presented Alex with an opportunity to enter a slice of his life that was very private. She knew it. He was opening up. Alex looked at her notes and circled 'emotional.' She felt herself getting close. She already knew about Will's tragic death from her dossier, but if she could get him to open-up and talk about him on a personal level she knew she would be able to probe his inner thoughts about anything. "When you speak of your brother I can tell that you two were very close. If you are comfortable, I would very much like to hear more about your brother and the impact he had on you."

Benjamin smiled. "Will and I were very close. I suppose I took care of him. My father was hardly ever home, and my mother tended to the ranch. Will and I spent all our time fishing, riding horses and playing in the meadows and the lake. He didn't get sick until he was almost nine. When he started to have breathing problems, I was the one who made sure he got his treatments on time; I was the one who made sure he went to all his doctor appointments; and, I was the one who did the research to find a place for him to get a cure. But, well, I was the one who failed."

Benjamin could feel the tears well up in his eyes. He knew what he looked like, but somehow it was okay. He knew he could give this part of himself to her. It felt right.

"I spent years beating myself up over not saving my brother. I became withdrawn and isolated. The day Will died I pounded the earth, cursed God, and cried until I had no more tears. That was it for me. Never again was I going to allow myself to feel that kind of pain, that kind of suffering. My brother became only a memory, trapped beneath the garbage I piled up over the years to keep him away. I completely locked him out of my mind."

Benjamin paused and took a sip of wine and the rich cherry and chocolate flavors sharpened his senses. Glancing back down at the table, his fingers cradled the stem and he slowly swirled his glass. "As an adult, I had the means to run all over the world. That was my way of coping. I began living life on the edge. I took on every kind of challenge that had death as a potential outcome. I was free diving from planes, mountain climbing and repelling from shear rock, racing in the Grand Prix circuit. . . anything really where I could keep myself on that cliff—that edge.

"I suppose I had a death wish. In some ways, I felt I should have died with Will. . . instead of Will."

Alex had heard every word from Benjamin's mouth and now her mind was flooded with memories of Christina, memories that she had suppressed for years. She remembered coming home from the hospital after Christina's death. She ran straight to Christina's room and threw herself on her bed and pounded the pillow with her fists. Her words were now fresh in her mind, "No. . .No. . .Christina cannot be dead. She cannot. . .This is not fair. . .Not fair. . .Take me. . .not her." Alex reached down and placed her hands on her thighs and clenched tightly.

Benjamin noticed a change in Alex's appearance. Her face was flush and her eyes had a far-away look. He leaned forward and asked, "Are you okay Alexandria? I am sorry if this is too much for you. I haven't really spoken to anyone about Will's death in years and I know it can be difficult. We can talk about other things if you'd like."

Alex placed her hands in her lap and slowly lifted her head until she met Benjamin's worried stare. She could see the concern in his eyes and she hoped he could not see the panic in hers. She held her breath as she reached deep into her consciousness and tried to patch the hole in her cracked blockade. Finally, she said, "Oh, I am sorry. I am fine. It is just that your story is very emotional and I was just thinking how difficult all of that must have been for you. How did you finally come to grips with everything? It seems like you are now able to talk about this so freely."

Benjamin sat back in his chair and tilted his head to the side. His lips parted with a hint of a smile and he said, "It wasn't until I was lying in a hospital bed after slamming my Formula One car into a stone wall that I was set free. I was forced to lie still for almost a month. I found myself doing a lot of thinking in that position. Every day, I saw Will's face. The image I had blocked years ago. At first I was angry. Then I slowly began to enjoy thinking about him and the times we spent together. I remembered his laughter and how he would spend hours practicing soccer, using the legs of the horses and sheep as a make-shift goal."

Benjamin bowed his head and tented his fingers in front of his mouth. He blew several deep breaths through his fingers-his two small fingers tapped together. Thoughts of Will skipped through his mind. He lifted his head, pressed his back into the chair and arched his shoulders. He felt the warmth of his memories. He was balanced.

Looking across at Alex, he continued, "The day I left the hospital, I went home, pulled out the old stained and dirty pictures of my brother, sat on the floor of my room and broke down. I'd never felt so much sorrow and so much love. For the first time since I was ten, I let myself *feel* the loss of him. I sat for hours on that floor, thinking, crying and remembering. That was the day I, I don't know, I let go, you know? It was like I unshackled those chains that had imprisoned my mind and my heart for so long. I could finally feel things again. *Really* feel things. I found myself enjoying life's simple pleasures like the beauty of a sunset, the feel of the warm sunshine on my face, and the smell of the wind from the ocean."

He paused and looked at Alex. He untented his hands, held them out and continued, "I didn't know it for several months, but that day in my room, on that floor, I released all the harbored guilt and the years of harbored shame over not saving my brother's life."

"I know this must sound strange to you. It's difficult to understand why a child would blame himself for the death of a sibling, but there sure isn't a lot of logic involved when you're ten years old." He slowly shook his head and continued, "I often think today, what a strong young lad I must've been to be able to care for my brother the way I did. I'm very proud of that now. I suppose that's the reason I set the William Hunter Foundation in motion; not only is it for him, but for the life he gave back to me."

When Benjamin first began to tell the story of Will, Alex took meticulous notes. She thought this was perfect—he's beginning to trust me, he's opening up—the key should be in here somewhere. As she listened and wrote, the pen took on a life of its own: I was the one who watched over *her*; I was the one who brought *her* the food; I was the one who protected *her*. I was the one who *failed*.

Alex's thoughts had shifted again. The same? No different. I failed—no, *you* failed Benjamin! You should have done more—why didn't you? You had all the money in the world to buy your brother's life. You fool. You stupid fool! Failed! Failed! The pen wrote the word over and over.

She stopped writing at that point and became transfixed in time: not here, not now—another dimension, another place, another time. As a child, long ago. I ran away too. I have lived my life on the edge, too. I am shackled by the same chains, too. I live in the same prison, too. But, *you* can see the sunsets; *you* can feel the warmth; *you* can smell the wind; *you can love.*

Benjamin again saw the far-away look in Alex's eyes. He knew his story about his brother had an effect on her—a deep effect. He reached for the bottle of wine and poured them each another glass. "Are you sure you're okay?"

Alex felt the mounting pressure from the salty dampness encircling her eyes. She glanced down at her notes, unable to see what she had written. She arched her back as if to pull her very being back from the depths of darkness, embedded her nails into the seat of her chair as if ready to take flight and dug down to the depth of her soul for the strength she needed to display. The hunter can never show fear—never back down.

She felt the comforting, reassuring coldness begin to return. She lifted her wine glass to her lips, took a sip and said, "That was quite a moving story, Benjamin. I see you have put your life into this work. I am so very impressed. Can I ask you now, do you feel private organizations, such as yours, do a better job in the arena of medical research than your own government does?" She was still struggling to come out of the darkness. No more prisons. No more Will.

Benjamin was calm. A sort of peace had come over him as he shared his life with this mysterious woman sitting across from him.

"I believe that the combination of the two is essential for any type of research, medical or otherwise," he replied. "They both seem to place checks and balances on each other. One should never be able to be the sole owner of any type of research. One obvious advantage private foundations seem to have over government funded research is that we can move at a much faster pace and with less paper to push."

Now totally composed, Alex was able to continue a focused and productive interview. She became even more business-like and rigid as she posed question after question, circling her prey. With lightening speed she scribbled page after page of notes, while Benjamin answered every question with a quiet sincerity and great wisdom.

They sat for another hour and a-half discussing the intricacies of private foundation work, and Benjamin, to no avail, tried several times to lead the conversation elsewhere. He did learn that she had two brothers and grew up in a small village in Italy. But that was it. As much as he wanted to help Alexandria with her work, he also wanted to know more about her. There was much more to learn about this mysterious woman who had entered his life.

"This has been so much help to me. You are certainly the right person to learn from," Alex was trying now to end the conversation. She was exhausted and it was time to leave. She needed to get back to her computer. She reached down and pulled the linen napkin from her lap, neatly folded it along the original creases and placed it back down on the table.

Benjamin's heart sank with her sign of departure. Don't leave. Stay with me. Be with me. "How long will you be here in the Bay Area?"

"I should be here about another week or so," she responded, knowing that it all depended upon whether or not she got the information she needed today. "I have a lot of work to do while I am here, but I hope I can also see the sights of your beautiful city."

It was the opening he had been waiting for.

"I do have some free time coming up and I'd be honored to show you around San Francisco. How about a swim tomorrow morning and maybe we can have lunch on the wharf afterwards?" Benjamin suggested, hoping she would agree to his invitation.

"I would love to join you for a swim. Maybe, 8:00—same place?"

Flashing through his mind was that still vivid vision at the Dolphin Club. The woman walking out of the water, her hair draped around her body. . . her body.

"Perfect. Works for me." You are perfect, Alexandria, he thought.

They both rose from their chairs and started to walk toward the elevator. Benjamin remembered, "Can I give you a lift to your hotel? My car is just out front."

The image of the view from her hotel room came suddenly into her mind—the bridge she could not cross. She replied, "Thank you. I need to make a few stops along the way back—but perhaps you could call me a cab?"

Damn. "Sure, I'll grab one out on the street for you," Benjamin offered.

The elevator doors closed and he could smell her fragrance. He pushed the lobby button, turned and looked back into those eyes.

"I hope I was of some help today. It was great seeing you again." Slower. . . go slower. . . what am I trying to say? Benjamin thought. Alone in the elevator he stood on one side and she on the other.

"Yes, you were very helpful. I really appreciate your time today," Alex said.

Remembering her intensity at the beginning of the interview, Benjamin asked, "I hope it didn't bother you. You know—when I was talking about my brother?"

Oh, God. Not again. "No, not at all."

The doors opened and Alex had to keep from running to the front door. *Leave me alone. Let me go.*

Benjamin caught up to her swift pace, walked down the stairs and opened the outer doors of the Club. He whistled out for a taxi. One pulled up immediately.

Benjamin opened the side door. Alex put out her hand to shake his and said, "Thank you again, Benjamin. See you in the morning."

The hand. . . the connection. Trying to hold on to her as long as possible, he said, "Goodbye, Alexandria. See you tomorrow."

She stepped into the taxi, sat down, turned to him one last time, smiled, and whispered, "Ciao."

He closed the door behind her. Don't go. . . wait. I have so many things I need to know about you. Why didn't you ask more about my brother? Why did your warmth turn to ice? What happened? I shared my soul with you and you rejected it. No, you ran from it. What are you hiding?

CHAPTER 11

THE DOSSIER PREPARED BY ANDRE CONTAINED information on the computer network used by GEN, its firewall capabilities, and types of Data Loss Prevention programs used with its centralized management framework and other filtering systems to limit intrusion into its internal network. The Transport Layer Security protocol surrounding this system was state of the art to say the least. Whoever the system administrator was who designed and monitored this system made sure that the front door was securely bolted. The only entry would be through the back door and that would take some finesse.

When Alex first arrived in San Francisco, she had spent several days running her own analysis on GEN's computer network. She ran port scans and portsweeps to find any active ports and to determine if there were any known vulnerabilities. There were none. Everything was locked and protected. Her attempts to insert a Trojan horse were rebuffed. The dossier prepared by Andre proved to be accurate—this system would take some time to break, but break it she would. Alex had done this before and she would do it again, one last time.

To gain access to Benjamin's computer, Alex created a bogus email and sent it to Benjamin's email address. The email suggested Benjamin go to a specific web site to check out some articles on Cystic Fibrosis research. The email was infected with a Trojan horse. Once Benjamin visited the site, the worm opened a back door to his computer and Alex gained the access she needed. She was set to begin her search for the password that would allow her into GEN's network.

Sitting at the desk in her hotel room, Alex's mind strayed back in time to a few years ago when she put on her black hat and crashed through a supposedly impenetrable firewall. It's not everyday that you can erase critical files and shut down over 300 computers for a 24 hour period—your target being none other than the United States military. The US Navy had developed a highly advanced Magnetic Anomaly Detector that could uncover the most minute variations in the earth's magnetic field. This allowed the military to spot submerged submarines well past their crush depth of 2400 feet. The military already had this technology, but this advancement alerted it to previously undetectable submarines, the ones built with titanium hulls. The detector was patterned after a geomagnetic survey device originally used by mineral exploration companies to determine the location and extent of deposits.

The irony in all of this was that Alex had been hired by a British mining and exploration company to obtain this new technology. The original magnetometer technology was developed and employed by the mining industry and the military had used it to advance its sonar detection capabilities. She reasoned at the time that she was doing nothing more than returning the original technology to its rightful owner.

Alex had buried her own prints and was never connected to the theft, despite widespread investigations undertaken by the UK National Hi-Tech Crime Unit and the FBI. She deflected the trail to lead to an unsuspecting system administrator for a Scottish based financial services company. She dubbed the administrator "Solo." He was indicted by a federal grand jury in the United States on nine counts of computer related crime. That was two or three years ago, and the poor dupe was still fighting extradition proceedings.

Alex turned on her laptop and waited for it to boot up. She was now in her element. The mission, the solving of the puzzle, and then the sting. Alex enjoyed the puzzle best. That was the creative part of the hunt—the time her intellect entwined with her intuition. That was when her adrenaline was highest. The rush of uncovering the key was addictive for her.

She had direct access to Benjamin's home computer, so she could retrieve any file and monitor any form of communication connected to it. Through Benjamin's computer she would access the GEN network, download the data she needed and return straight to Paris. She could then rid her mind of her past and start a new life. Again.

Uncovering a person's user ID and password could be as simple as using the last four digits of their Social Security number, or as convoluted as unleashing a sophisticated brute force attack. With the use of the right specially written software, it was possible for a hacker to uncover the proper password within seconds. If a person did use the last four digits of their Social Security number, a password could be discovered within .046 seconds. The longer and more complicated the password, the more difficult it was for the program to discover it. A password with 8 letters, all in lower case, would require 2.4 days for the computer to run through all of the possible combinations. Adjust just one capital letter and one asterisk, and the processing time for an eight-character password would soar to 2.1 centuries.

Alex had developed her own network login cracker. Patterned after the THC-Hydra program, she had added new modules and numerous protocols of attack, while enhancing the recovery speed. This was usually a hacker's last resort. If they unleashed this method of attack it meant that the targeted password was almost certainly more complicated than a Social Security number, a pet's name or a birth date. She named this program Hercules, after the slayer of the serpent-like Hydra of Greek mythology.

Alex opened the key-logging program that she had uploaded to Benjamin's home computer when she first arrived. This program was an enhanced version of a program she had developed when she worked at DGSE. It ran under the targeted system's operating system and automatically transported each keystroke used back to the attacking computer. Nothing, Alex thought, as she looked over the entries. In the past several days, since she set the program up, Benjamin had probably spent no more than ten minutes on his computer.

Running through her program files, Alex pulled up the Hercules program and kicked it into gear. She would unleash this as a brute force attack and the user ID and password would be hers. She could still input her own guesses at his password as she delved into this man's mind. But Hercules was her best hope for a quick triumph.

And so the work began.

Alex sat looking at her hi-def monitor, unable to make out any of the words scrolling down before her weary eyes. The program was fast, and she would now simply wait for it to spit out the prized access information.

She pushed herself away from the computer, and her bare feet skimmed across the plush wool carpet fibers as she drifted over to the window. She placed her open hands on the sill and leaned forward. Her forehead rested gently on the glass pane as she stared out at the bridge. She felt the stiffness in the muscles of her lower back creep upward, around her spine and all the way to her neck. Her thoughts were now clouded with images of Benjamin. She knew she would have to begin the transformation of matching her psyche to his. She must think like him, feel like him—*become him*—in order to find the access information. Hercules would work, she knew that, but if she could access the inner working of this man she might be able to finish everything sooner. What is the word? What would he use? Think, Alex. Think.

Still staring aimlessly out the window, she said to herself, now stop this. You listened to his heart. What did he say? He gave you the answer. Pay attention. Concentrate. . . now, *feel*, Alex. Feel.

A gentle warmth flooded the room, and slowly caressed her aching muscles. She wasn't conscious of her fingers tapping against the cool glass. This man, she wondered, how could he be so at ease with the loss of his brother? He seemed so grounded and sure of himself. Why didn't he ache from the loss? How could he stop it? A single tear fell from the corner of her left eye and landed silently on her cheek. The years of work she had done to protect herself from that ache; the years of laying the bricks and mortar that held her captive, out of reach and alone; the years of filling her mind with knowledge and intrigue; and the years of anger she had stored toward the parents she felt held her responsible—it all began to seep out of her soul that night.

She turned and pressed her bare heels firmly into the carpet and slowly slid to the floor. In a protective fetal position, Alex held her head in her arms, as if to rock herself—and Christina—once again.

Her thoughts were unstoppable. She had always been able to control her mind. Something happened. Something had to happen. She had to break.

Coiled up on the floor, from deep within the synapses of her memory links, Alex envisioned Christina. Beautiful, innocent Christina. She could see her running up the mountain and rolling down the long-bladed emerald green grass to the bottom where Alex waited to catch her. She heard her laughter, and felt her little arms and legs wrapped around her waist as she carried Christina on her back. Alex remembered braiding her beautiful long black hair so it twisted around her head to keep it out of her large dark eyes. How she had loved Christina, taken care of Christina, protected Christina.

After several moments, though it seemed an eternity, Alex uncurled her arms from around her head. She rolled onto her back and looked up at the ceiling. Christina loved me too, she thought. She would never leave my side. When other children wanted to play with her, she would always come to me first to see if I wanted to go along. She would look up at me and say how beautiful I was, and how much she wanted to be just like me some day.

Would you still say that today, Christina? Would you? Have I become what you would want to become? Have I led a life you would be proud of? Where are you Christina? Help me now. Be with me now. I need your strength, since I have none. I need your innocence, since I have none. I need your love, since I have none. Help *me* to see the sunsets. Help *me* to feel the warmth. Help *me* to hear the wind.

Her mind drifted back in time. A time when she had permanently wrapped her pain and guilt in an impenetrable shroud.

Secret 7 was a DGSE "deep" cover unit that focused on procuring intellectual property and technology from the aerospace and electronics industries. It consisted of eight agents, a support team of video and audio technicians, and specialists trained in chemicals, computers, electronic surveillance, forensic services and explosives.

Until Alex arrived at Service 7, it used less sophisticated spying techniques such as dead-letter-drops, digital scanners, non-technical intelligence collection known as HUMINT, or Human Intelligence, electronic intercepts, and aerial photography. Alex used her experience from the Tangiers operation to develop a software program that could be hidden in an email and installed by exploiting security vulnerabilities on the target's computer. The program, called Carnivore, acted as a keystroke logger and was also designed to steal encryption keys used to decipher encrypted files or messages.

Alex took Carnivore and her cadre of agents on a whirlwind tour to the United States, Japan, Germany and Korea. They infiltrated aerospace, computer technology, pharmaceutical and banking companies and returned with state-of-the-art technological riches, all shared with French companies. Thanks to the DGSE, and Alex, the glory days of Napoleon had returned.

Alex consistently butted heads over the Agency's strict regulations and protocol, but she did love her work. She engrossed herself in it with the same passion and inner drive to succeed that she honed so well from her younger years. Her secret life was her own and, following the standard practice of the Agency, she did not tell anyone about her double life. She had never been someone who needed to unburden her personal problems onto others. This new underground lifestyle enabled her to construct an impenetrable blockade around the sheer pain and guilt she still harbored from losing Christina. Following Agency protocol, she was periodically vetted by clinical psychologists trained to look for actual or potential personality disorders. Alex's barriers were by then so tightly packed and impassable that these skilled professionals couldn't penetrate the walls that encased her demons. The memory of Christina was securely bolted within her memory banks.

In spite of the accomplishments that Alex had achieved for Service 7, she was not without her critics. Many claimed she was not a team player, lacked judgment and was not committed to the DGSE because she was prone to going on 'frolics of her own.' Her colleagues had nicknamed her 'Renegade' in large part because she preferred to work solo.

When Alex returned from Hong Kong where she had successfully pirated core trading platforms from HKEx, the regions public stock exchange, she discovered that her swipe card would not allow entry into her office. The security guards immediately alerted her that it had been canceled, but offered no explanation. Her department head notified her that HKEx had publicly announced that $8 million had been illegally wire-transferred from client accounts and that they were investigating the matter. HKEx alluded to the possible involvement of a foreign intelligence agency. She was put under internal investigation for the possible disappearance of the funds and placed on an immediate leave of absence.

Infuriated by the false accusations and not trusting that the DGSE inquiry would be undertaken with her best interests in mind, Alex embarked on her own investigation. She soon discovered that one of the agents who was there with her, Alain Marrion, had used the Carnivore program for his personal benefit. The rogue agent had obtained the security codes from the HKEx wire-transfer room and in a series of transfers had dispersed the funds to several offshore tax havens.

Alex had cleared her name and was immediately re-instated, but by that point she had lost all confidence in the DGSE. While that was not the first time she had a run-in with the upper brass, she had decided to make it her last. The so-called 'honorable calling' that Andre so eloquently claimed, no longer existed. The inside politics, the constant defending of her actions and the lack of ingenuity within the Agency itself had taken its toll. The 'Renegade' turned in her resignation and ventured off alone into the world of corporate espionage.

Alex was trembling. She wrapped her arms around her body and squeezed tightly. She closed her eyes and held her breath and with all her remaining strength she willed the peace and calmness to return to her.

Benjamin began to trickle back into her thoughts. Their lives were parallel. There was no denying it and at the same time there could be no admitting it. He gave her his soul that day. Alone, she gave him hers that night.

Slowly, vivid images of the large overstated office with bay windows framing the Eiffel Tower crept into her mind. Andre was pacing before her, peering down at her, convincing her.

Did she pick the wrong prey? Had she made the fatal mistake? Would she be able to uncover the password? Was she too close. . . were they too close. . . was it too late to choose another?

Her thoughts were interrupted by a beep from her computer. A message had been received. Slowly, she picked herself up and walked back to her laptop and hit the message key.

TO:BENJAMIN HUNTER

FROM:MURRAY PAULSON

RE:G4G Security

Hi Ben,

The security people will be at your house by 9:00 am this Thursday. They will need approximately two hours to install the security measures we discussed. Your presence will be needed to show them where your computers, phones, etc. are located. Unfortunately, you will be unable to access high security clearance from your home after this. This should not be a problem, however, because your basic clearance should be enough for your personal purposes. If needed, you can obtain classified materials through me directly.

I hope this will not be an inconvenient time for you. Let me know if it is, and we can make other arrangements.

Thank you, Ben

Murray.

Yes, Alex thought. It was too late. I have to move now or it will all be over.

CHAPTER 12

Somehow Benjamin was not as cold from the icy Bay water that day. He didn't have the usual numbness of his skin or the tingling in his fingers. He took a quick shower after their swim that morning and hurriedly dressed to meet Alex for a cup of coffee in the Staib Room. This was a room used by the Dolphin Club members for social gatherings and where various trophies, pictures, memorabilia and Club lore were housed.

Benjamin swam like a champion that morning. Not bad at all, he thought. Normally, he would be exhausted from the fast-paced swim he had just completed however; he could not even come close to releasing the mounting tension that began the afternoon of his lecture.

Alex was slowly taking her shower. She was not in a hurry. She needed more time to think. More time to find the key. More time than tomorrow would lend her. She needed another day. But, she thought, I can finish this today. I have to. But, I need more time. I need to see him again. There is more to learn. Maybe the access is too difficult. Maybe *we* need to work on this a little longer.

She stood under the water with her eye-lids squinted shut, and allowed the warm shower to cover every inch of her body. The steam leached through her pores and began to thaw the chill of her inner core; her mind eased. She thought, what a great swim. What a beautiful morning. What a gorgeous city. What a wonderful man. He was nothing like anyone she had ever encountered in all her travels. If only this was another place, another time.

Benjamin was sitting in the rear of the Staib Room overlooking the swimming cove when Alex entered. He'd never noticed before, probably because he couldn't take his own eyes off of her, but every man in the room was staring at her. She had to know how beautiful she was. She had to feel all those eyes watching her every movement. Yet, she had a commanding, statuesque presence about her that would not allow for any foolish flirtations. As if raised by royalty, this woman, this mystery, had the enviable grace of a doe and the confidence of an eagle. Ah, yes, Benjamin thought—like an eagle.

"Hello, Benjamin. That was such a wonderful swim. I wish I could have kept up with you. You are quite good, you know," Alex teased.

Before he could stand she sat down beside him and he could see from the corner of his eye that her hair was still damp and clung tightly to the back of her neck. She wore a loose fitting lilac colored wool sweater and the sleeves were pushed up just enough to expose the strength of her slender, but shapely arms. He pressed his broad shoulders back, took a deep breath and he swore he actually felt the warmth coming from the aura that haloed this alluring woman.

Looking into those deep-set aquamarine eyes once again, he said, "You're pretty damn good yourself. I wish we could do this more often. I usually swim alone when I'm here, so it was a real treat to have someone alongside me out there today." He hoped that wasn't too forward, but felt he had so little time left.

"You know there's another spot I should show you. Twice a week I usually try and join up with some friends at China Beach just outside the Golden Gate. I think you'd love it there. The currents are stronger, and if you get a good read on them you actually feel like you're steering through the water. It's quite a rush. Some of the guys keep saying they've seen dolphins while they were swimming there, but I'm not so sure about that. A bit of unfounded swimming lore, I think."

"Oh, that sounds like a wonderful spot. I hope we can try it before I leave. But you have to promise I can have a head start."

"From what I saw today you're the one who'll be handing out head starts. Hey, I'll get us each a cup of coffee and we can plan our day," Benjamin said as he rose in anticipation of her answer.

"That would be nice. Thank you." Alex hoped she could accomplish her mission in just a few short hours, and would not need the whole day. But, she had to get the code—the key. As she watched him walk out of the room, she tried not to notice this giant of a man. He had a poise and composure about him that commanded respect and reverence. She needed to let him think she did not care about his virility or his sensitivity. She needed *him* to be the prey, not her.

When Benjamin returned with coffees in hand, Alex was standing, admiring some of the many pictures along the wall of the Club. She felt him behind her; she turned, pointed to a picture, and asked, "Is this you?"

Beaming, he said, "Oh, it's nothing. A while ago."

"Nothing? Swimming the Catalina Channel seems very impressive to me. Even I have heard of that one. You really are something," Alex noticed his flushed face and knew she had embarrassed him. She thought, my God, this man is amazing. He has everything, has done everything, yet, so humble, so sincere, so unaffected.

"Your time here of 9 hours and 34 minutes for 21 miles, that must be some sort of record? Am I right?"

"Well it's not really a record, but it was the second fastest crossing that year," Benjamin answered, with just a hint of pride in his voice.

Alex nodded toward the cove and continued the praise, "Very impressive. You surely are an accomplished swimmer. That was obvious from watching you out there today." She truly was impressed.

Benjamin continued, "I suppose I have accomplished a lot in swimming over the years. I'm flattered that you're impressed— even that you noticed. I'm sure, from watching you, that you have a few medals stored away as well."

"No," Alex said as she rose and walked toward the double paned window looking out to the cove, "I am not as accomplished as you. Shall we sit?" She sat down on the built-in window seat and Benjamin sat beside her—closer this time. He needed to get closer.

Alex asked a few more questions about San Francisco, and Benjamin sipped his coffee, answering in as great a detail as possible. Anything to prolong the close proximity he had managed to maneuver. He was able to get in some questions of his own and he did learn more about her, but not without some prodding. When she slipped in a few French words in their conversation he learned that she spoke several languages. She had enjoyed some success in her career as a journalist and had dreams of someday pursuing more investigative stories.

They sat on the window seat for an hour and Benjamin continued to speak in his thoughtful, effervescent style and Alex sat calculatingly, listening to every word. Was this it? No, what about this one? Maybe. Remember these words, she thought. Lock them into your memory. Stop looking in those dark eyes. Stop smelling his skin. Move away a little. Words—concentrate on the words.

"So, Alexandria," Benjamin continued. "Let me take you to Fisherman's Wharf first and we can have lunch at Scoma's. It's a pretty fair seafood restaurant overlooking the Bay." I know you want to be with me, just be with me.

"I have had such a great time with you this morning, but. . ." Alex hesitated.

But what? thought Benjamin.

"I have some work I hope to finish today. I just cannot make it."

Benjamin leaned toward her a little more so that his eyes were now directly across from hers. They were too close now—too familiar.

"I really want to continue today with you. Is there another time today when we could meet? There are so many things I'd like to show you."

Alex's thoughts rolled through her head as she listened to Benjamin. There are so many things I want to learn from you. What is the damn password? Just give it to me and leave me alone. I need the word; not your smell, not your warmth, not your soul. But, I may need you tomorrow. If I cannot break the code by tonight, you cannot install that security system. I may need you tomorrow. "I really do not have time today. But, I should be able to get most of my work done today and I will be free all day tomorrow. Maybe you can think of something fun we could do for the whole day."

It was better than nothing. He felt defeated, but tomorrow could be a very long day. With that sturdy outward composure, Benjamin replied, "Alright. That sounds great."

Now what? Where can I take her that will consume the entire day. . .and night? "I have a great idea. Let's drive up the coast toward Mendocino. Some of the cliffs and coves there are breath-taking." Like you. "We could spend the day sight-seeing and eating abalone and Dungeness crab. You'll love it. I promise."

"Sounds fantastic. Count me in," she said with half-feigned enthusiasm.

"So why don't I pick you up tomorrow morning at your hotel and we'll be off?"

Alex knew that if they did go tomorrow, she would have to control this part of the trip. She needed to get him away before the security people arrived. And she wanted to see his place—the clue, the code, could be there too.

"Oh, I think it would be easier if I just met you at your home."

Perfect, he thought. "Great. I'd love to show you my home." Just don't look for traces of the mistake I made years ago—the one that lives in the East.

"Where do you live?" As if she didn't know.

Benjamin reached into his jacket and pulled out a pen. He sketched out a map and began to explain the directions, "Well, you cross the Golden Gate Bridge, go to the Stinson Beach exit. . ." As he continued with the directions, Alex stared into his eyes, not hearing a word. No, she thought. I cannot cross that bridge. Is there another way? She knew the answer.

"So, are we set?" Benjamin asked confidently.

"Yes, Benjamin. I will be there," Alex replied. What time were those security people coming to his house? Oh yes—nine o'clock. "How about 8:00 sharp? Is that too early? I love to get going in the mornings." She loved to sleep in.

"Perfect. Would you like another cup of coffee?" Benjamin couldn't stand the thought of her walking away just yet. Just a little longer. . .just a little more. . .just a little closer.

Alex was getting restless. She needed to get away from his overwhelming presence. "Oh, no. I need to be on my way. Again, I had a fabulous morning. Thank you so much."

They both stood and, as if on cue, leaned into each other. Apparently an accident—or they were beginning to give into the force pulling them together.

"Sorry," Alex muttered, knowing that she couldn't possibly look in his eyes. Her right hand swept her hair away from her face one last time, and she paraded toward the door. Benjamin walked behind her, trying not to show her or any of the others watching her that he was totally fixated and taken by the sway of her hips and the flow of her ebony hair.

They walked out into the crisp San Francisco air and Benjamin began to regain some of his balance. Apparently, he needed the cold to counteract the heat. They walked silently to her car. She turned, pressed the electric key opener and said, "See you tomorrow, Benjamin." Maybe.

He held her door open as she slid into the driver's seat. The wind blew her fragrance toward him one last time. It was everything he could do to say goodbye and shut her door. They waved to each other as she drove away.

Even in that car, driving away, behind that tinted glass, she was the most beautiful sight he had ever laid eyes on. Tomorrow? Why not today? I need tomorrow to be today.

Alex drove up the steep hill of Powell Street, back toward her hotel. She was determined to get the information she had learned today inputted into the Hercules program. She was excited about what she had uncovered. They had spent a lot of time together. She knew the answer was there somewhere.

She arrived back at the hotel and hurried to her suite. She sat down at her mocked up workstation. She turned on her laptop, and noticed the wads of crumpled paper on the floor—then she remembered. They were her bed last night, her blankets.

The beep of the program opening on her screen brought her back to the here and now. Because the meeting was still so fresh in her mind, she wanted to enter as many of the words that she could possibly remember into the Hercules program. She stopped the program and hit the Special Option button. Here she directed the program to run all word combinations up to a maximum of four words; the speed of the Hercules program would run these combinations within fractions of a second. She typed the words directly into the program as fast as possible.

CATALINA ——— CODE DENIED

CHANNEL ——— CODE DENIED

9:34 ——— CODE DENIED

TROPHIES ——— CODE DENIED

TROPHY ——— CODE DENIED

She continued for the next several hours using almost every word he said and every word she thought he said. Fatigued, she finally turned off her laptop and edged over to the couch and leaned back against the armrest. Kicking off her shoes, one by one, and pulling the cashmere scarf from her neck, she slid down to the oversized cushions and stretched out. She took the burgundy blazer that she had earlier thrown on the couch, bundled it up and stuck it behind her head. She closed her eyes in search of the missing word. What was she not seeing? What had she ignored? What else was there? What now? Think. Think.

She was exhausted and her thoughts drifted off to her day with Benjamin. Most of their time together was lost in a conscious void; she could not concentrate on his words. She tried over and over to hear his voice, yet all she heard was her own: stay away, stay focused, don't look in his eyes, don't smell his skin, stop the desire, stop the ache. You need the password. . .his eyes. . .the code. . .his eyes. . .the job. . .his eyes. . .

Benjamin didn't hesitate to call Murray at GEN as soon as he got home. He needed to change the security installation tomorrow. There were no options. "Hello, Murray. This is Ben. How are you today?"

"A little pressed at the moment. How're you doing?"

"Couldn't be better. Listen, I need to change the installation of the security system at my home tomorrow morning. I have some things going on here I can't change. Could we reschedule it for another day?"

"We really need to get that installed Ben. Can you leave a key with a neighbor and they can come in while you're gone?"

"Normally that wouldn't be a problem." There was no way he wanted anyone at his house tomorrow. What if they never make it out of there? Nothing can go wrong. This can't be interrupted. Benjamin continued, "But tomorrow may be a potentially complicated day. I have some guests coming in from out-of-town tonight, and I don't want anyone to disturb them."

"Okay, I understand Ben. I'll reschedule it and give you a call with the details."

"Great. Thanks a lot. Talk to you soon."

They hung up.

Excellent. I'm free and clear, he thought. What a day this will be. We'll drive up the coast and I'll have her all to myself for an entire day—an entire evening—an entire night. Benjamin thought once again about her beauty, her innocence, her poise. Then he thought about her mystique. He still had so many questions. She had an uncanny ability to shift every question he directed at her into a question toward him. Every time he wanted to know something about her, she would learn something about him. Why was she doing this? Very clever. Too clever. This was odd to him. Here was a woman, well educated and obviously intelligent, who was here to write an article about foundations. There was much more to this story, much more to her. She was much more than a journalist looking for a story to take back to her country—much, much more.

A lex awoke suddenly to the sound of Benjamin's voice. Where am I? Benjamin? Is that you? She quickly sat up on the couch and looked around the well-appointed, but empty room. God, she thought, what is happening to me? She got up and wandered into the bathroom and splashed cold water on her face. She stood with her arms stiff against the sink propping herself up and stared into the mirror. She took a deep breath and held it, still staring at the image in the mirror. The air slowly escaped from her lungs and she heard the murmur of her own voice, "Alex, get a grip. You are losing it. Use this man. Use him."

She wiped the water from her face and walked back into the room. The clock on the nightstand read 6:30 pm. What happened to the time? she thought. Have I been asleep for six hours? Damn it. I have so much to do. The password—I have to get the password. I need more time. Tomorrow—the security installation—the phone.

She picked up her cell phone and dialed the number she had memorized on the plane. Two, three, four rings and then the answering machine picked up. Damn, she thought, he's not there. In between the machine's utterances and beeps, she heard, "Hello, hello."

"Hello, Benjamin?"

In his swirl toward consciousness he heard the accent.

"I am sorry, did I awaken you?" Alex asked.

Quickly, he said, "I must've fallen asleep."

You too, Benjamin? Alex thought. Are you as exhausted as I? In as much turmoil as I?

Benjamin was sprawled across the bright plaid couch in his den. He quickly threw his feet to the floor and sat upright. He rubbed both eyes with his free hand and said, "Nah, I'm awake now. How are you?"

"Fine, thank you. I just wanted to make sure we are still on for tomorrow morning," she said.

Are you kidding? Do you think I would cancel—that I *could* cancel? "Yep. In fact, I was thinking earlier about some of the places I want to show you. I think you'll love them. You have beautiful beaches in Italy, but I think you'll find the shoreline of Northern California equally spectacular. You're in for a real surprise"

"I am anxious to see what you have in store, Benjamin."

"I was thinking earlier about Italy. Have you lived there your whole life?" Benjamin asked in an effort to learn more about this woman.

Alex replied, "Well, yes. Have you lived here in California most of your adult life?"

There it is again. Clever woman, Benjamin thought. "No, not really."

"Where else have you lived?"

He wanted to move the conversation back to her, but decided that it was more important to keep her on the phone, so he answered, "I live part time in Montana now and I've lived in a few other countries over the years."

Montana; Alex wrote down the word. "That sounds exciting. I would love to hear about the other countries. Have you spent much time in Europe?"

"Yeah, in several countries and I've vacationed there numerous times. As I said the other day, when I was living life on the edge, that edge included lots of places in Europe. I loved the Alps. That was probably my favorite place. I skied often in Kitzbuhl and then went off to St. Moritz. Those were great times."

Alps, St. Moritz, Kitzbuhl, Europe, skiing, edge. She wrote them all down. Trying to quickly write the words and keep the conversation going, Alex said, "I went to school in Switzerland. I love it there too." What have I said?

What, he thought, you're telling me something about yourself and I didn't even have to ask? You were educated in Switzerland? I knew there was much more to you. "Really? When were you there?"

"Oh, when I was young, of course," she said, quickly. "I hardly remember it. I have done very little traveling," Alex lied. "It just was not something my family enjoyed doing, I suppose. Perhaps someday I will. This trip has been wonderful for me and you truly live in a beautiful area. Are there any special places in Europe that you would like to return to someday?"

"I've thought about returning to the place that saved my life. Remember I told you about my car accident and the month I spent in the hospital? Well, that was at the Grand Prix in Monte

Carlo. I've always wanted to return there but I've been afraid to. I suppose even though that place transformed my life, it's always held a painful memory for me. It reminds me of Will in a way that not even New Zealand could. It was in Monte Carlo where I saw Will again. It was there he spoke to me, and there I forgave myself. And it was there I began my journey back. My fear of that place probably has more to do with how close I came to losing my own life. Will would never have forgiven me for that."

Benjamin stopped and wondered why he felt so comfortable and why it was so natural to talk about his brother the way he did with Alexandria. What was this connection to this woman? he wondered.

Alex continued to write down word after word throughout Benjamin's disclosure. Trying to find the code, she wrote his words, his thoughts, his feelings, and his pain. From within that unconscious space, that frozen place in time, she suddenly, and without thinking, revealed her hidden secret that allowed him a brief glimpse into her soul, "You are right. Christina has never forgiven me." Her name. No, no. I mean Will. What the hell have I done? Hang the phone up now. Run. Get away. That was so stupid. . .

CHAPTER 13

EVAN WAS SEATED AT A SMALL ROUND TABLE IN THE corner of his office and Matt was seated opposite him. A "Do Not Disturb" sign hung on the door to Evan's office, where the two men had been huddled for the past several hours. Earlier in the day, Evan had heard from Isabelle and Henry that each had completed all of the preliminary tests and they were ready to proceed with the final tests with both products.

Henry was now certain the three synthetic genes he had created could be successfully carried by the virus. One of the genes he had created was designed to bolster cell resistance to death. The end result would be to increase the life span of a human being by at least 30%. He had run additional rounds of gene mutations to change the DNA sequencing and the gene alignment now matched the DNA data base.

"Henry has assured me that he has stitched the three synthetic genes together and his tests on the new virus are conclusive–the targeted gene will be attacked." Evan had completed reviewing his notes with Matt and he leaned back in his chair, his hands placed firmly on his knees.

"So, what do you think Matt?"

"This is great, Evan. I'm looking forward to testing things out. I haven't reviewed Henry's final results from the tests using the spider monkeys, have you?"

Evan replied, "I have, and everything is as close as we can hope for. We won't have any way to measure the precise effect on longevity yet, but his results are in line with the computerized model. Is everything ready on your end? I'd like to run these final tests simultaneously in the next day or two."

Matt pushed his chair back and stood up. He was just over six feet tall, rail-thin, neatly cut light brown hair, his eyes several shades darker than his hair. The jagged scar on the left of his protruding chin was the result of a lab injury inflicted by a spider monkey six years ago. The scar, or the scuff mark, as Matt referred to it, was just one of the perks that came with the business. At the same time it was the main reason that he was no longer concerned with testing new experiments on monkeys. They had their place in the evolutionary cycle.

With precise measured steps, Matt paced in a circular route, over to the window, around Evan's desk and back to the conference table. With each hand chopping the air for emphasis, he replied, "I'm really excited about where all this is leading us, Evan. We used 14 monkeys, and the results have been the same with each one. A perfect match. The virus spreads rapidly through the lymphocytes, and the targeted gene is attacked within 30 seconds after the virus is injected. In the specific cases where we used the mosquitoes to transmit the virus, they were able to draw the lymphocytes from the infected monkey and pass them on to non-infected monkeys with the same results. The virus will be transferable from human to human. No doubt about it."

Now standing behind his chair with his hands gripping the upper edges, he leaned slightly forward, looked directly at Evan and lowered his voice, "It's going to be a dead-bang winner, Evan."

The look on Evan's face revealed the mounting excitement this usually restrained and calm man felt. With more than a smile and a wink, he said, "Who would've thought that when we started this just over a year ago we'd be at this point today? Great job, Matt."

Matt took a bow and replied, "It's all in a days work, my man. Thank you."

Evan looked down at his cell phone to see who was beeping him. The HCL facility was equipped with its own cellular system so that people could communicate by text, email or voice within the compound. "I just got a text from Henry. He wants to see me. He must've got his call by now. Why don't you wait around and I'll tell him to come on down."

"Hi, Evan. Oh, hi Matt," Henry said as he walked over to the round conference table and stood behind one of the chairs. "You guys planning another project or the celebration party? You've been in here a while."

"Yeah, it seems that way. But we're done now. What's up Henry? No problems on your end, I hope?" Evan asked. His straight-laced unassuming facial expression had returned and he remained seated.

"No, no. Not as far as things go down here. Everything is just fine. I got a call a few hours ago, though, from my colleague in Alameda, and it turns out they want me back in the States as soon as possible. Something's come up and I'm really the only guy that can work through the analysis. This is kind of a mixed blessing. I'd love to head home, but we're so close to finishing up here I really should be here, too. Anyway, I told him I'd talk to you guys and see if something can be worked out on both ends."

Evan motioned to the chair where Henry was standing. An eyebrow raised. "Sit down, Henry. This seems kind of sudden. Is everything okay back home?"

Henry pulled out a chair and took a seat. He crossed one leg over the other and placed both hands loosely on his knee. "They really need someone like Matt, not me. This is more his area of expertise. They ran some follow-up analysis on the stored data we had, and abnormalities appeared that weren't in the original batch. Apparently some of the stem cells are infected with an external virus. It's going to require additional testing, and time is pretty important in all of this."

Matt spoke first, "I'll make you a deal," Matt said as he looked at Henry. "If I can help you on your end I will. There's no reason we can't use the nanocomputers we have here to run part of the analysis, and we can hook you in by teleconference for the final SyNAPSE testing. We definitely need your input and blessing on the final results, Henry"

"You know, Henry, I think everything is all set here, and I don't expect any problems when we run the final testing. Matt's right, we can hook you up through teleconferencing if we do have any problems. We may as well put the telecommunications system here to some good use," Evan added.

Henry had been looking out the window while Matt and Evan spoke. He heard every word, but his thoughts were directed elsewhere. He really knew he should be going back to headquarters. "Ok guys, I appreciate your understanding on this. I think I will go back to Alameda and work on things there. You need to promise me that you'll keep me in the loop, though. I've spent way too much time on this project not to see it through to the end."

"I promise," said Matt.

"Me too, Henry. You've been too integral to everything here not to keep you involved."

Evan took a sip of water, "There's a chopper due in tomorrow, the usual time. I'll go ahead and make the arrangements for you to go back to Manaus with them, and I'll get the rest of your travel arrangements in order. You should be home the same time we start our testing here," Evan said.

Henry pushed his lanky frame up from the chair and extended both arms out, palms down, "Thanks, Evan. I'll get some things completed in the lab this afternoon and go over some details with Isabelle, and tomorrow I'll get ready to leave. This should all work out just fine," He pivoted and walked toward the door.

Evan spoke, "Henry, you've been very valuable here. We wouldn't have gotten this far without all your help. We'll have a celebration together as soon as we all return."

"Thanks guys and I'll hold you to that celebration, Evan." Henry closed the door as he left.

Evan stood and looked at Matt, "Okay. It's just us now. We should have this wrapped up and be out of here ourselves within the week. Have you got your test subjects lined up?"

Matt's features darkened, "I have three plasmids that have the identical DNA sequencing to our three test subjects. I've made arrangements for the test subjects to be in the lab room when we're ready to proceed. They won't know what hit them."

CHAPTER 14

B ENJAMIN HAD A RESTLESS NIGHT. ANTICIPATORY anxiety has a way of not allowing the mind to rest. As he dressed, he was thinking about being with her: holding her, feeling that black mane on his face and becoming lost in her sea-green eyes. Images of her had run through his mind most of the night. But, their peculiar conversation had been just as provoking. Who was Christina? Benjamin went over and over in his mind what had been said. "Will would have never forgiven me for that." Then, "You are right, Christina has never forgiven me."

Then there was the afternoon at the Olympic Club. He felt her become more-and-more distant as he had spoken about Will. Before his eyes she had become ice. He had known she needed to stop the conversation. He had seen the tear in her eye and the way she had stared at her paper, unable to share the pain. He had recognized the signs—the fear, the struggle.

It must be Will. Is Christina a Will to her? Is that possible?

His thoughts were broken by the sound of a car pulling up the meandering tree-lined driveway. He moved to the side of his bedroom window and looked down at the circular entryway as the car pulled to a stop. He froze as he watched her step out of the car. She couldn't see him through the dense trees lining the north side of his home. The light was such that her silhouette replayed that image for him once again. She wore a long flowing dress that swirled around her as she walked. The sunlight penetrated completely through it outlining those sleek legs—where they began and where they ended. Her hair was flowing over a dark sweater that made it hard to differentiate between the two.

Unable to move, hypnotized by her sway, he no longer thought of Will. . . of Christina.

He watched her walk up to the front door and place her small hand on the button, but it wasn't until he heard the buzz of the doorbell that he came out of his trance. He bounded down the stairs two at a time and skidded to a screeching halt at the front door. Taking a long deep breath, he swung open the solid redwood double doors. He couldn't see her face. The sun was directly on her back shining into his eyes. Again, the dark, mysterious silhouette.

"Good morning, Benjamin." Those words seemed to have come from the sun itself.

Still unable to see her face, yet smelling her fragrance, hearing her accent, feeling her presence, he said, "Good morning to you too. Come in. Let me get you a cup of coffee before we take off."

Curious about whether the security installation time was canceled, and wanting to view his personal surroundings for a potential clue, Alex said, "That sounds great. Can I help you get the coffee?" She walked past him into the foyer.

He stood in the doorway as she brushed by him. Her right shoulder swept by his chest, close enough so that he needed to tighten his grip on the doorknob. . . balance.

"No. But why don't you join me in the kitchen and we can go outside on the deck with our coffee?"

"Sure," she said. "Lead the way."

As she followed him around the curves of the house, down the long hall lined with pictures and memorabilia, she thought over and over: God, I hope he does not ask me anything about last night. I do not want him to know anything about me. He is too close. This is too dangerous. Just do not talk about Will, about Christina.

He poured their coffee, handed a cup to her and led her out to the deck where the sweeping panoramic view was stunning that morning. The two towers of the Golden Gate Bridge jutted through the low creeping fog and the sun glistened on its shiny steel. She walked toward the railing and said, "I have never seen anything so breath-taking in all my life. I could stand here forever."

Forever. I could watch you stand there forever, Alexandria. I could wrap you in my arms forever. I could protect you forever. I could love you forever.

Alex leaned against the wooden railing and gazed out at the Bay. Benjamin moved closer to her. Somehow, he sensed it was now alright to be close. She stood sipping her coffee, unable to take her eyes off the vista, and he stood unable to take his eyes off her.

Alex carefully phrased the question, "I really appreciate you taking the time to show me around today. I hope this has not inconvenienced your schedule in any way?"

"Not at all. I had one appointment this morning but I was able to change it to another time," Benjamin thought she was just being polite.

"I hope it was nothing too important."

"No it wasn't. Just some people coming here to install a new security system. I really hate having to bother with it all anyway,"

"I really could stand here all day, but I am very excited to see your coastline." She also needed another look around his house. Maybe a clue.

"Then we're off," Benjamin said as he threw a hand in the air and motioned toward the house.

Alex pivoted around toward the house and a reflection from the sun caught her eye. She turned back and peered out to the tree-filled surroundings, and saw a peculiar mesh-like wire wrapped around a group of trees off to the right side of his property. Curious, she pointed and asked, "What is that over there?"

He knew where she was looking. "Where?"

"Is that some sort of cage over there in the trees?" Alex prodded.

"Oh, that. That's an old cage I used when I was involved in falconry." This was too important, too precious. Too soon. "Shall we?" He led her back toward the house.

Alex had too keen a sense of curiosity. What was in there? She knew she would have to find out. Falconry? That was one she had not yet tried.

In the kitchen, they set their cups down on the marble countertop, and Benjamin followed Alex down the long hall. She walked slowly and looked at as many of the pictures as possible. She saw one with him and Constance. In her briefing materials on the plane, she had seen pictures of Constance. At that time, it made no difference to her that Constance was beautiful and had her own distinctive and exotic look. Passing her pictures in the hall sent a piercing sting to her chest. She felt a quick flush of anger. How dare this man attempt to captivate me when he is not free to do so? No, wait. What am I thinking? Alex pondered. Even if I chose to be captured, and I do not, he is not even close—not even able. Her right hand brushed her hair away from her face and she continued on down the hallway.

When they reached the front door, Benjamin spoke, "Let's take my car. I'll drive and you can just take in the view. I'm parked on the side of the house. Why don't you wait out front and I'll drive around?"

He opened the front door and Alex passed close by him again—the sweep of her left shoulder, the brush of her hair across his chest. He watched her every move, her every sway as she walked down the front steps. He closed the large redwood doors, turned and quickly ran through the bends and turns of the house to the side entrance and out to his car.

He opened the door to his charcoal-gray Land Rover and vaulted straight into the driver's seat. He always loved four-wheel drives, long before they had become fashionable. He used them for the purpose they were built—to explore the mountains and off-roads.

He drove around to the circular driveway where Alex was standing, awaiting the ride she somehow knew would take her across the bridge—across time into a world of darkness.

He pulled up along side her, rolled down the window and said, "Hey there. I'm on my way up the coast. Need a ride?"

She giggled and mused, "Well, I do not know. What is up the coast?"

"Take a risk. You'll see."

Take a risk, she thought. That I will. She laughed and jumped in next to him.

He thought how wonderful it was to see her laugh. He knew this was a rare occasion.

"You have a beautiful laugh, Alexandria. You need to share that more often."

It was not often that Alex let anyone close enough to pay her such a compliment. But it felt good to her that day. It felt right.

They joked and laughed as they slowly wound their way through the narrow and twisting roads that led from Mill Valley to the vistas of the Pacific Coast Highway. Benjamin reached over and touched Alex protectively on the shoulder as he accelerated through the tight bends. Alex exaggerated each tug as they rounded the corners. She placed her hands on the front dashboard and pretended to hold fast as she wittingly swayed to her left. They were each finding a way to bring out the child-like sensations in each other. Laughter is sometimes an easier way to release pain than the anguish of tears.

Throughout the drive, Benjamin pointed out the sights. He loved talking about the beauty that had surrounded him here on this coastline. The tall redwoods of Muir Woods gave the drive an exciting, eerie feeling, as if they were meandering through a never-ending forest with all its magical legends and mystery.

They were becoming comfortable and more open with each other. Benjamin talked about the loss of his mother, what it was like to grow up in New Zealand and he revealed intimate details about the struggle he had with an alcoholic father.

Alex too, spoke freely about parts of her own life, although she remained careful not to include any details that would expose who she really was. She spoke about the loss of her own father and the life of her mother who remained in the family home in Italy. She visited her mother as often as she could and she talked on about how she worried so about her mother since her father died.

Alex leaned back in her seat, looked over at Benjamin and said, "You have done so much with your life. I am certain that if your mother was here today she would be beaming with pride over who you have become."

It wasn't the words that Alex spoke, but the tone of her voice that made Benjamin reach over and gently cup his fingers on her arm. He nodded, "Thank you for saying that. Like you are now, I was very close to my mother and she still enters my thoughts when I have tough decisions to make."

For a brief moment Alex closed her eyes and cringed. An image of the bridge outside her hotel room, the Golden Gate Bridge, appeared. To her, the symbolism of that bridge was clear. She knew she had now crossed over that one-way bridge that had kept her isolated in a place steeped with loneliness and guilt. A place where she was comfortable and where she knew she would not have to face her inner ghosts.

When she opened her eyes, she was not staring at darkness and there were no demons to torment her. Instead, she was surrounded by rainbows dancing on the horizon with dazzling beams of light trickling through the morning mist. Her eyes sparkled and her endless smile said it all.

The vertical cliffs and emerald-green slopes bordering the winding Pacific Coast Highway were awe-inspiring spectacles for Alex to behold. She continuously leaned over toward Benjamin to look down on the ocean below them. Amused, Benjamin was busily pointing down at the rocks—pulling Alex toward him every opportunity he could.

They stopped for lunch at Vladimir's, a little Czech restaurant in the small bucolic town of Inverness, just outside Point Reyes. There, they shared Vladimir's specialty of stuffed cabbage, along with a bottle of Merlot.

After lunch, they strolled through the quaint village and sat for several hours along the shore of Tomales Bay. Feeling a warm spin from the wine, Alex flirtatiously pressed her shoulder up against Benjamin, and spoke with exaggerated animation as they playfully chatted about their dreams, their sorrows and their hopes. No longer was she thinking about computers, genetics, Andre, the code, the password. This was her time. However brief, she felt she deserved the fun this man was sharing with her. Lost in time, she was what she had always wanted to be—happy.

Benjamin was euphoric. He felt her drawing nearer to him, and knew that she was beginning to open up. He so much wanted to grab her and hold her, to tenderly kiss her mouth and touch her skin. He had to wait-the time had to be right. He had grown used to that feeling of being off-balance. It was becoming his new sense of reality. He understood that he would forever swirl when she was near and ache when she was gone.

The Point Reyes lighthouse jutted out from the southerly point of the peninsula at the end of a narrow, windswept road. The tower was anchored to the rocks 294 feet above sea level, and since 1870, it had protected weary mariners from the dangers and perils blanketed by the dense, syrupy fog. It had served as the sole, steadfast sentry to warn against the huge waves, high winds, towering cliff faces, rolling sand dunes and pounding surf threatening this passageway.

Benjamin knew that this place held the evolutionary key to the mind—the ocean in all its mystery, the womb of all life. Its very meaning could shatter one's carefully constructed sense of reality.

They pulled into the small parking area overlooking the beaches to the north. Alex was giddy with anticipation. The views here were truly intoxicating, and she jumped out of the car as soon as Benjamin pulled to a stop. "A little excited, huh, Alexandria?" he said.

Alex coyly replied, "This is fabulous. You certainly are the romantic one."

Benjamin, without thought, walked around to the passenger side, gently took her hand in his and said, "This is one of my favorite places on earth, and I want to share it with you. Follow me and hold my hand tight. The winds here can be treacherous."

She felt his strong hand holding hers, and for a moment imagined living life here by the sea, without a care in the world, and with this man to protect and shelter her from harm.

They sauntered along the path toward the lighthouse and Benjamin suddenly stopped. He lifted his head, closed his eyes and whispered, "Listen. Hear the whistle of the wind through the canyon? Close your eyes. Listen."

Alex stopped next to him. She held his hand tightly, closed her eyes and leaned her head back. She could hear the eerie sound and she concentrated on storing this moment in her memory, as if knowing that this time and this sound would forever remain with her. As she stood silently next to Benjamin, he felt the warmth of her body next to his; he saw strands of her hair blowing in the strong wind; he smelled her fragrance he now associated with passion and, he imagined her wrapped tightly in his arms.

She opened her eyes, gazed into his, and said, "I will remember this sound all my life."

They began walking again, this time more briskly, toward the lighthouse, as if a new urgency had developed. Walking along the road through the Monterey Cypress and up to the narrow path leading to the 308 downward steps to the point where the lighthouse peered out over its world, the winds began to gust in unexpected spurts. They moved closer to each other for warmth, for stability, for balance.

There were a few people lingering around the lighthouse with binoculars and cameras, watching the whale migration. The Gray whales migrated to the south at this time of the year, and from this vantage point they watched the whales as they breached and played along the long trek to their spawning ground. They would give birth to their young in the warmth of the Baja lagoons and return home to the chilly Alaskan waters in the spring.

Alex was awestruck as she watched pods of whales swim off the coast in their southerly migration. She zipped up the front of her dark indigo blue wind jacket and slid a half step closer to

Benjamin. She placed her hands back on the iron railing and said, "I have never seen whales in their natural habitat before. How sad it is that we once hunted them and killed them for pleasure."

Benjamin wrapped his arm gently around Alex's back, his hand cupped tenderly around the nape of her neck. "Fortunately, they've multiplied over the past 10 years, thanks to the environmentalists bringing so much attention to their plight. It sickens me to think of man's selfish need to hunt down and slaughter one of nature's most beautiful creations," Benjamin said.

Hunt, Alex thought. The hunt. What an awful word. What have I done? What am I doing?

Her thoughts were interrupted by the loud guttural sound of the fog horn perched high atop the 16-sided pyramidal lighthouse.

Benjamin tilted his head close to Alex's ear and said, "That's the sound of safety, of reassurance. For over a hundred years that same horn has called out to sailors lost in the fog, lost in the night, those unable to come home."

Alex closed her eyes again. She listened for the next calling out to the ocean, to the whales, to where life began. This sound, too, would become embedded in her mind. It was now her sound of safety, of reassurance, and of a moment in time she never wanted to forget.

They stood overlooking the ocean for some time, their thoughts and emotions fixed on the migrating whales. The pounding of the waves against the rocks below them sounded like kettle drums in rhythmic tune to the symphonic caw of the gulls circling endlessly overhead. Benjamin stood close to Alex and occasionally put his arm around her when he wanted to point out a breaching whale or something off in the distance.

Hesitant to leave this wondrous view, yet knowing that he needed to take Alex somewhere to be alone, where they could talk and he could ask some of the questions he knew she did not want to answer, Benjamin said, "Let's go back now and we can sit on a knoll overlooking the beaches to the north. You'll love it there, too."

He took her hand once again and led her back up the wooden stairs to the upper vista point and then back down a steep dirt path that led to the long sandy beaches on the northern side of the peninsula. They stood at a deserted area overlooking the entire northern coast. This was a rare, clear day. Without the usual fog over the cliffs, they could see as far as their eyes would allow. Alex heard, once again, the whistle of the wind and the faint sound of the foghorn as if they were now one force, giving her the peace she needed.

They continued on the narrow dirt path to a small vista point. Benjamin pulled off his jacket and laid it down on the ground. The wind was not as strong on this side of the peninsula, and the rays from the sun provided warmth. They sat down next to each other. Alex, once again, was amazed at what she saw. The beach was lined with white foam. The breaking of the surf made the foam twist and curl along the shoreline. The cliffs above the foam were jagged and imposing. A few miles off the shore, an ominous fog bank threatened to descend upon them. This was a striking picture of parallels—the fog, the foam, the shoreline, the cliffs. . . and their lives.

They sat next to each other on Benjamin's jacket, and Alex asked, "Have you been here many times?"

No, Alexandria. Never have I been to this place before; never have I felt this before; never have I experienced life the way I am with you today.

"I've been to the lighthouse a few times over the years, but I've never sat down here before and witnessed the beauty that we're seeing today."

"Yes. This is breathtaking." Alex's arms balanced her as she leaned back, her long hair gently swayed as she slowly rolled her head from side to side.

This sight has nothing over you, Benjamin thought, as he continued to gaze at her. You take my breath away, Alexandria.

They sat in silence for some time, just staring out at the coastline and rolling sea. Benjamin's thoughts were racing. How do I begin this conversation about who this mystery is beside me? I have to do it slowly. She'll run if I ask the wrong question. Christina. Who is Christina? Who are *you* Alexandria? There was a part of him that wanted to know nothing. A part that was afraid if she answered him honestly, he would be cut out of her life forever. He felt so much was at stake right now, yet he knew he had to continue.

"Alex, I want to know more about your life."

Shivers ran up her spine. Her warmth turned to ice. Without hearing the question she asked, "Why did you call me Alex?"

"I'm sorry. Don't you like that name? It just seemed natural." Benjamin felt the door to Alex's inner-most thoughts suddenly slam shut.

She dropped her head. Her hair covered her face and she said, "No. It is just that name puts me back into another life. A life I do not want any part of right now."

Delicately, but knowing that this was the direction he needed to go, Benjamin took Alex's hands in his and inched closer to her. His voice was firm, but soft, "I'm sorry, but I have to ask—what does that mean? What life are you talking about?"

"Another world, Benjamin. Please do not ask me any more. Even if it is just for this one day, you have brought me out of that world. I just want to sit here with you and remain absorbed in this place."

Alex trembled. She didn't know what she felt anymore. She thought about what was happening to her. Why was she so terrified? She knew she could not say who she was, or where she was from. He would leave and this moment would be over. She had to stop shaking.

Again, Benjamin pushed. He had to know who this was beside him. He gently put one hand under her chin and pulled her head up so that her eyes met his soulful gaze. He brushed back the hair from her face. Their eyes were now fixed on one another—he recognized the fear. He wanted to just hold her and say it would be alright, and that he doesn't need to know anything else, but he needed to know.

As if his life, and hers, depended on it, he continued, "I can't let this go. There have been too many times I've felt you pull away from me when we begin to talk about your life. Today you have opened up and shared parts of your life with me. There is still so much more to you though, and I want to know everything. Please trust me, Alex. I want to be here for you, and I want you to be here for me, too. I see a pain in your eyes and I can feel your ache. It's a familiar ache to me. I know that it has something to do with Will—with Christina. Who is Christina, Alex? Who is she? Please. . . please tell me."

Alex couldn't pull her head away from him. Her eyes were frozen on his. . . they were his. He knew. She knew that he knew. The ache he once felt was now totally and completely a part of her. The ache she hated. The ache she had so successfully escaped all these years. The ache she could no longer contain. It was there, in her heart, in her throat, in her tears. She began to silently weep.

And so it began. The journey into Alex's masked world. The story she knew she would have to tell; the destiny she knew she would have to meet.

Benjamin sat in silence. He held her hands, wiped her tears and listened to the story of Christina. Benjamin finally understood.

Reliving the tragic story of Christina left Alex numb and weak. Never before had she shared the weight of her sister's story with another so completely, so honestly and so openly. The years of guilt and anguish poured out of her. On that vista overlooking the ocean, witnessing a wondrous migration as old as time, in Benjamin's arms, Alex took the difficult journey back to heal her wounds, her suffering, her loneliness—her soul.

When she finally finished, her head was cradled on Benjamin's shoulder, her forehead tucked tightly under his chin. Her body molded into his. Benjamin knew they had become one. The past they shared, the pain they knew, bonded them in a way no physical touch ever could.

Alex was dazed, and was in no condition to speak or move. Benjamin knew that. He put his strong arms under her and gently scooped her up as if she was a wounded animal—one that had once soared through the skies, run through the forests, and conquered the oceans, but had now fallen, stumbled, and was unable to breath. He knew he had to save her, protect her, love her. He knew it was time for her to heal. He would take the time to help her. He would take her there now.

CHAPTER 15

ALEX SLEPT THE WHOLE TWO HOUR DRIVE BACK TO Benjamin's home. He did a lot of thinking on that drive. His marriage to Constance was over years ago, and he had only a threadlike piece of paper that would eventually have to be shredded. Neither one of them had ever wanted to deal with the legalities of divorce. She had her career in Congress and needed to maintain an upstanding image. He never wanted to go through the hassle of dividing up his estate.

Everything was different now. Divorce did not carry with it the stigma it once did. Constance would survive. She would hold her head high among her colleagues in Congress. She would always have enough money to live the lifestyle she had grown accustomed to, and more than enough to fund countless campaigns.

Benjamin now knew that he needed to be free from Constance in order to be with Alexandria. He felt certain that he could convince her to stay with him; and if not, he didn't mind living in another part of the world, as long as it was with her.

When he drove up to his house, he was careful not to awaken her. He turned the engine off, eased out of the car and walked around to her side. He opened her door and stood fixed on her face, once again. This time it was different. He saw not just the physical beauty he had been so taken with, but now he saw her soul—the very essence of this person who was no longer separate from him. She was a part of him—she was him.

She stirred and looked up at him. He whispered, "Shhh. Close your eyes. Sleep. Shhh." Once again he cradled her in his arms and carried her toward his house.

Alex was barely conscious. Wrapped in Benjamin's arms, she felt safer than she could ever remember. The sense of peace and contentment was too powerful to resist. This was what she had been missing. In her dream-like state, she now began to understand why her mother stayed with her father all those years, why she had given up her life for him.

Benjamin opened the front door, still with Alex in his arms, and carried her to a large cushioned sofa where he gently laid her down. She moved slightly to her side and he grabbed the blanket draped over the back of the sofa. Placing it over her, he tucked it in around her the way a parent does to a child. She looked so peaceful, so perfect. He leaned over, kissed her forehead and whispered, "Sleep, Alex. Sleep."

He walked out of the room and Alex heard the back door open and shut. She wondered where he was going, but was unable to move just yet. She was in the throes of something much more draining than any kind of physical exertion—the healing of the soul.

Moments later Alex rose. She needed to be with Benjamin. She wandered through the house looking for him. From the kitchen, she looked out past the back deck where they had coffee that morning. She saw him standing by the wire—the cage. What is he doing? What is out there?

She opened the French doors, and he immediately turned to her. Briskly he walked toward her. Without words, they held each other in their arms.

He whispered to her, "I want to show you something now. I need to share this with you."

With their arms still around each other, he arched his back so he could look in her eyes. He continued, "You have shared with me your most secret thoughts and now, before I take you into my own secret world, you need to know a few things. What I am about to show you I've shown no one. What I am about to share with you I've shared with no one."

Benjamin tilted his head in the direction of the cage, and continued, "That bird you see is the part of me that I have healed—the part of me that I will soon set free. It's the most powerful and beautiful of creatures—the bald eagle."

Alex was hypnotized. Benjamin continued, "I found him several months ago in Canada. He had a gun wound in his leg and his wing was broken—probably from the fall. He lay on his side and tried to move, but the long struggle had taken its toll. His body was jerking, but he was unable to move. It was a horrible sight. What hurt me the most was to see his mate only a few feet away. She was shrieking at him, and probably at me. She was in as much pain as he was, and as terrified as I was. When she saw me, she stared at me with her eerie yellow eyes. Her beak opened and I knew she would attack me if I came any closer. She was protecting her injured mate and she wouldn't leave his side. I stopped about 20 feet away from them. Sitting still on the ground, knowing that she could attack and seriously hurt me at any time, I tried to hide my fear. For the longest time the three of us sat and watched each other.

"The big male stopped struggling and he watched my every move, my every breath. I could see the pain in his eyes. He had lost a lot of blood and I could tell he wasn't far from death. As I sat with the two of them, I knew they both understood. She tilted her head from side to side, studying me. I sat as still as I could. Then she moved back slightly, as if trying to tell me to come forward. He tried to stand on his one good talon, and moved his body toward me. I could see that his one wing was completely broken. He had been struggling there for hours and she had been protecting him for hours."

Alex buried her head in Benjamin's chest and embraced him tighter. He held her tightly, and continued, "I slowly inched forward. She moved around behind him. As I went forward, she retreated. When I got close enough to touch him, she shrieked at me. I looked in her eyes and she looked in mine. She was telling me something. She had already given me permission to come close—this was something else. I sat transfixed with her for a moment. She backed away a little more, again telling me to move closer, to help her mate. Then her stare became piercing—it went right through me. She jumped into the air and was off. She circled above us, silently continuing to watch my every move. I could feel her desperation, her fear. Then I knew what she was telling me. Almost as if her shrieks became the words in my mind. 'Take him. . . heal him. . . bring him back to me.'"

Benjamin's hands slowly wove through Alex's hair and he caressed her face. Holding her in his arms and feeling the beat of her heart against his was everything he had imagined, and more. He continued, "A lot of people believe that eagles mate for life and I knew what I had to do. I slowly placed a hand on his good leg and he continued to stare at me. Through his glazed eyes, and barely alive, I knew he would never understand, but I felt I had to make a promise to him—to her—before taking him away. I promised him that I would heal him, as I'd been healed, and I promised him that I would return him to his mate. He understood. She understood.

"As she continued to circle above us, I picked him up in my blood-soaked arms and carried him to my car. I laid him on towels and a blanket in the back. I shut the hatchback door, looked up to find her, and saw she was heading toward the mountain behind us. She landed on what appeared to be a nest. I wondered if their young were there waiting for him also. She was watching me care for her mate, watching my every move. I stared back at her for a moment, and then I heard her last shriek. This was the one that echoed through the canyon. This was the one that awakens me now at night in a cold sweat. Her heart was broken and so was mine. I know now that I will never truly be free until I release him back to her. . . until I fulfill the promise I made to the creature on the mountain."

Alex trembled in his arms. Tears streaked down his face as he told the story of his quest. Her head was tucked under his chin and she softly whispered, "Hold me, Benjamin. Hold me tight."

She felt the beat of his heart in her chest. She felt his breath become hers. Again, they were one.

He dropped his arms, took hold of her hands and said, "Come now. Come with me to the cage." He led her to the gate, unlocked the latch and escorted her inside.

Softly, "Are you sure it is alright for me to be in here with him?"

"Yes, Alex. Don't worry. He'll know who you are."

They heard the rustling in the tree just to their left. Benjamin called out to the eagle. The sight Alex saw silenced her breath. Not many people have ever seen this beautiful creature up close. The eagle swooped down onto a branch directly above them and flapped its enormous wings. As it sat peering down at the two of them, Benjamin said, "It's amazing that mankind thinks of himself as the greatest of species. Only in the presence of an eagle can you really know how insignificant we really are."

They stood holding each other, gazing upward. Benjamin knew that Alex now understood the meaning of his world. He had everything he wanted—everything he needed—his life was now whole, now fulfilled.

They watched the powerful bird for over an hour as it moved from branch to branch as if to get a better look at his savior's mate, as if it knew that the time was drawing near for it too to be with its mate. To Benjamin, the symbolism was clear that evening in the cage— he had introduced his mate to the eagle and showed it that he truly did understand where and with whom the eagle belonged.

As they walked away from the cage, Alex turned back to see the eagle on the ground—its golden yellow eyes tracking their every movement. She whispered, "Goodbye," and he flew upward again. Benjamin nodded, "He was waiting for you to say that." She felt it too.

They walked back to the house, arm in arm. Afraid of letting each other go, Alex asked, "When will you return him to her?"

"He's just about healed; probably in a few weeks. I want you there, Alex. You must do this with me—for me."

"I want more than anything to be there with you, Benjamin."

They walked in the house, through the kitchen and down the hall, past all the pictures. Benjamin turned, pointed to a black-framed photo on the wall and said, "Right here, Alex. This is the place where I found him. Along the forest line near a small village in the Queen Charlotte Islands, off the coast of British Columbia. That's where we'll release him."

They continued down the hall toward the living room. As they entered the room, Benjamin grabbed her shoulders, not wanting to be forceful, but needing her to hear what he was about to say. He turned her toward him so that she was unable to move in his arms. "Alex. You can't leave me tonight. I've never wanted anyone so much in my life. I've never needed anyone like I need you. God! I've never loved anyone the way I love you. Stay tonight, Alex. Stay forever."

She moved her head up toward his and his hands gently cupped her face. He felt her burn. He tenderly pulled her into him and kissed her with the growing passion he had been holding onto ever since he first laid eyes upon her. Ever since the day he had seen her in the sunlight; ever since he first heard the accent; ever since he touched her small hand; ever since he lost his balance. Now, finally, he was ready to release the burn, the ache and the longing.

Alex fell limp in his arms. As they kissed, locked somewhere deep in the catacombs of her mind, in the tangled web of her being, in the cold isolation of her darkness, came the desire of a lifetime. This controlled woman could no longer contain the yearning. Her breathing became short, her heart pounded, and her legs no longer held her up. She was unable to think, to reason, to stop.

Benjamin felt both her weakness, and her burning strength. He picked her up once again in his powerful arms and carried her upstairs where their worlds would collide in a way few have ever known.

CHAPTER 16

E AGLE... EAGLE... EAGLE. ALEX STIRRED NEXT TO Benjamin. A dream—the Eagle—wake up, she began to say under her breath. Then, as she opened her eyes to the soft light from the full moon glistening through the window, staring at it she thought, EAGLE! That's it. EAGLE!

Without thought of the warmth next to her, she slid, very carefully, to the edge of the bed. Gently, she rose up from under the covers and began to gather her clothes scattered around the room. She heard the whisper of sleep from across the room, turned toward it and was instantly hit by the reality of what she was about to do—what she must do.

She stood across the room, gazed at his face in the moonlight, and felt overwhelmed at the thought of what had happened to her over the past several days. Lying in this room was everything she had ever dreamed of, but thought would never exist in her world. This man brought her life when there was only death; light when there was only darkness; purpose when there was only aimless wandering; and love when there was only emptiness. Alex knew he had given her something she would take with her for the rest of her life. A gift so precious, so divine, and given only to her, in a way no mortal being ever could. From an eagle, Alex learned that love was not desperate and final, but instead was a mutual and willing bond sealed for eternity.

So began the battle within her being. That was an unfamiliar battle for Alex, the only one she had never fully prepared for. Struggle had always been second nature to her, and she was used to being the victor. This time was different. This was not the battle she had perfected—the one within her mind. She even knew how to struggle within her heart. This narrow intersection—where the mind crossed paths with the heart, where reason conflicted with emotion, where the intellect clashed with passion—was somewhere Alex had never been.

Alex took a single step forward and then stopped. No, she thought, there was no way she deserved someone like Benjamin. She had deceived the first and only man in her life who had lovingly opened himself up to her and shared his innermost thoughts. He knew nothing about her. Her past was littered with countless lives she had destroyed. She had come to his world to destroy it. Her whole time with him had been based on a lie, a ruthless deception. There was no way she was worthy of this decent, kind and pure man. She knew he loved her for who she pretended to be, but she knew she did not deserve Benjamin.

She gazed at Benjamin in the dim light and realized she had to leave. The battle was over. Silent and motionless, she struggled to keep her cluttered emotions sealed until she no longer saw the dim light coming through the window and no longer heard the whisper of sleep.

Carefully, she put her clothes on, trying not to awaken Benjamin. She knew she now had the password, and somehow it didn't matter anymore. She would go back to her hotel room, punch in the password, retrieve the documents and deliver them to Andre. It was now all so simple—so complicated. She knew Benjamin would never want her after he found out who she was and why she had entered his life. He would hate her. She had to leave. It was over.

Alex stood over Benjamin now, by his side. She knew she would never see him again, never be wrapped in those strong arms, never be touched so gently, and never be loved so completely. She wanted to tell him everything. . . she wished to tell him nothing. She bent down beside him as he lay in the bed. His face was turned away from her toward the window and the light. She stretched out her arm, but knew she couldn't touch him. With her hand only inches above his head and with the ache she knew would last an eternity, she softly whispered, "Goodbye my love. Goodbye."

CHAPTER 17

"GOOD MORNING, GARRAN." Murray was in his office early, going through some much-overdue paper work before the rest of the office crew arrived. The early morning hours in his office were what he called his "in-and-out-time." The unfinished work in his office would be finished and out of there in no time.

"So are you calling me to let me know that you're all done with our new security measures?"

"Murray, there's a problem." The worry in Garran's voice crackled over the phone line. "A major problem. One of my techs just brought me a report that shows the GEN computers were hacked early this morning. We don't know yet what files were taken, if any, but we do know that something was uploaded. Everything is still intact as far as your files go, but I'm coming up there right away to look into this myself."

Murray threw his feet off his desk and jerked upright in his chair. "What? I don't believe this Garran. Tell me again what you just said."

"I really don't know any more at this point, Murray. I looked over the report myself and it's correct. Something was uploaded to the system. We'll find out exactly what it was, but I know it'll take most of the day to get to the bottom of this."

"Jesus, Garran. Tell me this isn't happening." Garran's words sliced into Murray's gut. His air of confidence was sucked out of him and beads of worry formed on his brow. With a noticeable tremor in his voice he continued, "Did you finish installing the security system? I thought you said our data security would be bullet-proof?"

"Come on, Murray, you know that was never represented to you when we first talked about upgrading your system. Cyber attacks today have become so sophisticated that some degree of compromise is nearly impossible to prevent in *any* system."

Murray could hear his mind rattle in the lonely solitude of his office. His shoulders were bowed under the weight of this discovery and he felt a stiffness crawl though his body. How the hell could this have happened? he thought to himself. He knew this wasn't Garran's fault. He had known Garran for most of his adult life. There was no one more competent in the security field than Garran. No, Garran would get to the bottom of this and everything would work out. He hoped.

Garran Upshaw was a career military officer who often wished he was still serving in the military. If it weren't for the urging of a few good friends to hang up his uniform and take his expertise to the private sector where he could make some serious coin, he would probably still be serving. For a man in his mid-sixties, he still fit the poster image of a career military officer. His brownish-gray hair was cropped short and his physique still finely tuned from his daily running and weight lifting regimen.

During his 30-year military career, he specialized in clinical psychology, intelligence, special operations planning, and crisisresponse management. At the tail-end of his career, he had served as an intelligence officer with the United States Strategic Command, and was responsible for synchronizing human intelligence, measurement and signature intelligence, signals intelligence, imagery intelligence, and open source intelligence. It was his job to make sure there were no gaps in the national security operations. He took his job very seriously.

When Garran started G4G Security Solutions, he relied heavily on both his military training and his contacts to turn his company into a world-wide leader in fighting the daunting challenge of computer network security. His creation of the public key cryptograph was a milestone and was still the gold standard used by security companies today.

Murray sat back down in his chair, slumped forward and placed both elbows on the desk. With the phone wedged tightly against his ear, he said, "Okay, Garran, where do we go from here? If something has been stolen from our files it needs to be recovered, and we need to find out who was behind all of this. *And* we need to know what's been uploaded to our system. What's your next step?"

"As I said, I'm going to catch the next flight out of here and I should be in your office within a few hours. I'll bring some extra manpower so we can probe through your network for the information we need. I'm hoping we can complete everything today. Whatever we find, we'll decide what to do then."

"If you find that files have been taken will you be able to find out who did this? I'm afraid I can probably guess which files were taken. God, I hope I'm wrong. Whatever those files are we'll need them back."

"We'll get to the bottom of this, Murray. If any files were taken I am sure we'll be able to trace the theft to a specific location. The files had to end up on someone's computer. And yeah, I hope you're wrong too, Murray. There's always the chance that this was some random hacker of sorts."

"And you can track down that computer? You'll find this person?"

"We can and we will. You know over 25% of corporate data theft comes from a company's own employees. That may not be the case here, but I want you to give some thought to whether that may be a possibility."

"I don't think so but I'll think about it. Should I contact the authorities at this point? Maybe they could help in all of this."

"No! Don't do that yet, Murray. We don't know yet what's been taken, and we obviously need to find that out first. I'm probably better equipped to find the person who did this and get the data back, anyway. I'll make some calls on my way to the airport and have some people standing by. I know just the right guys who can handle this quickly, and quietly—very quietly"

CHAPTER 18

S ITTING IN THE SAME CHAIR WHERE SHE HAD ALLOWED the course of her life to change once again, Alex rolled her fingers across the armrests, bit down on her lower lip and waited—impatiently. She hoped this would be her last encounter with this miscreant of a man. Tight coils of anger were lodged within her as she looked out at the Eiffel Tower and all the beauty of Paris. What an awful city this is, she thought. What an awful country, what an awful man. He is ruthless and mean-spirited. He uses anyone he wants any way he wants. Why did he make me do this? Why did I let him? I hate him. Benjamin would hate him too.

This was the first chance Alex had to sit in silence, alone, with time to reflect. After she had left Benjamin's home, she had quickly cracked the code to GEN's classified files, extracted the targeted documents and had flown to Paris on the first flight that same morning. She had been exhausted on the flight home. She had slept the entire time, except for an occasional turbulence that startled her slumber. When she had arrived in Paris it was late in the afternoon and she headed straight for Andre's office.

Andre was in another meeting but was anticipating Alex's arrival. He had instructed his secretary to let her into his office as soon as she arrived. She hated this time alone, this uninterrupted time to think. She just wanted to hand over the hard drive and leave—forever.

As if she owed a debt—a sacred debt—Alex was forced to be alone with her thoughts in this pretentious office of greed and power. Time was all she had now. Time to think and confront the enormity of what had just transpired and how her life had been transformed over the past few weeks. As she closed her eyes she could see his face, hear his voice, sense his touch, feel his pain— *her* pain. At that moment she knew. She knew that the price she would have to pay for having stolen the documents and the trust of a selfless, loving man was to be tortured for the rest of her life, with only the memory. That was to be her penance. Her hell.

Alex slumped in her seat and dropped her head to her hands. She was exhausted. Her mind was racing with thoughts of Benjamin, Point Reyes, the Dolphin Club, his home in the hills, the eagle, the moonlight through the window. . .

Suddenly the large mahogany doors swung open. Startled, Alex jumped to her feet as if she was caught at something she was not supposed to be doing.

"Oh. Andre. You scared me!"

Andre, with a gleam in his eyes and an endless smile on his face said, "You did it, Alex? You brought me the material?"

He walked over to Alex, his arms outstretched as if about to embrace her. She forced a brown wrapped package in between them.

"Here you go, Andre. Everything is there," Alex curtly interjected as she handed over the package.

Andre was taken aback by the coldness in the room. Alex had always been kind to him, and either gave him a hug when they met or at the very least shook his hand. Something was wrong, Andre sensed. She did not even look him in the eyes as she forced the package into his hands.

"Are you alright, Alex? Is anything the matter?" Andre studied Alex's face as he attempted to engage her in some form of a conversation.

"I am exhausted, Andre. Please, I need to leave now. I am sorry." Alex was trying to hold herself together long enough to get back to the safe haven of her flat.

"I can see this must have been quite difficult for you. Can you tell me about it?" Andre's smile had faded and was replaced by his default facial expression—a frown, but his furrowed brow feigned a genuine concern about Alex for a moment.

Alex knew this concern was anything but genuine, and that he needed to make sure she was alright for his own protection, so she decided to give him a little information to pacify his selfishness.

"Yes, this was difficult. I had a very hard time getting the access code to enter the computer system at GEN. I spent many long and sleepless nights trying to crack it."

"Really?" Andre asked. "And how did you finally come about getting the code?"

How dare you, Alex thought. If you think for one minute that I am going to tell you anything that happened to me over there—you are crazier than I thought. You, of all people, could not possibly understand what I went through—what I am still going through.

"Andre, you know I never discuss how I obtain any of my information. Let us just say it is done, and leave it at that."

Andre felt her piercing stare, her hostility. Needing to know more, he continued to probe, "Did you take anyone down? Will anyone be implicated in the disappearance of this information?"

Alex knew exactly what Andre was driving at. He needed to feel safe. He needed to feel nothing could be traced back to him. She knew how to play out this hand. She knew how to keep him on edge, and because of her anger she decided to do just that. Playing a passive-aggressive role came easy to Alex.

"To my knowledge, Andre, I left no traces, but I cannot be one hundred percent sure. I told you this was extremely difficult. If you are a betting man, I would tell you to place a wager that this case has a 90 percent chance of complete and total secrecy. Those are damn good odds."

Alex stood tall once again. She had regained her composure and enjoyed watching as Andre began to nervously tap his foot and unknot the Hermes tie around his neck.

With a slight smirk she continued, "You know, Andre, every assignment has its own set of risks. You knew this when you made me take the job. It is over now, and there is no need to worry about me being tied to you or your company. I do not plan on being caught. And, no, no one was implicated in any of this. They will be hard pressed to figure out how the information was taken from their system. I was very careful to make sure that I left no prints."

As she spoke these last words to Andre, Alex began to wonder if in fact there *was* a trace left behind. Could this come back to Benjamin? No, she thought. I was careful to corrupt the log file and eliminate any trace of my entry. The access would be untraceable.

Andre's irritation wrinkled his usually calm appearance. With a slight crick of his neck he tented his hands, pointed his fingers toward Alex and said, "I am not following you, Alex. You tell me everything went well, and yet you leave a margin for doubt. This is not like you. You invariably seal these assignments up airtight. What is this talk of 90 percent assurance? That is not good enough." Andre's voice pitched higher and louder as he spoke. When he finished he walked over to the fixed plate windows and, in his typical fashion, began to pace back and forth.

Alex thought about how he looked as he paced. A wounded animal, she thought. No, a hunted animal. Now, maybe he could feel what it is like to be out of control, afraid of what is around the next corner. Now *she* had the power and the knowledge. He was where she needed him to be, who she needed him to be— another helpless animal—the prey.

Alex stood up, moved closer to him by the window and said, "Andre, you do not need to worry. You have what you need. This is the end."

"I hope for your own sake, Alex, this truly is the end. I would hate to think of what could happen if any of this came back to me, or my company. I must admit, you had me a little worried. This show of aloofness is quite troubling and very much unlike you," Andre continued his futile attempt to learn if she had done anything that could potentially damage him.

Alex had enough of this game. She was in too much pain to continue this charade. She knew she could outwit this man, and she began to relish the thought of watching him writhe in his own anxiety. She decided to give him one grand finale and leave his presence—forever. She wanted him to live from that point on with the fear that someday his life might catch up with him, and he would be exposed for who he really was. No different than a thief or a burglar, this man stole secrets and turned them into products for a living.

All of her anger toward him boiled over now, and all of the pain she felt over the loss of Benjamin fueled the words that would echo sharply in Andre's ears for many days and nights ahead.

Her voice was sword sharp. "I pity you. What a miserable existence you live, hiding behind your wealth and power, never able to create anything that is truly yours; always having to take what belongs to others. Take your package, and know that someday you will pay for the suffering you have caused others—caused me. May you live out your life as miserable as you are now, as scared as you are now and as alone. I will see you in hell."

Alex turned quickly away from this man—this mirror. She opened the paneled doors and walked down the hall toward the elevator. It was at that moment she realized she was not just admonishing Andre in that room, she was speaking to her own soul. And she was cursing him not only for the loss of her own soul, but for the two souls she left behind in the moonlight and in the cage.

CHAPTER 19

THE EARLY DAWN HOURS WERE ALWAYS A BEAUTIFUL time of day in Sidi Lahcen. A promise-of-sunshine color reflected off the red terra cotta roofs. The sun's first rays highlighted the different shades of brown covering the stark mountainside contrasting with the lush greens of the cultivated fields. It was the perfect time to savor the solitude and to lose your inner thoughts in the reflecting light. Alex sat at the kitchen table, sipping tea and waiting for her mother to awaken. She gazed around the small country home she had grown up in and the long-ago memories began to flood her mind.

Nothing had really changed in this house. It was as if time had stood still, and she felt herself drifting on a cloud looking down at her past. She looked around at the small, simple, box-like kitchen, and remembered all the mornings past when her mother would make breakfast for the family. How Alex and Christina loved to catch the smell of their mother's cooking before rising from bed in the morning. Since both Youcef and Thérèse worked long hours and were rarely home before supper time, that meal tended to be the biggest one of the day, and was one of the few times the family could all be together. Alex hated to cook supper, but always did so for Christina's sake.

Thérèse opened her bedroom door and walked over to Alex. Wrapping her arms around her, Thérèse said, "I am so glad you are here. I am sorry I could not stay awake last night, dear. I just cannot stay up very late anymore. Oh my," she said, standing back to look at her daughter, "you look so beautiful this morning."

Alex stood and greeted her mother with a warm hug and heard the soft sounds of tears as she held her close.

"I came as soon as I could. Are you alright, mother?" Alex loosened her embrace, afraid that her frail mother would simply splinter into a thousand pieces.

Wiping the tears from her face, Thérèse sat down beside her daughter, almost as if she was weary from a full day of work. "I am feeling fine, Alexandra. Certainly much better now that you are home."

"It is so good to be home. Let me get you some tea and we can get caught up. I so much want to hear how you are doing." Alex rose and walked over to the old wood burning stove and smiled when she noticed that the white enamel handle was still missing. She poured her mother a cup of tea and walked past the same tarnished metal pots and pans that hung from the ceiling.

"Here you go, mother." She placed the tea on the table.

"Oh, I think we both have so much to catch up on. I will go and get my brush so I can braid your hair this morning."

As her mother rose from the oak armchair and walked to the bathroom, Alex shook her head at the thought of how her mother continued to treat her like a child. She had resigned herself, however, to allow her mother those simple pleasures so that she would feel needed. Whatever gave her mother some form of joy these days was worth the light humiliation that went with it.

Alex sat patiently at the table as her mother began to brush her long hair. The task of braiding Alex's hair was quite tedious and Thérèse usually took quite awhile to complete it. She always braided it in an elaborate fashion that twisted and turned around the back of Alex's head. Without words, Thérèse worked on her daughter's hair.

The table where Alex sat had been built by her father—hand hewn from oak by his own hands. The faded patina reflected the many meals and family gatherings that had been held around this table. Alex rubbed her hand along a notch that had been carved in the table and smiled, "I remember when Christina and I carved this notch. We thought you and father were not looking. Why did you not say something to us? You must have known that we did this."

Thérèse's lips curved upward and her eyes had a far away look. "Oh dear, of course we knew what you two had done. But it is just a table, and we knew that someday we would all laugh at the memory."

"Being in this house always brings back so many memories. I know I have tried to get you to move to Paris and live with me, but I would miss being here. I was looking at that photo of father before you got up this morning." Alex pointed to the picture protected by an old wooden frame sitting prominently on the small rock mantel.

"I just love that picture. There is not a day that goes by that I do not walk over to it and give your father a kiss. I miss him so."

They both stared at the man in the picture and Alex thought about how much he reminded her of someone—something. She thought about how good he was to her mother, and to her and Christina; how broad his shoulders were as he carried her on them; how huge his hands always seemed to be as he held her tiny one in his; how deep and intense his eyes were as he stared at her from across the kitchen table when she got in trouble; how commanding and confident he always appeared; how warm, how gentle, how perfect, she thought. How much like Benjamin.

A hint of a smile appeared as she thought of how two people from completely different worlds could be so much alike.

Finally, Thérèse, standing over Alex and busily creating, remarked, "Your father always loved these bright sunny mornings. I remember you and Christina sitting over there by the window looking out at the sun. We used to laugh at the two of you sitting there, pushing each other out of the way—competing for the strongest ray of sunlight."

"Yes. That always bothered me how Christina seemed to get the spot that held the sun the longest. She seemed to know which spot would have the best sun each day," Alex said.

Thérèse balanced the hairbrush on her fingertips, sighed, and continued, "The two of you were so cute together. Oh, I wish so much we could all be together again."

"I miss those days too, mother. I loved having a sister to play with and to watch over. Remember how much Christina used to love to climb the grassy foothills and roll down into my arms?" Alex began to laugh as she reminisced.

"Of course, I remember. I was the one who had to wash out all those awful grass stains on her clothes every day. She was such an active child, before she got sick. I also remember how much you loved to braid her hair—just like I am doing to yours now." Thérèse was smiling, something she rarely did, as she continued braiding Alex's hair.

"I could never do it as well as you, mother. Christina used to laugh at how badly I would braid her hair sometimes. She would even take it all out when I was not around just so I would have to do it again and she could laugh at me one more time. She really enjoyed me messing up her hair. That is why I never let her do mine." Alex was now laughing.

Alex continued to reminisce about Christina. Thérèse listened silently as her daughter talked on about her sister, and watched with growing love and concern. Finally, she set down the brush, and took her daughters shoulders in her frail hands. Gently touching her cheek to Alex's, she whispered, "What has changed, Alexandra? You have said barely a word about Christina since she passed on, and today you have not stopped since we began talking."

Their faces were melded into one, like two children staring into a mirror. Alex thought, yes, I have changed. How can I possibly explain this to her? My life has been transformed. I will never be the same again. I no longer am afraid of that pain—the pain that paralyzed my heart for so many years. I have rid my soul of it, mother. Instead of living with the guilt and the pain of Christina, now I only have to live with a shattered memory of a love that could never be. . . a world I could never be a part of. . . an emptiness I never thought could exist.

Alex began an explanation that she herself didn't understand, "A lot happened to me while I was in America. I suppose I learned more about myself in that short time than all my years of education and travel. I wish I could tell you what I went through, but I am not even sure myself. I only know that I have begun to forgive myself for Christina's death. God only knows why I blamed myself for so many years. It is so comforting to finally be able to think about her and to openly talk about her. I really miss her so much, mother. It is as if I can still see her sitting here at the table with us. I can even see father."

Tears of joy poured out from Thérèse's weary eyes and streamed down her time-worn face. She was overwhelmed by the conversation she was having with her daughter. She rose slowly and continued to braid Alex's hair. With her eyes half shut, she said, "Yes, dear, I can see them both here with us. I can even hear them laughing. What fun times we all had together. Tell me, dear, what happened over there in America? Did you meet someone? Did *you* fall in love?"

Was it so obvious that the change in me could only happen through loving someone? "I did meet someone, mother. That person taught me a lot about myself. Through him I was able to love Christina again. Through him I lost the fears and guilt of a lifetime. I miss him, mother. Maybe even the way you miss father."

"You know," Thérèse said gently, "sometimes I wake up at night, feeling warm and safe and I know that your father is there beside me—like he never really left me."

Alex was staring out the window at the mountains in the distance. "Maybe he has not left mother. Maybe he will always watch over you and keep you from harm. Do you ever feel that he might be trying to say something to you?"

"I know he is probably disappointed in me right now. He would want me to be happy, like I used to be. He always worked so hard and loved the fact that I did too. I guess I should try to make myself happy. I just cannot. I do not know how. I am so miserable without him." Thérèse walked around the table and sat down directly across from her daughter.

They looked deep within the others soul and tears rolled out their eyes, not in drops but in sheets of moisture. Each felt the bittersweet emotions of sadness and happiness.

Alex reached over, clasped her mother's hands and gently shook them. "You should do what he would want you to do, mother. It is not that difficult. You can still have a good life without father."

"Can you have a good life without this man you met,

Alexandra?" Thérèse said. Her words were more of a statement than a question.

Alex stiffened. She pulled her hands back and propped her elbows on the table, her chin was buried in her hands. Thérèse stretched her arms out across the table and gently touched her daughter's face. Alex's hands muffled her voice as she whispered, "I am so frightened, mother. I have left the only man I have ever loved. In such a short time he became my entire world, the center of my life. I feel so lost without him. . . so alone."

Thérèse grabbed both of Alex's arms and pulled her hands down so that she could hold onto them. Alex looked up from her sobs into her mother's eyes, those eyes that gave her strength as a child; those eyes she looked to when she was scared or felt lost. This person across from her that brought her into this world and, when she was young, gave her the love and safety every child needed suddenly looked strong and powerful again.

Thérèse was holding Alex's hands tightly as if to squeeze her lost life back into her. She spoke in a determined manner that was unlike anything Alex could ever remember.

"Alexandra, listen to what I have to say. You are a beautiful and talented woman. You can have anything, can do anything and be anything you want. True love comes only once in our lifetime. If this is the man you love, you cannot be without him. Do not spend your life alone and miserable, like I am now. Please, do not end up like me. Your father is gone. I have no choice—but you do. Go back to America and be with this man. Nothing would make me happier than to know that you have found the same joy your father and I had together. Nothing."

"But mother, I cannot. He does not even know who I really am. If he knew, he would hate me. I deceived him. I lied to him. He How can I be with him now?"

"How can you not?" Thérèse asked. "I do not know what you did, Alexandra. Whatever it was why can you not just go to him and tell him the truth? If he really loves you, it will not matter, anyway. Lying is a terrible thing. I know you know that. But, if you tell him why you lied, maybe he will understand. What I mean is that if you do not try to fix this with him, you will only carry another loss for the rest of your life. Is this what you want, dear?"

A silence blanketed the room and Alex remained frozen in her thoughts. Her thoughts were of Benjamin. "I cannot go back there, mother. It is too complicated to explain to you right now, but I just cannot. I have to live with what I have done."

Once again, Thérèse pressed her daughter, "Please, Alexandra. Listen to me. This feeling of love is unlike anything else. You cannot shut it out of your mind or your heart. It has a way of tearing at you for the rest of your life. This feeling you have for this man in America, it is the same feeling I have for your father and it does not stop. It will continue even after death has separated you. I know you are strong and you listen to your head, not your heart. I know how much pain you have suffered over the years because of this. I have watched you. But, my dear, you now know that all the years of fighting against the pain of losing Christina has not been good for you. It has only tortured you. Your head became stronger as your heart became weaker. Listen to your heart for once dear—let it guide you to the happiness you deserve."

As Alex sat listening to her mother, she knew that they were healing each other. Alex would now fulfill her destiny and her mother would now listen to the man that woke her up at night; the one who would no longer be disappointed in her; the one she loved beyond all dimensions.

CHAPTER 20

THERE WAS NO FOG BLANKETING THE BAY THAT MORNING. Shafts of sunlight crept through the partially opened slats of the plantation shutters, warming the room and replacing the loss. Benjamin began to stir as the horned larks chirped their sharp-tempoed morning melodies. Not wanting to open his eyes in the bright sunlight, he moved closer, seeking the warmth next to him. In his slumber he heard the murmur of the accent, and he reached over to envelop her once again. In a place somewhere between conscious thought and the fantasy of a dream, Benjamin remembered what it was like to touch an angel, to make love with the stars, and to soar with the eagles. Slowly he pulled her into him as he did the night before.

Nothing. . . nothing. . .

Benjamin opened his eyes to the bright sunlight. He shoved the thick down comforter away from his naked body. He sat up.

"Alex? Alex?" In a daze he looked around the room. Alex? Alex? She must be in the bathroom or downstairs waiting for me.

He jumped out of bed onto the cold wood floor, rushed to the closet and grabbed his large blue terrycloth robe. In a panic, he ran down the stairs. Yelling, "Alex? Where are you?" The endless stairs became twisted into the sound of his own voice.

"Alex! Stop, Alex. Alex!"

He jolted awake in his now cold and empty room. As if he had just stumbled in a marathon, his heart pounded, his body wet with the remnants of the chase, and his spirit broken. Once again he lay in his bed staring at the ceiling, asking the unanswerable questions, Why? Why did she leave me? What in God's name happened that night—that morning? Where in the hell are you Alex? How dare you do this to me!

Lying in his bed three days after Alex's disappearance, Benjamin was still unable to flush-out the anger racing through his veins. His eyelids were plugged with crusts of sleep and he stared endlessly straight ahead. His face was painted with the tortuous twists and kinks that had dominated his waking hours since Alex had disappeared.

Waking up these past mornings without her was as devastating an experience as any Benjamin could ever remember. He felt betrayed and abandoned as never before. The pain of loss was a feeling all too familiar to him. The suffering he experienced all those years after his brother died was enough for one lifetime. He trembled at the possibility of reliving that horrifying experience.

Benjamin was angry, but knew he had to somehow find Alex. Just like the creature on the mountain, his mate, too, had to be returned.

Benjamin slid slowly out of bed. Still in a semi-sleep state, his clenched hands rubbed his eyes, he stretched his over-tired muscles and he shuffled aimlessly off to the bathroom. With a cold sweat lingering from his still-lucid dream, he turned on the shower's hot water nozzle and waited while the room filled with steam. The warmth from the heat and steam began to slowly soothe his restless spirit. After adjusting the water temperature, he stood under the pounding jets. He stretched his arms out in front of him and wrapped his hands around both sides of the shower nozzle for balance. With the blistering water cascading down the back of his neck, Benjamin bowed his head and became lost, once again, in the memory of Alex.

She was so beautiful, so perfect, he thought. Making love to her was unlike any sexual experience I have ever known. Her touch was as soft as the wind and as powerful as thunder. She took me to a place, a dimension, where I've never been before. Her lovemaking was slow and passionate, as if she wanted it to go on forever. Touching her was just as I'd dreamed it would be—her skin was as smooth as silk and as warm as the morning sun; her breasts were firm and tasted like honey; her rhythmic movements were perfectly in sync with mine; and when I was inside her it was as if she was also inside of me. We became one that night. We are still one now.

He looked up and felt the water stream down his face. He balanced himself on his arms and his thoughts continued, I cannot find you anywhere. Where are you Alex? What did I do wrong? What am I suppose to do now? Where do I look? Should I even look? What if I find you? What will you do? What will I do? God damn it! What am I going to do without you?

After toweling off, Benjamin began to get dressed then suddenly snapped to attention. Without thought, he dashed to the ringing phone in anticipation of the hoped-for accent. "Hello? Hello?"

"Hey, buddy. It's me. How you doing today?"

Disappointed, he gave a drawn out, monotone reply, "Oh, hi Phil. I'm okay. What's up?"

"I'm down at the market. Mind if I drop in?"

"I'm not very good company these days."

"I know. That's why I want to come over. You sounded pretty beat up last night. I can be there in a few."

"Yeah, okay," Benjamin was feeling low that morning. Maybe Phil could cheer him up.

"Good. See you soon. Down the road."

"Yeah. Bye."

Benjamin hung up the phone, finished towel-drying his hair and threw on some clothes. He drifted downstairs and started a pot of coffee for the two of them.

Phil Morgan was Benjamin's best friend. He had been a professor of Anthropology at UC Berkeley for 16 years. He was a child prodigy who completed his Ph.D from Harvard at the tender age of 22. He went directly to Berkeley after completing his degree, where he soon became the leading authority in the ancient cultures of New Guinea. A very eccentric man, Phil isolated himself from most people and worked incessantly on his career.

He originally chose UC Berkeley because of its long history of progressive social movements. He loved the era he was too young to experience—the 60's—and relished the thought of continuing its traditions, wherever he taught. By the 2000's, the conservative movement had engulfed much of the country's academic institutions. Phil slowly became disgruntled at the prospect of limiting his radical voice. When the Chancellor of the University personally requested that he no longer engage in open anti-government movements on campus due to the negative publicity the University received, he turned in his resignation. He was not one to compromise his beliefs under any circumstances.

Since he left the university, Phil had been living in Bolinas, in west Marin County. There he could grow his own organic vegetables and grains and remain in his small home for days on end without encountering a soul. Benjamin always told Phil he was trying to re-live his granola days. He claimed to now have the good life, but Benjamin had always thought he was only escaping the reality he detested.

Benjamin first met Phil a few months after he moved to the Bay Area. Benjamin began to get involved in open water swimming in the Bay, and Phil had been a fierce and well-known competitor in the sport for years. Benjamin always thought it odd that Phil was so into the competition of the swim and yet his philosophy on life was the polar opposite. Perhaps, Benjamin thought, this dichotomy created the equilibrium Phil needed to balance out his life.

Benjamin respected Phil's forthrightness and honesty. Whenever anyone wanted a straight answer, you knew Phil would dish it out. He often offended people, but Benjamin appreciated that Phil was his own person, and never looked to others for self-validation or recognition. Over the years, they had grown to become close friends. Benjamin had very few people in his life he could truly trust and Phil was one of them. He was always there for Benjamin when he needed someone to talk to about anything from his business ventures to his personal life. Even though Phil projected a very simple life, he seemed to have an extra sense when it came to understanding people. Benjamin always thought it was because Phil spent so much time studying other cultures in such great detail that he really knew what mankind was all about.

So, it was natural that Phil would pick up on Benjamin's dejected spirit. He seemed to carry it with him these days like a ball and chain. Benjamin did explain a little of what he had been going through over the past several days, but Phil knew there was much more to the story. He also knew that Benjamin needed a friend about now.

The loud rap on the door startled Benjamin, who was lost in thoughts about Alex once again. He always laughed to himself each time Phil came over because instead of using the doorbell like everyone else, he would pound his fists on the carved redwood doors and pretend they were Conga drums. Always the nonconformist.

Benjamin's lips turned up in what passed as a smile and he yelled out, "Door's open, Phil. Come in."

"Hey, Ben!" Phil marched into the entryway.

"I'm back here in the kitchen. Your coffee's ready."

Phil walked down the long hall to the kitchen. He grabbed Benjamin's shoulders and gave his friend a warm bear-hug. "Good to see you. Sure, I'll have some of that designer coffee you always make. Just make sure mine doesn't have all that fancy shit in it. Just black."

"Okay. Here you go. This'll kick start your engine," Benjamin said.

"Let's go outside. It's a sunshine get your ass outside kinda day," Phil motioned toward the deck.

Phil led the way as they moved through the French doors to the back deck. Phil was about six feet, four inches tall. He had a swimmers body—V-shaped, lean and defined by muscle and tendons. The creases in his leathery face reflected a man who had spent hours enjoying the rigors of the outdoors. His curly blond hair was beginning to thin around the edges, but for a man in his mid-forties, his head of hair was enviable. As usual, he wore khaki pants, a Greenpeace sweatshirt, no socks, and ratty-old running shoes.

They sat outside and Phil wasted no time with pleasantries. He began, "Ben, it's me, your old friend. I think you know that when I talked to you last night I knew something was cooking with you. You haven't told me everything about this Alex person. Something's happened to you. What is it? Let's hear it."

Benjamin sat slouched back in his Adirondack chair with one foot draped over the footstool and the other stretched out to the side. He stared down at the coffee mug resting on his lap, his fingers tightly interlocked around it and his thumbs rimming the lip.

"Phil, I don't know if I can get into the whole thing right now. From the day I first met Alex until now my life has been a real whirlwind. I don't even know where to start."

Phil dragged one of the Islander Sling Chairs from the corner of the deck over to where Benjamin sat and collapsed into its bright red canvas seat. He looked straight into Benjamin's eyes. "Well, how about from the beginning? This gal must've stuck you with voodoo needles. She's gotten to you big time."

Benjamin paused and looked up at Phil. "Phil, have you ever met someone who instantly absorbs your thoughts, your dreams and your life? From the first time I met Alex, I've been unable to think of anything else."

"Well, you know me—I've never had a relationship where I placed any woman on my same level. Not that I'm a sexist or have anything against women. Just the opposite—I respect the hell out of them. They've always had it much rougher than men in this society, but I've just never met anyone who's satisfied my intellectual side like they have my physical side." Phil spoke in his typical animated style, his hands chopping the air.

"This gal has a real hold on you. Come on Ben, I came over here to see if there was anything I could do to cheer you up. I'm your friend and I can probably make a good sounding board. Come on, give it a shot."

Benjamin stood up and walked over to the wood railing. He hunched forward and cocked his elbows on the railing. He looked out at the expanse of eucalyptus and watched the dark clouds, heavy with unspent rain, as they crept slowly forward casting their gray shadows over the hillside.

Phil could tell by looking at Benjamin that he was tired, not just physically, but there seemed to be something tearing at him, not allowing him to rest. Obviously, it was this woman. This mysterious woman.

"Well," Benjamin began as he turned around to face Phil and leaned back against the railing. He placed his mug down on the railing and continued, "You *are* perceptive and yes, you are a good friend. I guess it's easier and cheaper to talk to you than to go to some shrink and have to rehash my whole life history."

"Now that's more like the guy I know. Now you're talkin'." Phil bent his arms and pointed at Benjamin.

"I just don't know what happened." Benjamin took a sip of his coffee and stared off in the direction of the cage for a few seconds before continuing, "I know that I haven't known Alex for very long, but there's something between us that tells me I've known her forever, that I've found the one person who was predestined to be with me. Alex had a sister who died when she was young, and for years she shouldered the guilt of her sister's death."

"Ah. . .So your first link with this gal is Will, right?"

"Well yes, in a way, but not exactly. Yes, we both had siblings who died at an early age, and we both had difficulties in coping with that. But more importantly, we've each led our lives in such a way as to prevent us from finding what it is that can truly make us happy. Sure, I have money and I can do anything I want to, but I haven't been able to share my dreams and desires with someone I love, and that is important to me. Maybe for the first time in my life I realize it. I know Alex has felt the same way about her life.

And now I'm more lost than ever, because I don't know where she is, or even why she left."

Phil crossed one leg over the other, slurped his coffee and said, "Ben, what about Constance? I know you two don't have the typical marriage, whatever that is, who the hell knows, but I've always thought you were happy with your arrangement. And, she is your wife."

Benjamin tilted his head slightly to the left and with both eyes squinting half shut he looked down. In a voice that was barely audible, he said, "You know, I haven't really thought much about her since I met Alex. Oh sure, our arrangement seems good. We each come and go as we please and do what we want. I know that I haven't been married to Constance for very long, but you know, I've always remained faithful to her. But I don't think that I've ever loved her in the way I should—the way I feel about Alex. I'll have to face Constance and tell her about Alex. And whatever the outcome, I am sure that we'll eventually get a divorce."

Now, with both eyes open and standing erect, he continued, "In the meantime, Phil, I'm not sure what more I can do. From the moment I first discovered that Alex was gone, when I couldn't find her at the house, I've done everything I can possibly conceive of to find her. Do you know what's really stupid? I don't have the foggiest idea where she lives or how to find her. So I hired a private investigation firm to help me. They discovered that she'd registered at the hotel with the last name Pancini. But so far, they can't locate anyone named Alexandria Pancini anywhere in Italy."

"Look, this may not be what you want to hear, but how do you know that this whole thing wasn't just a fling for her, or that she isn't married, or that she isn't really someone else, or that you're not just getting carried away over a new piece of ass?"

"No. No. No way. For the same reason I now know that I need to share love with a woman in order to be truly happy myself, and I know that this woman is Alex."

Benjamin folded his arms and looked at Phil. "I've never told you much about the eagle and I appreciate your understanding my need for privacy about that. The night Alex stayed at my house, I took her over there to the cage," Benjamin looked briefly in the direction of the cage and then continued, "and I explained to her how I had found the eagle and why I'd brought it back here to heal. I'll tell you Phil, even though she wasn't there with me in Queen Charlotte, she felt the same feelings I felt when I watched the female trust me with her mate's life. Alex felt the same sense of commitment that I have to reunite the eagle with its mate. Although I felt strong feelings for her before that moment, it was then that I knew I could never be happy unless she was part of my life."

Phil stood up, walked over to Benjamin and placed a hand on his shoulder. Benjamin's grief and distress shot through him like static electricity. He had never witnessed Benjamin in such a state of emotional upheaval before. The man he knew and admired had always stood ten feet tall with an aura of confidence and invincibility. He was now lost at sea caught in the conflicting currents of love and emptiness. This gal really had an effect on him, Phil thought. He needs to find her and be with her one way or another so he can sort this out.

With a firm grip on his shoulder and his eyes locked into Benjamin's, he said, "Well, listen Ben, don't give up hope just yet. It's only been a few days, and in time I'm sure that the PI firm will come up with something."

"You know Phil, if I find her. . ."

"No," Phil interrupted. "*When* you find her—not *if*."

"Yeah, okay, *when* I find her, I'm not really sure what I'll do or what I'll say to her. I just know that I need to find her."

Phil released his grip and took a step back. Damn he admired this man's strength of mind, his determination. "I'm willing to bet everything that I have on the fact that you'll find her. In the meantime, you need to keep occupied with other things so you don't go completely whacko on me. You're already close. What do you say we drive up to Gualala this afternoon, grab our old buddy Jack, and do some ab diving? You probably haven't been diving in several weeks, have you?"

For the first time since Phil came over, Benjamin cracked a faint smile and replied, "You think it'll cheer me up when I find a bigger abalone than you?"

"It'll be a cold day in hell when you can out-dive me, my friend." Phil quickly responded to the challenge and raised his arms in a triumphant salute.

Benjamin picked up his coffee mug and started walking toward the house. "Come on in and let's get a re-fill."

Phil followed Benjamin into the kitchen. Benjamin poured them each another cup of coffee. "Damn. I just remembered. I'd better not go diving today because Constance is coming in this afternoon for a few days, and I suppose I should get ready for that ordeal. But you're right, it would be good for me to get away and do something to get my mind off Alex for a little while."

"OK then, I'll tell you what. I'll go ahead and call. . ."

Phil was interrupted by the ringing of the telephone and Benjamin's immediate leap to attention.

"God, I hope that's Alex, or at least some news of her whereabouts," Benjamin said as he reached for the phone.

"Hello?" Benjamin's skin crawled with anticipation as he anxiously awaited the accent.

"Ben, it's me. How are you?"

Benjamin slouched down on his stool, his shoulders drooped and he covered the phone with his hand as he whispered, "It's Constance."

"Hi Constance. Where are you?" Benjamin rose from the kitchen stool and walked over to the window. He bent his right elbow and leaned against the glass and with the phone cradled to his left ear, he waited.

"Well, I'm still in D.C., and I'm afraid I need to stay here longer. The Clean Energy Standard Act legislation which I'm co-sponsoring is coming out of Committee next week, and I've so much to do to prepare for the floor debate."

"That's too bad. How long do you anticipate you'll be back there?" Benjamin asked.

"Oh I don't really know, but I suspect that this will take up a good part of my time for at least the next several weeks," Constance replied.

Benjamin turned and walked back to the stool and plopped back down. He looked over at Phil and fidgeted in his seat searching for the right spot to set anchor before he forged dead ahead. After taking a deep breath, holding it and exhaling slowly to steady his nerves, he continued, "Constance, this isn't the right way to tell you this, and I'd prefer to talk to you in person, but I need to tell you what's happened recently in my life."

"Wait, Ben," Constance interrupted. "If this has something to do with my not being able to come out there again, I'd rather you wait until we can be together. There is so much I need to tell you about my life as well."

"Constance, please. Just hear me out." He leaned forward and held the back of his neck in his right hand as he drilled his elbow into the counter. With his head crouched, he continued, "I don't know any other way to say this but to just say it. I've fallen in love with someone else. I'm sorry to just dump this on you like this, I really am, but I don't see any other alternative. You and I both know that we haven't had a marriage in years, if ever, and something like this was bound to happen sooner or later. I don't know what else to say except that I think we should begin discussing a divorce."

There was no expected silence or lengthy pause, Constance launched ahead as if she already knew the script. "This is a lot for me to handle all at once and I don't know what to say. But, you're right, Ben. This isn't something we should talk about over the phone. We should try to get together either here or out there to talk about this." Constance continued on as if she were speaking to her aides about researching a Senate Bill, "Why don't I call you in a few days, and I'll see if I can change my plans and possibly come out there soon. We can talk then. Okay?"

"Constance, I would much rather talk about this in person but, you need to understand that my mind is made up and I feel we need to proceed as soon as possible.

Phil looked at his friend and saw the twin blades of raw emotion and brutal honesty cut away at his conscience. He knew at that point in time that Benjamin was truly driven to find Alex and he hoped that when he did he would find everything just as he imagined it.

"Alright, Benjamin, I'll call you in a few days." The line went dead.

As Constance hung up the phone, Benjamin stared at the receiver and heard the drone of the phone line. "Jesus, Phil. I'm not sure she heard a word I said. There was no emotion, no surprise—nothing. I don't know how I could've made myself any clearer."

Phil shuffled over to Benjamin. He put one hand on the counter, his other on Benjamin's shoulder and gave it a tight squeeze. "You were pretty direct Ben. You said what you had to say and there's no way she didn't get it."

"Yeah, but Phil, she didn't react at all. All she said was she'd see if she could change her plans and *maybe* come out here. That's it. Not a—what are you talking about, or, no I don't want that—nothing. I don't get it."

"Look Ben, this thing with Constance will sort itself out pretty quickly. Things like that do. But if Alex is everything you say she is, you need to focus on finding out just what the hell went on with her. You need to find her."

An enormous sense of relief engulfed Benjamin as he realized that he had finally done what he should have done several years ago.

"Phil!" Benjamin said with excitement this time, "Let's go ab diving!"

CHAPTER 21

D RIVING ACROSS THE GOLDEN GATE BRIDGE TO SAN Francisco was more tedious than usual that foggy September evening. Traffic was unusually backed up along the bridge. It must have been one of those nights where everyone in Marin had decided to head to the City.

Benjamin edged along in the bumper-to-bumper traffic and he began to chuckle as he thought about the day before when he brought home the largest abalone and all Phil could do was complain that he had too much equipment failure. His mask leaked. Yeah, that was a good one.

What a perfect day it had been for Benjamin. He loved to go up the coast and explore the serene and icy waters. Weaving in and out of the kelp beds and looking up at the sun rays glistening through the dark blue currents was always magical. When he and Phil would go diving, it was a serious endeavor. It wasn't possible to stay out in the ocean for too long; free diving could become quite exhausting, especially on a day when the swells were large and the currents were strong. Diving that day was very therapeutic for Benjamin, and he was able to take his mind off of Alex for those few hours. Of course, he talked about her most of the drive up and back and that was also relaxing as he could finally share the excitement he had felt being close to her as well as the pain of losing her so suddenly.

Earlier, just before he left, he placed a call to Constance. He wanted to talk to her again. He just couldn't understand her reaction to what he had said, and he was perplexed about her comment—there is so much I need to tell you about my life as well. What did she mean? Maybe she has met someone too? Maybe she's happy that I want a divorce? In any case, Constance didn't answer and he didn't leave a message. Phil was right, this would sort itself out.

That evening, as Benjamin drove into the City, Alex continued to be at the forefront of his thoughts. He received a call earlier that day from one of the investigators he had hired to find her. The only new information the man had on Alex was that a woman fitting Alex's description did fly to Paris, and the airline had confirmed a reservation was made for Alexandria Pancini. That was as far as they had been able to trace her at this point. Still, it made Benjamin happy that there was at least some kind of a lead. He told the PI to pursue the lead, to check further with the airlines and follow up on other leads for information on Alex. Just do whatever was necessary to find her, he told them.

Benjamin was convinced that there was something else going on with Alex that made her disappear the way she did. He knew she loved him the way he loved her. He knew that her disappearance had nothing to do with him, but was about something else— something bad—something she was afraid to tell him. Something she had come to America to do and then could not because she met him. He kept trying to fit the pieces together. That was the twist in the mystery that had begun to consume every part of his life.

Going to meet Murray was not exactly what Benjamin wanted to do that night, especially since his life was in such upheaval. The only reason he agreed to meet on such short notice was because Murray sounded so upset. He told Benjamin that GEN was in serious trouble and he could talk with no one else about it. Murray was typically calm and politically astute, seldom raising his voice or letting things upset him. He chose his words wisely when in the company of people of influence and was always very careful not to offend. He ran GEN with such grace and dignity that he had become one of the most respected executives in the Bay Area. Calling Benjamin late on a Sunday afternoon in such a panic was very much out of character for Murray. Benjamin didn't think twice about accepting Murray's dinner offer.

Benjamin walked into Tadich Grill in the heart of the financial district. Tadich's was a legendary old school restaurant where the weekend dress code matched the Art Deco ambiance: molded ceilings with rich wood paneled walls and the buzz of the bar scene. It wasn't exactly the spot for a romantic evening, but if you were looking for a night out to experience the roaring decorum of San Francisco's elegant past this would be your best choice. The place was steeped in the memories of the Barbary Coast, the gold rush era, the great fire of 1906, two world wars and the Summer of Love.

Benjamin was about fifteen minutes late and he knew the always-on-time Murray would have already grabbed a table. When he saw Murray sitting alone in a far corner, he walked over, placed his hand on Murray's shoulder and gave him a slight tweak, "Hi Murray. Good to see you. Man, traffic was murder on the Bridge. How you doing?"

Murray didn't get up. He pulled out the chair next to him and said, "I've been better, Ben. Have a seat."

Immediately, Benjamin felt the tension. He took a seat next to Murray who was staring at his menu.

"Figure out what you're eating first so we can talk about GEN uninterrupted," Murray said.

Even the tone of Murray's voice was different. His face was flushed and the lines in it seemed somehow deeper and more pronounced than usual. His right leg rocked back and forth—not in a relaxed fashion, but in a hurried, tense way. He looked as though any second he was about to implode.

Benjamin opened his menu as instructed. He wanted to just ask what the hell was going on, but he needed to play it Murray's way right now.

The waiter came over to the table and routinely asked if they were ready to order. Without looking up Murray said, "I'll just have a scotch on the rocks. Make that a double. Are you ready to order, Ben?"

"Are we having dinner?"

"I'm not. I think you should though," Murray said, still blindly staring at his menu.

"Um. I'll just have a glass of cabernet for now, please. House is fine." Benjamin was hungry, but he sensed that this meeting was not going to last into the dinner phase of the evening.

The waiter walked away and Murray began, "Well, Ben, I'm sure you know why I've called you here. Let's not bullshit each other. What the fuck is wrong with you? Why the hell did you do it?" He stared at Benjamin as if he had once studied the technique of eye contact, but lost the art.

Beads of sweat began to form around Murray's bushy eyebrows. He sounded angry. He looked defeated. He still could not look Benjamin directly in the eyes. His left hand was wrapped around the candle holder on the table and his right hand was clenched into a white-knuckled fist. Benjamin was confused as he looked at this man he had known for years. He was suffering and being eaten up from the inside out. Who is this? What's happened and what am I being accused of?

Benjamin was stunned. Uncertain about Murray's accusation, frightened by the way his mentor appeared, angry that he could be accused of *any* wrong doing, Benjamin could only respond with, "What are you talking about?"

With that question, Murray bolted upright in his chair, grabbed the outer edge of the table and looked ready to pounce on Benjamin at any moment. His large, dark brown eyes met Benjamin's in a threatening and aggressive way. He held the stare. Instinctively, Benjamin grabbed the armrests of his chair and awaited the attack.

Never before had Benjamin seen Murray so disturbed, so agitated. He knew this was very serious and whatever it was, he was about to be accused of it.

In a forceful, yet still quiet tone, Murray continued, "Don't insult my intelligence. You know exactly what I'm talking about. The thing I need to know from you is why? Why did you steal the information? What does someone like you have to gain from this? I thought you were my friend—I trusted you, Ben. I need to know, right now, how much you know."

How much I know about what? Benjamin thought. Carefully, he responded, "Murray, Jesus Christ, I have no idea what you're talking about. I need you to tell me plainly what you mean. I'm sorry if I'm insulting you. That isn't my intention, but I'm totally at a loss right now."

"I'm not going to sit here and lay out your entire escapade. You need to do that for *me*. All I know is that vital information was stolen from our database, and you stole it."

Confused and frustrated, Benjamin released his hold on the armrests and spread both hands on the table, palms down. "Stole what?" he asked. "How? This is crazy. Why would I need to steal anything I already have total access to?"

"Why indeed, my friend?"

"Come on, Murray. You know me better than that. This is total crap. You have me totally confused right now. Please, calm down and explain to me what you think I did."

"Calm down?" Murray's volume control had been turned up all the way.

The waiter appeared with the drinks, mechanically set them down and disappeared. Murray picked up his scotch and with one upward motion of his arm, emptied the glass.

Staring into his empty glass, he lowered his volume control a notch and continued, "I don't have the time nor do I have the patience right now to explain what you already know. The only reason I asked you here tonight was to look you in the eyes when you told me why you've deceived me all these years. Let me tell you, Ben, my career is over. I hope you can live with the choices you've made."

Unable to move, Benjamin continued to push Murray for answers, "Indulge me here, Murray. Level with me. What is this about?

"Fine. Genetic research methodology. Sensitive research. Shit, don't play me for the fool."

"Okay Murray, and how exactly did I steal this?"

"What a joke you've turned out to be. You want to play this little game right now when I'm about to lose everything I've worked my whole life for? God, Ben. I treated you like a son. I don't know you anymore. Maybe I never knew you. Maybe you aren't who you say you are." Murray lowered his head and his voice tapered off, "I just don't know anymore."

"Please, Murray. Just tell me how I got the information."

"Right off the computer network, that's how. I know you broke through the main security systems and extracted all the unpublished research. All our sensitive data."

Benjamin raised his bent arms, his palms faced in and with a half sheepish grin said, "I can barely run a computer—you know that. How could I have stolen this classified information?"

Murray's hands tapped against his thighs, his head was still bowed. "How the hell should I know? You probably hired someone to do it. Why don't you tell me!"

"Murray, I already know everything about GEN—remember, I'm a Board Member. I own most of the company, for Christ's sake. This is ridiculous. If someone *did* steal information from us, then we need to figure out who that was."

"I'm getting old Ben, but I'm no fool. I had Garran Upshaw come up from San Diego to investigate this break-in. He's the foremost expert in computer security violations and has worked with the government for years catching hackers who steal military or government secrets. He caught *you*, Ben. He doesn't know who you are—but he caught you. He told me that you tried—very cleverly—to cover your prints by getting rid of any sign of your password. He's too good—even for you. Whoever you hired wasn't good enough. So, now I have you and I have to decide what to do with you."

Earlier that day, Murray had met with Garran and received a complete briefing on the security breach. Garran had no way of knowing who the hacker was, but there was no denying that the data was uploaded directly to Benjamin's computer. The hacker was unaware that the security daemon running on a secondary server was not accessible by any network. The root disk on the backend database server was dual ported, allowing the daemon to take snapshots of various parts of the root disk every 10 seconds and store them on a machine that the hacker couldn't know about. A batch process ran every night comparing the daily snapshots with the disk they were taken from, and that's where the discrepancy was first discovered. After careful analysis, it was clear that the logs on the database server did not match the snapshots perfectly, and this could only be due to an intrusion. From the little pieces of unmodified log files that were captured in the snapshots, Garran's security forensics team determined that the only possible explanation was related to a mass data copy instigated by Benjamin's computer.

Benjamin's hand rubbed his forehead. He shot a puzzled look at Murray and said, "Wait a minute. You think I sat at my house and entered GEN's database and stole proprietary documents? That would be pretty stupid. Why wouldn't I just go to GEN and get the information directly from you? Or, why wouldn't I have done that years ago? Why now? Hell, I could just shut the company down if I really wanted to create a problem."

Murray's anger continued to simmer. He shifted positions in his seat. "I don't know where you sat or, maybe I should say, whoever you hired sat, when you stole the information. All I know is that your fingerprints are all over this mess."

"Why? How?" Benjamin shot back at Murray once again.

Murray reached up and loosened his tie even further. Shaking his head ever so slowly, he blurted, "Your password, idiot! You tried to cover up your intrusion by corrupting the log file and making it look like the corruption occurred several weeks earlier. Clever, but it didn't work. I guess the point here is that we need to be up front and you need to tell me exactly what you got your hands on and why."

Completely confused now, Benjamin asked, "My password? You found my password and that's how you figure I'm the thief?"

"It doesn't take a rocket scientist to figure this one out.

Garran gave me a complete report and there's no doubt that the theft occurred from the computer at your house. Give it up now. I'm tired of this game and my life is hanging by a thread. Just tell me what you know. I don't even care why you did it anymore."

Benjamin's head was now lodged in the soft spot between his thumb and index finger. His eyes were half shut and his brows were furrowed as his mind played out the course of events in reverse. Fragments of conversations, taken one-by-one, began to reveal a pattern as intricate and orderly as a spider web—a web that was cast over his own blind eyes. Stunned and now staring aimlessly out across the open dining area, his fingers drum rolled across the tablecloth. . .maybe you aren't who you say you are! I am such a fool, he thought.

"I know who stole your information."

"Yeah, I know you do," Murray almost laughed this time.

"No, Murray. I mean I think I know someone who could've obtained my password. I don't know about the other stuff you're talking about, but the password definitely."

Murray leaned back in his chair. He folded his arms across his chest and a deep frown controlled the lower half of his face. But he had seen something. He had felt something. Benjamin had reacted just as Murray would have predicted if in fact Benjamin *was* blameless. He had never known Benjamin to misrepresent anything. He had always been beyond reproach and never crossed that imaginary gray line. Everything was either black or white. Still, there was hesitation in Murray's voice as he continued, "Nice try. You want me to believe that someone got the password out of you and broke into GEN. And, even sat in your home to get the information?"

Benjamin responded before Murray's last words cleared his lips, "Yeah, why not? Think about it. What would I have to gain? I have all the money anyone could ever want. No matter what someone would pay for this so-called secret information, I certainly don't need it. Plus, I could've gotten this stuff at anytime. Most importantly, you, of all people, know how dear to my heart this research is to me. I have done nothing but promote GEN since I first acquired it. I even helped get you hired because I knew you'd be a great leader in this fight against congenital disease. I have nothing to gain and everything to lose if GEN goes under. I'm telling you, Murray, on my brother's memory; I did not steal anything from GEN. You need to believe me; I have a strong suspicion about who did though. I'll find this person Murray. Count on it."

Murray studied Benjamin's movements. There was a flow, an evenness to Benjamin that you wouldn't find in a man who was hiding from the truth. He took a deep breath and letting it out slowly, he said, "Boy, you're right Ben, you're right. Everything seemed so clear and it all pointed to you and I reacted. I just wasn't thinking through everything. It never made any sense that you would be behind any of this."

Murray reached down for his cocktail glass but it was empty. He shook his head half pretending he could magically make a fresh drink appear and then he looked at Benjamin, "We need to get this son-of-a-bitch, Ben. I'll get Garran on this now."

"I can't tell you who it is yet Murray. I don't even know where this person is right now, but I promise you I'll find out. It may take awhile, but believe me—I want this person as badly as you do."

"You've got to tell me who it is, Ben. Garran is the perfect guy to help on this."

"Trust me, Murray. I can help you. But I need to do it my way. I think the thief may have left the country, so it will take some time and work. I promise I will find this person."

Obviously relieved, Murray leaned forward and grabbed Benjamin by the shoulder, and said, "I can't tell you how upset I've been. Thank God it isn't you. I believe you now. We've got to find this person. The data can't get into the wrong hands—it'll have devastating repercussions on us if it does. Please let me help you. I know some people who can work with you to find this person."

"You need to promise me now that you'll leave me alone on this one. I'll find him but I have to do it my way."

"Can't you even tell me his name?"

Benjamin spoke in a more solemn tone now. "Sorry. If I'm right, then this was someone close to me and it will be hard enough for me to find him. The danger comes with too many people knowing his identity and he could flee—never to be discovered. He's clever. I don't want that and I'm sure you don't either."

Murray sat back in his chair, clasped his hands in his lap and looked at Benjamin. "I understand, Ben. But I won't be able to rest until this is resolved. Also, you can't repeat this to anyone. No one else at GEN knows about the break-in. It was discovered by Garran, and he brought in several forensic people to go through the system. I've left all the Board members and executive officers out of this. I felt the panic would escalate to a level where the media would catch the story and the expected distortions would ensue. Until we know what we're dealing with, we must keep it confidential."

"You mean no one knows about the break-in? Not even the inner circle of security people?"

"They know something happened," Murray explained. "But, once I brought Garran in to investigate, I closed all access to everyone at GEN. I explained that we had a small security break, but that it was no big deal and wouldn't hurt GEN in any way. Even Garran doesn't know whose password was used. I'm the only one who knows right now. My fear is that the genetic information has been stolen by another corporation and will be used very soon—before we have a chance to introduce it first. So, time is precious. If we can get this person and even pay him if necessary to give it back, no one will have to know it was ever stolen. But, if we can't find him, not only is my career over, but my biggest fear is that GEN will be shut down."

Benjamin pushed his chair back. He stood and said, "I understand the urgency behind all this. Thanks for trusting me Murray—and I can understand why you'd think I was involved. I need to get started right away. I'll be in touch as soon as I know something for certain. Don't worry, we'll find him."

Murray rose, and Benjamin extended his hand. Instead of a handshake, Murray reached out and embraced his friend.

"Bye, Murray. I'll call you." Benjamin walked toward the door as Murray sat back down and ordered another drink. When the drink arrived he slowly sipped the aged spirit and let its pungent flavor numb his already over-worn senses.

D riving back over the Golden Gate was dark and morbid for Benjamin. His thoughts raced around in circles—why did she do this to me? Where is she? Who does she really work for? She used me; she lied to me; she is so beautiful, so soft; she is so evil, so cold. Now, more than ever, I have to find her. I will not sleep until I have found her. I'll make her tell me first why she did what she did and then I'll hand her over to Murray. Was the whole thing a lie? Did she even have a sister who died, or was that made up only to seduce me? If this was all an act, I'm the biggest fool—the dumbest guy alive. There's no way it was all an act. What about Point Reyes, the eagle, the night in my arms? That was the most real experience of my life. I know she felt the same. Then why? Why did she steal from GEN—from *me*? At least now I know *why* I woke up alone that morning.

Benjamin's voice echoed loudly in his car, "I am coming after you Alex! You can't hide from me! If it takes my entire life, I *will* find you!"

Benjamin pulled into his driveway, a feeling of bitter emptiness festered inside him. How much she filled my life in that short time, he thought. How much I miss her.

He closed the door to his Land Rover and walked around the house to the back yard, toward the cage. Facing it, he rested his head against the steel mesh, and began to silently weep. What am I going to do? Maybe I should just let go; forget about what I thought we meant to each other; forget about what happened between us. Yes, I need to think of her as dead. Alex died and I'll never see her again. Never gaze into her eyes, touch her soft skin; never laugh with her or cry with her. I am alone.

Benjamin opened his eyes. Wiping the tears away he saw the eagle standing there in front of him. It was looking up with its glaring yellow eyes—the eyes that first pierced him that day on the mountain. Even in the dark, there was no denying the intensity of the eagle's stare. Benjamin stared back. The eagle stretched out its wings. What is he doing? Benjamin thought. What is he trying to tell me? The eagle stood motionless with its outstretched wings and its eyes fixed on Benjamin. Suddenly, the eagle shrieked as its mate had done the day Benjamin took the injured bird away from her. It was the same shriek of pain and loss—the same sound that was silently coming from Benjamin that night. The eagle then took flight up into the trees and Benjamin knew his friend was trying to help. Standing there against the cage, looking up to where the eagle was perched, Benjamin felt a cold chill run through him.

The message that came through, loud and clear to Benjamin, was that there was an order to all life and a greater lesson to be learned in a time of suffering and loss. Symbolically, with its outstretched wings and the shriek from the mountain, the eagle showed him that the laws of nature would guide us all and show us where we belong.

With a silent whisper, Benjamin thanked his friend and now felt reassured that he would somehow see Alex again.

CHAPTER 22

"I'LL HAVE ANOTHER ESPRESSO, PLEASE," ALEX beckoned to the waiter as he passed by her table.

Sitting in the Lapin Agile, a small bistro in the Montmartre District, Alex sipped her coffee and played her part in the age-old pastime of people-watching. Couples strolled arm-in-arm, shoppers bustled in and out of the small shops, and tourists stopped and admired the local artwork displayed on the easels that lined the chipped and foot-warn sidewalks. She loved this area of Paris with its cobbled squares and countrified architecture. This was her favorite restaurant in all of Paris. Originally one of the raunchiest haunts in the city, it served simple French country dishes during the day, and turned into a popular bar and cabaret each evening.

Somehow, this place had reminded Alex of home. The old woman who cooked the meals during the day often came out and mingled with the patrons and chatted about current events. She owned the bistro, and only employed family members and close friends. It had a homey atmosphere with its old, simple, rustic furniture, red and white checkered tablecloths and friendly service. The old woman, with her slight build, incessant energy, and jet black hair reminded Alex of her mother.

The Lapin Agile had an outdoor seating area that was perfect for such a beautiful fall day. The trees were completing their final rituals before the coming winter's long slumber. The leaves covered the remaining foliage of the grassy open spaces with a camouflaging array of rich color. The deep scarlet, brilliant orange and contrasting yellows of the Acacias and Sumacs eclipsed the pale yellow leaves of the thickly planted Sycamore trees with their tired-tan and cream-colored bark.

Alex was seated at a small round table nestled in a far corner of the patio area. She sat in the direct sunlight and let the beaming shafts of light warm her tired face. Periodically, she would close her eyes, lean her head slightly back and feel the sun's rays gently soothe her weariness, only to be interrupted by the image of Benjamin.

She wondered what Benjamin must think of her. He must know by now what had happened. When she left his bedroom that morning she had fled down the staircase and back to her hotel room. There, she had turned on her computer and accessed the Hercules program. She now knew that "eagle" was the password—or at least part of it. Hercules ran the word eagle with scores of other words Alex had entered previously. In less than five minutes she had pieced the puzzle together. Typing 9:eagle34, she opened up the login site at the GEN network.

GEN used a cluster of Linux machines for data analysis, with a single, primary Linux machine managing the backend database server. When she passed through the GEN firewall, she found herself on one of the front end Linux machines. Using a secure shell, or ssh, backdoor, she accessed the database server.

She had quickly scrolled through the pages of files until her eyes landed on the file titled "Cystic Fibrosis Research.' Opening the file, she had begun her search of the sub-files. She had searched file after file for the information that Andre needed, rather, demanded. CF Journal, CF budget, CF allocations, CF presentations, CF symposia. . .. She stopped at the sub-file, "CF Protocol." When she opened it, she had found numerous data files in ACCESS and SAS databases. She had continued looking and found the extensive protocol that detailed all the funded and non-funded Cystic Fibrosis research. This was the detail she had been looking for, and the fact that all the clinical trial data were present in the same sub-file had been an added bonus. She had closed the sub-files and copied the folder to one of the front end Linux machines.

She had continued scanning the rest of the folders and found two additional sub-files entitled, "Federal CF Project" and "Federal Annual Reports." She had copied those to the front end machine as well. She had then uploaded all of the data to Benjamin's computer and then on to hers.

When all the data had been safely filed away on her hard drive, she wiped Benjamin's computer clean of the data and cleaned his local ssh logs as well by corrupting the log file. This made it look like the corruption had occurred two weeks prior to the attack. She had cleaned the syslog and ssh logs on the front end Linux machines and the backend database server, substituting bogus log entries for the real ones she had created. She had been very careful not to upset any log entries created by others so it wouldn't be obvious that the logs had been tampered with.

Only when she finished did she pause and think and let the enormity of her actions wash over her. What had she done? She knew then that she had made the choice to throw away a chance for a life with a real purpose, focused on love, tenderness and heartfelt dreams, instead of one based on deception, guilt, and fear.

Alex opened her eyes as the waiter returned to her table with her second cup of espresso. She looked around at the people in the bistro and the crowds strolling along the artist-filled sidewalks, and wondered if any of them had been as unlucky at love as she. Is there anyone as miserable as I am right now? As alone?

She closed her eyes again. There was Benjamin, rising out of the ocean toward her, holding open the elevator door, leaning out his window and charming her into the car, cradling her in his arms up the stairs—up those stairs. She sat motionless imagining the melodic tunes of gulls and the sound of the foghorn on the cliff that had made her feel protected and safe. She imagined the feel of the wind swirling around. Finally, then, Alex had felt calm and happy.

The splattering crack of a dish on the stone patio jolted her to her senses, and pulled her away from her place of refuge.

For the past few days Alex had thought endlessly about the course her life had taken. Her life was nothing more than a series of stepping stones laid in random patterns to cover-up the destruction and carnage she had left behind. She had destroyed the lives, families and dreams of so many, simply because she could not, *would* not deal with her own weaknesses, her own failings, her own imperfections. She had re-played her life's destructive blueprint over and over in her mind and for the first time she was overcome with sorrow. She remembered back to that soulful day when she heard the guttural sounds of the foghorn calling out to the ocean, to the whales, and to where life began. There was no turning back to undo her sins, she knew that, but that sound of safety gave her the strength and compassion she needed. Just as she told her mother that she should lead her life the way her father would want her to, she would lead the rest of her life in a way that would make Benjamin proud—the way he led his life—with strength, compassion and love for others.

Her mother was right. Why couldn't she just go to Benjamin and tell him the truth? If she didn't at least try, she would carry the burden of losing him for the rest of her life.

Alex tightened the scarf that was draped loosely around her neck. It was an unusually cool autumn day and she was beginning to feel a chill. She looked around the bistro and her gaze stopped on a couple sitting in the far corner. They were nuzzled close to each other and she could hear their gentle laughter. She saw the tenderness when the man reached over and took the woman's hand in his and she saw the gleam in the woman's eyes when he smiled at her. In that moment Alex knew she could no longer live her life with only a memory, a dream. She must now do what her heart had been crying out for ever since she fled in the dawn's sunlight. She must listen to her mother and follow the twisted, yet only path back toward happiness, toward wholeness, toward love—Back to Benjamin.

With the strength and courage she had developed as a young child and used so successfully to flee from her guilt and pain, Alex rose from her chair and walked out of the bistro. She was taking the needed steps toward a new beginning of her life.

She pulled her cell phone from her purse and punched in the numbers to Benjamin's phone. She stopped for a moment, put down the phone and began to think once again. I must be very careful. His line is surely tapped. What should I do? I need to think of some way that we can speak openly.

Once again she began to dial his number.

The ringing of the phone roused Benjamin from his first deep sleep in days. Still hovering on the edge of consciousness, he rolled over to the table by his bed, thinking this must be Murray again, or maybe Constance. He picked up the phone, "Hello?"

"Benjamin. Do not say my name. Please, hurry and grab a pen and paper and I will give you the number where you can call me back."

Benjamin stiffened and sat straight up in bed the second he heard the accent. *Am I dreaming again?* He turned on the light, in an attempt to make this all real.

"Where are you?"

"Please, Benjamin, I promise I will explain everything but you must first do exactly as I say. Now, do you have a pen?"

Fumbling around, Benjamin found one in the nightstand drawer. "Okay. Go ahead."

Writing on the bed sheet because he didn't have time to find any paper, Benjamin took down the number he recognized as one from another country.

"Okay, I've got it."

Quickly, Alex gave him instructions, "Now, you must go to an unrecognizable phone outside of your house somewhere and then call me at this number. Hurry! Go now!" The phone went dead.

Frantic, confused, and trying to make this scene all real—not a dream again, please, God, not another dream—Benjamin shot out of bed and threw on some sweats. He ripped the part of the sheet where he wrote Alex's number and clenched it in his fist. Running down the stairs he wondered what the hell this was about. For a brief moment, as he began to drive away from his house, he felt that now familiar flush of anger toward this woman who had torn his life apart, but then a feeling of longing began to take over. *Thank God,* he said to himself. *Thank God she had finally called. Her voice was so beautiful and soft—everything I had remembered. I miss her so much. I hate how much I love this woman—whoever she is.*

Confused and in a panic, Benjamin pulled into a gas station at the foot of the hill. With his mind still a blur, he jumped from the car and ran toward the phone booth. Inside the booth he looked at his watch for the first time. Jesus, it's 3:30 in the morning, he thought. Please don't let this be another dream.

As he dialed the phone number scribbled on the torn sheet, Benjamin felt a mix of anger, love and curiosity. His curiosity was the strongest emotion as he waited for an answer on the other end.

"Hello?" the familiar voice said, "Benjamin?"

"Alexandria. What the hell is going on?"

"Do not say anything else. Give me the number where you are right now. Quickly."

"Fine, but you have to tell me what this is all about."

"I will, I will. This is critical. Give me the number there and I will call you back in a few minutes."

Benjamin gave Alex the number and she hung up, once again. He stood in the phone booth at the gas station waiting to clear up this chaos. What the hell was going on? She was acting crazy; Murray must be right. She did steal the GEN information and that explains all these untraceable phone calls. I'll play along for a little while, but only until I hear her explanations.

Ten minutes passed, maybe more, before the phone finally rang. Benjamin didn't hesitate—he grabbed the receiver from its cradle on the first sound of the bell, "Come on now. Enough already. Start explaining."

"I am so sorry. So sorry."

Benjamin could hear the soft sobs. "It's okay, Alex. Just tell me where you are and what happened."

Barely able to utter her words through the tears, Alex said, "I miss you so much. I cannot sleep at night. I am so sorry."

"You need to do better than that Alex. There're a lot of things I don't know at this point, but I do know that you have a lot of explaining to do. I'll try to give you the benefit of the doubt, but you need to level with me, Alex. Now!"

Alex took a few deep breaths knowing that what she was about to say might end any chance of a future with this man. The truth was going to be painful, but she needed to see exactly how deep the welts went.

"I have so much to tell you and am so afraid you will hate me for what I have done. I am so scared, Benjamin."

Crammed in the phone booth with his left hand holding the door closed and his head leaning against the glass side panel, Benjamin felt his own anger toward this woman pound against the closed door. He had played out this scene in his mind countless times—the scene where he finally pinned her in the corner—finally broke her spirit and the truth came spewing out. Now here he was, the scene was about to begin and he could feel the pain from the far end of the line. He needed answers, but until he had them he couldn't unleash his own anger. His voice was steady, reassuring and he said, "I know more than you think about why you were here. I just need to hear it from you. Tell me the truth, Alex."

With another long deep breath, Alex began, "I came to America to obtain the information on the eradication of disease through the use of genetic engineering. I was hired by a man here in Paris to infiltrate GEN and bring back certain research information. You need to understand that this type of work has been my line of business for many years. I am very good at it. But I have grown to hate what I do and to even hate myself. Yes, I targeted you as the one I was to work on to obtain the genetic research. You and I had so much in common; it was a natural choice. I had no idea I would become so involved with you. That was never my mission. I was only going to get close enough to figure out what your password was so I could pirate the documents from GEN. I could not tell you what I was doing because you would have either exposed me, or worse, never spoken to me again. I hate what I have done. You were so good to me. I cannot remember ever being as happy in all my life as I was with you. Please forgive me, Benjamin."

Benjamin was no longer wedged inside the phone booth. The folding glass door was jarred open and half his body hung outside in the cool morning air. He had listened to every word, every syllable and every emotion. The explanation from Alex's lips was real, he felt it, but the tattered thread that had stitched his splintered heart these past few days remained taut. "I figured out it was you who stole the research when Murray came to me and accused me of doing it. No one else could've figured out my password. I just don't understand, Alex. Why didn't you just tell me? Why did you leave the way you did?"

"I had no choice."

"I don't buy that. There's always a choice. You have no idea what you've done to me. What's so sad about this whole mess is that I would've done anything for you. But instead, *you* did everything *to* me."

Alex felt a stinging pain as she listened to those harsh words from Benjamin. In a last desperate attempt, she gathered her composure and said, "I have never loved anyone the way I love you. Maybe you will never forgive me for what I have done; I know that I can never forgive myself. I have thrown away the most precious thing in my life. I wake up at night calling your name. My dreams are full of you and every time I close my eyes, all I see is you. I had to call you this one last time to tell you the truth and to let you know that I am so sorry. I would give anything to do it all over again. I would still be with you, beside you in your bed. The morning I left you, only my body walked away, my heart and soul are still with you and will always be there with you. I will understand if you never want to see me again; I would hardly blame you. I only hope that someday you will forgive me and hold me in your arms once again."

Those words began to peel away the hatred Benjamin had felt for this woman. The yearning desire to hold her again, to love her again, began to swell within him. Yet, this woman's entire life was built on manipulation and deceit. He wanted to give in to the desire to once again feel her warmth and her love, but the emotional mayhem still festered inside and tempered his aching desire. "I don't know what to do, Alex. I hate you and I love you. I too wake up at night and reach over to the emptiness beside me. I only wish you'd have told me all this while you were here."

Benjamin had every right in the world to distrust Alex and hate her for what she had done—for who she was. She needed to be with him, to look deep into his eyes and search for that one passage where she could go, where he would understand, where he would accept her again.

"Please, come to Paris? Or can we meet in some other country? Anywhere? I just need to see you and be with you and explain everything to you. Please, Benjamin. Let's meet somewhere."

Even though she was six thousand miles away, Benjamin could feel her next to him. Her voice over the phone was enough to send him back to the night they spent loving each other and giving to each other. He wanted so much to say, yes, I will come and I believe you, but his wounds were still too fresh, too deep.

"How can I trust you this time? What if I come to you and it is all another set-up?"

"I do not blame you for thinking that way. I suppose I should not even ask such a thing from you. I probably would not trust you if the situation were reversed."

With a renewed strength and her mother's words still fresh in her memory, Alex continued, "You know what we have between us is real. There is nothing deceitful about that. Neither of us can deny that intensity and we both know we belong together. You will never be whole without me Benjamin, and I will never be whole without you. Yes, I lied and betrayed you for a job I loathe and a life I no longer live. I'm almost embarrassed to tell you, though, that I have never before been in love with someone. I mean *really* in love. It is a powerful force unlike anything I ever imagined and it has taken root in my heart. I have fallen completely in love with you, Benjamin and, I can't run away from that. I went to see my mother after I left you and she helped me to see what I have been missing and that I must go to you and at least try to make you understand. She said to me that this emotion of love is stronger than any other human emotion and if you ignore it, it has a way of tearing at you for the rest of your life. She was right, Benjamin. I am not prepared for that sort of ripping at the flesh. Are you?"

Benjamin's heart urged him to run—run to Alex and throw his arms around her and tell her that everything was okay, they were okay. This same heart urged caution. The fractures and cuts were too fresh, too fragile, to suffer more pain. He was lost in his struggle—his mind raced to find the path he should follow.

"Are you there?. . . Benjamin?"

The damp morning fog sent a shivering chill through Benjamin. Alex's voice brought him back to the here and now. He stood tall, gave a quick shiver and rubbed the sleeve of his sweatshirt to warm his body. After a deep breath he spoke in a calm and more loving tone, "Yes, yes, Alex. I'm still here. You may be right. In a lot of ways I feel we're destined to be together. It's just that I'm not sure anything *was* real between us. I want to believe everything you've said, I really do, but I don't know what we can do to fix the damage. Right now I know so little about you.

In fact, I really don't know anything."

The softening of Benjamin's tone gave Alex hope that he might someday understand. "Please Benjamin; please understand that I am sorry and that I will do anything to make things up to you. I wish I could reverse the course of events and start over. No, you do know so little about me, but I know so much about you and I love everything about you Benjamin. If you could see it in your heart to meet me somewhere, anywhere, I know you will understand and forgive me for what I have done. We need to see each other again, Benjamin."

Benjamin knew he needed to see Alex. He wanted to believe her. He wanted to hold her. He wanted to be with her, forever. He wanted to get the stolen information. "I think we should meet somewhere. I'll come to Paris."

"Thank you! Thank you, Benjamin!" Alex sighed in relief.

"I'll make a plane reservation as soon as possible this morning."

Something was beginning to nag at Alex. What was it that he said earlier that did not make sense? Murray. Murray was accusing Benjamin of stealing the research. That's it.

"Benjamin, I need to ask you a few questions. I am sorry, but a few things just do not add up. You said Murray thinks you stole the information and yet you remain a free man?"

"I convinced Murray that I knew who stole the research and he was comfortable with allowing me to do my own investigation."

Alex's instincts hurled warning after warning—Benjamin may be in trouble. He certainly didn't know anything about this repulsive world of hers, the danger that he may be in right now. "I am sorry Benjamin. There is something very strange going on. First of all, if Murray thought you stole this research then there must be others at GEN who also think you stole it. There is no way they would allow you to just deny it and lead your own investigation. They would have you in jail by now or at least under surveillance. No, no. I think there is more to this story. We must talk about that later. But for now, hurry, Benjamin. Get on the plane. And please be careful. This can be a very dangerous world."

"How do I find you? Obviously, you're afraid of being caught with all this crazy back and forth calling we just did."

"Yes, I need to be very careful. And so do you. It is best not to let Murray or anyone else know that you are coming to see me."

"Wait a minute, Alex." Benjamin's gut twisted when he heard Alex's last words. "You stole information from GEN and I need to get it back. I don't need to say anything to Murray, but it makes me uneasy to hear you say I shouldn't alert Murray or anyone else about my plans."

"I know. I know. Nothing makes sense. One ugly thing I have learned over the years in this business is you really cannot trust anyone. There are no friends in this line of work. I only said that about Murray because I am worried about you. I do not care what happens to me at this point, but I want you to be safe Benjamin. If you feel you must say something to Murray then go ahead, but please be careful, and I *will* return the stolen research to you. I have already delivered it to the man I worked for, but I have copies of everything. I will give them to you the moment I see you."

"Alright, Alex, I won't say anything to Murray at this point. I just hope that you aren't leading me down some one-way road where I don't want to go. I am trusting you and this had better not be another lie on your part."

"I'm sorry. . .again. I want you to be safe and I may be over-reacting. I just want to make things right."

"Alright, Alex I'll be there as soon as I can. Now, how do I find you when I get there?"

She gave him the number of the Hotel Montpensier and told him to ask for her by name.

After writing down the number, Benjamin asked, "I still don't understand why you left so suddenly. Why, Alex?"

"I promise I will explain everything to you, I promise. Just get on the plane and call me when you land. I am so excited, Benjamin. Thank you for understanding. I promise I will make this all up to you."

CHAPTER 23

"WHAT? WHO THE HELL IS THIS?" a voice mumbled over the phone.

"Phil, great news! I just spoke with Alex and. . ."

Phil quickly interrupted, "Jesus Ben, why don't you tell me about this at a decent hour, not four-fucking-o'clock in the morning?"

"No, wait Phil, I need to talk with you *now* because I'm leaving for Paris shortly and I need your help."

"Paris? What's this about?" Phil's gargled voice responded.

In a hurried and excited voice, Benjamin continued, "This whole thing is hard to figure out, and I'm sure I don't know everything yet, but I'm catching a plane to Paris at 7:30 this morning. Alex called me a little while ago and explained why she left. My involvement with GEN has a lot to do with not only why she was here, but also why she left. She's supposedly involved in some sort of an espionage operation that wanted to obtain some research from GEN and in the process she fell in love with me. Anyway, I'm not yet certain why. . ."

"Whoa! Hold on!" Phil interrupted again. "Back up a little, pal. You're telling me that you're supposedly in love with some woman who tried to use you to steal some type of research. I think you've gone overboard on this one."

Benjamin ignored the scolding and continued, "I know it sounds a little bizarre, but it's kinda complicated. I don't know yet why she wanted this information or who she'd been working for, but I think she may be in some sort of trouble and I need to do whatever I can to help her. Yeah, she did try to use me, but I know now that she does love me and I need to get to the bottom of this. Besides, Murray knows that the information was pirated through my computer and he has agreed to give me some time to solve this mess."

Phil was now wide awake and sitting on the edge of his bed. "You're crazier than I thought, Ben. You don't know the first thing about what you're getting into and it sounds like she may have implicated you in some way. What you *ought* to be doing right now is calling a lawyer!" Phil's voice expressed a fraternal concern.

"Listen Phil," Benjamin said, "I know this doesn't make much sense, but you have to trust me on this one. Alex sounded as if she was in trouble, and I need to help her. Besides," he paused, and took a tremulous breath, "I need to help myself, and this is the only way I can think how to do that."

"Trust you? Come on Ben. You call me at this god-awful hour and tell me you're heading off on some jaunt but you don't know what's going on. Why don't you wait a day, hell wait two days, talk to your PI and see what they can come up with before you go gallivanting off?"

"There's no time for that and I know what I'm doing. I need. . ."

Phil paced back and forth and again interrupted Benjamin, "This could be way dangerous. Let me just think about this for a sec. There has to be a better way."

"Phil you know what Alex means to me. I need to get to the bottom of all this and the sooner the better. Now I need. . ."

"Ok, then, let me go with you," Phil jumped in again. "I can trail behind you and keep an eye on things from a distance. In fact, get your PI to come along with us also too."

"Phil, I don't have time for this. I need to be off to the airport in a few minutes and I need your help here."

Phil had witnessed Benjamin's drive and determination before. Once he had made up his mind, there was no stopping him. "Well, I can't stand in your way, but I still think you're nuts."

"I may be. But I'm one happy nut!" Benjamin laughed.

"How long are you going to be gone? Do you have any idea?"

"No. Not really. When I get to Paris I have a phone number to contact Alex. I suppose I'll meet her somewhere and get to the bottom of this. I'm going to be winging it until that point."

"Ben, this whole thing sounds too dangerous to me. How do you know there aren't other people involved in this, or that she isn't just setting you up for something else? Come on, call that PI firm of yours and have it do a little more investigating before you fly off to never-never land." Things still didn't sit right with Phil, and he wanted to slam the brakes on Benjamin's hare-brained idea.

Benjamin felt rushed and no longer had the time to placate Phil or to fully explain the situation. Raising his voice a little, he said, "Phil, look, you're going to have to just go with me on this one. I know you think it's crazy, and to tell the truth, so do I, but I really have to do this. What I really need now is your help. Can I count on you?"

Benjamin had made up his mind—he was going one way or another. Phil wasn't sure if the romantic part of Benjamin or just his sheer willpower was driving his decision. Either way, Phil wasn't going to be able to derail his train. Reluctantly, Phil said, "Okay, you've obviously made up your mind. What do you want me to do?"

"Like I said, I don't know how long I'll be gone and I need someone to feed and care for the eagle. I'll leave instructions on the kitchen counter and the keys to the cage are in the middle drawer of my desk in the den."

Phil collapsed on his bed and leaned his head back. Staring at the ceiling he knew there was nothing he could do, but the concern he felt was not masked when he replied, "All you need me to do is feed a fucking bird while you wander off on some mission without a clue as to what you're doing? I think the least you can do is let me know where you'll be at all times and let me know how to get in touch with you."

"I'm sorry that I don't have time to explain more to you, Phil. I really am. But I will as soon as I can. In the meantime, the eagle is almost healed and I can't let anything happen to him. And it's not just a fucking bird—you know it means a lot to me."

"Alright, alright, I'll feed your bird. Don't they eat whole rabbits and crap like that?"

Laughing out loud now, Benjamin replied, "It's easy. He's on a special diet the vet gave me to help him heal. You may have to throw in a snake or two. I won't be gone long and hopefully I'll return with Alex. I can't wait for you to meet her—then you'll understand why I have to do this."

"Oh great," Phil said sarcastically. "I just love snakes. How do I get in touch with you?"

Benjamin reached into his shirt pocket and grabbed the torn sheet with Alex's number written on it. "I told you, I only have a phone number where I'm supposed to call Alex as soon as I arrive in Paris. It's a hotel called Montpensier. You'll need to ask for Alex. I'll have my cell phone with me too so you can always try that. But Phil, I'll be fine, so don't try to call me unless it's an absolute emergency. Besides, there's not much I can do if something goes wrong here."

Phil wrote the number down, and asked, "So what's her last name? I don't think hotels have a guest registry for first names."

"Oh. It's Pancini. I think. Wow, that may not even be her real name. But I'm sure she's using it since I have to call her when I arrive. If this number is changed or I can't find her right away, I promise I'll call you."

"All right Ben, I expect you to check in with me regularly and let me know what's going on. I still think this is crazy, so you be careful."

"Oh, and don't tell anyone where I've gone—no one!" He emphasized the 'no one'. "Thanks, Phil. I owe you one. I'll be in touch, I promise. When I get back I'll even let you get the bigger abalone next time."

"Jesus Christ, Benjamin. I'm against this whole thing, but I know you're dead-set on it. Just be careful!"

"Thanks for everything, buddy. Later." Benjamin hung up the phone and rushed upstairs to throw a suitcase together.

CHAPTER 24

"**M**ONSIEUR **H**UNTER?"

Benjamin turned toward the woman greeting him as he exited the customs area, "Yes?"

With an outstretched hand a woman with a heavy French accent said, "My name is Claudette. I am a good friend of Alexandria. She asked me to pick you up because she could not, but she will meet you at the Hotel Montpensier, instead. I live close by the airport and it is much easier for me to come get you. Besides, she had some last minute work she had to finish."

Puzzled and weary from his long flight, Benjamin looked at this woman and wondered how Alex knew her. She was close to Alex's age and her accent was definitely French. "Excuse me if I'm a little confused, but I'm supposed to call Alex when I arrive. She never mentioned anyone picking me up."

"She should be back at the Hotel Montpensier very soon and I know she is expecting you. I spoke to her just several hours ago and I know she is anxious to see you. I hope you do not mind a little change of plans? Besides, Alexandria has a little surprise for you."

"Okay. Is she alright?"

"Yes, yes, of course she is. She is dying to see you. She has talked about nothing but you. Please, you have had a long flight, let me help you with your bag."

"No. That's fine thank you. I've got it." Benjamin picked up his bag and, weaving in and out of the throngs of travelers, they headed toward the front entrance of the airport. He had spent most of the flight trying to piece together what little information he had on who Alex might really be and whether, as Phil pointed out, all of this might be just another trap . He waited until the French woman stopped and turned to him before he asked, "How did you ever recognize me?"

"She showed me a picture of you. Hurry, we should go."

He thought for a moment and figured she probably had a lot of pictures of her potential victims. "I should give Alex a quick call before we leave, but my cell phone battery is dead. Do you know if there's a phone around here I can use or maybe I could borrow your cell?"

Waving her hands and motioning for him to follow her, she said, "The phones here are such a pain. You can use my cell phone instead. It is in the car. Please, we are wasting time. She is anxious to see you."

Carrying his luggage, Benjamin continued to follow the petite Frenchwoman through the maze of corridors in Orly Airport. They exited the building onto the street, where cars were stacked bumper-to-bumper to pick up and drop off travelers. Claudette led him to a black limousine parked only a few feet from the exit doors. A driver jumped out and opened the back door for them. Inside Benjamin saw a man sitting at the far end of the passenger compartment. Claudette immediately said, "This is my husband, Antoine. He also wanted to meet Alexandria's American man."

From inside the dark, "Hello Benjamin. Nice to meet you. Please, please, get in."

Benjamin handed his luggage to the driver and stepped into the limousine. He sat across from Antoine. Claudette stepped into the car, sat beside her husband, and said, "We are not too far from Alexandria's hotel. It should not take long. Can I offer you something to drink?"

"Thank you, but I'm fine." Still somewhat confused, Benjamin began to wonder why Alex had changed the plans. Maybe she thought it was better for me to be escorted rather than mess around with car rentals and directions? Actually, this was quite nice, Benjamin thought. If only she were here too.

"Are you comfortable?" Claudette asked.

The plush surroundings were more than comfortable, but something made him uneasy. The limousine was dark and the windows were tinted so no light came through and no one could see in. It felt like a chamber moving along unrecognizable roads to a place just as dark; just as cold. His nerves began to quiver as if his body were telling him something his mind had not yet recognized. Oh God, he thought, this doesn't feel right. What have I done? Who are these people? How could I have been so stupid? Alex, where are you? What have you done?

Answering Claudette, Benjamin said, "Yes, thank you. Could I use your cell now?" He reached for the phone sitting on the small car seat table in front of Antoine.

The large man across from him known only as Antoine, leaned slightly forward. His dark eyes were set deep in their sockets and wider apart than seemed natural. A single bushy black eyebrow ran from one side of his head to the other making it tricky to focus on his eyes. His face was dotted with pock marks, and he bit down just slightly on his lower lip. It was difficult to tell how tall this man was, but judging by his thick neck and the bulging biceps beneath his tight fitting sweater, he was the type of man who would get his way, one way or another.

He placed his large calloused hand over Benjamin's outstretched fingertips before he was able to pick up the phone. Now releasing the bite on his lower lip, he leaned even closer to Benjamin and in a dull, drawn-out monotone voice said, "You will not be needing that right now."

The faint knock at the door startled Alex. "Who is it?"

"Room service, mademoiselle. Champagne and flowers from a Monsieur Hunter."

Without thought, Alex opened the door. A man immediately jammed his shoe against the foot of the door, grabbed Alex and pushed her back inside the room while another stormed in behind. They shut and locked the door, pointed a gun at Alex and ordered her to sit down on the bed.

Taken completely by surprise, Alex immediately blurted, "What is going on? Who are you?"

One man pointed a gun at her while the other began looking around the room, in the closets and the bathroom. "It's okay. The place is empty," said the smaller blond-haired man to the apparent leader who was holding Alex at gunpoint.

Alex knew immediately that the man with the gun meant business. His right hand cradled the 9mm Compact Glock 19 with a familiarity that can only come from constant practice. The small 4 inch barrel on this gun made it easy to conceal and Alex guessed he had a shoulder holster under the slightly oversized gray sports jacket that hung loosely from his broad shoulders. His trigger finger was cocked, but fully relaxed. This wasn't the first time this man had pointed a gun at someone.

Clutching the bed sheets, Alex asked again, "You need to tell me what you are doing and what you want."

The man standing over her wielding the power of the gun angrily snapped, "Shut Up!" He leaned over and put his face inches in front of hers, his breath smelling like curdled milk. The man exuded depravity. She looked up at him as he spoke. He was actually a handsome man. His hair was neatly trimmed to just over his ears, but his eyes were the most frightening, the most wicked thing, she had ever seen. His eyes were dark brown, flecked with a lighter color. His dark eyebrows were narrow and well trimmed and without any curvature. They ran straight across the top of each eye socket. His eyelids were thick and drooped down over his eye, giving him a squinting appearance like that of a tiger peering through the tall grass, about to pounce on its prey. If, as Alex's father always said, the eyes were the windows to the soul, truly, this man's soul was from hell itself.

"I give da orders here, not you. Ya got some infamation we need, so hand it over—now!"

Reeling from the stench of this man's spitting breath, Alex replied, "I do not know what you are talking about."

Out of nowhere came a hand across Alex's face. His hand felt like a block of cement. The sting masked the warmth that began to flow from the corner of her mouth. She instinctively reached up to her jaw and caught the blood dripping down onto her lap.

The man took several steps back, his gun still pointed at Alex's imaginary third eye. "Give us da infamation and ya walk. If not, we'll kill ya and yur American boyfriend."

"My American what? You must be mistaken—you must be in the wrong room." Alex remained calm on the outside as she heard this man's words. Inside her blood began to boil.

"Listen up lady, I can add a few bruises to dat bloody face of yurs. No problem." The man kept the gun pointed at Alex, moved a few steps to his left and pressed on, "Now give us da infamation. If not I can order Benny boy's burial."

"Where is he god damnit? I don't care what you do to me, but he knows nothing and has done nothing."

The man raised his hand up once again to inflict pain on the other side of her face when she suddenly shouted, "Go ahead, you coward! Go on. Hit me again." Alex pushed herself up off the bed to confront her tormentors. The blond-haired one, the one with the overgrown Rambo like stubbles protruding from his narrow pointed chin, reached over, grabbed the back of her sweater and jerked her back to her place. "Easy, lady."

The man with the gun began to laugh loudly, but he quickly stopped. Again he pressed his face into hers, "Yur a feisty one, huh? Well listen lady, if ya want Benji alive, hand it over."

"Where is he? How do I know you have not already hurt him?" Alex's glare lasered into this man's dark pupils.

"Our partners picked him up at da airport. They're talkin' ta him right now. They'll kill him, I know dat, if I don't call dem real soon. Alexandra, right? Hand over da infamation. Now!"

Alex was stunned. Continuing to wipe the dripping blood from her mouth and barely able to remain calm, she attempted to speak without showing the paralyzing terror clamoring to take control, "Tell me exactly what it is you want."

"No, no, lady, stop with da bull shit. Yur a smart lady and ya know what I need. Yur startin' ta make me mad and ya won't like me when I'm mad. Let's finish dis. Yur runnin' outta time and da trigger finger on my friend holding yur American lover boy is gettin' itchy." He stretched his left arm out so Alex could get a clear view of his watch. "Shall I make da call?" He reached into his left coat pocket with his free hand and brandished a cell phone back and forth.

Oh God. What am I going to do? Alex thought. I need more time to think—to plan. My back-up hard drive is at the bank. . . maybe there. "Fine. I will get the information you need. But first, what assurances do I have that Benjamin will not be harmed?"

"None. You'll get 'em back if ya do as I say."

"I could give you what you are asking for and you could still kill him—and me. I am not a fool either."

The tall dark man grabbed a chair from the small seating area and dragged it over to the side of the bed, next to Alex. He sat down and pressed the gun into her chest, jabbing into her heart that was now pounding to pump the oxygen she needed to at least appear calm. "Listen lady, we were hired ta do a job. If dat means we kill a few people, we don't care. Our boss though, he don't want a big mess. He never does. But pretty lady, if we don't get our hands on dat infamation, den no problem. We'll kill ya and Benny boy. From where I'm sittin', ya don't have a choice, do ya?"

This man gave Alex the creeps. It was clear to her that he didn't care who stood between him and his paycheck. He was all business. "Then we must go. The information you want is on a hard drive. It is in my safe deposit box at the bank."

Alex no longer cared about what was happening to her. Benjamin was in danger and she needed to find a way to get to him somehow. She started to get up and the man sitting in the chair twisted the gun so that it bore into her chest, even harder; his voice croaked, "Not sa fast. What 'bout other copies? Sit down. Now, tell us who ya work for."

"I have no idea," Alex replied.

"I'm dis close ta bein' mad." The man held up his left hand and his thumb and index finger were squished together.

"I am telling you the truth. I was hired by someone from Germany. I only have a contact man whom I have spoken with several times. I know him as Roland. I am to meet him here in a few days. He has my hotel phone number, and called me yesterday to set up a meeting. I have the only hard drive. There are no copies."

"I'm suppose ta believe dat?"

"You do not have to believe me. If you wait here for a few days he will show up with my money and I will give him the hard drive."

"Okay, Okay. Let me warn ya, lady. If ever any copies appear anywhere den we'll know it. If ya lie ta me, den we'll know dat too. We'll track ya down, yur boyfriend—and Thérèse."

"My mother! How dare you. You bastard!"

"Don't dare me, Alexandra. Don't do it." The man lifted his foot up and stomped it into the floor. He again twisted the gun in her chest—even harder. "Ya don't look dat stupid ta me. Now, get up. Let's go collect what we came for."

The man pulled the gun from her chest and Alex stood up. She felt a little dizzy from the adrenaline rushing through her veins, but tried not to appear affected. The blood had stopped dripping but the pain in her jaw was becoming worse. Pain she could deal with. Benjamin was all that mattered at this point. She walked forward to grab her purse on the table, she turned and asked the evil looking one, "How do I know Benjamin is alright?"

"I said we don't want ta kill nobody. Just give us da infamation. We'll be on our way and Benny boy and ya will be rumblin' under the sheets tonight."

He instructed the other man to escort Alex out of the hotel, but to keep a close eye on her. They all walked single file out into the hall with Alex stuck in the middle. She felt the presence of the leader up against her back. She smelled his rancid breath as he whispered in her ear, "Remember, if ya try anything, we'll kill da American, and ya, too, of course."

They moved through the downstairs lobby undisturbed. The men escorted Alex into a blue two-door Peugeot 206 parked in front of the hotel. Even though these men spoke broken English with no discernable accent, she had already guessed they must be locally based. Now she was certain. You can't rent a Peugeot 206; they stopped making that car some five years ago.

Within a few short minutes, they pulled up alongside the Bank of France. Alex began to get out of the car when those wicked eyes turned to her and said, "Don't try nothin' funny, lady. Remember, we have a gun ta old Benji's head while ya walk around dat bank. Hurry back, pretty lady."

Alex exited the car and walked toward the tall glass doors of the bank. She opened the right side of the double doors and turned toward her captors. There they sat in the blue coupe, glaring and watching her every move.

Inside the bank Alex began to feel safer. Even though she had been in this very same bank many times over the years she still paused to look around—to get a feel for what was going on around her. She stopped for a moment by a desk on the left side of the room. Think Alex, think. What to do? I cannot hand over that hard drive, and I cannot allow them to kill Benjamin. What a mess I have gotten us both into. Damn Andre! That's it! I'll call Andre. Maybe he can get me out of this.

Alex walked over to a loan officer sitting at one of the desks in the bank. She asked, "Is there a phone I can use here?"

The woman's head was buried in stacks of paperwork. She shuffled a few papers and without looking up said, "I am sorry, but the phones here are for bank personnel only."

"No. Please. This is very urgent! I must use a phone now. I am here to pick up some materials from my safe deposit box and must make a call before doing so."

"Very well," the loan officer said, "you can use one of those phones." Her head was still buried in her papers and she pointed to the three empty desks next to hers.

"Thank you, madam." Alex moved to the desk in the corner hoping for some privacy and punched the tiny buttons on the phone.

"Mr. Broussard's office, may I help you?" Andre's secretary said.

"Hello. I need to speak with Andre, please. Tell him this is Alex."

"I am sorry, he is in a meeting right now. I can ask him to return your call as soon as he has finished."

Alex snapped, "You must interrupt him. I may not be alive for him to call me back. Go get him now!"

A smug irritation rang from the secretary's voice, "Let me try then. I will be right back. Please hold."

After only a few seconds Andre picked up the phon. "What is it Alex? What is so important it cannot wait until my meeting is over?"

Alex spoke in a hushed voice and began to explain, "I am so sorry for what I did the other day. I need your help right now. I am standing in a bank calling you before I have to go to my safe deposit box and hand over the genetic research to a bunch of thugs."

"What is going on? Do not do that! Where are you? I will come get you," the sound of Andre's voice escalated with each word.

"Quiet, Andre. Listen. There are two men outside this bank in a car. They have guns and will kill me if I don't come out with the hard drive."

"What hard drive? I thought you gave me all the information. Forget all that—just leave another way and I will come get you."

"Andre, there is a lot I never told you. I fell in love with a man in America. Actually, he was my target, the one I used to obtain the password to break into GEN's computer network. He was on his way to see me today, and these people picked him up at Orly. They have a gun to his head this very minute. Even if I escape now, they will kill him."

Silence. The sounds of the customers in the bank, the rattling of chairs and the swinging of doors were all muted as she cupped her hand over her free ear and leaned forward to hear Andre's words. The silence dragged on.

"Andre, are you there? Are you still there?"

Finally, "Yes I am Alex. Is this man's name Benjamin Hunter?"

"How did you know?" Alex stiffened and gripped the receiver even tighter. "There is no way. . ." She stopped mid-sentence. How *did* he know?

"Alex, wait. . .wait. . .I do not know how to tell you this, but a man was shot in the vicinity of Orly just hours ago. Apparently, he was shot and thrown from a car. I found out his name is Benjamin Hunter."

Trembling, Alex forced herself to ask the next question, "Is he dead?"

"I do not know. I can find out. The important thing now is that you can escape. Get out of there and I will pick you up somewhere."

Holding onto the hope that Benjamin was alive and that she could go to him if she escaped from these thugs, Alex said to Andre, "I will make a diversion, somehow. Go to Jardin des Tuileries and I will meet you by the Rue de Rivoli gateway. Hurry, Andre."

"Be careful, Alex. I will be there in a few minutes." The phone was already dead.

Staring out the window now, Alex felt the coldness of her skin, the warm blood retreating to protect her vital organs. Fear had crept into her consciousness and her breathing slowed, her heart skipped its rhythmic beats. Her mind struggled as the words "a man has been shot" drifted in and out of her thoughts. She fought the battle within herself. Unwilling to allow the possibility that Benjamin was dead to even enter her mind, she quickly walked back over to the woman at the first desk who she spoke to earlier.

Alex was already very upset so she didn't have to try and convince anyone of her fear.

"Madam? Please help me. I have been trying to call someone to come help me, but I think maybe you can assist me instead. There are two men outside in a blue Peugeot, parked in front of the bank. They have been following me for several blocks and I even saw one of them with a gun. I am afraid to go to my safe deposit box and leave because I think that is why they are following me. Could you please call security?"

The woman flinched and dropped the stack of papers she was holding. She looked up, "Absolutely! Stay here and I will get our guards to take care of this." The woman quickly rose and waved in the direction of a security guard standing near the teller windows.

Alex watched as the security guard talked to the loan officer. The guard looked over at Alex and motioned to two other guards. After several minutes, they all walked outside together. Alex followed them to the front door, stood to the side and waited for her opening.

The guards appeared to say something to the men in the car and then backed up a few steps as they watched the men exit the car. The guards put them up against their car and began to search them for weapons. Alex made her move.

She darted quickly out of the bank and as she turned to flee she heard one of the men yell, "Alexandra! Alexandra! Dat's not such a smart idea."

She continued to walk straight ahead, her pace quickening with each step, until she turned the corner, away from their line of vision. Confident that they would be detained for some time, she slowed her tempo down to a brisk walk. Intent on getting to Andre as quickly as possible, she threaded her way through the crowded street. Her mind was racing, trying to make some sense of all this. These men have called me by my real name. How would they know that? Suddenly, it hit her again—how on earth could Andre have known about Benjamin? If he was shot it could have happened only a short while ago. There was no way Andre could know this. Unless. . .

Alex froze in her tracks. Andre, she thought. Is he tied up in this? Why? Then she remembered their brief conversation a few moments ago when he sounded very surprised that she made copies of the research and was holding onto it. Oh God, Alex thought. What am I going to do now? If Andre is after me, I am dead. And my mother. I have got to warn my mother. I have got to go find Benjamin. I have got to get out of here!

Alex picked up her pace again, reached into her purse and pulled out her cell phone. Quickly she dialed the familiar number, "Hello?"

"Mother. Listen carefully. Please do not be frightened. You have to pack very quickly and leave Sidi Lahcen. I am in danger and so are you. I want you to go to Uncle Djamel's house. I will call Royal Air Morac and have a ticket waiting for you at the airport. You need to get to the bus in the village right away and it will take you to the airport."

"Honey, are you alright?"

"Yes mother. I am fine. Please do not ask me any questions. There is no time. I promise I will explain everything later. I will call you at Uncle Djamel's tomorrow. Right now you need to pack—do not take too much—and get to the airport. Please, mother, hurry."

"I am afraid, Alexandra. None of this makes any sense."

"I know. I am so sorry to do this to you. A ticket will be waiting for you under your name. Do you understand? I must go now. I will call you tomorrow."

"Alright. I will go. You sound very serious."

"I am. Please, go now mother. Hurry. You need to leave in the next few minutes. Okay?"

"Alright. I will do what you ask."

"Bye, mother."

"Bye, dear."

Alex hung up the phone. Next she called the airlines and booked her mother's flight. She was now only a few short blocks away from the Jardin des Tuileries.

Standing in a crowd of tourists, Alex watched Andre exit his car and walk to the gateway where they had arranged to meet. Observing him for a few moments, she noticed the familiar nervous pacing back and forth along the sidewalk. Surrounded by the moving crowd she monitored Andre's every move and scouted his immediate surroundings. He was alone.

She walked slowly toward him. When he saw her, he rushed to her, his arms outstretched. She raised her arms and caught the inside of Andre's arms, pushing them away. Taking a step back Andre appeared flushed. "Alex, what is going on?"

She moved in close to him and began the inquisition, "I do not have much time. You need to answer my questions first. How did you know Benjamin was shot?"

Alex's eyes drilled into Andre. He was direct, "I was in a meeting when you called me, remember? That meeting was with reporters from Le Monde. In the middle of it Jean Petain was paged. He used my phone to answer it and found out that an American had been shot and taken to the hospital. One of the other reporters asked the name of the American, and that's when

I heard the name, Benjamin Hunter. I immediately knew who he was because I put together those files for you when you went to America."

Convincing, but probably a lie, Alex thought. "What is so important about this genetic research that Benjamin has been shot and they are after me as well?"

"That is a mystery. The financial gain from this research is immense and that quite possibly could be the motive."

"Have they come after you, yet?"

Andre winced. "No, they have not. The only link they would have to me is through you. As a matter of fact, we are both being very naive to be standing here in plain view. You must be careful, Alex. I must be careful as well."

A bit more at ease now, but still guarded, Alex continued, "This whole thing makes no sense to me. Are you sure there is nothing more to this research? I find it hard to believe that Benjamin is now involved and is in danger. Oh God! I have to find him, Andre. He must be at a hospital by now. Do you know where he is?"

"No. But I can make some calls and find out for you. Come with me and we'll find him."

Alex threw her head back and said, "No. I will find him myself. I have to go. I will call you later."

"Are you sure I cannot take you?"

"No. Bye." Alex ran toward a taxi parked at the edge of the park.

"Call me, Alex!" Andre yelled out as the door to the cab slammed shut.

Alex instructed the driver to just drive, anywhere, and hurry.

After a few blocks and when Alex was certain that she was not being followed, she quickly punched the phone number for the local police into her cell phone.

"Service de Police. May I help you?"

Alex began, "I am looking for someone who flew into Orly a short while ago and I cannot find him. He may be missing. With whom should I speak?"

"Just a moment, mademoiselle," the voice droned.

After a few clicks another female voice spoke, "Missing persons, may I help you?"

"Yes, I hope so. I went to pick up a man at Orly who flew in from San Francisco today. I know he arrived, but now I cannot find him. Can you help me?"

"It does not sound like there is any cause for alarm. He has probably just been delayed in the airport—customs and all. You should give it some more time."

"No, you do not understand. Let me explain further. I heard there was a shooting near the airport and the police have recovered the victim. I need to know if this was the man I was to meet."

"What is his name?"

"Benjamin Hunter. He is from San Francisco."

The deafening pause while Alex waited for a reply seemed endless. Andre's words continued to ring through her conscience 'shot. . .thrown from a car. . .' Finally the long silence ended, "Mademoiselle,, there was a Monsieur Hunter who was taken to Hertford British Hospital about an hour ago. He is an American."

Without hanging up, Alex abruptly said to the cab driver "Take me to Hertford British Hospital. Please, hurry."

CHAPTER 25

"I AM LOOKING FOR MR. HUNTER, MONSIEUR Benjamin Hunter. Can you please tell me where I may find him?"

As Alex spoke to the woman seated behind the large white counter, her eyes scanned the hallways and corridors of the maze she had just entered. Where is he? Which elevator? Which door?

The cold, sterile walls of the emergency room waiting area felt like death itself to Alex. The people sitting in the small card table fold-up chairs waiting for word about their loved ones all turned their eyes toward Alex as she spoke. Their collective dreary affect showed no signs of conscious awareness. There was blunt terror in their eyes as they awaited a message, any message, from a doctor. Alex shuddered at the thought. Here she was, about to wait with the others, to stare at the double doors where the doctors and nurses shuffled in and out aimlessly, ignoring the nameless family members in the metal fold-up chairs waiting for the words they hoped would not come.

Alex remembered sitting with her mother in another crowded hospital. She drifted back in time to when they sat and waited to hear if Christina had survived the long drive from their home to that tiny hospital. Her eyes locked on a woman holding a small child on her lap in the corner of the waiting area and she suddenly felt her mother's arms around her squeeze tighter as the doctor came through the door to tell them about Christina. "Dead" was the only word Alex remembered. Death was too final, too painful, and the waiting room in this hospital was full of it.

Alex wanted to scream and run out into the cool crisp air, but she turned her eyes back to the woman behind the counter when she heard, "Mademoiselle? Mademoiselle? Excuse me, mademoiselle."

"Sorry," Alex said as she pulled herself from her mother's invisible arms. "Please, help me. I need to find Monsieur Hunter's room, Benjamin Hunter."

After shuffling through papers and looking on her computer screen, the nameless, elderly woman looked up at her and, with a robotic smile, said, "I am not sure. You need to have a seat and I will get someone to help you."

"No! I need to know if he is here. Yes or no? Tell me now!" Alex demanded.

The half-smile disappeared, "I said I will get someone to come out here for you. Now you must have a seat."

Alex clenched her hands and reacted, "I do not have time to sit here. If you do not tell me now, I am going through those doors to find him myself." She spun around and began to move toward her threatened destination.

"Look mademoiselle, I said. . ." before the woman could finish her sentence a uniformed police officer came into the waiting area from one of the locked, side doors. He put a hand on Alex's shoulder, and said, "Please, come with me."

Without hesitation, Alex followed. As they walked through the back corridor, Alex asked, "I just need to know if he is alive."

"Please, just follow me and all your questions will soon be answered," the officer said without missing a beat of his measured cadence.

Alex was led into the hospital administrator's office. Four police officers immediately stood, apparently awaiting her arrival. A uniformed woman placed her right hand on the back of a chair, pulled it out and motioned for Alex to come over. Despite her petite frame, she spoke with a firm and commanding voice, "Please, have a seat and tell us who you are and what you are doing here?"

Alex stood her ground, stared right back at the woman and said, "No, I think you all need to tell me who you are and why you have brought me here."

The other plain-clothed officers looked at one another, shifted their weight a bit, and the tall thin man with his shirt tail hanging half way out of his khaki trousers replied, "My name is Inspecteur DePaul. This is Inspecteur Bergeron, Inspecteur Durand, and Officier Levesque." Reaching into the inside pocket of his tattered, but well-tailored blue sports coat, he pulled something out and stepped forward. "Here is my badge. Now, what is your name?"

Still standing rigid and becoming more agitated at the thought of wasting time, Alex said, "I am sure you are all nice people and have meaningful intentions, but I have to find someone, and I have no more time to stand here chatting with you." Alex spun around and headed toward the closed door.

A heavily accented French baritone stopped her in her tracks. "Excuse me, mademoiselle. How do you know Monsieur Hunter?" Inspecteur DePaul said.

At the sound of his name, Alex stopped, turned back and glared at the man with the barking voice. "He is a friend of mine. Why?"

"Look, mademoiselle, we are investigating an attempted murder. We know nothing about this man, and you come walking in here asking for him. Do you not think it is obvious why we need to know who you are?"

Attempted, Alex thought. Benjamin is alive. "I am sorry. I just do not know who to trust right now. The same people that did this to him tried to kill me, too. I just need to see him."

Inspecteur DePaul moved closer to Alex, his bark mellowing to a soft tenor, "We have placed guards outside and inside his room. You must understand that we need to make sure that his visitors are not also his killers. If you are involved in some way and have information about who may have done this, we need to know. Now, please sit down, and the faster you cooperate, the sooner you will see him."

Alex sat restlessly on the front edge of the chair the officer had pulled out for her. Knowing that she would get out of here if she gave them a story about who tried to kill her, she told the Inspecteurs about the men who came to her hotel. She explained that Benjamin came to Paris to see her and that they were in love. She told the Inspecteurs that she accidentally downloaded some confidential information from a company she was working for while in America. She had absolutely no idea she had this information until Benjamin phoned her from California, and he decided to come to Paris to help her figure out what to do about it. She needed to give them just enough believable information so that she could go to Benjamin and then buy some time to figure out what to do next. The fact that she loved Benjamin helped to convince the Inspecteurs that she was not there to kill him.

After about an hour of repetitive interrogation, the Inspecteurs decided they had all the information they would get from this lady. She had deftly sidestepped around the questioning about the information she had downloaded and no, she did not keep copies of the information.

"Go now with Officier Levesque. She will show you to Monsieur Hunter's room. After you have spent time there you need to return here so we can get a sketch of the men who came to your hotel today."

Alex stood and shook Inspecteur DePaul's hand and said, "Thank you. I will be back later." She turned and followed Officier Levesque through the door.

The anticipation of seeing Benjamin, of holding him, of hearing his tender voice and gazing into his eyes was too much to bear. Alex walked briskly down the hallway and pleaded with Officier Levesque to please hurry.

After twists and turns and climbing up one set of stairs and down another, Officier Levesque ushered Alex into a corner room in the Intensive Care Unit. The room was small, and she was overwhelmed by the smell of antiseptic and emptiness when she entered. She stopped in her tracks and her hands fell limp to her side at the sight of Benjamin. Lying motionless in a bed, his skin was deathly pale; his face bruised, cut and bandaged. The bed sheets rose and fell so slightly with the cadence of the beeping respirator sitting by his side.

With the carefully placed steps of a small frightened child, Alex inched closer toward Benjamin. Leaning over him, she held his right hand in hers and tenderly stroked his bruised face. "Benjamin, I am so sorry. This should be me lying here, not you. Can you hear me? Do you feel me next to you?"

Stroking his battered face Alex began to shudder at the sight of all the narrow plastic tubes running in and out of his body.

The sound of the respirator next to her, the rhythmic pumping of life in and out of Benjamin's lungs was what brought Alex to release her terror of losing the only man she had ever loved. She began to cry, uncontrollably. She cried as she had only cried once before, the way she did that day at Point Reyes. With her head resting gently on his chest, listening to his faint heartbeats, she was overcome with the guilt about the secret and the deception of her life which she had not yet explained to Benjamin. Without thought, Alex began to softly whisper the twisted tale that brought her into his life.

As she spoke to Benjamin, watching as each breath was pumped into him, she continued to tenderly stroke his face and tell her story of the hunt. She talked about Andre, and how she was indebted to him from years ago, about her duplicitous work and the life she had led. She talked about how she set her sights on him as her target for obtaining the GEN data and about how she stalked him—his speech at Stanford, the encounter at the Dolphin Club were not just happenstance. Then she began to talk about the eagle, and what that experience meant to her, and about Point Reyes and how he helped her to release the guilt that was embedded within her for years.

"I am so sorry for everything, Benjamin. It seems like I keep saying that over and over but I truly am. I am sorry for what I have done to you and to so many other people. I have learned so much from you in such a very short time. I want to right the wrongs I have committed over the years and I want to spend my life with you." She laid her head on his chest and closed her eyes. She felt the rise and fall of his chest with each whooshing sound of the respirator. She felt his forehead and the lines of his years and thought, what a brilliant man this is. She moved her hand to his eyes, the ones that looked at her with longing and desire, that were honest and humble. Placing her fingers on his mouth she remembered his deep masculine voice that soothed her when the fear began to take over. The mouth that whispered I love you in the cold night air. Her head sank back down again on his chest as she thought about how wonderful it would be to hear him say those words again.

"I hope you do not hate me for all the lies I told you. I only wish you could tell me it is alright now. Please, Benjamin. Be strong. You must pull through this. I cannot live this life without you." Alex began to cry once again as the reality of this room engulfed her. The sound of that awful machine, tubes everywhere, and the slow blip on the small screen over Benjamin's head showing that what remained of his soul within this room was still fighting. Alex's heart pounded in her throat. Her skin tingled as if thousands of tiny needles were piercing through her.

"Mademoiselle?" The nurse said as she peered through the opening in the curtain. "I think that is enough for now. Monsieur Hunter needs to have a few more tests and we need the privacy."

"Alright. Give me a few more moments, please."

The nurse nodded, closed the curtains and walked away. Alex turned back to Benjamin and put her face directly in front of his. Her voice regained the strength she needed and she whispered to him again, "I know you can hear me. They tell me I must leave now. I promise you I will find who did this to you, but you must promise me that you will fight and come back to me—to us. You cannot lie here forever, and you must not die. Be strong, as you have been strong for me and fight this machine you are on." She stood up and leaned over one last time as she did the morning she left him in his home, only this time she leaned further and kissed his forehead and whispered, "I will be back, Ben, my love, and we will go home to the creature from the mountain."

Alex walked through the exit from the intensive care unit to find Inspecteur DePaul waiting for her. "Are you alright, Mademoiselle Boudreau?"

She was visibly shaken. She had lost that unwavering composure that so often served as her shield against the forces that tore at her sometimes fragile core. Her eyes were crimson red and her cheeks tear-stained as she somehow found the courage to lift her head up and respond, "No. I can hardly breathe. What are you people doing to find the men who did this?"

"Actually, I need to take you to our headquarters, where an artist is waiting to sketch those men from your hotel. Will you come with me?"

"Yes. How long will this take? I need to get back here soon. Benjamin looks so awful." Her voiced softened as the words trailed away.

"Not long mademoiselle. This will help us a great deal. Follow me."

CHAPTER 26

"**M**ADEMOISELLE **B**OUDREAU, **D**R. **V**OEKLER will be here in a few moments. He needs to see you." The young nurse at the attendant's desk informed Alex.

Alex took a seat in the waiting room just outside the ICU. The cold, off-white walls, the assemblage of worn-out and uncomfortable furniture, did little to ease the anxiety churning up within her. On the wall directly across from her hung a picture of a crucified Jesus, that same picture found in every hospital, morgue or other place where death was the center of conversation. Oh God, Alex thought, please Benjamin be alright. I need you.

"Mademoiselle Boudreau, I am Dr. Voekler." Alex looked up and saw a young man, perhaps in his early thirties, standing over her with his hand extended out to her.

Alex knew something was wrong. She jumped up, ignored the doctor's outstretched hand and asked, "What's wrong? Where is Ben?"

"Please, have a seat." He motioned for Alex to sit back down.

Without moving she blurted out, "Oh God, No. It cannot be. No!" Pushing past the doctor she burst through the unit door and ran toward Benjamin's room.

The doctor turned and protested, "Please. Wait!"

Standing in front of Benjamin's door were Inspecteurs DePaul and Durand, Officier Levesque and several hospital personnel. "Oh my God, what has happened?" Alex screamed as Inspecteur Depaul's outstretch arm halted her charge.

"Mademoiselle, please, return to the waiting room and I will be with you shortly," Inspecteur Depaul said, as he moved to his side to block the door.

"I will not, and I insist on seeing Benjamin this very minute. What is going on? Why will you not let me in?"

"Mademoiselle, monsieur Hunter is not in his room. To be frank, we do not know where he is. Neither the guards who were posted at his door, nor the hospital personnel know of his whereabouts. We are doing everything we can to get to the bottom of this, so please let us do our work and I will talk with you shortly."

"Do your work! If you were doing your work to begin with this never would have happened." Alex took a step back and with her arms tightly folded across her chest she glared at the Inspecteur. "I was here only several hours ago and there is no way Benjamin could have gotten out of bed and walked out of here. No way. You must have some idea what has happened. What are your own guards saying about all of this? Tell me what you know. Tell me!"

"Mademoiselle, please, we are doing everything we can to. . ."

Inspecteur Bergeron appeared in the doorway and interrupted. "The forensics boys are just finishing up dusting, but it doesn't appear we'll find any solid clues here. His clothes and other belongings are here. There's no evidence of any foul play, so all we may have at this point are some prints. But I doubt we will even have a match there."

"Mademoiselle," Inspecteur DePaul stood firm with his legs spread wide, his hands loosely cuffed in his front pockets and he continued, "at this moment we consider this to be a crime scene and we cannot allow you to go in. I think it best that you go with Officier Levesque back to the room where we first met; perhaps there is something you can recall that will help us with all of this? Time is very important here, and any information you can provide to us would be most helpful."

Alex's eyes darted from man to man. She looked for a clue, any clue that would give her the information they were withholding from her. "Inspecteur, if there is anything I can do to help find Benjamin, I will gladly do it. You have my word. I need to go in the room first and look around. Then I will gladly go with Officier Levesque."

Inspecteur DePaul looked over at Inspecteur Bergeron who gave a slight nod. "Very well. You may go in, but only briefly and please, do not interfere with the team that is inside."

Alex walked into the room and saw the opened curtains and the empty bed. There was no whooshing of the respirator, no beeps of the intravenous fluids pumping into his veins, no more blips on the screen. Everything was turned off. A cold chill crawled through her bones. She walked slowly over to the bed and stared at the wrinkled sheets. This cannot be happening, she thought.

"Excuse me. Is your name Alex?" a soft voice asked.

Without turning toward the woman, Alex muttered, "Yes, why?"

"Monsieur Hunter spoke your name just after you left here."

She whirled around and saw the same nurse that had asked her to leave earlier. Alex's eyes were red-rimmed, but a single sparkle appeared around each green iris when she heard the nurse's words. She pleaded, "What did he say?"

"He started to wake up and was trying to breath on his own so we took the ventilator tube out of his throat. He coughed a little and then began to say your name."

"What did he say?" Alex insisted.

"It wasn't very clear at first, but he said your name and then said something about meeting you on a mountain with an eagle. Does that make sense to you?"

Alex couldn't speak. She trembled even more and then sank to the floor beside the bed. She tucked her legs up against her chest and buried her head in her knees.

Then the nurse said one last thing, "I think he thought I was you because he grabbed my hand very hard and said, 'It's okay Alex. I understand why you did what you did. I will be fine and will wait for you. Go to the mountain and I'll be there.' Then he looked up at me and said, '*I love you Alex.*' He must have loved you deeply, because he struggled to come out of his coma to tell this to you. It was interesting because the whole time he was here he looked determined as if he knew what was going on and he was trying to wake up. You should know that he looked very peaceful after he was able to say those words to me."

Unable to lift her head and her arms still tightly wrapped around her knees, Alex whispered, "Thank you. You will never know how much this means to me."

"No, mademoiselle. I think I do." The nurse turned and left and Alex remained on the floor tightly coiled to keep the overwhelming pain from seeping deeper.

She rose up slowly and sat on the side of the bed. "You did hear me. You heard everything I said. I knew it. Thank you, Ben, for forgiving me and for loving me so much that you sent this message to me."

The once-impermeable shield that surrounded her composure and protected her vulnerability were beginning to again, provide the protection she would need. She rose from the bed. The silence in the room was broken when Alex raised her arms and an echo filled the room, "All I have left now is the promise I made to you. I will find who did this to you. Whoever you are, I am coming after you! You cannot hide from me! If it takes my entire life, I *will* find you!"

PART TWO

CHAPTER 27

"Russell Senate Office Building, please. I'm running late, so any time you can save would be most helpful."

Paul Brewster closed the door to the taxi, laid his briefcase on the cracked and faded vinyl seat, took a deep breath, and let out a heavy sigh. He was tired. Not just physically tired, that he had learned to live with over the years. Sleep deprivation was nothing new to him. He was tired of making these routine trips to the Hill where he had to exchange pleasantries and answer mindless questions from politicians who really had no understanding of the profound importance of his work. "Mr. Brewster, how can I justify these expenditures to the American people?" The inevitable question that he would have to answer with the same political acumen as his questioners.

Paul Brewster was the Director of The Defense Advanced Research Projects Agency, or DARPA as it was known within the defense and scientific communities. DARPA was a unique research organization established to maintain the U.S. military's technological preeminence. Essentially, it was the Defense Department's intellectual playground. With few bureaucratic impediments to deal with, it was free to pursue whatever innovative applied research it considered to be within the realm of national security. Over the years, it met the various technological challenges thrown at it and developed technologies that have many useful purposes in the civilian world. It created ARPANET, considered by many to be the forerunner to the internet, the Global Positioning System and the Hypermedia System. In spite of its successes, it was not without its detractors, and many of its efforts had been quite controversial.

Any scientific research agency in need of a Director to guide it through the political perplexities of Washington, D.C., would be ill advised if it did not bring a credentialed person of Paul Brewster's prominence onboard. Even before Mr. Brewster was awarded his doctorate degree from Princeton University, he was heavily recruited by some of the largest private companies and most prestigious academic institutions in the country. His doctoral thesis on Recombinant Monoclonal Antibody Technology had gained worldwide recognition and although he had his skeptics, there were many companies and institutions that were willing to gamble on Mr. Brewster's theory on monoclonal antibodies. The potential economic windfall if his theories were correct was unimaginable, not to mention the upheaval it could create within the international political communities.

Paul Brewster chose to begin his career as the Staff Director for the Senate Armed Services Committee; the same Committee where he was on his way to testify. That was a long time ago, and while the people he knew from those earlier days had all moved on, he remained acutely aware of the highly political nature underlying any Committee hearing. He knew that the real objectives of those hearings were not to unearth the truth, but for the Committee Members to each craft tough-nosed questions and pithy 'one liners' that they'd disseminate to their constituents in glossy-coated brochures, showing that *this* elected official was someone important. He was always mindful of the need to never embarrass the questioning Senator when he answered those questions, although he was often tempted to counter with a few mocking one-liners of his own.

After mulling over a few last-minute thoughts, he reached for his briefcase when the phone rang. "Yes, Julie?" Paul instinctively answered as he did dozens of times each day when he knew it was his assistant trying to reach him. She wouldn't be calling if it weren't important.

"Sure, put him on."

"Morning, Nate. I'm on my way to the Hill for another show and tell session."

Nathaniel Brooks, known as Nate to his close friends, had known Paul Brewster as a friend and business associate for more years than he cared to remember. As the current CEO of MIS Holdings, Nate had received dozens of federal grants from DARPA. In a deep throaty voice reminiscent of James Earl Jones, Nate began, "Give 'em hell Paul, or at least tell them what they want to hear. Look, we're on the closing end of wrapping up the final issues with SyNAPSE. I think we'll have it packaged and ready to go in just a few days. I'd like to get things moved out of here and into a safer spot as soon as we're done. So we need to get together. What's your schedule today and tomorrow?"

"Isn't this ahead of schedule? I thought the contract still had a few months left."

"Yeah we're ahead of our delivery date by a couple of months, but as important as this project is to all of us, I want to get it wrapped up and out of here before those auditors of yours show up." There was just enough of a brusque edge to Nate's voice that Paul knew there was some urgency to his request. This wasn't business as usual.

"Okay, I'm fairly certain I'm free this evening, so perhaps we can meet for dinner. I'll check with Julie and she can confirm things with you and make the arrangements. Does that work?"

"Sure. Sure Paul. Good luck today and see you tonight."

Paul sent a text to Julie and stuffed his iPhone back in his inside coat pocket. He seemed to be wondering aloud about the urgency in Nate's voice. Nate was a meticulous CEO who knew all the minutia of every project MIS was involved in. Not many people were aware of the SyNAPSE project. It was a Top Secret program aimed at developing electronic neuromorphic machine technology that scaled to biological levels. Mind-boggling, where we have come, Paul thought.

"Hey, here we are sir, and I got you here with time to spare." The taxi driver skidded to a stop at the front of the Russell Building and turned to face Paul, "What do you think?"

Looking down at his stainless steel Breitling Mark VI watch, Paul smiled, "It looks like another 10 minutes was just added to my day. Good job." Paul paid the beefy cab driver with a crisp bill and exited the cab. "Keep the change."

Walking briskly up the steep marble steps that led to the tubular shafts surrounding the imposing entrance, Paul thought about his future. Things were coming together quickly. Maybe this is it. Maybe I'll be out of here sooner than I think. Paul was muttering to himself as he swung open the large brass doors leading to the lobby of the building and he hurried down the hallway to Room SR 222.

"Maybe. . .just maybe. . ."

CHAPTER 28

LEX PUSHED THE LOBBY BUTTON IN THE ELEVATOR and the doors sealed shut. She stood on one side and looked over at the elderly couple and a nurse holding onto the back of the gentleman's wheelchair. When they reached the ground floor, the doors opened and Alex stood against one door as the nurse pushed the elderly man into the lobby. She stepped away from the elevator and a cold chill ran up her spine. She turned slowly and locked eyes with the man from her hotel room. The anger, the rage and the hatred all welled up within her as she faced the man who had taken her hopes and dreams from her.

Over the years, Alex had done many things which had brought hardship and financial ruin to others. Perhaps some of those people had despised her so much that they would stalk her and kill her if they had the opportunity. Never had she felt a desire to physically maim someone, but now, she could think of nothing else. Kill. Kill. The anger poured from her wounded heart and shot directly at this excuse of a man.

"Well, well, I think ya have pulled yur last stunt, pretty lady." The man whispered as he stood, his feet braced, blocking Alex's retreat. His hand was stuffed inside his jacket and Alex knew what he was holding.

He cannot do anything to me here in front of all these people, Alex thought, as she side-stepped toward the center of the lobby.

The man in the wheelchair dropped a bouquet of flowers and Alex rushed to his side and scooped them up. She offered to carry them outside to his car and she tagged along beside him. She exited through the electric glass double-doors of the main entrance to the hospital and her eyes landed on the other man across the street leaning against the familiar blue Peugeot. When he saw her walk out with the elderly couple he jolted upright to a nervous attention, not wanting to look obvious, but unwilling to let her flee again. She looked toward him and he put his right hand inside his coat and patted his rib cage a couple of times.

Alex helped the man climb into his car and tried to make conversation with his wife all the time knowing that she must do something, anything, to distract these men. A cab was parked several cars in front of where she stood. She knew this would be her only escape. She walked slowly to the front of the car and then turned and sprinted toward the cab. By the time she reached the cab, the man from the lobby was running after her. He stopped and screamed at his accomplice across the street, "Hurry up! Get in da car!"

"Okay, I need you to drive and drive fast!" Alex shouted at the cab driver as she dove into the back seat of the taxi.

She slammed the door and looked through the rear window and saw the rising clouds from burnt rubber as her pursuers spun around and sped after her.

Alex reached over the front seat and dropped 200 Euros next to the cab driver. "Listen, this will not be a long ride, but I need you to do exactly as I say. I need to get some distance between myself and that blue Peugeot tailing us."

The cab driver didn't look the adventurous type—he was more like a guy who would be content to sit for hours in some out-of-the-way bar drinking a beer, or maybe cheap whiskey. He was dressed in what was probably his daily uniform of old corduroy pants, a dark blue sweater and a canvas hat pulled tightly over his hairless head. He was overdue for his weekly shave.

The driver looked into his rear view mirror, "Anything you want, mademoiselle." He responded to Alex's demand, but more likely to the 200 Euros, by accelerating and changing lanes like he was on the lam with his own demons tailing him.

Alex shouted out directions as they raced through the streets of Levallois-Perret. It appeared that they'd gained some distance on the trailing car, but it was clear that they were not going to lose it.

With another plan in mind, Alex instructed the driver to turn right at the next corner, and to pull over in front of the first building. Alex knew this building well and remembered that she could cross through the lobby and onto the opposite street. She used to frequent the Veress Building when she attended high school in Paris. One of her best friends lived in that apartment building and she had dinner almost every Sunday with her and her family. Hopefully, nothing had changed.

Alex was halfway through the steel-framed entry doors before the cab screeched to a halt. She looked over her shoulder as the doors closed and she saw the Peugeot skidding around the corner. She raced through the lobby and exited as planned on Rue Aristide Briand. Looking frequently over her shoulder she quickly blended into the crowd of everyday Parisians. She knew she had lost them, but only temporarily. Surely they would know she had crossed through to Rue Aristide Briand.

The Hotel Hermes was a quaint, out-of-the-way boutique hotel that was just up the street. There, she would be able to regain her thoughts and to plan her next course of action. She continued walking up the street, and as she turned to enter the hotel, she paused, one last time to look around. Nothing. She had made it.

Alex was stretched out on the bed, staring aimlessly up at the ornate crystal chandelier dangling from the ceiling. Her mind grasped at the fractured pieces of information that spun endlessly in her head. The down feather-bed slowly began to soften the knots twisting around her spine.

What happened? Who are these guys? My life has been threatened. Oh God, Benjamin! What has happened to you? For the first time since the two men entered her apartment earlier that day, she had the time to wrestle with her thoughts, to question what had happened. Why was Benjamin suspected of pirating the information, yet he was still free? How did he disappear? Why would someone do this to him? Surely the GEN information could not be that important? What about Andre? Was he really telling me the truth? Andre has the GEN research information, why has someone not tried to come after him?

Alex rose from the bed and walked over to the window that framed the interior courtyard below. She bent down on her knees and opened the window. She closed her eyes and let the gentle breeze cool her flushed face. Think Alex. Think. Time is so important here. She mentally raced through her past assignments, thinking maybe there was some connection there. Someone could certainly be after me and they are using Ben to get to me. And my mother!

The police? Maybe now is the time for me to call them and tell them what I know, Alex thought. Maybe they can help me. Jesus, who am I kidding? The only thing the police will do when they find out what really happened is stop me from doing what I need to do—find Ben's real kidnappers. These two men that are after me may be connected to Ben's disappearance, but they are not the real brains behind this. No, someone is using Ben to get to me and somehow the GEN research is connected to all this.

She pushed herself up from the floor and crept back to the bed. She threw her tired body on it, and rested her head against the fabric-covered headboard. Her hands gripped the back of her head and she mumbled to herself, "Damn, this clouded past of mine has finally caught up to me. Everything I have done, everyone I have ruined has come back to me. I should have seen this. How could I have been so naïve?"

Pulling another down pillow out from under the pink Jacquard cotton bedspread, she placed it behind her head, leaned back and closed her eyes. She thought about the DGSE, and wished there was some way to get them to help her. But she had burned all her bridges there. It wasn't just that her sudden resignation had wrinkled the suits of her superiors. No, that wasn't the first time the DGSE had lost one of its top agents. On more than one occasion Alex had managed to infiltrate lucrative corporate technology just before the Agency was ready to pounce.

The Frankfurt Stock Exchange used a Linux-based trading system named CAAC 40. It was considered the fastest trading system in the world, with trade completion speeds of up to 132 microseconds. Her initial surveillance uncovered what she knew were DGSE agents looking for the same technology, but Alex struck first. She stole the computer code that allowed the Exchange to engage in those trades. She encrypted the files and transferred them over the internet. She then deleted the program she used to encrypt the files and deleted the computer's "bash history" which records the most recent commands executed on the computer. The Exchange suffered a three hour trading outage and untold embarrassment. While human error was the public version of the problem, the international tension between Germany and France that arose over this event told another story. To bury her own tracks, Alex had re-inserted commands in the "bash history" that led investigators directly to the DGSE central computer system.

No, the DGSE wouldn't lift a finger to help her.

She needed to find out what was on that hard drive. She needed help.

There was a fellow she knew in graduate school at the University of Paris who majored in genetics whom she thought was now a professor at the University. What was his name? She sat up and swung her feet around to the side of the bed looking around the room for a telephone book. She found one in the nightstand on the side of the bed.

"Good afternoon, University of Paris. May I help you?" A pleasant voice came over the line.

"Hello. May I have your science department?" Alex asked.

"Hold on, I will connect you through."

Waiting for someone to pick up the line, Alex wondered what she was going to say. Hi, there was this guy I knew a long time ago. I cannot remember his name, but he was tall with dark brown wavy hair, and always wore funny wire-rimmed glasses.

A soft spoken male voice said, "Science Department."

"Hello. I am looking for a professor there who teaches genetics. He has been there for about 10 years and could be teaching several other courses as well. I know he is a geneticist. I am doing some genetic research myself and I am sorry, but I just cannot remember his name." Alex sounded confident and assertive.

"Let me see," the man replied. "We have a Dr. Vimont, a Dr. Appel, and Dr. Belanger. There are also two part-time faculty members who teach here and at a few other universities. They would be Dr. Kress and Dr. Diderot."

"Is that Charles Diderot?" Alex's voice rose.

"Why yes, yes it is."

"Could you connect me with him or give me his extension number please?" Alex asked.

"I just saw him a few moments ago so I am sure he is around somewhere. Hang on and I will see if he is in his office."

Alex clenched the phone so tightly that her hand was sweating and her fingertips turned white. Please be there, she thought, please.

"Hello, Dr. Diderot here."

Now what? Alex thought. "Hi, Charles. I hope you will remember me. We were in graduate school together. I am Alexandra Boudreau."

"Alexandra. . .Boudreau. . . Ah, of course I remember you. We used to study together at times. How could I forget?"

Alex remembered how warm and friendly Charles always was. He was a classic nerd in every sense of the word with his oversized eye glasses that always slid down his nose. She always did like him. He was a genius, and she knew he was the right person to help her.

Alex began, "I am so glad you remember me. I have a huge favor to ask of you. It is rather sensitive, but I do think you will find it very interesting."

"I must say, I am intrigued already. Go on."

"I have some genetic engineering information I cannot decipher by myself. I could pay you for your time and it is very important that I find out what all this means right away." Alex waited for his answer.

"Of course I can help you. Anything for a fellow Sorbonne alum. I can meet with you tomorrow if you like. Can you tell me anything else about this?"

"I would rather explain it all when we get together. Can I stop by your office tomorrow?"

"Sure thing. I have all morning open. Can you come early? Say 8:00?"

"That would be great. What is your campus address?"

Alex gathered the details of where to meet her old friend Charles. "I will see you tomorrow morning, Charles. Oh, and Charles? Thank you."

CHAPTER 29

WINDING THROUGH THE STREETS TOWARD THE University of Paris reminded Alex of her college years. She remembered riding her rickety old bike up and down those narrow cobblestone streets to her classes each day. Not much had changed over the years. The small family-owned bakeries with the aroma of freshly baked croissants; the old ladies still walked the streets peddling their fresh cut flowers; and the children darted in and out of the parked cars playing their games of tag. What wonderful memories. She wondered how her life could have changed so much—how it could have turned so many agonizing corners and how she ended up here today, running from the authorities and Benjamin's kidnappers, unable to trust anyone, and so alone.

Alex sat in the back of the cab and stared out the window at the world that was now so meaningless to her. As they approached the University, she asked the driver to drop her off at the Curie Building. She thought about what could possibly be on that hard drive. Clearly it was something very disturbing or Charles wouldn't have phoned her at 6:00 am that morning and insisted she meet him again right away.

She quite enjoyed seeing him yesterday. He had lost most of his hair, but still wore those same wire-rimmed glasses that never did fit his nose. She had to keep herself from giggling several times as they slid very slowly down his nose until he would finally push them back up to the bridge where they belonged.

He seemed quite interested in what she had to tell him about the genetic research information she had obtained from that company in America. She explained that she was working for the French government and went to this company in America to find out more about the research they were doing on Cystic Fibrosis, but thought she may have obtained some other, more sensitive, possibly even illegal, information. She told Charles that before she handed this over to anyone she wanted to know what it was. She said that she didn't trust the government's motivation and was suspicious of their intentions. She knew that would get a rise out of Charles, and he'd be aching for the chance to get involved in some sort of secret government operation. She remembered he was always into anti-government groups in college, but mainly because he was so disheartened that the government wouldn't provide the needed research support to the universities and other scientists involved in cutting-edge experiments. She explained to him that this was very top secret information and he couldn't tell anyone about it. He promised to help her and said he'd get back to her in a few days. So, the fact that he called so early the very next morning was a bit disturbing to Alex. It meant there was more to the contents of that hard drive than what she knew.

The cab stopped in front of the large, gray, stone-carved Curie Building. Alex paid the driver and quickly walked toward the building. Even though it was still early in the fall season, this was a cold, dark morning in Paris. A bone-chilling dampness hung in the air that penetrated her clothing and stung her covered skin. Alex could barely eat these past several days and felt light-headed each time she stood up. So, walking from the cab seemed to take more effort for her tired and weary body.

Once inside the building, Alex felt warm and protected. She rushed up the stairs to the second floor. The mottled teak door to Charles' office reflected the untold years that this prestigious institution had served as a model for higher learning. She knocked on the door and heard the shout, "It is open," from within.

"Hello, Charles," Alex said. She was smiling not because she had any reason to be happy, but because she was glad to see a familiar face.

With his glasses at the bottom of his nose, Charles placed his index finger on the middle iron piece and pushed them back up to where they belonged. He turned toward her and motioned to the chair beside him, "I am glad you are here. Come, sit down."

Charles' office was in such disarray that Alex wondered how he could possibly find anything in all the mess. He had books lying in all different directions on the two large bookcases surrounding his desk. One book would be turned backward so you could only see the pages, the next was lying on its side, and the next three or four were placed so you could read the jackets, but two were upside down. His entire bookcase was organized in what must have been his own systematic design. At the top of the shelves were stacks and stacks of loose papers. On the ground in one corner were two stacks of loose papers about two and three feet high. His desk was probably some sort of old oak, but you could barely see it, as it, too, was covered with books and papers. His old wooden swivel chair swung in endless circles if you'd let it and was the type that would lean way back for a good nap on a warm summer's day. A large glass paned window captured a view of the northern quad and showcased the stately and historic old gray stone buildings protected by majestic Elm trees.

Alex pulled a chair over to Charles' computer screen and sat down beside him. "I know you may not understand some of this, but I want to try to explain what I have found on your hard drive. I am not done yet, but you must look at this with me." Charles was not looking at Alex and his slow serious tone differed from the animated and jovial person she had met with yesterday.

"If I am reading the expression on your face correctly, Charles, this is not what it is supposed to be, is it?" Alex asked, as she watched Charles nervously rubbing his hands together. He looked frightened to her.

"Well, I do not know really." Charles shuffled through a pile of papers stacked on the far corner of his desk, pulled out a notebook and continued, "First, this hard drive of yours does contain some very interesting information offering new cures for Cystic Fibrosis. If this information proves accurate, someone has developed the first method of gene therapy to accurately fight and possibly eradicate this disease. Cutting-edge stuff, really."

"That is the information I knew I had, but there must be something more to all this," Alex insisted.

"There certainly is, but I do not yet have all the answers. There is some research data for a project involving the creation of a synthetic, mutated virus that can actually be injected into human beings. Once injected, the virus will replicate, the DNA host genome is altered and new gene sequences are expressed. The research is actually a type of genetic engineering of human beings. This type of genetic engineering has been successful in plants and several laboratory studies with rats, but nothing, and I mean *nothing* like this, has ever been remotely considered to be possible with human beings." Charles tilted back in his chair with such force that he had to catch himself on the edge of his desk to prevent a sure fall.

Righting himself, and without missing a beat, Charles continued, "Without getting into all the details, and I have not studied all the contents just yet, this research could potentially be a breakthrough that was once thought to be unachievable—genetically engineering a human being that can be resistant to death itself. This is very tricky stuff. Scores of research teams have made stabs at this, trying everything from starvation to hormone treatments. Gene therapies, where artificial genes are inserted into an organism to boost cell life, are the latest and greatest in life-extension science, but they have only been proven to extend a lifespan by 20 percent in rats. Nothing like this was ever thought to be achievable."

Alex stood up and brushed her fingers through her hair. Clutching the back of her head, she asked, "Who do you think would want to develop a synthetic virus of this nature?"

Charles held his hands out, palms up and said, "I cannot say for sure. All the data has been encrypted and I have to decrypt it piece by piece. This is a very slow process, but I will get through everything I have as soon as possible. So, while there are many beneficial medical and other scientific uses this could be used for, there is a rather heated, on-going debate within the scientific community that man might be overreaching when we create viruses that never before existed. This debate is shrouded with moral, religious and ethical beliefs about what is our proper role in the natural world, a debate largely about non-physical harms or harms to well-being."

Alex walked around to the rear of her chair, bent over slightly and gripped the top. "I probably should not ask because I do not know if I really want to know the answer, but you mentioned that this synthetic virus can alter the DNA host genome. If it is possible to produce positive results from these alterations, would it not also be possible to produce alterations that could be used for other purposes? Maybe military uses? Do you know anything about this whole process and how it works, exactly?"

Charles looked intense. His brow was furrowed, and Alex could tell that she was not going to like his answer. "There are potentially unlimited uses for this discovery. What really concerns me here is that the virus has encoded loyalty right into the DNA, by developing genetically programmed locks to create "tamper proof" virions. Should this virus somehow not respond in its intended manner, it has a biological kill switch built right into it. Someone, somewhere, controls this and if the human does not perform as directed—ZAP—it, or he, or she is dead."

"Oh, God. I cannot believe I have stumbled upon something so utterly horrifying," Alex muttered as she returned to her chair and rested her chin in the palms of her hands. Her fingers were cupped around her lips.

"Utterly horrifying is putting it mildly, Alexandra. Where exactly did you get this information?" Charles was sitting on the front edge of his rickety chair. His head was cocked to one side and he bit down on his lower lip as he awaited Alex's answer.

Alex remained statue-like for some time, still trying to absorb the gravity of this information. She leaned back in the chair and crossed her legs. "Listen Charles, this is a very long story and I still have not put all the pieces together myself, but if I am going to figure all this out, I am going to need your help. I obtained this information on the virus purely by accident and already one person is in serious trouble—a man who is very special to me." At the thought of Benjamin, Alex paused, and again leaned forward in her chair. Her hands still held her chin and she felt a stinging pain jolt through her once again.

Charles watched Alex. He reached over and placed his hand on her shoulder, and said, "Something is going on here, and maybe I do not need to know everything. I do want to help you, Alexandra, but how do I know that I will be safe? And I will not find myself in some kind of trouble, as well?"

Alex looked up at him and chose her words carefully, "You must know that you *are* potentially in danger. And I suppose the fact that I have gotten you involved this far could mean that you are already in danger. I can guarantee that I have told no one about you, and no one could possibly know that I have come to you for help. Only you and I know about this potentially lethal organism now, except of course, those who created it and are already after me. It is your decision, but if you do not help me, the danger here is too great. This virus can potentially be delivered to a rogue nation, or countless others who have the sole intention of using it for its worst-feared consequences. I cannot live with this knowledge and do nothing about it. . . can you?"

Charles knew better than Alex the potential for harm, even devastation, if this information were to fall into the wrong hands. His response was immediate, "No, I cannot either. I will do whatever you need me to do. But I have to admit, I am scared." His voice tapered off ever-so-slightly, and his glasses again slid down to the tip of his nose.

"I am really sorry to involve you this way. I have nowhere else to turn, nowhere else to go."

"I said I was afraid, but I am also very excited. This is some amazing stuff and I would love to be a part of deciphering this data in some way—maybe I will even be famous someday." They both laughed for a moment, easing the tension somewhat.

"Great," Alex said. "I need you to keep looking over this information and to make sure you have it all translated for me. I need to go back to California. I can keep in touch with you from there." She reached into her purse and grabbed a cell phone. "When we need to communicate make sure you only use this phone and keep it on you at all times. It has a pre-paid phone service, and is registered to an untraceable name. Our conversations will be secure on this line."

She handed him the cell phone along with her own cell number and continued, "We can call each other at anytime, but our calls must be brief, less than 60 seconds at the most. We can call back, but each call must be brief."

Charles took the phone and held it out in front of him. The corners of his lips rose sharply and he continued to stare at the cell phone. "Okay. You know, I have thought for a longtime that I need to do something different—you know, do something new to bring a little excitement into my life. I guess this ought to do it."

CHAPTER 30

"**G**OOD AFTERNOON. I AM HERE IN TOWN ON some business. I wonder if Mr. Paulson may have a few minutes available to see me?" Alex stood before the receptionist at GEN.

"I believe that Mr. Paulson is in a meeting at the moment, but if you will please give me your name, I'll check with his assistant."

Alex knew she might be taking a chance by using her real name or even her assumed name, but she needed to see Murray. Standing tall with her hands crossed and clutching her purse, she responded, "Yes, I am Alexandria Pancini."

Alex walked over to the row of chairs in the reception area and sat down where she had a clear view of the receptionist and the offices down the hall.

After leaving Dr. Diderot's office yesterday, Alex phoned her mother and was relieved she had made it to Uncle Djamel's without any problems. Alex tried, unsuccessfully, to ease her mother's concern. She would have to try to make it up to her when this was all over.

Before she left, there had been little time to do anything other than purchase some clothes and other items for this trip. On the red-eye from Paris, she drifted in and out of consciousness as she attempted to piece together the barrage of events thrust upon her which had forced her to once again assume the role of the predator stalking its prey.

Over the years, Alex's intuition had served her well. It had become a part of her arsenal, sort of a sixth sense, and she relied heavily on it when the need arose to make an on-the-spot decision. With some people, this was an innate quality—you either had it or you didn't. With others, it was something you eventually recognized and learned to trust over time. With Alex, there was no difference between conscious thought and instinct.

In one of her early assignments, she had been asked to probe the inner workings of a financial institution suspected of laundering hundreds of millions of dollars through off-shore banks. It was one of the rare times she had actually been retained to uncover unlawful activity instead of create it. It was also one of the very few times she had worn the white hat. She found herself in Philadelphia. She had routinely uncovered the footprints that led her from the dirty money hiding in several Cayman Island bank accounts back to the targeted institution. The problem was, those footprints were more like hoof marks left by a stampeding herd of cattle. Nothing could be that easy, she had thought at the time.

She was just about to download the information she needed to take back to her client when a wave of indecision made her hesitate. It was in that fleeting moment of indecision that her inner instincts swelled with alarm. Had she proceeded with downloading the incriminating evidence it would have triggered a set of safeguards that the institution had put in place in the unlikely event something like this were to occur. Most of the funds held in the various accounts would have automatically been dispersed in a series of wire transfers designed to land in different accounts, in different banks, in different financial havens. The incriminating trail and the funds would have all but disappeared, except for a small amount which would have been held in the name of Alex Romano, her assumed name at the time.

Now, Alex's intuition led her to conclude that Benjamin had walked innocently into the middle of this collapsing web she herself had created. If Benjamin was in fact accused, or even suspected, of pirating the Cystic Fibrosis research he would not have been allowed to come to Paris on such short notice. No, the police would have certainly detained him for questioning and possibly not permitted him to leave the country. At the very least, they would have taken his passport. But with Benjamin now missing, it became easier to lay all the blame on him so that the theft would not be further investigated. Whoever had undertaken the research and development of the synthetic virus would have no problem killing Benjamin or anyone else who stepped in their way. The only possible way to clear Benjamin's name from all this was to find out who was behind the development of this wicked organism. What better place to start than the source of the information itself.

"Ms. Pancini," Alex lifted her head, "if you'll please follow me I'll show you to Mr. Paulson's office. He does have a few minutes available now, and he said he would very much like to see you."

As they walked down the hallway, Alex noticed the sparse surroundings. The building was an old industrial warehouse that had been converted to GEN's particular use. There were very few windows, and the interior walls were thinly partitioned. Obviously, everyone who worked here would have little privacy since sound carried everywhere.

Upon entering Murray's office, Alex stopped and peered around. This was certainly different. Not only was his office neatly organized and laid out, but he had all the latest gadgets spread out around his desk. State-of-the-art computer system, video conferencing capability, digital office boards, and everything else an older man needed to have in the way of executive toys. This office was more likely to be found on the upper floors of an office tower in a major city than an old converted warehouse in Alameda. Alex helped herself to a seat at a small conference table.

She scoured her surroundings trying to see if there was anything—a picture, a knickknack, a plaque—which would mean something to her. "Well, Ms. Pancini," Alex heard as she turned toward the door. "This is a surprise. I'm Murray Paulson. It's nice to meet you." Murray walked through the door and over to where Alex was sitting and extended his hand.

"Mr. Paulson, it is nice of you to take the time to see me on such short notice," Alex replied as she clasped Murray's hand firmly, but remained seated. "I am in town on some business and I wanted to stop by to meet you. You may know that I am a friend of Benjamin Hunter's." Alex had already decided there was no need to play cat and mouse. She needed to be direct.

Murray moved around to the side of the conference table, pulled out a chair and sat down facing Alex. With his left hand resting comfortably on the table, he bowed his head slightly and replied, "I still can't believe what's happened. Ben is the rock behind this company, and I love him like a son. I am simply devastated by what has happened."

Raising his head and now looking directly at Alex, Murray continued, "You know, Ben told me about you. In fact, wasn't he on his way to meet you in Europe?"

"Yes, he was. He telephoned me just before he flew over to Paris and he had some very disturbing news. That was the main reason he had come to Paris. He wanted to talk to me about it." Alex remained calm with her legs crossed, her left hand gripped her right forearm. This, she thought, will be interesting to see how he responds now.

"Well I must tell you, Ms. Pancini, I didn't know very much about Ben's personal life. As you probably are aware, he is the controlling shareholder of this company, and we have worked together very closely, but outside the office we didn't socialize together. We each had our own separate lives. So I don't know why you have come to me to talk about this so-called disturbing news."

Okay mister, Alex thought. She stiffened in her chair and her sharp gaze caught Murray's eyes. He instinctively lowered his head to deflect her piercing glare. "Look Mr. Paulson, I am not here to discuss anything about anyone's personal life, and I think you know that. Ben told me that certain research information was stolen from GEN and that you thought he may have been involved somehow. Ben knew who may have taken this information and he was coming over to talk to me about it. He said he might possibly need my help. I am here for only one reason—to find Benjamin, and to see that he does not get falsely accused for any of this."

Murray remained calm. "Ms. Pancini, we do have a problem here at GEN which centers around some missing research. But I am hardly at liberty to discuss that with you or anyone else, except with my Board of Directors and the authorities. Why would Ben want to discuss this matter with you?" Murray placed both hands on the arms of his chair, his fingers gripping the ends. "It seems to me that you need to be a little more specific about your involvement in this whole situation."

"As I said, Mr. Paulson, I am here to find who has kidnapped Ben, and to see he does not get his name smeared. He did not take this research information, and you know that, as well."

"I am a bit confused," Murray offered as he continued in his attempt to pull information out of Alex. "How do you know he didn't take the research? How do you even know that any research may have in fact been stolen? What are you really doing here?"

"Mr. Paulson, I am not going to discuss any details about how I know what I know. I came to you for help in finding Ben, and clearing his name. Do you not care about that?"

Sitting forward and peering directly at Alex now from across the table Murray said, "Look Ms. Pancini, I am truly shocked at what has happened. I just can't believe any of it. But how do I really know that Ben did not steal our research, and that you aren't his accomplice?"

Alex laughed at this finger-pointing. "If that were the case, would I be so dim-witted as to fly back here from Europe, come to your office and ask you for help? You know that Ben in no way had anything to do with this. Why can we not work together? I am sure we could help one another."

"I want to believe that Ben was not involved in any of this. I want him back as much as anybody. I understand that he was thrown from a car or something?"

Alex shivered at this statement.

Murray stood and asked Alex if she wanted a cup of coffee. He began to walk to the door and Alex quickly rose from her chair, "If you leave this room, then so will I." She now knew not to let this man out of her sight unless she was safely away from him.

"Oh, no, please, you don't need to leave. I'm just going into the next room to grab some coffee. I'll be right back." He reached for the brass plated door knob on his office door.

To make a phone call, Alex thought. "I am ready to leave now. I will call you in the next couple of days." In those split few seconds Alex had figured it all out. There was no way he could have known about Ben's car accident. The French authorities were very careful not to release any details while they were investigating what they now classified as an attempted murder and a kidnapping. As she stood facing Murray, it took all the strength she had not to scream out at him or hurt him in some way. She looked in his eyes with all the hatred and anger any human could possibly muster and opened the door to leave.

"Oh excuse me. I didn't know you were busy, Murray." The sudden opening of the door before he could knock startled him. A casually-dressed man with a salt and pepper beard jumped aside as Alex whisked past him.

Murray watched her march down the hallway. Her footfalls landed on the concrete flooring without making a sound. He shook his head and let out a long sigh——a sigh of relief that her powerful persona was gone.

"Let me guess. She's a disgruntled saleswoman that hasn't met her quota this month, and you didn't help her out?" the bearded man said with a grin.

"No. No, Henry. It's nothing quite that horrific. I need a few minutes alone. I'll buzz you when I'm ready." Murray stood staring down the empty hallway. In that instant, he knew she knew.

Henry saw the color of fear painted on his boss's face. "Sure thing, boss." Henry turned and closed the door.

CHAPTER 31

FROM HER HOTEL WINDOW, ALEX COULD SEE THE EARLY morning fog roll in as it blanketed the Bay and hid the still slumbering morning sun. She sipped her coffee and stared blankly out the window. She was able to get some sleep last night, but her mind remained focused on Murray. Benjamin had spoken of him several times to her and she also knew from the dossier prepared by Andre that Murray and Benjamin were very close. Why would Murray do this? Using GEN's facilities for the research was one thing, but kidnapping Ben made no sense. Still, how else could Murray know that Benjamin had been thrown from a car unless he was somehow involved? Somehow. Maybe there was still someone else other than Murray? Perhaps he is not acting on this by himself?

Alex stood up and walked over to the small parquet-topped writing desk across from the foot of her bed and quickly booted up her laptop. Pulling up her email server she addressed an email to Murray and with that now familiar anger and rage locked tightly within her, she began to type.

Murray -

I now know who you are and what you have done. Yes, I know what the information is you are really seeking. I have it. I have absolutely no interest in your research. I have three demands and if they are met, I will leave you and this country forever.

- Where is Ben?

- Who else is involved in Ben's kidnapping?

- Clear Ben's name - permanently

If these demands are not met, the information I have will be turned over to the authorities and you will have to figure out how to clear your own name.

A piece of advice - do not come after me. If anything happens to me, I have left specific instructions with various people to deliver this material you seek to the media. I could release this information now, on my own, but then I may never find Ben or learn who masterminded this scheme. You would be the only one implicated in this dreadful nightmare. If there are others involved, I believe we both know that you have no alternative,

I will contact you shortly.

After re-reading the email, Alex's index finger lingered on the send button for a few short moments. Left with what she believed to be no other choice her intuition made her decision. She firmly pressed the button. In an instant her screen was blank. Now, she thought, this should set everything into motion. If Murray was involved with someone else, this should start to flush them out.

Alex walked into the bathroom and looked in the mirror. Now that everyone knows what I look like, she thought, it was time to look like someone else. She reached across to her travel bag and pulled out a pair of scissors. Very carefully, she cut. Strands of her long black mane fell to the bathroom sink. As she cut, she looked in the mirror with a sheepish grin and chuckled, I wonder what the housekeepers will think of this? With her new hairdo in place, she went into the bedroom and rummaged through her clothing. She chose a pair of old blue jeans with holes in the knees, a baggy, long purple sweatshirt and high top white Adidas sport shoes. She stuffed what remained of her hair into a brown wool tweed Newsboy cap, tilted just slightly to the right. Her green eyes were hidden by a pair of morning-after-the-party shades. She crammed the rest of her belongings in an unassuming black leather backpack and took a last look at herself.

She headed down the hotel stairs. When she reached the lobby, she turned right and made her way toward the side entrance. She exited the hotel and walked briskly up the sidewalk. It was only a few days ago, she thought, I was walking in the streets of Paris doing the same thing—running, hiding.

She hailed a taxi and slid into the wrinkled black vinyl seat before the driver had come to a complete stop. "Listen," Alex instructed the driver, "I need you to take me to Mill Valley. I will show you where I need to go when we get closer."

CHAPTER 32

"Mr. Brewster, we've been expecting you, sir," intoned the nattily dressed Maître d' as Paul calmly, but vigorously, shook the lapels of his tan, London Fog trench coat. It was a typical September evening in the City, with sheets of rain sending people scurrying to their dry havens.

"Thank you Donald. Whew, another one of those nights. I'm expecting one more person to join me this evening." Paul instinctively handed his trench coat to the man with the extended arms.

Paul was unconsciously scanning the dining area for familiar faces when the Maître d' interjected, "Your party has already arrived Mr. Brewster. Please, allow me to show you to your table."

The Caucus Room was not one of Washington's power restaurants steeped in rich political history like the Willard Intercontinental Washington, where Senator Henry Clay introduced Washington, D.C. to the mint julep, or the Article

One-American Grill & Lounge, where on- lookers could spot the "who's who" of Washington. No, as the restaurant critics say: The Caucus Room is expensive, leathery and meaty. A new restaurant by Washington standards, the dining room reflected the power structure of Washington: congress men and women, sports stars, lobbyists, media celebrities and anyone looking to make a connection to the ever-changing inner power circle. Yes, this was a town where deals were made around the clock, and everyone had a smug sense of importance that just couldn't be satiated.

As Paul was escorted to his table, he made a point of stopping at each table to shake hands and share good-natured remarks with those he knew. And he knew everyone. The seemingly endless walk was halted when Paul was seated at his table across from Nate.

Paul had deliberately chosen this restaurant. The din echoing from the walls served as a perfect muffler for these types of conversations. "Good to see you, Nate, although if I've judged correctly from the tone of our earlier conversation this isn't purely social. There is some urgency to this meeting." Paul was careful to always channel conversations to his advantage no matter whom he was with, and he could tell by simply looking at Nate that this was a meeting where trivial platitudes were unwarranted.

Nate had been leaning back in his leather-padded chair with his arms evenly placed on each armrest. Though he appeared calm, the inner stiffness of his muscles filtered through to his frozen expression. He looked anything but the relaxed and carefree businessman he tried to project. "Your perceptiveness hasn't changed over the years. If anything, I would have to say that you've become more discerning."

Nate leaned forward in his chair, his eyes fixed on Paul's deadpan gaze. "We've done it, Paul. We have actually done it." Nervously rolling his eyes from side to side to assure absolute privacy, he continued, "I spoke to Evan, and they've corrected the minor glitches they encountered last week. All of the new tests have been run, the safety measures are effective. We have created the synthetic virus that we intended, and it can effectively be inserted directly into the human system by a mosquito. I really couldn't believe this, but everything checks out, Paul. We're ready to deliver this now."

The corners of Paul's pursed narrow lips turned ever so slightly upward and he found it impossible to conceal the triumphant elation running through his inner seams. The two men sat motionless and their minds raced to absorb the magnitude of this giant leap. The din of the room had vanished, and each man was surrounded by his own unfathomable thoughts.

Paul ran Nate through a litany of questions on the procedures used to evaluate the effectiveness of the protocol, the safety measures that had been implanted in the synthetic organism, the security measures surrounding this discovery and other questions intended to validate the entire project.

To most anyone familiar with the SyNAPSE program, it was to design and develop a method to insert electronic circuit probes into insects to create insect cyborgs that could demonstrate controlled flight. The insects would be used in a variety of military and homeland security applications. This contrived perception of the SyNAPSE program was artfully created by Paul and he had covertly pushed through a grant for funding this project and made sure that it was awarded to MIS Holdings.

The reality of the SyNAPSE project was quite different. MIS Holdings was awarded $52.5 million and they were to manage the project and monitor the results. What Nate had successfully developed, through MIS Holdings and its co-researchers, was the creation of a new, synthetic virus containing selected genes that could be turned on and off at will. Insects were to be used as the vector for delivering this virus. The insect would be implanted with a circuit board that was just 8 x 7 mm, with a total weight of 500mg and a battery capacity of 16mAh. Once inserted into the human system by a mosquito, the new synthetic viral genes would make it possible to create tamper-proof cells. This would remove the randomness of evolutionary advancement and give birth to genetically engineered, living, breathing human beings. The virus encoded the genes with protein products that bolstered cell resistance to death. These bio-engineered humans could ultimately be programmed to live well beyond the normal life span of normal humans. In the unlikely event that these super-human specimens ever fell into enemy hands, their DNA was encoded with a "loyalty" factor.. Additionally, the synthetic virus would be traceable, using DNA sequence information, similar to a serial number on a handgun. And if that didn't work, the fail-safe was a genetically coded kill switch.

"Let me be the first to congratulate you on this pioneering discovery Nate. I must admit that I didn't expect things to progress quite this rapidly, but I will most assuredly direct all my attention to this project now so that we can securely deliver the final product." Paul's mind was galloping ahead as he spoke. There was certainly much to be done in a very short period of time.

Nate again leaned forward and spoke in a hushed tone, "I've had a couple calls from Alan Price in the past few days, and he's been asking about the missing files. I don't know how he found out, but I think I've put his worst fears to rest."

Paul raised an eyebrow. "What'd you tell him?"

"He wanted to put some of his guys on this to find out what happened, but when I told him that Garran's taking care of everything, he seemed okay with things. Garran supplies the outside security for Starling Defense Applications so he knows the best guy possible is on it."

"What is the latest news from Garran? Are our files safe?" Paul asked.

Nate took another look around and spoke softly, "No. All our research was embedded in several files in GEN's system and they were part of the files that were stolen. They're fully encrypted so they would need the key to decrypt the data into a readable form. Garran knows who took the files and he has some of his people on it now. He expects things to be cleared up quickly."

Paul paused to reflect upon what he just heard. He had utter and complete confidence in Garran, otherwise, this disturbing news would have sent him reeling with a fury of indignation. "We do have either the original research materials or copies somewhere, so at least we still have what we need, right?"

"We do," Nate said. "By the end of the day tomorrow, all of the research, including the new results, will be secretly embedded and safely dispersed throughout several new files. This should provide us with the security we need, but I still want to deliver the product as soon as possible so we can scrub our own files. I don't know why, but I just feel that those auditors of yours are due to pay us a visit."

"When are we supposed to deliver everything, Nate? Any update on that?"

"Since we're ahead of schedule, I've moved the delivery date up. Right now, everything is planned for a week from today."

Paul sat and contemplated everything Nate had said. With his fingers loosely gripping the edge of the table, he looked at Nate, and said, "We have a lot riding on this, and if we don't find out who took those files and get them back, then I'm afraid our payday will disappear. In fact, I'm certain of it. You can bet that Alan will be all over this until it's solved."

"You're right, Paul. Garran and I are in constant touch and I'm willing to bet my share of the take that Garran fixes things shortly— Very shortly."

With a hint of a sparkle returning to Paul's eyes and a renewed crispness to his voice, he raised his wine glass and proposed a celebratory toast. "To the past, to the present, and to our prosperous future."

The two wine glasses were raised and quietly, but forcefully, the two men confidently cemented their future with the links of the past.

CHAPTER 33

THE CAB DRIVER WOUND HIS WAY THROUGH THE streets of San Francisco toward the Golden Gate Bridge, and Alex closed her eyes and processed Murray's remarks yet again. How could Ben's father-like figure be involved in something so destructive? She knew what this deception would mean to the countless children and families who placed so much hope and faith in this new genetic research on Cystic Fibrosis.

An offhanded comment from the driver interrupted her thoughts, "A beautiful day, 'ay madam?" Alex looked out over the bay to her right, at Alcatraz and the Berkeley Hills. She turned slightly around to glimpse the City now just beginning to glimmer in the reflection of the morning sun. Then the pounding in her head came once again. The bridge, she thought. . .this bridge. How she longed to be driving her car once again to meet Benjamin, to be taken on another journey, to release her demons.

With her window completely rolled down, the memories flooded her mind as the sound of each cable stay whirred past her like the tick-tick-tick of a clock. She could almost feel him, smell him in the fresh salty air. This was all so intoxicating. For a brief moment, Alex was lost in Benjamin's world.

The jolt of the cab crossing the metal grate from the bridge onto the highway jarred Alex from her trance.

She instructed the driver how to get to the Mill Valley address. Once on the road, Alex asked the driver to drop her off at a home about a half mile below Benjamin's. She needed to be careful, and didn't want to drive up to the home where people could be waiting. She paid and thanked the driver.

She walked up the hill and turned into a heavily wooded area several hundred yards below the driveway. She pushed her way through the brush and took in the smells from the Eucalyptus trees still coated with the mist from the morning fog. When she came to the large opening in the backyard, she knelt down and concealed herself behind the shrubs. Unable to see anyone in the house, she decided to remain hidden for a few hours. If someone was in the house she wanted to give them enough time to wake up.

She sat down on the damp leaves and nestled herself comfortably behind the row of California Lilac shrubs lining the rear perimeter of the yard. The profuse blue intensity of those blooms was unlike anything Alex could remember. Here, she was hidden from any unwanted eyes and the lingering fragrance calmed her senses and kept her mounting anxiety in check.

In the near distance she heard the eagle bristling around in the cage. She could hear the leaves and branches rustle as he flapped his wings. I cannot let him see me right now, she thought. Not yet.

Then a loud shriek filled the air. . . then another and another. She parted the bushes and saw the eagle standing on the ground looking straight at her. The last shriek drew Alex to her feet and she ran to the cage and fell to her knees, her fingers clenched tightly around the chain link fence. The eagle flew upward to the branch above and she stared up at him. The emotions of that night, not long ago, filled her heart, and she whispered, "You know." Grabbing the links in the fence Alex pulled herself to her feet, unable to glance away from those turbulent yellow eyes. The eagle shifted his neck and head from side to side as he continued to gaze down at Alex. This shifting felt to Alex as though he was trying to understand her, to listen to her.

With her fingers white from clutching the wire links, she continued, "You are all I have left of Benjamin right now and I am all you have left. I came back to take you home and I know Benjamin will be there. . . I will find him. . .somewhere." Then the noble bird twisted its head upward into the sky above as if watching something—someone. He sat motionless on his perch. Alex watched intently, feeling the eeriness of the moment. A sudden gust of wind came from above blowing through the creature's long, symmetrical feathers and then into Alex's face. She tilted her head back, closed her eyes and let the wind flow through him to her. She felt the presence and so did he. When the gust of wind went by them, Alex opened her eyes and saw the eagle still looking upward with its outstretched wings in full view. With its mouth wide open, the creature shrieked at the heavens—at Benjamin. He jumped from his perch, swooped down toward the ground and then up again into another tree, out of Alex's sight. She stood there motionless, not wanting to lose the connection.

Suddenly, a large hand grabbed her shoulder from behind. Startled, Alex spun around. With her back against the fence she yelled in protest, "Get your hands off me!"

The man visibly relaxed at the sound of the accent. "You must be Alex," said Phil.

A furrowed brow. "And who are you?"

"Not so fast. What are you doing here?" Phil demanded.

Alex reasoned that this couldn't be one of Murray's thugs because she probably wouldn't be standing at this point. He seemed gentle and moved away from her as he spoke. After a quick measurement of this man, she said, "I am a friend of Ben's. I wanted to come here to see if I could be of any help."

"Help with what?" Phil's anger began to surface. His right fist jammed into his leg and his lower lip began to quiver. All he knew now was that Benjamin somehow disappeared when he went to find this woman.

"Could you please just tell me who you are, and maybe I could explain further?" Alex asked.

"Phil. That's all you need to know."

Phil was a frequent topic of conversation with Benjamin. She knew he was his best friend. Alex fell backward against the fence. Exhausted, she said, "Oh God, Phil. I know who you are. I am so sorry. I feel like Ben's kidnapping was all my fault." Unable to look into Phil's eyes, her eyes remained closed, and she continued, "I wish they had taken me instead of him. The only thing that keeps me going is my hatred for those people who kidnapped him. That is why I am here. I need to find out who kidnapped Ben and get him back."

"Jesus Christ," Phil bellowed. "I'm so pissed about all this, I can't even see straight. What the hell happened over there? Kidnapping! We're only getting pieces over here. Tell me, what the fuck happened?"

Alex found strength in talking about Benjamin. She went into great detail about why she originally came to America and how she was finally going to tell Benjamin everything when he was coming to see her. She told Phil bits and pieces about the research she obtained and that the people who kidnapped Benjamin were probably after her as well. She also explained that he would now be in danger if they knew she had spoken to him.

Phil's anger subsided, but his senses were cocked and on alert. He was not yet ready to fully embrace this woman. They walked toward the house together. Phil explained, "I have the only other key to Ben's house, and I've been here talking with the authorities. I guess you know about his bird, too?"

"That is another reason I am here. I promised Ben I would release him in Canada where he found him."

"He's a beautiful specimen. I've been feeding him and his wing sure looks healed to me. Anyway, I want to help you find Ben. I don't give a shit how dangerous it is. There's nothing I wouldn't do for him. So, tell me what you've found so far," Phil requested.

Before reaching the back porch, Alex stopped and turned to Phil, "I just cannot go in there yet. I cannot explain what I am feeling. I just ache all over." Then Alex looked over at Phil, and said, "One thing I know is that we had better get away from here now. I am sure this place is on the top of the list for Ben's kidnappers to look for me. Can we just leave and figure out what to do later?"

Phil motioned in the direction of his car. "Let me lock the house up. Head over there to my car and I'll come out the side door."

Alex walked around the side of the house toward the garage. Phil's old chocolate brown Karmann Ghia 1600 was parked near the garage. Phil came out the side door and hollered, "Jump in."

Phil turned the key, the engine sputtered a few times and then kicked in. Over the hum of the engine Alex said, "I have been very careful to watch everything and everyone I pass by. I do not think we should leave here the normal way. Is there a back road or something?"

Phil chuckled, "I wish Ben was driving. He'd take us up over that mountain." Then in a serious tone, he continued, "There is a dirt road that leads to another main road down the back side over there." Phil pointed toward Mt. Tamalpias. "We'll go that way."

They raced off in his tiny car down the dirt road. Alex thought what a strange small car for such a large, lumberjack-looking man. A longing smile filled her face as she thought about how happy Benjamin would be to see the two of them on the hunt together.

CHAPTER 34

"DO YOU KNOW OF ANYONE THAT BEN WAS close to that could help us find out more information about Murray, or the inner workings of GEN?" Alex inquired of Phil as they wound their way through the narrow roads and the towering groves of redwood trees down to Highway 1.

"I'd have to think about that one, but I'll tell you one person who can help us—Constance, Ben's wife." Phil glanced at Alex as he spoke looking for some type of reaction. Seeing none, he continued, "She knows a lot of people, and I know she'll want to have Ben's name cleared from all this."

Constance, Alex thought, I will need to see her. What will she be like? How could any woman not truly love Ben? "I suppose you are right Phil, she would be very useful in a lot of ways, but I do not think she really wants to meet me, especially now."

"I was sitting with Ben in his kitchen when he was on the phone with Constance, and he told her that he was in love with you. He didn't actually mention you by name, but he told her he was in love with someone else and that he wanted a divorce. She actually took it pretty well. I don't think it came as any great surprise to her. They really didn't have your normal marriage, if there is such a thing. I'll bet they spent more time apart than they did together. Anyway, Constance will help us, I'm sure. She has her own ambitions and it won't help her any if Ben somehow gets stuck with any of this."

Phil's heavy foot showed that this was not your standard Ghia as they sped through the turns and twists of Highway 1 toward his home in Bolinas. The last year they made that particular car was 1974, and it was equipped with a standard 50 horsepower engine. Alex knew that this engine had been souped-up. They'd already exceeded the original engine's maximum speed of 85 mph on several of the straight-aways. It handled the corners with the precision of its cloned successor, the Porsche 914.

The winds had picked up that afternoon, and Alex reached in her backpack and pulled out a simple gray hoodie. Pulling the sweatshirt over her, she responded, "Okay, I am willing to talk to anyone you may think can help us. How much longer until we arrive at your house?"

Phil pointed out the window, "Ten minutes. It's just on the other side of this lagoon, but we have to drive all the way around it."

They walked into Phil's house and Alex's eyes methodically panned the room, taking her customary mental inventory. Always size up your surroundings, she had learned over the years. The house was small, with a definite lived-in look. Bamboo wood flooring covered the entryway, kitchen and living area and several tattered throw rugs were tossed about. The rugs were definitely not for aesthetics, but more likely a drop off point for the dirt collected after walking up the front entry path. A black wood-burning stove was set just off the entryway with a large copper pot, stacked with wood, sitting next to it.

The living area was furnished with garage sale decor. Bookshelves crammed with books and artifacts from Phil's work covered one entire wall. Wooden carved figures, masks and musical instruments, original pieces from New Guinea, filled the nooks and crannies. I need to ask him about these, for sure, when I get a chance, Alex thought. Over the bookcases, abalone shells were nailed into the wall like some kind of trophy display. A sliding glass door opened to a redwood deck with a large, weather-worn burl-wood chair nestled in the corner. She imagined this was where Phil sat and read when the weather permitted.

Alex set her things down on the kitchen counter, turned to Phil and said, "I probably ought to call Dr. Diderot in France and see if he has come up with anything new."

"No problem, make yourself at home. I'll put on some coffee," Phil replied, as he circled around to the kitchen and grabbed the coffee pot.

Alex took her cell phone from her purse, punched in the numbers and walked over to a half-stuffed green corduroy chair in the living area and sat down. She reached over and turned on the nearby lamp, its narrow wood pole stuck in an abalone shell as the base. Definitely homemade, she thought.

Alex stared up at the ceiling as she spoke with Charles. It took several calls for her to ask her questions and to listen intently to the long and detailed answers, until finally she said, "Do not worry Charles, I will be careful and, thank you—you have been a tremendous help. I will be in touch with you again shortly."

Phil walked over to the counter separating the kitchen from where Alex was sitting, placed both hands on it and said, "That was intense. What'd he have to say?"

"He has not yet finished going through everything, but what he has found so far is anything but good." Alex stood up and walked over to the glass slider. Her shoulders were hunched and her hands were crammed into the front pocket of her sweatshirt. Staring intently out the window, she continued, "He said he believes this synthetic virus was designed for one specific purpose: to alter the randomness of the natural evolutionary process in such a way that human beings can be controlled in the same way that lab rats can be controlled. The economic windfall connected with this is beyond calculation. And the impact this could have on the world order, as we know it, is beyond measure."

Still staring out the window, she continued, "He is still going through the data, but there is a reference to a meeting scheduled just five days from today. The research and final product are going to be delivered at that meeting."

Phil cocked his head, "Who's going to end up with this?"

"He does not know. He just hopes it is not someone who will use it for its worst nightmare. We only have five days at the most, Phil."

Alex turned and walked over to the counter where Phil was still leaning, and continued, "He did find something else interesting, though. I had asked him earlier to see if there was any reference to who was behind this research. He said a particular name surfaced throughout the files. The name "Rush." He thinks it is a code name rather than a real name, but he is quite certain that this is the person in charge of the project."

"Did he say anything else about this Rush guy?" Phil asked as he straightened up.

"No. But, he is very upset about all this. He described it as the most hideous weapon developed by man, and feels that whoever is behind this is surely just as dangerous. I must say I agree with him."

"Yeah. Amazing. I don't know if this gets us any closer to finding out who is behind this, but there has to be something to it. I'm going to call Constance and see if we can see her as soon as possible. The coffee's hot, help yourself."

"If you do not mind, I think I will try and get a little rest. Is there someplace I can lie down?"

Phil led Alex down the hall and showed her the bedroom at the end. "This is all yours. I'll wake you when I know anything about Constance."

Her slumber was awakened when she heard the drum roll on the bedroom door. "Time to get up. Constance will be here in a few minutes," Phil bellowed through the door.

Rubbing her eyes and staring up through the skylight, trimmed in water-stained wood, she responded, "Okay, thanks. Give me a few minutes."

Alex walked down the hall to the kitchen. "I think," she said, "I am ready for that coffee about now if there is still some ready."

"There's always a pot brewing at my place, but I think I just heard Constance drive up. Let me get the door and I'll get us all some." Phil headed straight for the front door.

"Hello, Constance." Phil called out as he opened the door and watched Constance strut up the front entry path. "Thanks for coming over." He stood aside and Constance crossed the threshold without breaking stride.

Leaning against a wooden post that separated the entryway from the living area, Alex came face to face with Constance. She noticed Constance was several inches shorter than herself. Her jet black hair cascaded down her neck and disappeared just over her shoulders. Alex had seen pictures of her before, but looking at her in person she noticed her eyes for the first time. They were shadowy brown eyes that deflected another's inquisition without giving any clues. There was no penetrating the thoughts of this woman through her eyes.

"Constance, I want you to meet Alex Boudreau," Phil said as he closed the door and moved between the two women. "Alex, this is Constance Hunter."

Instinctively, both women extended their right hand toward the other. They clasped hands, but no words were spoken.

"Why don't you two each have a seat over there?" Phil pointed toward the living area. "I'm going to get us all some coffee. Alex, maybe you can fill Constance in with some of what you've told me."

Constance brushed past Alex, the distinctive scent of her perfume lingering behind her, and took a seat in a large wooden slat chair in the corner near the bookshelves. Alex noticed her walk—long, purposeful strides, wasting little effort or motion. She was dressed in an ebony-colored, tailored suit that fit like a glove, accentuating all the right curves. A bright paisley scarf accented her finely tapered neck. The size of her heels meant she was clearly more than just a few inches shorter than Alex. She was definitely a woman who was comfortable with her own looks.

Alex sat down in the same chair she had sat in when she called Charles. The same chair that was located on the exact opposite side of the room from Constance. She began the explanation, the same explanation she had given to Phil about why she was there, and what she knew about Benjamin's death, and what she needed to know. Only this time, there were no tears, no sorrow, and no touching definable moments. She was focused.

Phil handed them each a cup of coffee and assumed a yoga-like position on the floor. "Constance, we need your help. I think Alex is definitely onto something here and none of us want to see Ben saddled with this whole mess. We know he didn't do anything. We need to find him, and get all of this cleared up."

Constance turned from Phil and glared directly at Alex with her steely brown eyes. Her designer lips parted, "You're that Italian woman who was fucking my husband, aren't you?" The tension was broken.

"I think you need to know. . ."

Alex was cut off by Phil as he held his hands out toward each woman, like a referee signaling each fighter to retreat to their corner. "Listen, both of you. We're not here to discuss anything, and I mean anything, other than how we can collectively work to find Ben. Do I make myself clear? If not, I'll repeat myself, only louder."

Alex broke the silence first. "Phil, if we are all going to work together, and I hope we can, I need to tell you, Senator, that I do love your husband. In the days I have spent with him, he showed me all the beautiful things in life that I had been missing for so many years. I miss him more than I would have ever thought it possible to miss anyone. None of this has anything to do with you. Yes, you are Ben's wife. I truly envy you for that. But you know much better than I do what really existed between you. Please, I do not want to argue with you over Ben, or trade turns disparaging the other. I need help in finding him, and to find out who is behind this terrible injustice. And if you believe anything I have said here today you can see that whoever is behind this will stop at nothing. We are all in danger."

Constance gave a prim nod, "I must say, Ms. Boudreau, I find you to be a very clever woman. I can see why Ben may have been smitten with you."

Constance's flawless light brown complexion was all natural. The only make up she wore was dark eyeliner just underneath her lower lashes. She tapped her left index finger, very slowly on the armrest of the chair where she sat, and continued, "But I still don't know what I can do to help. I've already told the authorities everything they wanted to know, and as far as I'm concerned, they are better prepared to handle this sort of thing than either of you."

"The authorities can continue to do their thing and that's fine. I will tell you though Constance, I think the government may have some involvement in this in some way, and that is where you can help." Phil re-crossed his legs, looked at Constance, and continued, "You have contacts in Washington that you can lean on for help. Alex's friend who uncovered the virus information has found a name or code name of the person in charge of this operation. Rush. The name is Rush."

The left index finger stopped its measured tapping and Constance's fingertips turned white as she tightened her grip on the armrests. Alex glanced over at Constance and noticed the color had drained from her cheeks, her breathing stopped. She looked in her eyes, but the same impenetrable shield still deflected any indication as to what Constance was thinking.

"Constance. Did you hear me?" Phil asked as he straightened up and looked at her intently.

"Oh. I'm sorry, I was thinking about something you said earlier. I guess I didn't hear everything you said." Her left index finger began to tap—faster and faster. The creamy color had left her complexion and she appeared ashen, the energy drained from her very essence. She slowly pushed herself up from her chair and her knees buckled. She looked disoriented. She leaned back against the bookcase.

"Constance!" Phil jumped up and clutched her arm. "Are you alright? What is it?"

After a few exaggerated breaths, she said, "I think it's just everything catching up to me. I do want to help you. You know that. But I'm going to need a day or two to see what I can do."

She turned now to Alex and walked toward her. Her composure was back. Her eyes deflected. Her look was as black as midnight. "Ms Boudreau, I suppose I should thank you. Not for being in love with my husband, but for what you've learned about the circumstances surrounding his disappearance. For that, I do thank you. If you should learn anything new, you will contact me, won't you?"

Alex held her ground, and said, "Of course. Of course I will and, thank you for helping."

Constance pivoted and marched toward the door. "I'll let myself out. And, thanks again," she muttered as she closed the door behind her. The perfume of self-importance trailed behind her.

Alex turned to Phil and said, "There is something she is not telling us."

CHAPTER 35

"THERE. THAT SHOULD TO DO IT," ALEX murmured as she stood up and looked at her laptop screen. Phil had never owned a computer, although he knew the basic, rudimentary procedures behind operating one. He believed that if you couldn't solve something by using your brain, then it probably wasn't meant to be solved in the first place. The need for this computer was different—it was to help Benjamin.

The night before, Phil and Alex had talked into the early morning hours. It was obvious to both that Constance knew something. The mention of the name Rush had altered her equilibrium. Her poise, her self control, her purpose had left her if only for a brief moment, but it had clearly left her. They both knew that Rush meant something more to her than she would say.

First thing that morning, Phil had driven Alex to the Best Buy store over the hill in Novato, and she quickly purchased the necessary equipment for what she had in mind. She had an extra Wi-Fi card which she plugged into the USB port of the computer and connected to the internet over cell channels.

"Come here, Phil," Alex said as she motioned to Phil, who was standing on the outside porch.

Phil spun around, walked back inside and over to the makeshift computer area that Alex had set up. She used Phil's coffee table, a rickety old wooden plank door fastened atop two half wine barrels, as their new base of operations. "I'm glad you know what you're doing," Phil said, as he crouched down over his knees looking intently over Alex's shoulder. "Do you really think this is going to help us?"

"I sure do. There are a lot of people who patronize the Internet who will get a charge out of this. I do not know for sure if this will help, but I have a hunch that someone out there can help us." Earlier, Alex had reasoned that it would be worth a try to put some feelers out into cyberspace to see if anyone could help them crack the Rush code name, if that was what it really was—a code name.

The Outlaw Forum sprang from an original group called Masters of Deception. Masters of Deception was a New York based hackers' group that originally collaborated to hack the Bell Atlantic phone switches and the various microcomputers and mainframes used to administer its telephone network. The membership in this group was impossible to track, but through a joint task force, six of the members were eventually indicted and within months each had plead guilty. The Outlaw Forum was believed to be an extension of the Masters of Deception group, but they had remained untraceable through the use of code names and sophisticated trail cover-up techniques.

Alex had used the Outlaw Forum in the past to help her find information and to find it quickly. She knew that if she could rouse someone's interest out there, then maybe she could recruit some much-needed reinforcements.

Phil peered over her shoulder as she carefully typed a message which would begin her search.

ihav3 an intrugguing questino i n3ed infor/\/\Aion on someone wh0 ahs Been invbolved n a cofvarto par4tiom using genet1c reasearch tHis laMer si probably 1n america and they have za codE namme – rush. help!!!!!~~~~~~ OLOLOOLOLOLOL. . . ttime Is vary important///

Andromeda

"There. That is done. Now, before I call Murray. . ."

"Hold on." Phil waived his arms and walked around to the side of Alex. "Just what's that gibberish? That makes no sense."

Alex took a quick glance at Phil and smiled, "You do not speak leet? What rock have you been hiding under all these years?"

"I guess I haven't been out in a while. I'm sort of behind the times. So what's this all about?"

"There was a hacker group called the Dead Cow Cult that developed a nasty software program that allowed them to remotely control thousands of Windows 95 computers. They developed their own language to bypass censorship programs. The leet language has evolved since then and is used by hackers and serious gamers. Anybody that can help us on this forum will know what I am asking."

Alex motioned to Phil to look at the screen. "Here, let me show you some technical sites you can access and some other areas where you can do some research." Alex began taking Phil through the steps to go online and access the targeted research sites. Phil crouched down and wrote down all the information on a legal pad. With Alex's computer knowledge and Phil's tenacity, not to mention the fact that he could be a fast learner when he wanted to be, Phil was online and browsing by himself in less than fifteen minutes.

Phil rose from his crouched position and stretched his legs. "There's not much to this when you know what you're doing. I need to make a sandwich. Want anything?"

"Yes, that sounds nice, but I should give Murray a call shortly. I think it would be a good idea if we used a pay phone somewhere. I would expect that he may be attempting to trace any call I make to him. I may need to keep him on the line for more than the 60 seconds he would need to have the call traced to this location. I don't want him crashing in here. Where can we find a pay phone?"

"You're probably right. There's one here in town, down by the gas station. I think we'd be better off, though, driving over to Stinson Beach and using a phone there. I'm pretty sure there's one there. Anyway, it's about fifteen minutes away."

"Okay. Good idea. Maybe you should make a couple sandwiches and I will throw a few things together. We can eat on the way." Alex turned and walked to the counter where her notes were piled.

The Karmann Ghia pulled into a parking space across the street from the Stinson Market. Alex stepped out of the car and looked through the pine trees toward the ocean. She closed her eyes, took a deep breath and held the salt air deep in her lungs. Someday, she thought, I will be able to take the time to enjoy these moments.

The pay phone was fastened to the wall outside the entrance to the market. Alex handed her backpack to Phil and then lifted the receiver from its cradle. As she dialed the number she looked at Phil, "This had better work."

"This is Ms. Pancini. I would like to speak to Mr. Paulson." Alex's pointed tone clearly indicated she would not take no for an answer.

The delay seemed endless. Are they tracing this? Is that what is taking so long? He has to speak to me. Then a bellowing voice, "Ms. Pancini, I didn't expect to hear from you so soon." Murray spoke as if he were addressing some intruder who he was trying to discard.

"You have received the email I sent to you, I am sure. I only have a moment to talk to you so I will simply ask you, do you know what I have?"

A few moments of silence and Murray replied, "I do believe that you have something I need, and I'm willing to discuss with you any reasonable demands you may have. If it's money you're after, perhaps we can talk?"

"You know exactly what I am after. I have made that perfectly clear. It is time that you and I meet again, only this time it will be in neutral surroundings."

"Ms. Pancini," Murray interrupted, "I think you should come to my office and we can discuss everything here, in private."

"I am sure you know where the Ferry Building is in San Francisco?" Alex parried.

"Meet me in front of the entrance to the ferry boarding area in exactly two hours. We can discuss everything there, in private." She placed the receiver back on the cradle before any reply was audible.

Alex was dressed in the same sweatshirt and frayed jeans she first put on in her hotel room two days ago. She only had a few changes of clothes with her and she wanted to get full use out of each outfit. She stood behind a small statue of Gandhi where she commanded a full view of the rear of the Ferry Building, the entrance to the ferries, and the docks which routinely served as fishing platforms for half a dozen anglers. This vantage point permitted her to see, but not be seen.

She spied Murray walking out from beneath the underpass which led from the Embarcadero to the ferry loading area. She glanced at her watch and noted that he was on time. His gait was rapid, with short, but deliberate steps. He looked straight ahead as he walked over to the boarding area. He stopped and looked around. His eyes panned the surroundings and they passed right by Alex, unnoticed.

Alex sat in the protective shadows of the statue—watching— watching Murray and his every movement. He walked over to a newspaper stand and bought the Examiner, folded it neatly and tucked it under his right arm. He was alone, Alex surmised. She stood up and looked around. No one appeared to be watching. She moved quickly over to the ferry entrance and without skipping a stride her elbow shot into Murray's lower back with just enough force that he stiffened and shot forward a step or two. Looking back, she motioned, "Follow me. We are going sightseeing."

Alex followed the commuters and tourists through the ticket turnstile and handed the uniformed man two tickets. "The other ticket is for that man in the pin-striped suit with the newspaper under his arm," she told the man as she pointed to Murray. "Come on Murray, I do want to get a good seat." She turned and walked up the boarding ramp to the Sausalito Ferry.

Murray walked up the gangplank and stepped onto the ferry boat. He saw Alex standing aft with her back against the white metal railing, staring directly at him. He walked over to her.

The boat at that time of day was filled mostly with Marin County commuters. They crowded around the bar area inside, each waiting their turn to grab a drink for the thirty minute journey across the turbulent waters of the Bay. Alex took a spot outside where they would be noticed, but not bothered by the locals who preferred the confines of indoors, away from the wind and cold.

Alex turned around, placed both hands around the cold metal railing, leaned into the barrier, and said, "Well Murray, here we are, just you and me." She continued to look out at the Bay, not interested in looking at this man she now loathed. "What are you going to do about my demands?"

"Come on, Alex. I can't possibly give you any names. You're smart enough to know that I will end up like our friend Ben."

With this comment Alex snapped her head toward Murray, narrowed her piercing eyes and glared into his. "Do not ever again refer to Ben as a friend of yours."

Murray began to stammer and Alex quickly cut him off. "Do you have any idea how much Ben admired you? He spoke of you almost like a father. He trusted you. Do not believe for one minute that wherever he is he is not looking down on you right now, cursing your name. How do you live with yourself, anyway?"

Probably for the first time in his life, Murray could not speak. He genuinely liked and respected Benjamin, yet he had a job to do that was beyond any feelings he may have had for others. For a moment, Murray wanted to explain it all to Alex. He knew he never could.

Leaning against the railing, Murray tried not to sound as guilty as he looked. "Look. I may be able to figure out a way to clear Ben's name and to help find him. In fact, I'm sure I can. But, I can never give you any names of the people involved. I might as well shoot myself in the head."

"It is your decision, but I do not make idle threats. I promise you that if you do not give me the name of your boss or partner or whatever, I will make it known that you personally gave me enough information to launch a full investigation by the American government. Not to mention the American media. What do you think would happen to you if your friends knew you were cooperating in this investigation? Do you think you could run far enough and fast enough to lose them? I doubt it, Murray."

Murray turned toward Alex and she saw beads of terror on his brow. "Listen lady, you have no idea what you've got yourself involved in here. These people kill for the fun of it, and if you implicate me in any of this, you're a fool to think that you could run and hide. You're in much more danger than I could ever be."

"Maybe," Alex calmly replied. "The difference is that I do not give a rat's ass. I had better find Ben, and he had better be unharmed. Each day I find out new information, and I get closer to his kidnappers. I will find out what I need to know—I always do. I do not care what happens to me in the process. How about you, Murray? Do you have family? Children? Is your life as meaningless as mine?" Alex chuckled inside. She knew the answers.

"God dam nit! What am I supposed to do?"

"I can protect you, Murray. I know that your government or mine will protect you if you help us to find Ben and lead us to the lunatic who developed this gruesome weapon. Please, Murray. For Ben's sake, can you do something good to redeem yourself from all this ugliness you have created?"

"I did not create this," Murray snapped. "These are old friends of mine. They saved my life once." Murray leaned forward and placed his elbows on the railing as the Ferry chugged along the bay. His forehead was cradled in his hands. The mist and spray from the waves crashed into the hull and passed by unnoticed.

Alex felt this awkward man's balance shifting. She put her hand on his shoulder, and said, "Murray, you have to help me. You have no choice." No choice, she thought. Just what Andre would say.

Alex turned again toward the water and thought about how close she was. "Look Murray. I promise you that you will be protected. Think about this, and I will call you very soon. We have very little time left. Do not try to find me, you will not. Do not try to hurt me, you cannot. Do the right thing Murray."

Alex felt a peculiar combination of hatred and pity for this man. He looked pathetic to her as the waves rose and fell on the bay and the ferry bounced in rhythm. It was dusk and Murray blended into the overcast gray sky.

Alex brushed past Murray and made her way to the pier. She disappeared in the crowd. Murray never even looked in her direction. As she walked down the pier, she stopped and turned around to see if she could spot that defeated man. Like a tarnished statue, there Murray stood, slumped over on the starboard side looking out to the far end of the pier. She watched him for a moment as the passengers swept by. Then she whispered to the wind, "Almost. I am almost there."

CHAPTER 36

"GOD DAMNIT HOW IN THE HELL COULD THIS have happened?" Paul was ranting on and on as he frantically paced back and forth in his townhome. Normally, when Paul was home and peering out his second story floor–to-ceiling window at the gray waters of the Potomac River, he was able to rejuvenate his psyche from the heavy-going rigors of his day. This was his sanctuary, his refuge from the meaningless yet persistent uproar that had become a part of his everyday life. At this moment, the Potomac River was just a river and its soothing magic was asleep.

With his cell phone tightly crammed against the left side of his face, he thunderously barked, "Just how the hell could this have happened, Nate?"

The deep-baritone voice responded, "She slipped away somehow. Garran has some of his best people on this and they have re-located her. He's bringing in a few extra people so all of his resources are directed on this right now. I still think that we have encrypted the information in a secure enough way, but we'll just have to wait and see."

"Wait and see!" Paul continued to pace about. His temples were throbbing, he loosened his tie and stretched his neck. "The last time we talked about this you told me that everything would be okay. Well, it's not. We need to do whatever it takes to retrieve that research. I don't care what it takes—just do it!"

"Paul, Garran is on top of this and he's doing everything that he can. You know that. We have a back-up of everything so we still have all our data and we can deliver everything we need. But somewhere out there someone has a copy of all this, and if they can decrypt the codes they may just be able to trace it all back to us. That's our real risk at this point."

"Well that's a hell of a risk. . . for all of us." Paul's voice echoed the same anxieties that were apparent from his white–knuckled, clenched fist twisted into the back of his neck. "I suppose Alan Price is still all over you about this?"

"Yeah, he is. I think his full time job now is dogging me about this. He's everywhere. There's not much I can do about that, though. We're going to have to satisfy Alan that there aren't any copies floating around before I can get rid of him, and then we can safely deliver the product."

"We have to deliver our final package in just four days. If this research somehow surfaces in the hands of someone else, we'll not only lose millions, but our careers will be over. We've worked too damn hard to lose everything now. Those are huge risks, Nate."

"Like I said, Garran has tracked down the people involved in the theft and he'll have everything under control very quickly. I'll keep you up to date on everything the second I learn anything new."

"I expect that. Keep me posted if you learn anything and I mean *anything*. I just can't believe this has happened."

CHAPTER 37

A
LEX WAS PROPPED ON THE EDGE OF A STOOL, slouched uncomfortably forward as she scrolled through the screen on her laptop. Patches of morning sunlight filtered through the glass sliding door behind her. The kitchen counter in Phil's house with its cold, but colorful, talavera tile with cracked grout and the muted florescent overhead lighting, were not the ideal surroundings to sit and focus. But to Alex, the surroundings were invisible.

Alex and Phil had wasted no time when she exited the ferry the night before. Phil was no stranger to rush hour traffic in Marin. With both hands clutching the Karmann Ghia's washed-out wood steering wheel, he slalomed through the slow moving commuters as if he was living out a fantasy of blazing through the open countryside at 150mph, or racing three-wide at the European Grand Prix. Alex sat calmly in the passenger seat, her hands gently pressed to her thighs and her fingers tapped with each flickering thought as she sorted through the information that she had learned.

She had received several interesting responses to her earlier query posted on the hacker forum. Most of the responses were pointless, just some wannabes wasting the only thing they probably had—time. One response was puzzling and caught Alex's immediate attention. Someone calling themselves Cyberclaw had sent a brief note that she couldn't decipher.

"Phil, come here. Look at this," Alex cried out as she peered at the response.

Phil's hands were wrapped around a half-filled mug of coffee and he stood behind Alex as she isolated the response on her screen in large print. The screen on her Powermaster had an extra bright Crystal Blank display with high definition and contrast ratio. The lucid image glared at them. Their vacant and voiceless stares gave no hint to what they were each thinking.

IHZPHBGESIF.WPILOBBS.
TGUPAAZPUO=5331GZBBYZAUFHZC

3

"I've always been good at crossword puzzles and I can finish a Sudoku once in a while, but this is beyond my capabilities. What do you think Cyberclaw means? It has to have some meaning to it." Phil was ranting out loud and Alex remained fixated on the computer screen.

Alex leaned back and placed her hands on the inside of her thighs to steady herself. She looked at Phil and said, "This looks to me like some type of Monoalphabetic Cipher. A code, if you will that we are going to have to break."

"And just how do *we* do that?" Phil was waving his hands in small circles to emphasize that he was of no help in all of this.

"These codes always have a key that we need to find, and then we use that key to rearrange the letters of the alphabet. If this person used a simple key, then all we have to do is find which letters in this code correspond with the letters of the alphabet. We just have to do some rearranging."

"That could take forever. Why don't you just send a message back and tell this guy to respond in simple English? That would save us a lot of time."

"It will not be as hard as you think. We do not need to figure out each letter. Here let me show you something." Alex leaned forward and punched her keyboard. "Come here and look at this." She spun her laptop around toward Phil and motioned for him to read what she had just typed.

> It deosn't mttaer how the ltters are tpyed, jsut taht the frist and lsat ltteres are at the rghit pcleas. Eevn Pihl wlil get tihs.

Phil leaned close to the screen and within seconds his puzzled look turned to a triumphant smile. "Damn. I wish I knew about this when I was teaching. Do you know how much fun I could've had with my students with this? So what do you do now?"

"Well the letter E is the most common occurring letter in the English language, so I need to run a letter frequency analysis to see if that is the case here. If it is then at least we have a pretty good place to start." Alex opened her Program File and hit a program titled "Black Chamber." When it opened on her screen, she continued, "All I do here is copy and paste the message in the Plain Text box and hit Enter. This will run the letter analysis for me."

She hit Enter and the following appeared on her screen—

	A	B	C	D	E	F	G	H	I	J	K	L	M
Ciber%	5	9	2	0	2	3	5	5	5	0	0	2	0
Eng %	8	2	3	4	13	2	2	6	7	0	1	4	2

	N	O	P	Q	R	S	T	U	V	W	X	Y	Z
Ciber%	0	2	9	2	0	3	2	5	0	2	0	2	9
Eng %	7	8	2	0	6	6	9	3	1	2	0	2	0

Immediately, Alex knew the answer. "Well this won't work. The letters B, P and Z each appear in 9% of the code." Alex placed her hands on the top of her head, locked her fingers together and continued to stare at her computer screen. She muttered out loud, "I'll have to play around with a few other possibilities."

"So the 13 under E in this means that the letter E appears 13% of the time in most English writings?"

"Yes, but believe it or not there is a little known book called "Gadsby" written in 1939, a novel of over 50,000 words and the letter E does not appear even once in the whole book."

"In this cyber text here, there just are not enough letters to rely on the frequency analysis. But BB does appear twice consecutively, and AA is another consecutive pairing, that is something. Maybe. I need to find the key in here somehow, and then we can make some progress. It sure would have helped if they would at least have put spaces in between the words. Oh well. Give me some time, Phil. I want to play around with this for a little longer. I do not think that whoever wrote this would have sent it off to us if it did not have some type of useful information. I hope that is the case anyway."

Phil headed to the kitchen to get them both some food and some more coffee. He reached the kitchen, opened the refrigerator and silently mumbled to himself, "Utterly useless. Under what rock does she pull this stuff from?"

Phil returned with two cups of coffee, some stale pretzels and something resembling salami and placed it all on the counter next to Alex. "Hungry?"

"Just a sec." Alex was hunched forward and scribbling nonstop on a white legal pad. After a few more minutes she stopped, looked up at Phil and with her pen tapping the paper over and over again, she said, "Got it!" She reorganized her papers and continued, "See the number 3 at the bottom of the message? Well, that is the key, and in this case it is telling us to arrange the letters in such a way that we have 3 corners."

"It took a while, but look at this," Alex said as she angled the pad in Phil's direction.

P

BZG

HAZPE

PAYCAUS

ZPBZHFUOI

HUBZG5331=F

IGT.SBBQLIPW.

She pointed her pen at the diagram in front of them. "The 3 was telling us to arrange the letters with three corners like this." She paused for just a moment so that Phil could keep up with her pace. "You then rearrange all the letters, starting at the lower left corner and moving up the left side, back down the right side, across the bottom, up the next left side and so on. From this triangle you start at the top and read down, left to right and here is what you get."

PBZGHAZPEPAYCAUSZPBZHFUOIHUBGZ53
31=FIGT.SBBQLIPW.

"And we're right back to square one." Phil stood tall by the side of Alex with his outstretched palms facing up. "Are you starting over, or does this mean something that I should possibly know?"

With a glimmer of a smile Alex now took Phil's sarcastic tone to task, "Answer me this. How many letters are there in the alphabet?"

"Twenty Six."

"Now, divide that by two."

"Thirteen."

"Okay. There you have it. You just solved the code. Congratulations." Alex reached over and grabbed her cup of coffee with both hands and took a long sip.

"Come on, you're holding out on me. What is it? What does this all mean?"

"These types of codes have uniformity to them. All you need to do is find what that is, exactly. Through trial and error, I eventually came up with 13. You take each letter in the rearranged code and count back 13 letters in the alphabet. P becomes C, B becomes O and so on. With the numbers you count back by the Key, or 3."

Alex flipped over a page on the pad and handed it to Phil.

Constance   Campaign   Contributions   2008 =   Rush

PBZGHAZPE   PAYCAUSZ   PBZHFUOIHUBZG   5331 = FIGT

Good Luck
SBBG LIPW

Reaching across the kitchen counter, Alex grabbed her phone and quickly punched in a number firmly ingrained in her memory.

CHAPTER 38

"THANK YOU FOR COMING OVER HERE. I REALLY don't have much time right now. I'm already late for a fund raiser, so meeting anywhere else on such short notice just wouldn't have worked." Constance sat with her legs crossed, her back arched and her right arm dangled over the armrest of the green corduroy sofa. She appeared calm and at ease, as if she was entertaining a close friend.

"Well thank you for seeing me like this, but we are, after all, looking for the same answers, are we not?" Careful, Alex thought. She is shrewd. She did not get elected to the U.S Senate by her looks alone. After all, Stuart Weitzman black pumps, sleekly tailored gray gabardine pants and a white silk Anne Klein blouse is a stylish combination and they certainly tempted one to linger on Constance's finer features a bit too long. Alex knew she was not headed to a fund raiser looking like that.

"Miss Boudreau, if you. . ."

"Please call me Alex. I much prefer that—and may I call you Constance?" Alex quickly interjected.

"Yes, Constance would be fine. Now Alex, as I was saying. In fact, maybe you can tell me the importance of seeing me on such short notice? You did project a rather urgent tone when you called earlier." The tempo of Constance's ever so slightly tapping her right heel against the wooden leg of the sofa mirrored a soft musical score played in perfect legato.

"The importance of seeing you on such short notice is that as I uncover more and more information about Ben, and why he was kidnapped, I get closer and closer to finding out that *you* have certain ties with all of this. I had hoped that we were both interested in finding out who was behind Ben's disappearance, but now I am not so sure." Alex remained composed, and continued to look intently into those opaque and guarded eyes for any telling movement.

Constance huffed, "The nerve of you!" She bolted from the couch, took one step forward toward Alex and with her left index finger cocked directly in front of Alex's face, she readied her assault, "The nerve of you. The absolute nerve! You come prancing into my house and insinuate, no, you *accuse* me of having some type of involvement with the kidnapping of *my* husband. You tramp! You have been having an affair with *my* husband, probably right here in *our* house!"

"Constance, please, we. . ." Alex tried to intervene and direct the conversation, but Constance continued on, her voice lowered to a note that seemed venomous, "You think you love Ben? You don't know the first thing about him. He is a very complicated man." Constance stopped in mid-sentence, turned to her right and inched slowly over to the French doors that led to the back deck. Stopping inches from the door, she placed both forearms against the glass and with her head tightly tucked between her arms she continued, "I think we're done here. You know the way out. Please go."

Alex was caught between the crosshairs of the hurtful realities of what this woman was saying. Yes, it was an affair by some definitions, and yes, she did love Benjamin. Yet here she was, sitting in Benjamin's house, looking at that same door that Benjamin carried her through the night that their souls joined and soared together in unison. Before her was someone who could lead her directly to what she wanted—Benjamin's kidnappers.

Alex rose to her feet, pulled herself to her full height and reacted, "Constance you have said some things, some hurtful things, and some of those things may be true. But I do not really care at this point, and it does not really matter. All I care about is finding out who kidnapped Ben." With her right hand, she brushed back what remained of her clipped hair that had slipped over her right eye and she continued, "I do not know what it is that you know. Maybe you do not even know. But I know that you can help. Please try. Please."

Constance remained motionless, frozen against the glass door. I will bet there is a crack in the armor covering those steely eyes now, Alex thought.

Alex pressed on, "It may be nothing, but right now we are combing through your campaign contributions from 2008. We were told that there may be some link between certain contributors and the people involved in Ben's kidnapping."

Constance spun on her left heel and now faced Alex, her hands pressed tightly on the glass behind her and her head was still leaning against the glass, "And just who is we? Who is it that you work for?"

"I do not work for anybody, but you need to believe me when I say that I know what I am doing. My entire career has been spent getting exactly what I need. And I mean, exactly." Alex paused for a few moments to assess the reaction of her prey. "I received a response to a query that I sent out that has led me to your campaign contributions. Right now Phil is checking into those records."

The two women were stock-still. The only noise was the warm air lightly wafting through the overhead heating vent. Finally, Constance appeared to relax and walked over to the back of the green corduroy couch where she had sat earlier. With her left hand placed on top of the other to steady herself, she leaned forward and broke the exaggerated silence, "I don't think I can ever forgive you for what you've done. Believe it or not, I love Ben. It's not easy having a marriage where both people are consumed by their work, and the rare time we do spend together is not intimate time where the closeness we once so embraced is shared. No, we have our troubles, our own separate lives for that matter, but I do love him. Yes, I still love him."

Constance looked up and caught Alex's gaze, a vacant awkward air of uncertainty that was focused far away from the present. Chaotic thoughts randomly spun through Alex's mind as if twisting out of control, falling endlessly into some hidden abyss of her past. The house where she now stood was where she rid herself of the emptiness that once stalked her. Not by herself, but through the passion and oneness she shared with Benjamin that night; through the gentle lion of a man she discovered as she laid bare her guilt-ridden past and he embraced and tamed her quivering naked body; through the lonely eagle outside in the cold cage that ached to reunite with its departed mate. For the first time in her secluded and loveless life, she had no longer felt cut off from hope and compassion. She had a chance to be whole. To understand the loss of Christina and to cherish the thoughts of the short time they did spend together.

Alex barely heard Constance once again asking her to leave. Her hands clutched the top of the crisp beige leather chair next to her. The same chair where she imagined Benjamin often sat when he had reason to clear the useless clutter from his own mind and to refocus on the tasks at hand. Her breathless trance faded and she once again regained her balance. Balance. Once again she began to focus her thoughts on her prey. She circled. She crouched. She waited and she lunged. One last lunge, "I am leaving now. But first, one last question. There is one thing that you can help me with I am sure. There is a name or a code that is connected to all this. Tell me, where will the name *Rush* lead us?"

The hook was set, the line was drawn taut. Alex didn't blink. She absorbed herself with Constance's presence. She focused on Constance and watched intently as her hands tensed, the blood heated in her veins and a rapid pulsing ignited near her right temple. She seemed to hold her breath. And then those eyes. Ever so quickly a breach appeared that allowed Alex to see beyond the steely brown spheres that served as the armor masking this woman's emotional being.

Alex spun and walked with a weighty purpose toward the front door. She turned one last time toward Constance and then she knew. Constance remained frozen. She had not moved except for her eyes. That brief gap in her armor had closed, but it was too late. Alex had already peered into the veiled depths of this woman's secrets.

"Finding Ben and clearing his name is all we *both* care about at this time. The rest can wait." The door closed and only emptiness remained standing in the house.

CHAPTER 39

"WE NEED TO LEAVE HERE NOW. DO NOT ASK me why because I do not know, but we need to leave." Alex was propped on the now familiar stool next to the kitchen counter waiting for her laptop to boot when Phil appeared in the hallway. His arms stretched from wall to wall holding his six foot four inch frame steady.

"What do you mean, we need to leave?" Phil asked as he wiped the sleep from his eyes with his wrist.

"I will fill you in on everything once we get out of here. I know Constance has some involvement in all of this. I do not know exactly what yet, but she knows we are working together, so I suspect we will have visitors shortly. Pack some clothes, and whatever else you need, and then we will go."

"Alright. Alright. I catch your drift. Give me five, and then we're out of here." Phil spun around on one heel and headed directly to his bedroom.

When one works as Alex does, alone, it is difficult to trust anyone or anything. She had honed certain innate skills more than others and her hyper vigilance was alerting her to unknown dangers. Her internal alarm system had sounded and she responded without a shred of doubt. Before she left though she had two things she needed to accomplish.

The monotone hum of her laptop was broken briefly only after her mind sorted through the many things she needed to transcribe. She needed to get a message to Cyberclaw. Whoever this person was, they knew more than they have told us so far. She opted to send a message back in the same coded design as the original message. She typed:

T.PEKFEH?EFBYSZU.LAGMZA.B

3

"The guy knows something more I am sure," Alex thought out loud. "I need more to go on if I am going to figure out what "Rush" means.""Phil, have you seen my cell phone?" Alex yelled as she hit the send button and watched her coded message disappear. "Where is it?"

Phil's voice echoed through the hallway, "Check out the chair by the bookcases. I think I left it there."

Finding her phone, she punched in the number and pressed the phone to her ear. "Murray Paulson, please," she quickly blurted out before the receptionist could say good afternoon. "Tell him this is Alex Pancini and it is urgent."

Moments later Alex heard Murray's voice and she cut him off in mid-sentence, "I need your cell number and I am going to call you back very soon and you need to answer it."

Without hesitation Murray gave Alex his cell number.

"Now very quickly, what have you decided? Are you going to help me or not?"

"Alex I've thought of nothing else since we met on the ferry. You've really turned my life upside down. I need more time to make a decision and to sort. . ."

Murray only heard a dial tone on the other end of the line.

Phil appeared at the end of the hallway with a stuffed denim backpack slung around his shoulder. "Okay, I'm packed. You may want to turn off your computer if you're going to bring it along."

"I am just getting to it. I sent off a message to Cyberclaw. I sure hope he is monitoring the site."

"What'd you say to him?"

"I just asked if he knows anything else. I do not mind telling you, Phil, I am worried. We only have three days left before this viral weapon is delivered. I know we are close, but there is still so much more we need to find out. I am afraid that after the research is delivered these people will no longer have a need to keep Ben alive. We must figure this out now."

Phil put his hand on Alex's shoulder and gave a gentle squeeze. "Then let's get the hell out of here. We've got work to do."

They stuffed a few belongings into Phil's car—Alex's laptop, the few clothes that she had with her and Phil's tattered knapsack. Minutes later they had driven a few short blocks and Phil pulled into a driveway that led to a house landscaped with the same haphazard abalone and driftwood pattern as Phil's front yard. He parked next to a new Volvo XC90 with magic blue metallic paint and Galateria Alloy Wheels.

Phil looked at Alex, and with a feeble smirk on his face said, "Since you make it seem that we're going undercover or something, I thought we could use some different wheels."

Alex's expression softened and her lips parted revealing the amusement that was hidden somewhere deep inside of her. "Upgrading are we?"

"Nah, not really. It does handle a little better than this baby, but its lines aren't as sleek." Phil reached for his door handle and said, "This is a friend's car. He won't mind. I know where he keeps the keys. I'll be right back."

Alex exited the Ghia and stood next to the Volvo. Using her cell, she dialed Murray's cell phone and when he answered she began, "Murray there is no more time, and this needs to be quick. Are you going to tell me who is behind this hideous synthetic virus and who kidnapped Benjamin?"

"I don't know who kidnapped him. I don't know anything about that. Yeah, I do know some things about the virus, but I'm as good as dead if I say anything. You don't know these people, they're. . ."

"I want to know those people. I want to see them pay, and I want to see them suffer. Just tell me who I need to find and I will take care of them. You will be protected."

"Alex, I need another couple days, and I think I can find a way to get you what you need. Just a couple more days."

Sensing too much time had already elapsed and this call could already have been traced by now, Alex concluded, "If I need anything further from you I will contact you. If not, you will hear directly from the authorities."

The dial tone buzzed in Murray's ear once again.

"Get in." Phil remotely unlocked the car as he approached. They got in and backed out of the driveway. They drove slowly down the lane and as they drove past Phil's house, he glanced into his rearview mirror and Alex looked over her left shoulder. Three men exited a white Ford Taurus and walked directly toward Phil's house. They weren't dressed like Mormon missionaries, and they weren't coming for a social visit.

Phil and Alex looked at one another and each felt the other's relief. "Woman's intuition. Always go with it. It never fails."

Alex leaned her head back against the cashmere leather headrest and gently closed her eyes. "Find us a cheap motel in the middle of somewhere—somewhere busy."

CHAPTER 40

THE TRAVELODGE NOVATO WAS NOT A RESORT destination hotel one would pick for its ambience or sparkling architecture. While not quite classified as seedy, it was dated, in need of some stucco repair and paint, but best of all the front desk clerk accepted cash for the room payment and didn't ask for any identification. The perfect hideaway to sketch out the next course of action, whatever that would be.

Alex and Phil were in a third floor room that overlooked the main entrance to the motel off of Redwood Blvd. With the window slightly ajar, they could hear the creaks and scrapes of footsteps at the far end of the rickety and stained outdoor hallway.

Alex hadn't slept much that night and it wasn't the lumpy mattress or the constant wail of passing sirens that kept her wide awake. That morning, blotches of sunlight filtered through the draped window and her mind was still locked in a state of faraway meditation as she channel-surfed through the events that had taken place. She played the events backwards and forwards looking for any hint, any trace of evidence she might have overlooked. Each episode played out in her mind as if she were rehearsing for her first solo appearance at the Philarmonie De Paris. She needed every clue, every piece of evidence to be placed in perfect order. Failure here was not an option. She needed to fit these pieces in perfect order if she was to fulfill her promise to Benjamin. The image of Benjamin faded in and out of her mind as the weariness and fatigue began to weigh and take control.

"It's your cell," Phil repeated several times before Alex was able to bring her conscious thoughts back to the here and now. She picked up her cell and immediately recognized the number.

"Charles. Yes. Do you have anything new?"

"Yes, I do. Is everything okay on your end?" Charles asked, with the worried and self-important tone of someone hoping he was considered a vital part of the operation.

"Everything is fine, Charles. Just fine. What do you have?"

"A couple of things, really. Both interesting and puzzling. First, my initial findings about the creation of a synthetic virus were correct. The information does contain the research showing how this can be done. Are you familiar with DARPA?" Charles inquired.

"Unfortunately, yes. I know it is a research group connected with the United State military." Alex placed the phone between her right shoulder and her cheek. She grabbed a pen and some paper and scribbled the letters D A R P A. "Don't tell me they have something to do with this?"

"You are right, it is part of the United States Government Department of Defense. It stands for Defense Advanced Research Projects Agency. You might say it is an agency that conducts research in the hopes of coming up with the next almighty weapon that can be used to destroy the enemy. DARPA has funded this research, Alexandra. I am not a big fan of theirs, and the very fact that we have something they are involved in scares me."

Charles' voice was steady and assured, but his usual tone of frivolity and excitement was gone. "It's almost impossible to find out the inner workings of that Agency and what any details are on the projects they are involved with, but I think the research contained here has exceeded even the depraved expectations of the minds at DARPA. This research contains detailed scientific data on the creation of a new virus, which, if it is successful, could be used to kill a selected group of humans. The researchers have identified the DNA gene combinations which determine uh, uh, God, Alex, I do not even know how to say this. Race, Alex! It determines a specific person's race! Alex heard the heavy sighs.

Alex's eyes were squeezed shut and her face was pale, "Do you mean to tell me that there is. . ."

"Wait, Alexandra, let me finish. There is more, and you need to hear this as well." As Charles spoke his voice cracked with each succeeding word, "The virus can search out a specific DNA pattern which makes up a specific race of people. This virus can be altered by its manufacturer to seek out *any* specified race. All other humans would be immune from this virus. The virus, aptly named the G-16 Virus, because there are 16 separate genes which determine one's race, could literally wipe out whole populations within a matter of a few weeks."

As Charles continued, Alex stopped pacing. Her head was bowed and she stared blankly at the stained carpet. Her left hand gripped her cell tightly to her ear and her right hand clutched a tangle of hair on the top of her head. She backed up to the foot of the bed and sat down on the plaid bedspread and leaned forward, her right elbow rested on her thigh and her hand cradled her head as she listened intently.

"The virus attaches to a host lymphocyte which contains the targeted DNA sequences. It injects into the targeted cell and immediately begins to replicate; over and over. The oxidated metabolism is poisoned and dumped into the mitochondrion. Other cells are infected and the first cell is destroyed. This process repeats itself at geometric speeds and, once the process begins, well, oh, geez Alex, the outcome is horrible."

Alex heard a long sigh. "What, Charles? What happens?"

"Well, the victim's capillaries clog with dead blood cells, the skin begins to bruise, blister and then dissolve much like wet paper. The blood begins to flow freely from the eyes, ears and nose and the victim begins to vomit the black sludge of his internal tissues. Death will usually occur within five days, at the most."

When Charles finished relaying the horrors of this discovery, the phone line was silent. No one spoke as each contemplated the atrocities of this dreadful virus. Finally, Charles spoke, "I'm scared, Alex—really scared. This is beyond anything I could possibly imagine. We need to tell someone about this *now*, before it is too late!"

"I cannot believe this, Charles. This sounds like Nazi Germany!" Alex stood up from the foot of the bed and turned toward Phil who's probing eyes searched for the reason that Alex's face was the color of chalk. Still clutching the back of her head, she asked, "So what do you think the relationship is between Cystic Fibrosis and this G-16 virus?"

"The cure for Cystic Fibrosis is real. I do not personally know if it works, but the research is there, and the supporting evidence is there. It needs to run its course through clinical trials, but it is all very positive."

"I suppose that is the good part of all this. But Charles, we cannot go to the authorities, or anyone at this point. We only have two days left to find who is behind all this before the research is delivered into the hands of whoever intends to use it. We don't have the time to spend with the authorities bringing them up-to-date on everything."

"But, Alexandra," Charles interrupted, "this can cause irreversible destruction. Thousands, even millions of people could be killed if this is unleashed. We have to do *something* before it is too late."

Alex sat dead still, her head slightly cocked upward, and she said, "I am getting closer to finding out who is behind all this. We have only two days, Charles. I am not going to take any time to bring anyone else up to speed here. You need to keep going through what you have, to see if you may have missed anything. You need to do that, Charles, and we will find whoever we are looking for in time. I just know it. Can you do that, Charles?"

"Oh, Alexandra, this has me so scared I do not know what to do. I wish I never got myself into this whole mess to begin with." Alex imagined Charles slumped over in his chair with his fingers tightly curled around the end of his droopy moustache.

"I am sorry about that, Charles. But without you, none of this would have ever been discovered in time. We can do this, Charles. I know we can."

"I have gone along with you this far but, oh God, what am I doing? Okay, I will keep doing everything I can on my end, but just hurry up, Alex. Please, hurry."

"I will, Charles. Believe me. My whole world rests with my finding out who is behind all of this. You have given me a lot to absorb and I will call you right away if I have any questions.

"Oh, one last thing. Can the G-16 virus spread by itself from human to human? Or does it stay with the injected target?"

"Well, that is another frightening part of this new virus that I have not told you about yet." Charles' voice had a renewed strength, but it still reflected the utter horror of what he had uncovered.

"Once the virus is inserted in the human, it spreads geometrically from lymphocyte to lymphocyte. It looks like they are using the controlled flight of mosquitoes to carry the virus from one human to another. By using thousands of mosquitoes, this virus could be spread throughout a population very, very fast. Although the virus spreads very rapidly, it remains dormant in the human system. In fact, it will remain dormant until it is activated externally. The viral genes are equipped with what is called a promoter switch. This type of switch is not all that uncommon, but whoever is behind this research has other things in mind. They have developed special promoter agents, or activating materials that would be placed in the water supply. Once someone who is infected with the virus comes in contact with the water, the switch is turned on, and the virus becomes live. At that point, the cell replication begins and the results are, well, I think you know what they would be." Charles paused for Alex's reaction.

There was no audible reaction.

Alex's finger flipped her lower lip. Her eyes were nailed shut and she asked, "What kind of testing has been done on all of this? If this is such ground-breaking research, as you say, do you know if it even works? It just doesn't seem all that possible to me."

Charles responded, "Alexandra, all the research supports the conclusions I have given you. They originally used monkeys to develop and test the results, and when they reached a point at which they believed everything would work as intended, they exceeded what would be normal scientific protocol by anyone's standards. Alex, uh. . .uh, oh, God, Alex, this has already been tested on three *human* subjects. Each person died within five days."

"Oh God, Charles, I cannot believe something like this is really possible. What have we have stumbled onto?" Alex's voice trailed off as she imagined the potential destruction from this vile creation.

Charles broke the silence, "Now there are still some other items here."

Charles' monotone voice began to take on more of his usual animation. "I do not really know for sure, but I surmise that DARPA funded the research for its SyNAPSE program and this research somehow went out of control."

"Do you have any idea who, specifically, conducted this research?" Alex asked.

"Not exactly. I was able to find out that DARPA awarded a research grant for the SyNAPSE program to a company called MIS Holdings. It's not a true scientific research company, but more of a consultant that oversees research. This research was carried out in several locations, but the final results were tested at the Health Containment Laboratory in Brazil. It's a top-level facility owned by the United States government that I need not get into now, but there is a whole story behind that facility. That is as far as I can get on this now."

Alex thanked Charles, reminded him again not to speak to anyone about this, and then hung up the phone.

"Well, what the hell was that?" Phil leaned against the closed bathroom door with his elbows pressed into his sides, his arms extended and his palms facing upward, "What was that all about?"

Moving in slow motion, Alex slid down to the floor. Her back was pressed against the foot of the bed. Her arms were coiled tightly around her bent legs and her head was propped on her knees. Not knowing if she should open her eyes or close them, she replied, "Well, it looks like Cystic Fibrosis may now have a cure, but it's wrapped in the veil of Eschatology. Phil, are you familiar with the first Book of Enoch as it relates to the Jewish and Christian religions?

"Not really, but what does that have to do with any of this?"

With her eyes wide open she looked directly at Phil, and said, "Eschatology is a theological science that covers the last four things of life: death, judgment, heaven and hell. Part of the Book of Enoch describes Enoch's visits to Heaven in the form of travels, visions and dreams, and his revelations."

Alex stared straight ahead. "If we do not get to the bottom of all this soon, very soon, we will find out if the Book of Enoch is really true."

CHAPTER 41

"PACK UP. WE NEED TO BE OUT OF HERE IN THIRTY seconds. I just saw what looks like the same white Taurus that we saw parked by my house. Now it's out front." Phil had just returned with a bucket of ice from the machine down the hall. Alex could tell by the grittiness in his voice and the speed of his words that he meant now, not thirty seconds.

With ten seconds to spare they were packed and out the door. They used the outside stairwell next to their room and both descended two stairs at a time. Rounding the stairs from the second to the ground floor, Phil collided head-on with a man and his young son. The three tumbled to the ground, and Phil instinctively used his body as a cushion to break the fall of the young boy. The Burger King sacks and the large sodas the man and his son were carrying flew through the railing and landed on the ground below. The young boy who couldn't have been any older than 6 let out a startled cry and tears streamed down his cheeks.

"Hey. Look what you've done!" the father screamed as his eyes bore into Phil and then he leaned down, "It's okay, Curt. It's okay."

"I'm so sorry, I really didn't see you." Phil reached into his pants pocket and pulled out a $20 bill, "Here you guys, buy some more food. I really am sorry, but I'm in a hurry." Phil continued his descent with Alex trailing a half a step behind.

The noise from the stairwell didn't go unnoticed. Two men standing alongside the Taurus turned and saw Phil and Alex as they reached the ground level and they immediately made their way toward them. They were not yet running, but their hurried, long strides meant there was little time to react.

"You get the car and bring it around front and I will delay these guys until you get here."

"Whoa!" Phil said as he clasped his long fingers on Alex's shoulder. "I think *I'll* delay them, and *you* go get the car."

"Nope. Here." Alex peeled Phil's hand from her shoulder, thrust the car keys in it and closed his fingers. She turned and walked defiantly toward the two men.

"Do you guys know where we might find a Starbucks in this neighborhood?" Alex stood directly in front of the two men who were now stopped on each side of her. "The coffee in this place just does not cut it."

The man on Alex's left appeared to be the one in control. His bland, nondescript clothes meant he didn't want anyone to pay much attention to him. He wanted to surround himself with a cloak of invisibility. The fact that he was the size and shape of a dumpster made that impossible. "Jake and I were just heading over to a coffee shop just down the street. Care to join us?"

"Your car is parked over there and you are walking this way. I do not think so. I think I will just wait for my ride. Thanks anyway." Alex stepped forward between the two men. Jake, the shorter of the two reached out and grabbed Alex by her right forearm. "Not so fast. We've been looking for you, and I think you'll be coming with us. We don't really care about your boyfriend." The man pulled Alex's arm toward him, and she reacted. She swung around and her left hand landed open-palm directly in the man's exposed thyroid cartilage sending him writhing to the ground gasping for air. Her left leg cocked and exploded, landing directly in the boss man's groin. He doubled over and she spun and lifted her right knee into his rib cage. He was out.

Phil pulled up and the brakes screeched as he leaped from the car. "No. Don't tell me you carry an army in that backpack of yours. This is really your work?" He stared incredulously at the two men lying motionless on the ground. The only movement was an occasional groan and each man's fast twitch muscles sporadically searching for a connection to activate their memory panel. He reached down and took the 9mm Beretta PX4 Storm Sub-Compact that had fallen from Jake's shoulder holster.

Alex stood up after she retrieved the other man's Beretta and the remaining magazines, and chortled, "That felt good, really good. It has been a long time since I have been able to land some kicks on someone who actually deserved it. I think our thirty seconds are up though. We should leave—now!"

Alex and Phil sped out of the motel entrance and onto Redwood Highway just as the third man exited the motel office. His proud smirk faded when he looked to his right and saw his two companions lying in arthritic poses on the oil-stained asphalt.

CHAPTER 42

"THIS IS SOMETHING OUT OF MISSION IMPOSSIBLE. We need to find Tom Cruise, maybe he can solve this." Phil was half joking, but his mind had difficulty wrapping itself around the reality of the situation they faced. Alex had brought Phil up to date on her conversation with Charles on the drive from their now-abandoned safe haven in Novato to a small coffee shop in Mill Valley where they took up temporary refuge. La Coppa Coffee was in the heart of the bucolic and yuppie downtown area of Mill Valley. It was considered a local haunt and was frequented mostly by local residents who could sit at their laptops for hours and be ignored. For that reason alone, Phil had driven directly there.

Phil sipped on a large black coffee, while Alex rested her hands against the mug of her double espresso. There was a lot of work to be done. They needed to find out everything they could about MIS Holdings. Who they were; who owned them; who ran the company; its board of directors; past projects; current projects—

anything that would lead to some type of connection to the chain of events as they now knew them. MIS Holdings was not a public company, so their records were limited. An initial Google search revealed mostly press releases that only generally described the company's work. There was no mention of DARPA, SyNAPSE or anything remotely connected to what they were looking for.

"DARPA" revealed similar results. Its inner workings were only known by a select few government agencies and it was not even certain that those agencies knew much. There were a number of public interest and conspiracy theory groups that were highly critical of the work DARPA undertook. Those groups referred to DARPA as the intellectual sandbox for depraved scientific minds. Maybe they could be helpful? If only they had the time.

Constance's campaign fund-raising filings were voluminous. It would take days to go through that information. They didn't have days. They didn't know if they even had hours.

The incoming beep. . .beep from Alex's computer had not even finished when she swung around, grabbed her mouse and clicked on her inbox icon.

A message from Cyberclaw -

> Must meet you at the pier at Horseshoe Bay, near the Coast Guard Station at 13:00 hours today. Last info must be delivered in person.

Cyberclaw

Alex and Phil stared intently at the message. One o'clock was only two hours away. How did this person even know that they would read the message before then? How did they know where they were?

Phil spoke first, "We need to be there, but we should consider getting some help. We don't know who this Cyberclaw is, or what he wants. We've already had guys with handguns looking for us, for Christ's sake."

"Yeah. Maybe. But I think I am better off going on my own. Whoever Cyberclaw may be, he or she has given us some helpful leads. We do not have much time to figure this out, and my instinct is that we, or I mean I, need to do this."

"Nope. I'm going with you. Look, you were great back there at the motel. Those guys didn't see anything coming, but we need to have strength in numbers on this one, even if that number is only two." Phil pounded a clenched fist down on the table for emphasis. "This point is not open for discussion."

Alex leaned forward in her chair. With her elbows placed squarely on the table, her fingers clasped tightly, she cradled her chin on her thumbs and looked straight into Phil's weary, but still alert eyes. "You do not really know much about me, about my past, about what I have done or what I am capable of doing. You do know, because I told you, that if it were not for me pirating certain information from GEN, Ben would be here today. I have to live with that for the rest of my life. I will dwell alone in an isolated cell that houses only broken dreams. That is my penance."

Alex paused. Her own words stung. She knew that if anything had happened to Benjamin, she would be occupying that isolated cell soon—very soon. She tilted her head and continued, "We are close, Phil, to finding out what we need to know. I know we are. I will go and meet this person, and you should stay here and see what you can come up with on MIS Holdings."

"This just doesn't sit right with me. We're better off doing this together. We can come back here afterwards and continue our search for information on MIS."

Needing to reemphasize her point, Alex leaned back in her chair; her arms tightly crossed in front of her chest, and said,

"Phil, you need to go along with me on this. This is not about my safety. I can take care of myself. Whoever this Cyberclaw is, he or she is expecting me, not you. We do not want them getting nervous or scared and going underground again. They have information, and we need whatever information we can get. I will be careful. I will not get out of the car. And remember, I am now armed which makes me dangerous." Alex patted herself just under her left breast to underscore the point.

She reached across the table with her left hand, her open palm faced upwards, and she continued, "Now give me the keys. We still have some time here to get some research done before I need to leave."

The buoyant aura that typically surrounded Phil was gone. Instead, his appearance reflected a somber and grave man uncomfortable with the verdict he was about to reach. With his eyes fixed firmly on Alex's unwavering stare he slowly, but forcefully, slid the keys across the table.

"Be careful," was all Phil could say, but he meant every word.

CHAPTER 43

Alex found a secluded spot along Murray Circle where she pulled over to the curb and parked. To her right, the three-story whitewashed building with its red shingled roof had a stately, but complex elegance. It was distinguished from the other buildings set evenly back from this tree-lined street only by a single dormer extending from the midpoint of its gabled roof.

From this vantage point, she could see the pier jutting out near the Coast Guard station. Horseshoe Bay was located in Ft. Baker at the southern tip of Marin County and at the foot of the Golden Gate Bridge. The heart of Ft. Baker was the large grass-covered parade grounds surrounded by stately Colonial style buildings constructed in the early 1900's. Some twenty years ago, the military transferred Ft. Baker to the Golden Gate National Recreation Area. The post looked exactly the same as it did 100 years ago, its original design still intact.

The day was overcast and blustery, not uncommon for a mid-September day in the Bay Area. The dampness in the air was ripe with the distinctive and fragrant aroma of the Eucalyptus trees that lined the streets. She spotted a few tourists milling around, so the place didn't appear to be totally deserted, but it wasn't the crowded square swarming with bustling and gawking tourists she would have preferred.

She had arrived at the rendezvous point thirty minutes early, wanting to get a good look at the place before she met up with Cyberclaw, or whomever. She drove around the park and located the two street exits leading out of the area. If she was looking for a place to set up an encounter with no escape route this would be it. The entire park was located at the base of steep hills with San Francisco Bay bordering its south end. The two street exits both led to Alexander Avenue, a two lane street often gridlocked with cars coming to and from the tourist town of Sausalito.

Alex remained in the borrowed Volvo and her head rested comfortably against the padded headrest. She mapped the park layout in her mind, knowing that she might at anytime have to make a split decision—a decision that could cost her dearly. Her eyes scoured the landscape and she selected landmarks and committed them to memory. Her methodical scrutiny came to a screeching halt when her eyes landed on the Golden Gate Bridge to her right. Her memory no longer recorded her visual sightings. It catapulted back in time. It seemed like so long ago, a lifetime or more, when she drove across that bridge, her mission completed, but her life-altering events just began. *Why did I not just walk away from all of this when I could? I had the chance that night at Ben's to forget about Andre and my so-called "sacred debt." I know he would have understood if I had told him who I really was. Oh, Ben, how could all this happen? How could I have done this to you?*

Alex's internal quarrel ended without warning when she felt the vibration in her hip pocket. She impulsively shook her head and felt the warm waves flood through her body as she brought herself back to the moment. She recognized the number immediately. "I am here. Nothing going on yet."

"You were supposed to call me when you got there. I'm five miles away worrying my ass off here. Is everything ok?" Phil was anxious and concerned, but his voice echoed a tone of relief when he heard Alex's voice.

"I am sorry. I have been looking over the place trying to get a lay of the land. I have not seen anyone yet. Have you come up with anything on MIS?"

"Nothing yet, but I may be on to something I'm just not sure yet. You'll call me in half an hour, like we agreed?"

"Yes, I will remember this time. Thanks." Alex placed her phone back in her hip pocket.

The chilly on-and-off drizzle had just ended again, but an icy wind had picked up. Alex turned on the ignition and started the car. The warm air from the heater began to take the edge off the damp chill of her skin when she spotted a man walking toward the pier. She watched this person slowly edge out to the midpoint of the pier and with one hand resting on the metal railing he gazed out toward the bridge. The other hand anchored a black baseball cap to his head so it wouldn't soar off with the gusting winds. The cap was pulled down in front and would block any clear view of his face if he were to turn in her direction. His back was to her and she was still too far away to know if she recognized him. He wore blue jeans and his red flannel shirt was exposed through his partially zipped, light-weight black windbreaker. He was alone. She couldn't see any signs of others who might be staking out the meeting point.

Within minutes her car was parked next to the Coast Guard station. She wasn't able to appreciate the irony of the fact that this particular station was active in search and rescue missions and homeland security. She wondered why the place wasn't packed with security personnel. Halfway out the pier was a man who may have more information affecting homeland security than all those prisoners housed at Guantanamo.

She stepped out of her car and slowly moved to the foot of the pier. Her eyes continued to dart about, scouting for any signs of movement. Her arms dangled by her side, but they remained flexed and on alert. The man on the pier turned and saw Alex. Alex appeared to remain calm on the outside, but inside she simmered as rage spread through her limbs. Andre! It is Andre! He cannot be here to help me!

Alex was startled again when she heard the sound of car doors slam shut behind her. Keeping an eye focused on Andre, she turned to see two men mechanically advancing toward her. They had parked directly behind her car, so it was of no value to her now. Whoever those two men were, they weren't there to help her. Andre had moved several feet to the side and was standing behind a large round bearing piling.

"Alexandra. Let's just do this the easy way. Come with us, and everything will be okay." The man's shoes squished in the rain puddles and he stopped in front of Alex's car. His right hand clung tightly to his turned-up lapel and Alex could see the bump underneath his raincoat. The flaps of his left eye lid drooped down and partially obstructed his vision. The stubbles covering his chin showed he hadn't slept in several days. This was not a man known for his patience.

"And what if I want to do it the hard way? What are you going to do—shoot me?" Alex knew there was no escape from this pier, and she wasn't going to wait around for the Coast Guard to show up. She was on her own.

The man tipped his hat. "It makes no difference to us. Our orders are to bring you in. Nobody told us you had to be alive."

The larger of the two men bristled as he made this remark, and he began to slowly trudge toward Alex. She knew she could out-run this man if it came to that. His bulky frame may have had some muscle somewhere, but it was well hidden and probably hadn't been used for anything other than shoveling food. Anyway, this wouldn't come down to a foot race. That much was clear.

Instinctively, Alex made her play. She leaped to her right, grabbed the metal railing and hurled herself over the side. She landed in several feet of water and without breaking stride moved to the exposed rocky shoreline underneath the pier. The tide was ebbing and she stood still under the solid concrete pier with her borrowed Beretta drawn and cocked. She had jumped around fifteen feet. Her only escape from here was to hope they would leave—or to kill them. She doubted they would leave on their own free will.

She heard the men's footfalls overhead as they moved to the point where she had jumped and they looked over each side of the pier. "Not a good move, Alexandra. You have to come out sometime, and we're not planning on going anywhere soon."

About halfway down the pier at a point where it made a 90 degree turn and jutted out another 100 feet, Alex saw a ladder that ran from the waterline to the top of the pier. She quickly moved toward the ladder taking extra care not to make any splashes. The only thing she had in her favor now was the element of surprise. She scaled the ladder to just below the decking of the pier, and raised her head over the top to see the two men still leaning over the sides and walking slowly out the pier. She saw no sign of Andre. She climbed up two more steps and made sure that the loud clump of her feet hitting the steel rungs would be heard by the men. Their heads snapped and they ran toward her. Alex slid down the ladder and prepared to wait.

"Alright, lady, you want to do this the hard way? We'll show you how it's done."

Alex heard the men talking above her, but their voices were muted by the lapping of the ocean waves beneath them. Several minutes passed before Alex saw one foot descend on the ladder, followed by the second foot. Her fingers stiffened as she clutched the solid copper water pipe attached to the overhead concrete planking that ran the length of the pier. She had to plan this just right. Slowly she began to swing back and forth. Each swing brought her closer and closer to her intended target. Finally, just as the man's head cleared below the decking, she tightly coiled her legs and with her forward momentum behind her she heaved her legs forward and her heels struck the man in his groin. The force of Alex's kick sent the man reeling backwards from the ladder. His shrieks of pain only stopped when his head sank below the surface of the water.

Slowly, Alex sidled hand over hand down the water pipe back toward the shore. When she reached the shoreline, there was no sign of the man with the concave groin rearing his head from the choppy waters. The other man, the one with the robotic walk, oversized girth and stubbly face, was somewhere nearby. Alex remained crouched in the sand, her eyes closed to heighten her other senses. The beating waves lapping against the shoreline and the cawing of gulls were the only sounds echoing in the damp, still air. He was up there somewhere. She was certain of that.

Alex crawled along the sand making sure she remained under the planking of the pier. When she reached the foot of the pier, she lifted her head and saw him. He was still half way out the pier standing near the ladder. By his baffled expression, she knew he was just as lost as his partner. Whatever patience he had had before was drained by now. She needed to be careful. She crawled, jumped from rock to rock and eventually found herself looking in the driver's side window of her pursuer's white Buick Regal. The keys dangled from the ignition.

Jumping in, Alex started the car, put it in reverse and cranked the steering wheel hard left. The tires spun, and cakes of mud flew. As she sped forward and peeled away she heard the shots: one, two, three shots and the rear window shattered, hurling razor-sharp shards of glass through the car. The last shot landed inches from her right shoulder and splintered the gear shift handle that extended from the steering column.

She pulled onto Alexander Avenue and headed to the 101 Freeway. She punched in a three digit number on her cell phone. When a person answered she calmly, but convincingly said, "There has been a shooting at the Coast Guard pier at Horseshoe Bay." She placed the phone on the passenger seat and wondered to herself, what are the odds that Homeland Security will arrive before the local police?

CHAPTER 44

ALEX ABANDONED THE BUICK IN FRONT OF THE Safeway at the Strawberry Village Shopping Center. Someone would be looking for that car and she wanted to be far away from it—the sooner the better. She hopped a Marin Transit bus to downtown Mill Valley. There was still a drizzle in the air when she exited the bus on Throckmorton in the heart of downtown. Standing under the canopy of the Mill Valley Market, she had a clear view of La Coppa Coffee about one block to the south. She couldn't see Phil from this vantage point so she followed the sidewalk, being careful to stay behind the window-shoppers that were moseying through town. Standing in front of the Bank of America building across the street from the coffee shop, she spotted Phil, still sitting where she had left him.

She entered the coffee shop and stopped across from where Phil sat. His left hand was scribbling away on his white legal pad. His right hand was half closed and pressed against his lips and he breathed with evenly measured pants through the opening. His eyes were glazed and locked on the computer screen. An invisible shield protected him and he was oblivious to the clamor and ambiance of his surroundings.

Finally, Alex pulled a chair out and sat down. Her hands were placed evenly on the edge of the table with her thumbs locked underneath, "Nice to see that you are worried about me."

"Christ. Alex. You're here." He glanced quickly at his watch. "I was just about to call you. I've been worried. Are you okay?" He reached over and placed a protective hand over Alex's. The warmth of his hand chased away the chill she was somehow growing accustomed to.

"I would not call it a walk in the park, but yes, I am okay."

Alex looked down at the three empty porcelain coffee cups next to the laptop, smiled and said, "I think you drink more coffee than anyone I know. I am surprised you can sit still in a chair this long."

Phil took a gulp from a half-filled cup, nodded, and said, "Well, I look at it this way. When your car is low on oil, you add just enough so that it gently purrs again. Right? When I'm growling and testy, I add just enough coffee to make me sweet and lovable. Right now, I'm sweet and lovable, but it probably won't last long. So, let's hear it. What happened?"

Alex ordered an espresso for herself, and then brought Phil up to date on her outing at the pier. She gave him all the details, except the part about the bullets that she could still hear ricocheting in the hollows of her ears. Some things were best untold.

As Alex spoke, her mind weighed and balanced the facts, but she was unable to make any sense out of the presence of Andre. What was he doing there? If he was Cyberclaw, why was he trying to help us? And what about those two men? They did not seem to pay any attention to him. Where did he go? The whole episode left her with more questions than answers. But she was sure of one thing—whatever the truth might be, Andre has something to do with all of this.

Alex leaned back in her chair, lifted her chin up and stretched her arms high above her head, like a diver parting the water. She exhaled slowly. The warm air escaped her lungs and kneaded her knotted and aching muscles. She was riding on the edge of stress overload. She needed sleep. She needed food, and she needed to shed this mysterious and secretive life she had been living for too long.

The long stretches eased her tension, and her heart rate began to drop as her mind circled back to that warm night when her head was nestled against Benjamin's chest and his arms completely enveloped her. She remembered the softness in his voice as he told her about the eagle; how he had worked to repair its broken wing and how its mate was waiting for its homecoming. These birds picked their mate for life, he said, and each day together was cherished as if it were the last.

"Alex. Alex? Are you okay?" Phil's hand gently shook her shoulder.

"Oh. Whew. I was just daydreaming a bit. Wondering how all this happened." Alex pulled the sleeve on her sweatshirt down over her hand and reached up to catch a tear that had not quite dampened her cheeks. The floodgates had not yet burst, but she was just moments away from sobbing uncontrollably.

"Anyway, I am fine now. By the looks of things, you have been busy. Did you come up with anything helpful?"

Alex shifted in her seat, shook her hands and clenched her fists a few times. She felt the blood begin to flow and the color return to her face.

Phil's head was cocked to one side, and his hair was ruffled more than usual. The whites of his eyes had a distinct red rim that reflected the fire smoldering in his gut. Like Alex, he was dead-tired too, but he was now certain that they were in the closing minutes of identifying Benjamin's kidnappers. Part of him was afraid of how he might react when the answer finally flashed before his eyes. Phil had always been a non-violent person. In fact, some would identify him as the ultimate pacifist. But this was different. Benjamin was his best friend, and probably the closest friend he had ever had. If anything were to happen to Benjamin, it would be the first real loss Phil had endured and somehow he already knew that his life would be altered because of it. What would it be like when he needed to pick up the phone and hear that reassuring voice that had become a part of his routine mental therapy? No, maybe there were times when it was necessary to expend all your energy to pummel and tear apart another human being, limb by limb.

"I'm not sure where to start, so just hang with me here. I may ramble on, but I think we have some good stuff." He picked up his legal pad and began to thumb through the pages. "First, I did some background searches on some of the cast of characters here, and I started with Murray. I figured that since I know him, it may be easier to sift through stuff about him. Anyway, it turns out that Murray was a private first class in the U.S. Army in Viet Nam. In 1967, he and other members of his battalion were involved in a battle called the Battle of Ong Thang. That group incurred huge losses in the early minutes of the battle. When it was over, nearly all their men were dead or injured. Murray was injured in that battle, and received a Purple Heart. His commanding officer saved his life. He carried Murray on his shoulders for close to a mile until they were rescued by a chopper. This same commanding officer also saved the life of Nathaniel Brooks, who is now the Chief Executive Officer of MIS Holdings." Phil paused and lowered his legal pad and looked at Alex, "Well? What do you think so far?"

"I am still digesting all this. Who is the commanding officer? Anyone I have heard of?" Her hands were outstretched, palms up and her fingers were tugging with a "come on, let me have it" motion.

"The commanding officer is none other than Paul Brewster, the man who is now in charge of DARPA. Brewster even received a Medal of Honor for his heroic efforts that day. He's a regular war hero.

"Hold on, though, we have one more guy involved in all of this. Another guy was there in that same battle. He wasn't injured, but he was part of the same battalion and he flew out on the same chopper. Garran Upshaw. Heard of him?"

"No! You are not talking about a Lieutenant Colonel Garran Upshaw, are you?"

"I don't know his rank, but he was a military career guy. You know him?"

Alex shook her head. "Maybe. I do not know him personally, but he was in charge of computer security for a military system that I shut down some time ago. I ended up with the specs for a Magnetic Anomaly Detector and I am sure he ended up with a good tongue lashing or two. So what's his involvement here?"

"Well, it seems he left the military a few years ago and started his own company, G4G Security Solutions. It's a hi-tech security company that handles a lot of contract work for the government. They have patents on certain security software and hardware that enables all of the monitoring to take place in a central location. It's pretty cost effective, so the articles say. Anyway, MIS Holdings is wholly owned by G4G. MIS has no real function, other than it obtains government grant funds, disburses them, and then monitors the progress. Pretty slick. They do it all for a slice of the pie."

Phil pushed his chair back, slid his notepad toward Alex, and stood up. "I'm going to get a muffin and maybe a banana. I'll give you a minute to think about all this. Want anything?"

"No, I think my plate is pretty full as it is. This is a lot of stuff Phil. You have added a lot of pieces to this puzzle that need to be carefully placed. I do mean carefully. This may involve bigger players than I originally expected."

Alex's mind was again churning through the evidence, whittling through the compound pieces that had a multitude of meanings. Her elbows were squared flat on the table and her hands clasped together covering her mouth and nose. Her thumbs pressed against her jawbone. Her small fingers tapped together gently. This was her own interpretation of Rodin's famous bronze bust, The Thinker.

Phil returned with a plate loaded with muffins, fruit, chocolates and whatever else he could find. "Here. You need to eat some of this anyway. It's actually pretty good, I've been eating it all day." He reached forward and placed a blueberry muffin in Alex's hand.

"So, did you finish the puzzle or would you like me to tell you about Rush?"

CHAPTER 45

"I'M NOT SURE HOW WELL I REALLY KNOW HER OR if anybody really knows her, but I just can't believe that she has anything to do with this." Phil's eyes were locked on the three story multi-colored Victorian house where he thought maybe, just maybe, it's possible they would get the answers they needed.

Phil and Alex had taken a cab across the Golden Gate Bridge into the City to the upper reaches of Vallejo Street, a ritzy, leafy area that housed the City's privileged elite. Phil suspected that they would find Constance here at the home of a friend. She was now in their crosshairs.

"Phil and. . .uh, what are you two doing here?" Dressed in a pair of blue Cal sweatpants, a faded, but plain matching blue hooded sweatshirt and looking like sleep was a long lost friend, Constance staggered backwards when Phil pushed the door aside and he and Alex stomped through the entryway.

Slamming the door shut behind him, Phil's eyes glowered down at Constance, "We're going to talk. Now! You'd better sit down."

The standoff was broken when Constance turned and without a word, walked back to the den. She sat down on a red velvet arm chair and with her hands placed on the armrests, she asked, "I don't really know why. . ."

"Stop! At this point all I want to hear out of your mouth is answers." Alex walked toward Constance and knelt down in front of her. Small tremors ran through Alex's muscles and the repressed force deep inside her was about to be unleashed.

"I have just been shot at by some men who will themselves pay dearly for missing me. Whoever they work for does not want me walking around. They will not stop until everyone that knows anything at all about them is dead. I am going to tell you what we have learned and what we know. That way you can either cooperate with us, or these men will kill you as well."

Alex rose and took several steps back. Her arms were crossed in front of her, and her hands gripped her elbows. She paced back and forth like a scorpion dancing around its prey. She shot an occasional glance at Constance.

Her tone was sword-sharp, "It turns out that GEN was conducting genetic research well beyond the scope of its Cystic Fibrosis model. Without going into great detail at this point, the research involves the creation of a new virus which can be used to target a select group of humans *and* kill them. This particular virus can attach to a specific gene combination that determines a person's race. Within a matter of days an entire *race* can be eliminated. They have tested this on human beings already--it works!"

Alex paused and let the harshness of her tone linger in the dead silence. Constance looked up and met Alex's stare. "I know that Ben would not have had anything to do with any of this. I don't think he paid all that much attention to the day-to-day workings of GEN, but there is no way he would have permitted this to happen if he knew anything about it."

"You are absolutely right. He did not know anything about this particular research, but Murray was deeply involved."

"But, if Ben knew nothing about this then there would've been no reason to kidnap him. His kidnapping must have been an accident, or it had to do with something else."

Alex tempered her tone, but continued her verbal assault, "It was no accident, Constance. All the data for this research was pirated from GEN using Ben's password and access information. That much we know, and so do the people behind all this. All the evidence around the theft of the research points directly to Ben. The fact that we know he had nothing to do with this is not important at this point. What *is* important is that the people behind this research have the capability to do anything to get what they want. We know that you are very familiar with DARPA, The Defense Advanced Research Projects Agency. You must know about the SyNAPSE project as well?"

Constance's rapid tapping of her left forefinger came to a sudden halt, and her light brown smooth complexion was drained of color. She crossed her legs and placed the palms of her hands face down on her thighs. She slowly let out a deep sigh, met Alex's gaze, and said, "Of course I'm familiar with them. I'm on a Committee that has certain oversight responsibilities on DARPA. You're not suggesting they are involved?"

"That would be the Armed Services Committee, and yes, while that particular committee does not have budgetary oversight, it does have project oversight and several times a year the Director, Paul Brewster, appears before your Committee to report on project developments."

"Look, I don't know where you're going with all this, and from what I've heard so far I don't think you really know either." Constance appeared to have regained part of her composure. She stood and her right hand motioned toward the front door. "I think it's time that you both leave. We're finished here. And Phil, Ben adores you. I can't believe that you've got yourself all tied up in this conspiracy thing, or whatever you two want to call it."

Phil moved in the direction of the front entrance, but he had no intention of leaving, not yet. He rubbed his hand several times over his stubbly whiskered chin and then looked up. Staring harshly at Constance and with both fists tightly clenched against his sides, he said, "Constance, you're not running for office in this room today. Everything we've told you is true, every word of it. A deadly weapon has been developed, and the effects of this weapon are far beyond the comprehension of any of us. You need to stop the bullshit and tell us what you know about DARPA, and Paul Brewster. Brewster, Paulson and two other guys, Nathaniel Brooks and Garran Upshaw, all served in the military together, and the four of them have their fingerprints all over this mess. They're behind Ben's kidnapping for Christ's sake. Doesn't that mean anything to you? Don't you want to see these men pay? I sure as hell do."

Phil eased over to Constance and placed a hand on her shoulder. Leaning down so he could look directly into her eyes, he whispered, "Somewhere inside you is someone screaming, screaming to help us here, to help find Ben and to clear his name from what may just become one of the largest terrorist disasters in history. *Please*, Constance."

Her legs trembled and she reached for the armrest on the red velvet chair. She slumped back down and the tears began to stream unevenly down her cheeks.

Alex and Phil exchanged glances and anxiously waited in the stillness of the room. Alex's thoughts turned to Benjamin. She fought to keep those conflicting emotions away. She knew she needed to stay focused on the moment and not get lost in the emptiness that would swallow her if anything had happened to him. She had tried over the past few days to keep all this at bay, but now, watching the tears flow from the wife of the man who had taught her how to embrace her past, and to once again love Christina and all that they shared, the grief that she fought to keep away began to creep through her veins toward her heart. Quickly, she took several deep breaths. She held each breath in as long as possible and exhaled as slowly as possible. She looked over at Phil and saw that he was firm and unyielding. His presence steadied her.

"I had no idea any of this would happen. Least of all that anything could ever happen to Ben over any of this." Constance's eyes were shut, she was slumped forward in her chair and continued, "I was involved in helping DARPA avoid the investigative arm of the State Department in its responsibility for overseeing the Biological Weapons Convention Treaty. Paul Brewster had convinced me that the State Department was being overly aggressive in its enforcement procedures, and he had asked me to intervene on his behalf. That's exactly what I did. I knew about the SyNAPSE project and its implications. I was assured that the project was safe, and conducive to peaceful and covert uses only. At that time, that was all I knew and I was able to get the State Department to halt its investigation."

Constance leaned back in her chair and with the sleeves of her sweatshirt wiped the tear stains from her cheeks. She stared at the ceiling and after several loud sighs, she continued, "It wasn't until a few weeks later when I was at the offices of DARPA that I learned the rest of the facts. I was in Paul Brewster's office to discuss an upcoming fund raiser I was having and he had agreed to assist in putting it on. We were going over some of the details. He was called out of the office for a few minutes and while he was gone I noticed an email on his screen. The email was from Murray Paulson so I opened it. That email contained enough information that I knew the SyNAPSE research had gone far beyond its intended purpose. I didn't know about targeting a particular race, but I did learn from the email that they were creating a virus that would attach to human genes.

"When Paul returned to the room I confronted him about Murray's email. He didn't bat an eye. He swiveled around in his chair, opened the email, read it and deleted it. He looked me right in the eyes and, as only he can do, he said, "We owe a lot of this success to you, Constance, and that's why we keep the campaign funds pouring in for you. We have not only completed the SyNAPSE program, and way ahead of schedule, I may add, but we have taken it to its ultimate extreme. Very shortly, we will have created the most powerful weapon ever. It is beyond anyone's comprehension."

"We argued over this, and I eventually left. So, yes, I did know something about all this, but I never thought that Ben would be involved. Surely not kidnapped."

At that point both Alex and Phil were sitting down and had absorbed every bit of Constance's confession. While the wheels of their brains turned to reflect upon everything, their stomachs churned over the thought that this woman would sit on this information.

"Why didn't you do something at that point, Constance? You, of all people. You could have brought this to the attention of even the President," asked Phil.

"I started to. I called Ben and I wanted to talk to him about GEN and to see what he might know about SyNAPSE."

Constance hesitated, "We never got to the SyNAPSE issue. That's when Ben told me he was in love with another woman and he wanted a divorce. I really didn't see that coming, but I knew I needed to talk to him about all of this before I went to anyone else. I rearranged my schedule and I came out to California several days later, but by then it was too late."

Phil looked over at Alex. By now, he knew her well enough that he could tell her thoughts had drifted somewhere back in time to when all this was happening. He stood up and tucked in the tail of his brown T-shirt, and queried, "Constance, you knew the importance of all this. You could have gone to somebody right then. I just don't understand. Why didn't you? Or why haven't you by now, for that matter?"

"Is everything that simple Phil? I don't think so. There have only been two men in my life that I have admired and loved and I haven't done a very good job of that. I love Ben. I haven't been a good wife, and he deserves someone far better than me. I can't deny that. The only other man I have loved is Paul Brewster. He's my father."

CHAPTER 46

A FTER MEETING WITH CONSTANCE, ALEX AND PHIL had taken a cab to Novato in northern Marin County and checked into the Econo Lodge on Alameda Del Prado. Constance had acknowledged that her father was called Rush by a select few of his friends. The rescue mission at the Battle of Ong Thang was called Operation Rush, and the few survivors from that mission used the code name admiringly when referring to their commanding officer.

Both Alex and Phil had both managed to get some much needed rest, but not before Alex had put together a complete chronicle of events and strategically placed it in several discreet blogs that she knew were regularly monitored by intelligence agencies. Going directly to the major media outlets was out of the question. They would move far too slowly for what was needed here and the government would have the ability to blackout any disclosure the mainstream outlets may want to initially make. No, if one of those blogs went viral, then this would get all the attention it needed.

That morning, Alex had gone out to collect a few newspapers so she could sit down and do several crossword puzzles. When she returned to the room, she did a quick check of the blogs on her computer and she suddenly yelled out, "Get up, Phil. We did it! Read this article." Phil jumped out of bed and they both stared at the screen where in large bold print they read the headline –

FRANCE ACCUSES U.S. OF WARFARE TREATY VIOLATION.

Phil began to read the article out loud to Alex.

> The French Government intends to file a formal complaint with the United Nations alleging violations by the United States under the terms of the Biological Weapons Convention Treaty of 1972. The allegation will charge the U.S. with conducting undisclosed genetic viral research aimed at creating new warfare weapons with the capability of destroying mankind.

Phil continued to read the article out loud until he came across Andre's name. Alex quickly pulled the screen toward her and began to read:

> In cooperation with the French Government, Andre Broussard, President of CS Generale, was instrumental in uncovering the viral research being secretly conducted by Mr. Paul Brewster, the Director of The Defense Advanced Research Projects Agency, known as DARPA, and in cooperation with MIS Holdings, Inc., of Alexandria, Virginia, and Genetic Engineering Nexus of Alameda, California. When questioned about his heroic efforts, Mr. Broussard would only respond, "Please print that Cyberclaw

wishes to thank Andromeda." He would not elaborate
further as to what this statement meant.

Alex laughed out loud with Phil. "It was him all the time. That
clever bastard! I will bet he has not told anyone about the Cystic
Fibrosis research that he ended up with. I have never known him
to help anyone unless there was a profit in it for him."

Alex reached for her phone and placed an overseas call.

"You son-of-a-bitch! Why did you not tell me?"

"Well, the least you could do is give me a thank you, or
perhaps a how are you?" Andre laughed as he began to unravel his
involvement. "I was contacted several months back by the French
government to assist them in confirming their suspicions that the
U.S was conducting this type of research and they explained if it
were in fact true it would be a direct violation of an international
treaty. I, of course, felt it was my patriotic duty as a Frenchman,
to assist."

"Yeah, right, patriotic duty, my ass. I know all about that. You
ended up with some completed research that provides a cure for
Cystic Fibrosis. Was that your patriotic duty as well?"

"Alex, Alex. Please do not insult the patriotism of a Frenchman.
I looked into GEN myself and I knew what they were working
on, and what I believed was that if they were involved in this
particular clandestine research, they would be shut down. I could
then step in and purchase the research for pennies on the dollar.
I had no way of knowing that you would hand it to me so readily,
and for a pretty low price I might add."

Alex chuckled, "Where have I heard that before?"

She now spoke in a serious tone, "Look Andre. I do not really
care how much money you make off all this. I have never really
cared about that. But what has happened to Ben? That is all I
really care about at this point."

"Please, Alex. I know where you are going and I would like to explain a few things to you. I was first contacted by Director Jean-Claude Imbot of the DGSE. He mentioned that the Agency had very credible information that led them to believe the United States was developing this particular virus and he wanted my help in recruiting *you* to help them. Even though there is bad blood between you and the Agency, they knew you were the best person for this job. They asked me to help recruit you. That is exactly what I did. The Agency put together the plan to take the Cystic Fibrosis research."

"How did you know that the virus research would be stored in those files?"

"DGSE had an inside man working with GEN and he was directly involved in all the virus research. He knew the files were encrypted and stored in the Cystic Fibrosis files, but he could not access them. The firewalls and security codes required someone with far more talent—someone like you. In fact, the man said he saw you coming out of Mr. Paulson's office and that you were surrounded by a "storm of anger." Those were his own words."

"Yeah, I do remember him. Where is Ben, Andre? Has the DGSE found him?"

"No, they have not, unfortunately. Not yet, Alex. You laid out a perfect road map for them when you posted your chronology online. They, along with the FBI, have each of the men in custody. Thanks to you, they will get to the bottom of things very quickly, I am sure."

"If anything has happened to Ben, I am responsible. If I had not got involved in this, he would be safe. I need more information, Andre. I must find Ben and make sure he is safe. That he has not been harmed."

"You need to know, Alex, that Mr. Hunter's bullet wounds suffered in that car were an accident. DGSE had agents following the car and they intended to monitor every move, to protect him. Mr. Hunter was involved in a fight with the man that held a gun on him in the car. He tried to jump from the car and the gun went off accidentally. I know that is not any consolation to you, but his being shot and hospitalized was, in fact, an accident. It was never part of DGSE's plan for any harm to come to him. Those people were after you, Alex. They were looking for the research material. That is all."

"I never thought I would ever have a reason to be involved with DGSE again. But now here I am. Who do I speak with about this, Andre? I cannot stop until I find Ben, and if they know anything that I do not, I need to know. I do not trust that DGSE will move quickly enough."

"I will call Director Imbot as soon as we are done, and see that you get everything you need. You may not realize it yet, Alex, but you have saved countless lives. Your deeds will not go unrewarded."

"Unrewarded! Jesus, Andre, I do not care about anything like that. Just get me in touch with the Director."

"You will hear from him shortly. I will make the call right now."

CHAPTER 47

ALEX WAS ONCE AGAIN SEATED IN THE PASSENGER seat of Phil's Karmann Ghia as they pulled up the familiar driveway. They had become good friends in a very short time. On that difficult drive, they were each able to talk about how much Ben meant to each of them. In their own special way, they missed him and he would forever be lodged in their hearts. Not just for the uncertainty surrounding his whereabouts, but for the energy and direction he had given their lives.

Standing on the front porch, Phil reached in his pocket and pulled out a key to the front door. Touching Phil's hand, Alex said, "Phil, if you would not mind, I would really like to be alone here for a while. I think it would help me sort through my emotions and give me the time alone I need. I hope you understand."

Phil handed the key to Alex. "Take your time. I don't have my cell phone with me, naturally, so how about I just plan on coming back in a couple hours?"

"Thanks, Phil."

Alex walked through the house as she had that night they were together. At each corner she stopped, closed her eyes and brought the image of Benjamin into that room.

Walking up the stairs she could feel him carrying her in his strong arms, kissing her forehead and saying, "I love you." She entered the room where they had made love. The same room where she gave him a gentle kiss goodbye as she fled from her dreams. The same room that would be a vision permanently imprinted in her mind.

She looked out the large bay window facing the driveway and her tears were stopped by the gentle pursing of her lips. She laughed softly as she remembered pretending not to notice Benjamin staring at her as she walked up to the front door that first time. He never fooled me, she thought. Then she turned and walked down the stairs that once led her to a place of unparalleled proportions.

She sat down at the bottom of the stairs, leaned back and rested her head on the steps. Her meeting with Director Imbot had been quickly arranged, but she left with more questions than answers. What she did know was that Paul Brewster, Nate Hawthorne, Garran Upshaw and Murray Paulson were all in custody, and each of them had been thoroughly interrogated. The two men who came to her hotel room, and the two people from the limousine where Benjamin was injured, were also in custody.

Unfortunately, Benjamin's whereabouts was still a mystery. No one knew how he was smuggled out of the hospital, but they did know that he was transported by car to London where he was held in a vacant row house for several days. The house had been searched, but no forensic clues had surfaced, except two pieces of wadded up paper with the word 'eagle' scratched on them.

Director Imbot said that the American defense contractor, Starling Defense Applications Corporation was an interested party in all this, and that the whereabouts of its CEO, Mr. Alan Price, was unknown. In the 1990s there were rumors that Israel had attempted to build an "ethno-bomb," and the Agency believed that Starling Defense Applications was attempting to acquire the means to produce such a weapon. That was all the evidence or information DGSE had been able to dig up at that point.

Alex stood up and walked into the den and came to an abrupt halt. She thought she could smell his body—the body that brought her fire and serenity; passion and peace; pain and love.

She stood in front of the large, bulky desk that was a gift to Benjamin from his grandfather. Her hands stroked the inlaid leather that was burnished by the passage of time. She felt Benjamin's hands move in sync with hers. The rhythm continued as she felt every scratch, every corner and every copper rivet. She knew that Benjamin loved his grandfather deeply. He had told her many wonderful things about him. How sad though, she thought, he never explained what had become of his grandfather. Almost as if he were embarrassed, he would not tell Alex where he lived, or even if he were still alive.

She opened the middle drawer and there she found the key she needed. As she picked up the key she noticed a newspaper clipping with a picture of a handsome, elderly fellow. Curious if this was Benjamin's grandfather, she picked up the clipping and began to read:

> Prominent mining executive, imprisoned for the past eleven years, was released today due to health concerns. Denis Wilkinson was convicted in 1999 for violating the Customs Act of 1901 in a scheme involving the illegal exportation of uranium. . .

"Oh, God! No! This cannot be!" Alex clasped her hands around the back of her neck, squeezed her head with her forearms and collapsed onto the desk. Her head swirled with each sputtering breath.

This was the very man she set up for Metallges, a former client, so many years ago.

Again, Alex pled with Benjamin, as if he were standing next to her, "I am sorry, Benjamin. I cannot believe what I have done." And then she made a promise, "I will find you, Ben, and I promise I will clear your grandfather's name—I promise!"

CHAPTER 48

I N QUEEN CHARLOTTE CITY, ALEX RENTED A LARGE PICKUP truck and headed up to the mountainous area near the Masset Inlet, on the north end of the island. With the large cage tightly secured in the back bed, she slowly traveled the winding dirt roads to the secluded spot Benjamin told her about. She stopped at an open meadow surrounded by native Shore Pine and Nootka Cypress. The timbered mountains loomed off in the distance. To the north side of the meadow, she saw the shear jagged rock where the eagles nested.

The eagle's wing had healed, and Alex knew she needed to return the creature to the wild. It's what Benjamin would have done. It's what he would have wanted.

She opened the rear door of the truck's bed and slid the metal cage back. She set it on the ground and pulled off the solid brown cloth to expose the beautiful creature. The instant she removed the cloth, the eagle looked at its surroundings and a powerful shriek alerted the wilderness that it was home.

She knelt down beside the bird and allowed the yellow piercing stare to go right through her. She began to weep as she said, "I have brought you home. Your healing is complete. Go now, find your mate, and breathe in the freedom you lost. Thank you for teaching me that we all exist within each other, and that we are all a part of one another's soul."

She opened the cage door, and watched the eagle hop out into the long-bladed meadow grass. Only a few feet away now, its body turned away from Alex, toward its home, the eagle slowly turned its neck and looked in her eyes. She said again, "Go, my friend. Take the part of Benjamin that is yours and fly far away, back into the mountains, back to the one who is waiting for you, back to your birthright, back to your home." Alex knew he understood her. Spreading its wings, he jumped and flew onto the top of the truck. Looking down at her, the same way he did the night Benjamin took her into the cage, his eyes fixed on hers, he suddenly shrieked louder and stronger than she had ever heard. The cry echoed through the narrow valley.

He flapped his enormous wings, and soared directly above her in the sky. He began a slow circle, bellowing loud shrieks at the end of each revolution. She stared up at him and knew he was crying out for Benjamin. She yelled up at him, "I know he is safe, and I will find him. He will always be with you. . .be in you. Take him with you, and be free." With those last words, the great creature swooped down close to Alex and then flew off toward the jagged rocks. She watched him until she couldn't see him anymore. Then she heard his last shriek. Holding her arms in the air, tears streaming down her face, she yelled, "Goodbye, my friend. Goodbye."

Epilogue

SYDNEY MORNING HERALD
August 12, 2012

Prominent Australian industrialist, Denis Wilkinson, was released early this morning from the New South Wales Penitentiary. Scheduled to serve a total of 15 years, Mr. Wilkinson was released early after the Commonwealth Attorney General announced it had received credible information exonerating Mr. Wilkinson from his earlier conviction. . .

The next Alex Boudreau
Adventure will be out in 2013.

Will she find Benjamin? Alive?
Safe?

What will happen to the G-16
virus?

What new and challenging
conflicts must she overcome?

Feel free to contact us and
offer your thoughts.

www.PaulHLandes.com

ACKNOWLEDGEMENTS

Creating and writing our very first novel has been an experience like none other. We embarked down this road soon after we first met in 1995 and we spent our first 4 months totally engrossed in this project. As so often happens, life events intervened and our hopes of completing this novel were shelved. In July, 2011, one of us dusted off the old floppy disks and found a way to convert the saved manuscript to modern technology. Interestingly enough, the story still captivated our interest and that same desire was renewed to finish our very own novel. The rest of the year was spent writing, writing and writing.

Along the way there have been so many friends and family members who read the various drafts and provided not only brutal criticisms, but words of encouragement, imaginative thoughts and unlimited support. Bill Rogers, Jim Sauve, Nancy Holman, Chris Rogers, both Dave and David Landes, Bud Whisler, Colleen McDonald, Rick Rogers, Therese Tiab, and Hunter Holman—your support in this project was so very helpful.

The creation of a genetically engineered virus that would be a potentially lethal weapon was way beyond our abilities, so we turned to a friend and recognized expert in this field. Murray Gardner is an Emeritus Professor at the University of California at Davis. He reviewed draft after draft and had the patience to explain the intricacies of this science in a way that ultimately made some degree of sense to us. The creation of the virus in this story is not something that is possible today, but it does rest, uncomfortably on the realm of probability.

Computer science and the methods employed for espionage purposes are complex and ever changing in today's technological world. By tomorrow many of the methods used in our story will be outdated and a thing of the past. Bob Upshaw was invaluable in sharing his expertise with us so that we could write about computer hacking and infiltrating with real terms and real procedures.

We were so lucky to find Nancy Roberts, our editor. We had completed so many drafts of this story that we actually lived and breathed the events. Nancy took our labor of love and found the rough edges (there were many) we were unable to see and smoothed and polished them in a way that we never could. This story is infinitely so much better because of all the effort and skill put into it by Nancy—Thank you! Thank You!

www.ingramcontent.com/pod-product-compliance
Lightning Source LLC
Chambersburg PA
CBHW070758180626
46818CB00001B/12